THE BEST LIES

TITLES BY DAVID ELLIS

Look Closer

The Last Alibi

The Wrong Man

Breach of Trust

The Hidden Man

Eye of the Beholder

In the Company of Liars

Jury of One

Life Sentence

Line of Vision

THE
BEST
LIES

A NOVEL

DAVID ELLIS

G. P. PUTNAM'S SONS
NEW YORK

PUTNAM
— EST. 1838 —

G. P. Putnam's Sons
Publishers Since 1838
An imprint of Penguin Random House LLC
penguinrandomhouse.com

Library of Congress Cataloging-in-Publication Data

Names: Ellis, David, 1967– author.
Title: The best lies: a novel / David Ellis.
Description: New York: G. P. Putnam's Sons, 2024.
Identifiers: LCCN 2023055275 (print) | LCCN 2023055276 (ebook) |
ISBN 9780399170935 (hardcover) | ISBN 9780698162006 (epub)
Subjects: LCGFT: Thrillers (Fiction) | Novels.
Classification: LCC PS3555.L59485 B47 2024 (print) |
LCC PS3555.L59485 (ebook) | DDC 813/.54—dc23/eng/20231204
LC record available at https://lccn.loc.gov/2023055275
LC ebook record available at https://lccn.loc.gov/2023055276

Printed in the United States of America
1st Printing

Space-break illustration by nikiteev_konstantin/Shutterstock.com

*To my kids, Abby, Julia, and Jon, who have given me more love and joy and pride than any person has the right to experience.
Now please stop fighting.*

VALENTINE'S DAY

2024

1

Leo

I hear them coming up the back stairs, the fire escape off the alley. Their footfalls are harsh, trudging, deliberate. So they're not coming to kill me. That's the good news.

The bad news is they're coming to arrest me.

You should reconsider your life choices when those are the only two possibilities.

Cops. Local or federal? I'm not sure which I should fear more. I'll know soon.

I pull out my phone and dial my law partner, Montgomery Morris.

"Happy Valentine's Day," he says.

"You busy?"

"On my way to the Bulls game. Why?"

"I'm gonna need a lawyer, Monty."

"You—what? Why?"

"It's a long story. They're about to take me into custody."

"Well . . . when?"

"In about eleven seconds," I say.

"Eleven sec—the Bulls are playing Giannis tonight. Is it serious?"

"Umm . . . probably. It depends on which crime they charge."

"There's more than one to choose from?"

"Depends on whether it's FBI or local cops."

"You don't even know that much? What did you do now, Leo?"

The fire escape from the second story to the third, where I live, is 14 stairs. Seven stairs, then a landing, then another 7. You'd think that would mean that, combined with the flight from the ground to the second floor, the total number of stairs is 28. But it's 29, as there's an extra step on the bottom. And 29 is not only a prime number but the sum of three consecutive squares (the squares of 2, 3, and 4), which helps me not at all right now but . . . yeah.

Three . . . two . . . one.

Two people appear at my back door. One is a guy I don't recognize. The other is Mary Cagnola, a sergeant with DPPD. Both with their badges out so I can see them.

"Deemer Park P.D.," I tell Monty and punch out the phone before he can object.

I slide open the door, a shock of cold air invading my condo.

"Leo Balanoff?" Sergeant Cagnola does the talking.

If I were cool, I'd say something like *What took you so long?*

"And here I didn't get a valentine for you guys," I say.

"No valentines, Leo. We have a warrant for your arrest for the murder of Cyrus Balik."

The booking process at Deemer Park P.D. is a real treat. They photograph me, swab my cheek for DNA, and fingerprint me. But the highlight is the cavity search. It's always a moment for self-reflection when someone's snapping on rubber gloves and ordering you to bend over and spread your legs. On the bright side, it's the most action I've had in months.

Interview Room A of the Deemer Park police station is about as exciting as a sensory deprivation tank. The room is paneled wood, if you can believe it, painted off-white. I sit at an old rickety table in an uncomfortable wooden chair that has uneven legs. Uneven, like the imbalanced scales of justice? Maybe I can work that into a line.

Cagnola and Dignan sit across from me. First time I've met Dignan. Ruddy complexion, decent head of hair, a face that's starting to surrender to age. Late forties, I figure, so he's close to his twenty if he wants to hang it up, and I'm betting he does. Beneath the false bravado, the show of authority that these cops try to project, he's nervous. His leg is bobbing up and down under the table.

He should be nervous.

"Are you willing to talk to us, Leo?" Cagnola will lead, apparently. Interesting. Frankly, I'm surprised she's in this room at all. She looks tired but otherwise the same as the last time I saw her—steely blue eyes that dominate her face, dirty-blond hair pulled back, kind of an overall go-fuck-yourself air about her.

"I didn't kill Cyrus Balik," I say. "I'm willing to listen to what you have to say, but this is a . . . gross miscarriage of justice."

It felt like that needed to be said.

Cagnola suppresses a smile. Shoots a look at my lawyer, Monty, and nods back toward me, as in *Do you believe this guy?*

The answer to that question, by the way, would be no. Monty probably doesn't completely believe me. That's not usually a healthy start to the attorney-client relationship.

"Okay, well, you can start by listening." Cagnola settles in. "But you already know what I'm gonna say."

I'd cross my arms, but that's not easy in handcuffs, unless I had the dexterity of Houdini.

That would be cool, to contort yourself like that.

"First off, nobody in this room is mourning the loss of Cyrus Balik. The guy was the worst of the worst. Human trafficker, gunrunner, drug dealer, and who knows how many murders. He lured in women, turned them into addicts and prostitutes, chewed them up and spit them out. He's what we call a destroyer. He's ruined a lot of people's lives. Truth be told, you did the world a favor, Leo."

You're welcome.

"So sentencing on something like this—if you cooperate with us, tell us what happened, I'd be prepared to recommend a lenient sentence."

I nod, like I'm considering it. I'm not.

"This isn't your first offense," she continues. "You punched that cop back in college."

"I didn't punch that cop," I say.

"Of course not. Of course you didn't. You just pled guilty to something you didn't do, right? That happens all the time, right?"

It happens more often than people think.

"But the good news for us," she says, "is your arrest back in college gave us your fingerprints and DNA. Those ended up being very helpful."

Yeah, more on that later, I assume.

"Then there's that stunt you pulled once you became a lawyer. You perpetrated a 'fraud on the court.' You lost your law license for . . . What did they give you—a nickel?"

Yes, a five-year suspension. I've been reinstated for a year now. Long story.

"And you were—the bar disciplinary committee, they had an expert who diagnosed you as a pathological liar. Right? You're a pathological liar?"

In other words, go ahead and try to talk your way out of this, but no one's going to believe you.

"That's what they said," I answer, which is not the same thing as yes.

Cagnola seems pleased with her summary. "So let's talk about the reason you're here. We know you were trying to get law enforcement to go after Cyrus Balik. We know that your, uh, client, Bonnie Tressler, was going to testify against him. And we know she died."

"She was murdered," I correct.

Monty puts a hand on my arm. "We're just listening right now."

"She was *murdered*," says Cagnola, happy to use that. "Murdered by Cyrus, you figure? I mean, that's the thing, right? You think Cyrus murdered Bonnie."

Of course I think he killed her. That's what we in the legal profession call my "motive."

Monty interjects again. "Just listening right now."

Cagnola nods, but she's looking at me, not him. "And we know you went to see Cyrus Balik afterward—after Bonnie's death."

That's true.

"And we know that your meeting didn't go well."

That's an understatement. That's like saying the maiden voyage of the *Titanic* fell short of expectations.

"And then, not long after that, Cyrus ends up dead from a fatal stab wound."

Roger that.

"Then, the forensics," she says, looking at me for a reaction. "We found your blood—your DNA—on Cyrus's shirtsleeve."

I'll be the first to admit, that whole thing didn't go quite as smoothly as expected.

"And we found your fingerprints on the knife sticking out of Cyrus's neck."

That was just plain sloppy. I'm not gonna sugarcoat it.

"So?" Cagnola parts her hands. "We have all kinds of motive, and we have forensic evidence putting you at the scene with the knife in your hand. We got you, Leo. You're done. Anything you'd like to say?"

Not really. I have an alibi, but it wouldn't hold up under close scrutiny. And the odds of a mistake in DNA profiling are one in a billion.

"Maybe it was self-defense," she says, prodding me.

No, it wasn't. She knows that. Not under the legal definition, at least.

"Maybe it was a moment of panic," she tries.

It was anything but a moment of panic.

"This is a chance to help yourself," says Dignan. "Explain how it happened."

I look at Monty. Nothing I can say will help me. He knows it, I know it.

For the first time in my life, I can't talk my way out of something.

ONE YEAR EARLIER

JANUARY 2023

2

Leo

"I still have nightmares. I'm still afraid of him. Is that weird?" Her knees up on her couch, the shadows playing on her face, Bonnie Tressler chews her thumbnail while she looks outside at her scenic view of a brick wall on the other side of the alley. With the dim lighting and her sunken eyes, she looks far older than her forty-nine years. Decades of drug use didn't help, either.

"It's not weird at all," I say.

She smiles, appreciative but sure I could never understand. "I'm tired of being afraid of him. I mean." She lets out a breath. "I got away twenty years ago. He's forgotten all about me. I'd be no use to him, anyway, at this point. I mean, look at me. A middle-aged junkie?"

There's nothing wrong with Bonnie's appearance—her mouse-colored hair streaked with blue, the multiple piercings on her face—but she does have the look of someone who weathered her share of storms.

"Ex-junkie," I say.

She has three hoops in each ear, a stud above her lip, one in the side of her nose, and one on her left cheek at the dimple. She has five visible tattoos—one on each ankle, a small heart on her right cheek, a cross on her forearm, and a skull on the back of her neck. She has crossed or uncrossed her legs six times since we've been sitting together and has licked her lips—a nervous habit—seven times.

Sometimes I count things.

"You don't have to tell us." Trace, sitting next to her, puts his hand over hers. "I know I've been pushing, but you don't have to, Bon. It's okay."

She gives him a kind smile, her eyes welling up. "No, it's *not* okay. You know why it's not okay? Because he could be doing it to other women right now. He probably is."

He probably is. Whoever he is, if he's not dead or in prison, he's still preying on women. Human trafficking is too profitable to give up. And the people who do it are not the kind who grow consciences.

"Fuck it." She sits forward, pins back her hair with her hands. The overworked radiator picks that moment to bellow and hiss. "Cyrus," she says. "His name is Cyrus." She messes up her hair and lets out a decisive breath, a breath she's been holding for twenty years.

"Cyrus Balik."

"We take this to law enforcement. I'll go with you," I quickly add, seeing the look on Bonnie's face. "I'll be your attorney, so they'll have to work through me."

"You can do that now? You're back to being a lawyer?"

"My license was reinstated last week."

Last Friday, the five-year suspension ended. My law license is reactivated.

Long story, but here's the short version: I fucked up.

"We know a cop in Deemer Park, right?" says Trace, peeking at me for a reaction.

"Oh, of course—Andi." Bonnie lights up. "Of course! But . . . you've been on the outs."

"On the outs for the last five years." I shoot Trace a look. "Without a single word to each other since. Andi would welcome a call from me like she welcomes gridlock traffic."

"Well, but she's the obvious person to call." Trace opens his hands.

I roll my neck. "I was thinking federal," I say. "FBI."

But Trace is right. Andi is the obvious person for this, and Deemer

Park—her jurisdiction—is where Bonnie thinks Cyrus still does some of his business.

"Okay, I'll reach out." I pull out my phone and type a quick note to Andi:

> Law enforcement issue for a client. Need your assistance.

That's as much as I'm willing to say over text. I hit "send," then type a second message:

> This is Leo, by the way, if you've deleted my contact.

"She might have a different number now," I say. "And even if this is the right number, I might be hearing back . . . never."

"You can't really blame her," says Bonnie.

I never said I did. I don't blame her. I'd have dumped me, too, after the stunt I pulled.

"Hell yes you can blame her." Trace to my defense. "You did a good thing. You did the right thing. Who cares if you broke some stupid lawyer rules?"

The state supreme court cared, for one. A five-year suspension isn't a slap on the wrist.

My phone buzzes. Andi. That was fast:

> I left the department. Private security now. Call Sgt Mary Cagnola, DPPD. I trust her.

I do a slow burn. Andi quit the force? The Andi I know would never. I feel it in a way I never have before—I no longer know her. We're over. She's gone. Forever.

"Seriously?" Trace says after I show him the text, rereading it like it's written in a foreign language. "Andi's not a cop anymore? The fuck is *that* all about?" He throws the phone down on the floor. Then he kicks it.

"That's my phone, T, not yours."

3

Chris

"Let me see if I understand this." Special Agent Christopher Roberti sits across from Bonnie Tressler and her lawyer, Leo Balanoff. On his side of the table is Sergeant Mary Cagnola, Deemer Park Police—his sister— who brought him in. "Ms. Tressler—"

"Bonnie," she says. "Everyone calls me Bonnie."

Bonnie and the lawyer are both looking him over, or at least that's how it feels to Chris. He knows his hair is only half-grown back, in thin, wispy sprouts. That the skin on his face sags from the significant weight loss. That his clothes don't quite fit—the shirt collar too wide, the shoulders of the suit hanging. They're thinking—crash diet, or illness? The hair usually tips it to the latter.

"Okay, Bonnie," Chris says. "You're saying you ran away from your home in Indiana when you were fourteen. Cyrus Balik took you in. He kept you. He gave you drugs. He raped you repeatedly. And then you got pregnant."

"That's right." Bonnie plays with her hands, keeps looking over at Balanoff, her lawyer. "I cleaned up after I found out. I didn't take drugs when I was pregnant."

"Okay, gotcha." Chris smiles. "Then you gave birth, but Cyrus still kept you at his place."

"Right. He didn't really—he didn't really let us leave the property.

There was a courtyard, sort of, in the middle of the building. He let us walk around there."

"Us. There were other women he kept there?"

"Yeah, several. I don't know how many. I'd see some of them. Maybe six, ten?"

"Okay, and—and when your son was four, Cyrus took him."

She winces, nods.

"You think he sold the child."

"We know he did," Balanoff says, speaking for the first time.

Chris looks at him. "To who? Black-market stuff? A pedo ring?"

"That's something we can get into when the time comes."

Chris sits back in his chair. "The time has come, hasn't it? I mean, you came to me."

"We'll tell you more about her son when we know that something's going to come of it. Bonnie's not going to risk giving up her son's identity until then."

Chris glances at his sister. "Look, Mr. . . . Balanoff?"

"Call me Leo," he says.

"Leo, I've been trying to find a way to put away Cyrus Balik for the last five years. If you have something for me, then I'd love to act on it. But so far—look, I believe you. I believe you, Bonnie. A hundred percent. But I'm not sure what that gets me. For one thing, it happened over thirty years ago. Which means all I have so far is a he-said, she-said with a serious statute-of-limitations problem."

"First of all," says Balanoff, "there's no limitations problem. There is more than one federal human trafficking statute that doesn't have a limitations period at all. And as for proof, it's not he-said, she-said. Bonnie gave *birth* to this child. We can prove that. We can prove the child is hers by DNA. And we can prove when he was born. We can prove how old Bonnie was when he was born."

"Right, understood. But how can we connect it . . . Oh." Chris does a grand nod; he gets it now. "You're saying Cyrus is the father?"

"Cyrus is the father. Get a DNA sample from him. That proves that Cyrus and Bonnie are his parents. The child is now thirty-four years old. Bonnie is forty-nine. So then—"

"Then it's just simple math." Mary slaps her hand on the table. "Forty-nine minus thirty-four gets you fifteen. You were fifteen when you gave birth."

Bonnie nods. "Fourteen when he got me pregnant."

"Wow. That could actually . . . work." Mary looks at her brother.

"But I can't get PC for a search without the child," says Chris.

"Probable cause," Leo explains to Bonnie. "He can't just take someone's DNA from them. He needs a warrant. And he's saying he can't get a warrant without talking to and testing your son."

Bonnie shakes her head, more from exasperation than anything else.

"Get creative," Leo tells Chris. "You can get someone's DNA plenty of ways. He drinks from a glass and you're there to scoop it up. He discards a cigarette or a wad of gum. You don't need a warrant for any of that."

Chris mulls it over, warms to the idea. "Get creative," he says. "I can do that."

Three weeks later, Chris pulls up his collar, bracing himself against the wind before stepping under the police tape. "Where are you?" he says into his phone.

"Basement. Set of stairs by the back."

The two-flat looks, by all accounts, to once have been a promising starter house in Humboldt Park that has gone to shit since the foreclosure. The city tries to board these places up, but the junkies are resourceful. A roof over their heads during a frigid winter like this, and a quiet, dark place to shoot up? Too good to resist.

The smell alone, when Chris enters the house, badging his way past Chicago P.D.—the smell alone says it all, thick and acrid, more like a zoo than a place that houses human beings. Take away running water, though, and people will just shit and urinate wherever's convenient.

He holds his breath and finds the stairs, passing more officers on their way up, keeping his credentials out, though they don't even look.

Mary is standing in the corner, her badge hanging around her neck, shining a flashlight on a woman who lies on her side, eyes vacant, foamy mouth. Just three weeks ago, she'd looked very different.

"Positive ID for Bonnie Tressler?"

Mary says yes, but Chris can see for himself, that distinctive hair colored blue, the piercings and tats.

"Think she went back to using?" she asks Chris.

"Shit, no. Three weeks ago, we meet with them, she's clean, she's sober, she's determined, got a lawyer and everything. And now she ODs? This was Cyrus. Dammit." Chris spins in a small circle. "What—what did I do wrong? How'd he get wind of us? We kept the circle small. Tight as a drum. But he found out anyway."

"Yeah, these guys have eyes in the backs of their heads," says Mary. "And ears. Ears everywhere. They're good. They're damn good."

Chris looks into Bonnie Tressler's dead eyes.

"Then we've gotta be better," he says.

THE PRESENT DAY

JANUARY 2024

Six Weeks before Valentine's Day

4

Leo

Judgment Day. I hope. I need this to end.

We arrive in the courtroom after battling our way through a throng of reporters and TV cameras. It takes us—or me, at least—43 steps to travel from the elevator to the courtroom. 43 is the smallest prime number expressible as the sum of 2, 3, 4, or 5 different primes. I wish I didn't know that.

The prosecutors, the assistant United States attorneys, are already there, two men and one woman. The "funeral directors," Monty always calls them, sober to a fault, dark suits and white shirts, nary a smile among them. Young lawyers from fancy law schools with a plum job to polish their trial skills before they saunter over to the private side and make absurd money representing defendants as (wait for it) "former federal prosecutors." For now, though, they have bought hip-deep into their role, the just-the-facts sobriety, the holier-than-thou sanctimony.

Our client, Peter Sahin, who walked in with his wife, Eva, greets their grown sons in the courtroom with double cheek kisses. He unbuttons his coat and reaches for his cuffs before remembering that he's not wearing a shirt with French cuffs. No cuff links, we told him. No tiepin. Nothing fancy. Basically don't look like a rich slimeball.

The phone in my left pocket buzzes. Not my regular iPhone. My burner. I pull it out and check it from my lap, below the desk. It could only be one person—Trace.

Did you win? Can we get on with it?

I type back, **Patience, grasshopper,** and slide the phone in my pocket.

Peter is too nervous to sit. His expression is implacable—he prides himself on not showing emotion—but his anxiety reveals itself in other ways. Like now, as he rubs his fingers together like he's trying to create fire.

"She's late," he whispers.

"The judge is never late," I remind him. "She's the judge."

I pull out the phone in my right pocket, the iPhone, for the first time. Four minutes past the hour. I don't like the number four. I prefer my numbers odd. And divisible by three.

Peter, radiating nervous energy, looks at me. "I can't stand the waiting."

(Then maybe you shouldn't have bribed an alderman.)

"Today would've been my mother's ninety-fifth birthday," he says, unable to sit still.

95 is a semi-prime number, its only factors 19 and 5, both primes themselves.

"Maybe that will bring me luck." He turns to me. "Are you close to your mother?"

I don't really like talking to people. Especially about myself. But really just generally.

"My mother passed," I say.

"She must have been young."

I nod. "She was killed in Afghanistan."

"In combat?"

"Yeah. She was a CIA paramilitary officer. Her convoy came under attack in the Shah-i-Kot Valley during Operation Anaconda. She rolled over a land mine while taking a defensive position."

I wonder if anyone's ever actually died that way. At least you'd have a cool story.

"That's . . . I'm sorry to hear that."

"You and me both."

"All rise," the bailiff calls out as the judge enters. The time is 9:06 a.m.

A strobogrammatic number, 906, rotationally symmetrical. It reads the same when flipped 180 degrees. Maybe Peter Sahin's life is about to do a 180, too.

"I've reviewed the submissions at length. I'm prepared to rule, unless either side wishes to add anything beyond the papers." The Honorable Miriam Blanchard looks over her glasses at both parties. When a judge says she's prepared to rule, it means she doesn't want to hear any oral argument. But she makes the offer anyway, to protect her record. Monty wilts ever so slightly in his chair, whether out of relief or disappointment, I'm not sure.

"The court is persuaded by defense counsel that the evidence falls short of an explicit quid pro quo, namely an exchange of campaign contributions for an official act. The government has offered no evidence of any meeting of the minds—any evidence, for that matter, that the defendant ever so much as communicated with Alderman Francona before the campaign contributions were provided. Under these circumstances, a directed finding is in order. The defendant is discharged."

Twenty-seven seconds, a judgment read as dispassionately as a principal giving announcements at homeroom, and Peter's life has changed forever.

Peter blinks hard, stunned, as if he were just punched. He turns to me. "We . . . ?"

"It's over," I say.

Monty puts his arm around him. "Congratulations, my friend."

Peter finds my hand, squeezes it hard, gives me a soulful look, mouths a *Thank you*, before he turns to Monty to do the same thing.

And a man who paid off an alderman goes free. The law protected him. He deserved to win under the law, because he and the alderman were smart enough not to say the quiet part out loud—Peter gave a whopping contribution to the alderman's campaign but only asked for the zoning variance after the election was over. Nobody ever explicitly tied the quid to the quo.

Peter didn't hire us for a civics lesson or a morality lecture. He hired us to find a way out, and we found it. That's why we never deem someone innocent. We just say they're guilty or not guilty.

I pull out the burner phone and type, Victory is ours. But don't come. Let me handle it. I hit "send."

Within eleven seconds, Trace responds:

Fuck that. Give me two days to get there. And buckle up.

5

Leo

Two days later. I've caught up on sleep and done some thinking. A lot of thinking.

I leave work early and take an Uber. I get out a block from the apartment in Old Town. It takes us 31 minutes to drive from my office to this spot. If you add up the first 31 prime numbers, you get 31 squared. The sum of the first eight digits of pi is 31. Stop it.

The sky is smoky gray. Remnants of last week's snowfall linger with the chilly air, the sidewalks littered with invisible ice patches. January in Chicago.

I do a once-over up and down the street. Nobody casually loitering. No tailpipes kicking out smoke, and in this cold, nobody could sit in their car for any period of time without the heat blasting. So at first glance, at least, it looks like nobody's staking out the apartment.

Out of caution, I enter through the alley. Same first reaction—nobody's sitting on the place in a parked car, nobody's standing around pretending to be focused on something else while they wait for a man to walk up or down the fire escape of the building at 1441 North.

If you ever need to hide somewhere, winter in Chicago has a lot to recommend it.

I pull out my phone and send a text: Here. Knocking in thirty.

Clutching take-out Mexican in one hand, my briefcase in the other, I walk with caution, as the ice in the alleys has a longer shelf life than on the sidewalks. I do my best audition for *Disney on Ice* as I slide across a particularly nasty and thick patch of frozen water in the shape of an armadillo. I'm not sure how to factor that slide into my step count, which now registers at 134. Life is full of conundrums.

By the time I reach the fire escape at 1441 North, my steps reach 162, which is interesting, because last time I came here the count was 166. Maybe the Uber dropped me at a different spot.

I wasn't thrilled with 1441 for an address, but at least it's a palindrome and an odd number. Could be worse. Besides, the place was cheap and allowed for month-to-month rental.

I take the fire escape up to the second story and set down my briefcase, poised to knock, but the door opens before I can pound it.

"Hey." Trace lets me in and closes the door behind me. "Were you followed?"

"Yeah, the bad guys are right outside," I say. "I gave them the apartment number, in case they lost me."

"You can't just answer me straight, huh?"

"It's a dumb question. If I thought I was followed, would I have led them to you? By definition, my being here means I *don't* think I was—"

"Jesus, fine, I'm sorry I asked." He turns the deadbolt, thumping it closed after a sharp whine. "This entire system needs an upgrade," he says. "Starting with a double-cylinder bolt right here. Probably the 626 in chrome."

Trace runs a business that supplies all kinds of doors for residences, warehouses, commercial offices, you name it, but his personal specialty is locksmithing. He can't pass a door without commenting on the quality of its security.

"Or you could just wedge a chair under the knob at night," I suggest. "How was the drive?"

"Brutal." He rubs the back of his neck. "And this weather sucks. I can't believe I ever lived here."

He lived here, in the great state of Illinois, his entire life until four years ago. That's when his boss, Hector, a guy from northern Mexico, took over his father's door business in his hometown, a village just outside Chihuahua. He asked Trace to run the day-to-day down there while Hector stayed here in Chicago. Trace needed the change of scenery, so he said yes.

I drop the bag of tacos on the breakfast bar of the kitchenette. The smell of grilled chorizo makes my stomach churn.

"I live in Mexico, I'm in Chicago for maybe a week, and you bring me tacos," says Trace. "Not Greek. Not a beef sandwich. Not chicken parm. Besides, why can't we go out?"

"First of all, please don't whine like a puppy," I say. "You're always whining."

"I'm just saying—"

"Waah, waah, waah." I make a mouth out of my hand and flap it. "And anyway, it's not safe to go out."

Trace pulls out the food, takes his portion and one of the bottles of water. "You really think I'm in danger?"

"What kind of a question is that?" I put out my hands. "The only reason you aren't six feet underground like Bonnie is that they don't know who you are."

"But that puts *you* in danger. You're our lawyer."

"Yeah, no shit. We're both in danger. But I can't help it; they already know who I am. You, on the other hand, *can* help it. By staying anonymous."

He makes some guttural noise of dissatisfaction and takes his food to the couch. Trace looks good, trim and hard and happy, much better since he moved south of the border. He got sober up here in Chicago, but the usual temptations abounded; I always thought it was more of a struggle than he would admit. Moving to Mexico, the change of scenery, switching up everything, has made the road to permanent sobriety easier, even if it's a road filled with daily off-ramps of temptation.

"So when does it happen?" he asks me.

"Soon as possible," I say. "I'll need to set up the meeting."

"You don't have to do this," he says. "You shouldn't do this. You should let *me* do it."

"You're the one who should be nowhere near this thing," I tell him. "I told you not to come. You should've stayed in Mexico."

"Hey." He waits until I look at him, we have eye contact. "Seriously. Let me do this. Not you."

I get my food and lay it out on the breakfast bar in the tiny kitchen. "How long have you known me?"

"Since I was five," he says.

"Have you ever talked me out of anything? Besides, I've done crazier shit for clients."

That sparks a laugh. "True, but risking your *career* is one thing. You've never risked your life."

"First time for everything." Like I'm cool with it, like I'm some action hero.

"Trying to negotiate with a guy like Cyrus Balik is suicidal," says Trace.

I open up my first taco. They put cilantro on it. I hate cilantro.

"You're overreacting," I say. "I'm sure Cyrus will be a perfect gentleman."

6

Andi

George McLaughlin is having a good time. Who wouldn't, dining at Gibsons Italia, with this pricey bottle of champagne chilling on ice, the fancy tablecloths and gorgeous view of the bend of the Chicago River as the sun hits the water?

Andi is sitting at the bar, alone, which can be painful not because she minds being alone (she doesn't) but because men think she's looking for companionship (she isn't). She sits with her phone against her ear as if in conversation.

But the only person she's talking to is through a bud in her ear, connected wirelessly to a radio on her belt. The bud is obscured by her hair, which she's wearing down straight. Her suit coat covers the radio.

"It's about to happen," she says as George McLaughlin reaches inside his sport coat.

"*On it,*" says Jack Cortland, in her ear. "*Lights, camera, action.*"

George McLaughlin is sitting across from his friend at a four-person table not far from the picture window overlooking the river. Andi reaches the table and catches the attention of George and his companion while said companion is stuffing an envelope inside his coat pocket.

"George?" she says, using her corporate-friendly voice.

George has a long face and coils of bushy hair the color of rust. The tweed coat perfects the professorial look, though the guy's spent his career in sales and marketing.

He just retired last week at age fifty-four, after twenty years with QCI, claiming he'd take some time off, do some traveling with his wife, then maybe look into some internet sales ventures.

Yeah, or maybe not.

"George McLaughlin?" says Andi. "You don't remember me, do you?"

He has a decision to make. He makes the right one by coming clean: "I'm sorry, I'm not placing you . . . ?"

"Andrea," she says. "Andi Piotrowski. We met at the IHM conference in Portland last fall. You're still with QCI?"

Quigley Crowe International.

"Actually, I just announced my re—"

"Mind if I join you a second?" she says, helping herself to one of the two vacant chairs.

"Uh, sure," says George, looking across at his companion, whose name is Richard Jaconti, for confirmation. "This is my friend Rich."

"Nice to meet you, Rich. Andi Piotrowski. Don't mean to interrupt."

"Uh, no, not at all." George looks Andi over, a different sort of smile creeping in. "I must have had way too much to drink in Portland if I don't remember *you*."

Oh, gee, George, bet you say that to all the girls.

"Piotrowski," he says. "That's . . . Polish, right?"

"Sure is."

"Your married name?"

"Nope," she says.

People hear that last name and expect a white, blond woman, not a Black one. Biracial, technically, but most people see Black when they see Andi.

"Ah. So one of your parents is Polish?"

Yes, that's usually how it works, George. Want me to draw you a chart?

Now comes the apology in three . . . two . . . one . . .

"I mean, it's fine," he says. "I—didn't mean offense."

If she got offended every time somebody wondered how a Black woman could have a Polish last name, she'd be nothing but angry. She usually finds it amusing, sometimes exhausting.

"No offense taken," she says. "So, Rich, what do you do?"

He starts to answer, pauses a beat, then says, "Oh, just a boring sales job."

Richard Jaconti, age forty-two, is an executive vice president and head of domestic marketing at Jenner3D Labs, a direct competitor of Quigley Crowe International.

"And you?" he asks, changing the subject.

"Me? Oh, I work at QCI, too." Andi smiles. "Surprised I never saw you around the office, George. Then again, I'm in the security department."

Judging from the expressions on each of their faces, you'd think she just told them she has a bomb strapped to her chest.

Andi removes her credentials from her suit coat, shows them her badge. Just a gold star with the corporate logo; she's still getting used to having one that doesn't say "police" on it. But the pay's much better.

"Oh?" George manages, though he's losing color quickly. "Security? That sounds . . . That sounds interesting."

"Some days it is," she says. Today being one.

"Would you two excuse me a second?" says Richard, pushing back his chair.

"You should stay right where you are, Mr. Jaconti," says Andi.

First time she's mentioned his last name. Now, at least, they all understand each other.

"I'm sorry, what—what's going on?" George asks, a quiver in his voice.

She turns to George. "Richard will be arrested by the FBI before he has a chance to ditch that thumb drive you just gave him, George. That thumb drive containing the FY25 sales projections for, what, Hematology, Incontinence Management, Infection Prevention—am I leaving any product lines out?"

During her short speech, George has taken a quick tour of emotions, from shock to horror to partial recovery. "I don't know what you're talking about," he says, chin up. "Yes, I downloaded that sales data."

See, he knows he can't deny that part. He knows that QCI's security department can track downloads on every computer.

"But that's because I was concerned about those lines, and I wanted to make sure I left things on an upward trajectory."

Right, that was probably the explanation he always had planned and long rehearsed if confronted. It's not a bad answer and impossible to disprove. That's why Andi had to wait until he handed it over to a competitor.

"George thought he was clever," she tells Richard. "He downloaded the IM data the Wednesday before Thanksgiving, hoping we wouldn't notice. Nothing happened, so he felt safe, so he downloaded Hematology's projections the second week of December. Then IP, he downloaded on Christmas Eve. Y'know, spread 'em out, wait for a reaction, when you get none, you keep going. Then he tenders his resignation last week. And suddenly he's having this late lunch with a direct competitor!"

Richard, who looks like he's about to pass out, as if every ounce of blood has been suctioned from his face, leans forward and manages to whisper the one word that resonated most with him: "FBI?"

"If you try to run or destroy that thumb drive in the envelope you just put in your coat pocket—yes, Richard, the FBI will arrest you," she says. "And I have to tell you, nothing would make me happier. So please, go for it. By the way, if one of you gets arrested, the other one does, too. This is either a criminal investigation or it isn't."

Richard's eyes work the room while he tries to keep his hands still.

"You're saying there's another way . . ." George can't finish the sentence. Nervous throat closure.

"George, you've violated your confidentiality agreement with QCI, not to mention your noncompete agreement, for which you received a substantial signing bonus. And you've committed federal offenses. If you come clean right now and cooperate fully, and Richard hands me back the thumb drive, we will not turn either of you over to the authorities."

George and Richard look at each other.

"So . . . all would be for—" George swallows hard. "Forgiven?"

"You won't be prosecuted for commercial espionage, either of you," she says. "Are you wondering if you can keep your stock options and pension and health care?"

George nods, chewing on his lip.

"That's up to QCI," she says. "Not me. If it were up to me, you'd both be in handcuffs."

"Oh, for fuck's sake, George." Richard pulls the envelope out of his pocket and hands it to her. "I, for one, accept that deal."

7

Andi

Jack Cortland returns to his office, where Andi's sitting with her feet up on his desk. "I think George will look back on today and wish he'd worn a set of diapers."

He throws his sport coat over a chair. Jack's the kind of guy who only dresses up when required. If it were up to him, he'd wear a button-down shirt and khakis to work every day. He looks like a guy who's worked with his hands all his life who has now reached grandpa stage, a decent build but an expansive stomach, a weathered face, and flyaway white hair.

"I gotta hand it to you, Andi. Beautiful *and* brilliant." From a desk drawer, he pulls a bottle of Dewar's and two glasses. "Join me?"

When it comes to interpersonal relationships at the office, Jack hasn't quite made it into the twenty-first century, routinely commenting on Andi's looks and outright flirting with her. There are a lot of ways to deal with a guy like that, and once upon a time Andi probably would've been a lot more aggressive, but she's opted for low drama, chill and easygoing.

"I'm good, thanks." Don't encourage him, but don't make a big deal of it, either.

Agnes had a line for that. What did she always say? *It is harder to say no the second time than the first.*

"Not a Scotch girl, eh?" he says.

"Not a drink-with-the-boss girl."

"Well, can't blame me for asking."

Actually, I could, Jack, but I won't.

He pours himself an inch. "You had that guy pegged all along. I wouldn't have believed it. Cheers to you." He takes a sip, lets out a satisfying smack. "You miss being a cop, don't you?"

She answers with a shrug. She misses the romance of it, good guys catching bad guys. But that ship sailed a long time ago, well before she left Deemer Park P.D., when she realized the bad guys aren't always as bad as you thought, and the good guys definitely aren't as good.

Here, at least, there's no pretending. Quigley Crowe International sells medical products for a profit. Sure, big picture, they're making products that help people, but in the end, QCI is a private corporation trying to make money and protect its own interests.

"That FBI bluff, too," Jack says. "I didn't think they'd fall for it. But you knew they would."

"Look at it from their perspective," she says. "They were on the spot, caught red-handed. They had to make a quick decision. They don't realize that an FBI arrest would embarrass QCI as much as it would them. All they're thinking about is being perp-walked out of Gibsons Italia in handcuffs, losing everything, having to face their wives and children, spending time in a federal penitentiary. That fear crowded out any other rational thought."

He purses his lips, nods with approval. "You think like they think."

"I have to."

"Mm-hmm." Another swig of the Dewar's. "Andi, I'm going to assign you to Project Nano. You've heard about it?"

Of course she has. Though few know the details, everybody at QCI has heard of Project Nano. The game changer. The white whale. Not quite ready to submit for FDA trials but, when it's done, it will be the biggest thing QCI has ever produced. One of the greatest innovations in cancer treatment in decades. Estimated to be worth about three billion dollars in revenue over the next twenty years.

A lot of people—competitors, foreign governments, corporate pirates— would pay a lot of money to get their hands on the specs for Project Nano.

And as of now, it's Andi's job to stop them.

8

Andi

Saturday morning, Andi completes the first half of her run outside Sal's Diner. Her head is pounding from too much vodka last night—an evening with the girls—but she's too stubborn to give up her morning run. She removes her headphones and stocking cap and heads inside.

"Morning, Andrea!" says Sal from behind the counter. "How we doin' this fine morning?"

"You know me, Sal. Every day's a gift."

"Ain't it the truth. Your pop's in the back, big surprise."

She waves and walks to the rear of the diner, the scents of fried meat and pancakes making her stomach growl after three miles of running through slush and water puddles.

Brando's in the booth, wearing a tracksuit, an open newspaper blocking his face, while a waitress refills his coffee mug. "Andi!" he sings.

"My father is a dying breed," Andi says to the waitress. "The only person on the face of the earth who still holds the actual morning paper in his hands."

He looks over the newspaper at her. "Do me a favor—don't use the word 'dying' when describing your old man."

Andi snatches a slice of crispy bacon off a plate and bites off half. Brando always starts with bacon, what he considers an appetizer.

"Sure, help yourself." He folds up the newspaper and tosses it on his seat, then turns to the waitress. "She gets her looks from her mother, if you're wondering."

The waitress seems to be enjoying this exchange. Andi orders orange juice only, as she has three more miles to run. Brando wants eggs with Tabasco.

"How *is* your mother, by the way?" he asks.

"Same old Marni. How are the ponies?"

Brando makes a face. He hasn't showered yet. What's left of the hair atop his head looks like a victim of static electricity. His face is a mosh of eye bags and razor stubble.

"Ponies don't always do what I tell 'em to do," he says. "I was a net-plus yesterday, though. Caught a long shot in the fifth. It passes the time."

"A gambling problem isn't really a way to pass the time."

"Who said I have a gambling problem? Guy my age can't do something he enjoys?"

She sits back against the cushion. "You don't look so good, Dad."

"Yeah, worrying about you, I don't look so good." He gives her a once-over, eyes narrowing. "Right back atcha, by the way, my dear. You tie one on last night?"

"I . . . may have had a few too many cosmos."

"Did you at least get laid?"

"Oh, for God's sake." She hoods her face with her hand. Brando has no filter. The waitress has returned with her juice, just in time to catch this last question. "We, uh, don't have a traditional father-daughter relationship," she explains. The waitress just smiles and walks away.

No, she didn't get laid last night. It's been a dry spell. She hasn't had a serious relationship since Leo, since that Hindenburg crashed and burned, what, six years ago. Six years of occasional dating, even less occasional sex, only one guy who seemed promising until Andi learned that his wife was pretty fond of him, too.

Probably the married-to-her-work thing. That was a bigger problem when she was a cop in Deemer Park. The shitty hours, for one. But more so, coming home with all that stink on her, then trying to wipe it off and put on a pair of heels and act "normal" for some guy who usually compared unfavorably to a novel or a show on Netflix, if not a night out with the girls.

You're not married to your work, Mama always tells her. *You* hide *behind your work.*

"Anyway," says Brando. "How's your investigation going with that guy stealing the whatchamacallit, the sales figures?"

"Caught him in the act. He gave it up. The whole thing."

"No shit? Good for you. Bet Jack Cortland was happy."

"He was. You know how happy?"

"No, how happy?"

Andi leans forward. "Happy enough that he assigned me to Project Nano."

"Ah, Andi, that's great!" Brando falls back in his seat, a look of pride on his face. "Look at you, moving up in the world."

9

Chris

Special Agent Christopher Roberti, just out of the shower, thwacks the syringe, removing a large air bubble, then slides it from the vial, setting both on his bathroom countertop.

He glances at his phone, still open, the article from the *Tribune*, a long-form piece about "what went wrong" with the feds' prosecution of Peter Sahin, who walked on federal corruption charges earlier this week. The *Trib* article doesn't do justice to the evidence, the case his colleagues in Public Corruption put together or, better said, *didn't* put together. He can recite error after error, things the boys in PC could have and should have done, moves they made that backfired.

His phone buzzes. His sister, Mary. He puts his phone on speaker.

"What are you up to, little brother?"

A welfare check, basically. He gets a lot of those from her. He leans forward on his left leg, exposing the right side of his rear end. He draws an imaginary cross on his right glute, then wipes the upper right quadrant with an alcohol pad. "Gotta work a corner tonight. Meanwhile, I'm reading about how our office screwed up the Sahin case."

"So you're stewing."

He picks up the syringe, poises the needle over the spot, draws a breath, then shoots the needle into his skin in one smooth, dart-like motion. "I'm not stewing."

"Let me guess. Those guys in PC can't find their asses with a compass, but they turned you down for a transfer again. Something like that?"

It's annoying, how well she knows him. He cranes back his head to see the syringe. No blood inside. Good.

He plunges it forward, empties the contents.

"I'm just tired of Organized Crime. Tired of chasing low-level drug dealers."

"You're still just getting back on the job, Chris. Give it time."

Mary always says that; the line is growing gray hair. He isn't "just" getting back on the job. He's been back over a year now, and still he hasn't moved from OC, despite his requests for transfer. They still see him as wounded, fragile. They won't say it, but they think it.

"You should call Levi," she says. *"He always cheers you up. Have you talked to him recently?"*

"No, but I did make an appointment with a psychic for next week. Only she called back and told me I wouldn't be able to make it."

A groan from the other end. But that was one of "Levi's Rules" that Chris has tried to follow ever since. *A dumb joke a day keeps the bad thoughts away.*

"Guess I need to work on my delivery." He kills the phone, drops the needle in a hard case, then opens the bottle of Diana on the counter. He pops a pill, swallows it with water from the sink, and winces. It tastes like shit.

He throws a toothpick in his mouth and settles on his bed. He goes online to his medical records, the results that came back last week that he's read and reread. The charts and numbers and terms—CBCs and CMPs, lipid panels and MPVs and hematocrits—they all blur together. All he sees is the word at the end of each line: Normal.

And the note from Dr. Quaresh, his oncologist:

Christopher: Well done! One year healthy! Keep up the good
work and see you in a couple weeks.

He's read it every day, multiple times, like a security blanket, to know that it's real, not a dream.

Dr. Quaresh is a small man with big ears and a tuft of gray hair, the same man who delivered the words that changed Chris's life three years ago: *Well, the tumor was malignant, which means we have some work ahead of us.*

So far, it's Christopher Roberti 1, Cancer 0.

You won, said his chemo partner, Levi, when Chris got his first clean bill of health. *Now act like it. Live! Go out and take what's yours.*

He closes his medical file and pulls up his electronic surveillance of Cyrus Balik, the bug he planted inside Cyrus's office at his strip club, *Seksi.*

Cyrus Balik runs the trifecta of guns, girls, and drugs. White guy, Baltic by birth, who supplies the street gangs in Calumet City and Deemer Park. Human trafficking is his main thing these days, girls from Eastern Europe but also homegrowns, runaways mostly. Owns a bunch of businesses—dance clubs, a strip club, two car washes, and a burger joint—to launder his money.

Some call him "Cy-Bal" because of his artificial left eye. Word is, he lost it in a knife fight in his hometown of Tallinn, Estonia, after getting crosswise with some higher-up in organized crime over there. Came to the States for protection and took the opportunity to start building his own criminal enterprise here some thirty-five years ago.

And boy, did he build one.

Five years ago, Chris had Cyrus dead to rights on an arms purchase, AR-15s coming in from Central America. Chris had flipped the courier, the go-between, a lanky guy named Arturo. They found Arturo's head in a ditch off Pulaski Road two weeks later.

Three years ago, just before the C-word entered Chris's life, just before he had to go on leave for chemo—he had an informant inside Cyrus's operation, a Latvian teenager, Lucija, a sweet kid who got duped into coming to the States and was forced into the life, selling sex and dancing at Cyrus's club. They never did find her body. She just disappeared one day.

Then, of course, there was Bonnie Tressler, a year ago.

People who cross Cyrus seem to fall on awfully hard luck.

Chris hits "play" on the audio surveillance, fast-forwards through dead space. Cyrus doesn't usually spend his days at the club, just nights. The audio first starts playing at a little after 7:00 p.m. last night:

"Viin, mida me teeme, maitseb nagu piss."

"Kedagi ei huvita, mida me müüme. Nad on naiste jaoks olemas."

That's most of what Chris picks up on this intercept—Cyrus speaking to one of his men in their native tongue, Estonian. Of no use to him, even if he took the time to translate. He went to the trouble once, parsing through hours of conversation to learn that the topics covered by Cyrus and his idiot lackeys consisted entirely of tits, blowjobs, vodka, soccer, and dick size.

"Ütle sellele rumalale hoorale, et täna õhtul raha teenida."

"Ma ütlen talle, et ta peab oma perset veel natuke raputama."

He fast-forwards more, continuing to pick up nothing useful—only dead space or Estonian. He closes the audio and keeps it saved on his computer.

He doesn't care what Cyrus says to the thugs who surround him. Cyrus doesn't tell them anything that Chris could use. He's only interested when Cyrus clears the room and gets on that burner phone and makes a private call to the one person higher up on the food chain than him, the only person to whom Cyrus answers.

Nico.

Nico Katsaros, the invisible man, the Greek Ghost, Mr. Teflon.

And fortunately, Nico doesn't speak Estonian. Cyrus talks to him in English.

Like in the call Cyrus made eight days ago. Chris pulls it up and listens:

"I need to talk to you about that thing. No, not that one. About Nano."

Project Nano, some new cancer breakthrough developed by a private medical technology company called Quigley Crowe International. Nico plans on stealing the formula and selling it to Chinese operatives. And Cyrus is supposed to help with the delivery, handing it off.

"Yes, this. I should not be involved. What happens if I am caught? This is what you always say, yes? Prepare for worst? Yes, of course, I would say nothing, but I am close to you. They will try to make connection. Would it not be

better for someone with no connection? Okay. Okay, all right, yes, I will, but—but consider what I am saying."

The call ends there. Oh, what Chris would give to hear the other side of that conversation, Nico's words. But he only has a bug in Cyrus's office, not a tap on the burner phone.

Sounds like Cyrus is getting cold feet. He doesn't want to be the courier—the guy who will deliver the formula to the Chinese government agents. He's trying to convince Nico to use someone else. And it sounds like, so far, Nico isn't budging.

Chris kills the audio and closes his laptop.

Cheer up, Cyrus, he thinks to himself. *It will all be over soon.*

10

Leo

The nightclub is on Erie near the river, a place called X, one of the clubs that Cyrus owns. There's a line of people shivering in the cold to get in. I wore a decent jacket so I wouldn't look too out of place. It doesn't work. I look out of place. There is no article of clothing I could have worn that would make me look anything but out of place. The median age of the people in line is at least ten years younger than me.

I go up to the front of the line and approach the doorman. I can hear dance music from out here.

"I'm here to see Cyrus," I say to the guy, about two inches taller and a hundred pounds heavier than me. I hand him a card.

"It's business," I say.

"What kind of business?"

"Business I want to discuss with Cyrus."

He brings a radio to his mouth and turns his back to me. Between the dance music and the buzz of the people in line, I can't make out what he's saying.

He ignores me after his radio call, working the door, letting people in and flirting with women who are freezing out here and trying to get inside.

In round numbers, it took me 27 minutes to get here by Uber, which cost me $18; I've taken 39 steps since leaving the Uber; and I've been standing outside for 19 minutes. Two more minutes outside and every number will be a multiple of 3.

The man nods at me and juts his finger behind him. "Back there," he says.

Oh, well.

Then I turn back and see a door open, a door I didn't even know was there. A bald man with a tired face waves me over. I reach him in 11 steps, which is screwing with my math. At least it's warm inside.

"I need to talk to Cyrus," I say, shaking off the cold.

"Uh-uh." He shakes his head. "Doesn't work that way."

I figured. "Tell him it's about Bonnie Tressler."

But Cyrus will know that as soon as he sees my business card. Bonnie Tressler was my client. Bonnie is now dead because of it.

The man gives me a full appraisal. He pats me down, checking for wires or weapons, finding none. "Stay here," he says. The door closes. I bob my toes to warm them up. Finally, the door reopens. "Come in," the man says.

We walk down a long hallway. He sends me into a room. Inside that room, another man, also bald but wearing a full beard, sits behind a desk, reading his phone. "You are Leo?" he says with a thick eastern European accent.

"Yes. Are you Cyrus?"

I know he's not Cyrus. But better I don't let on.

"No, I am not Cyrus." He peeks up at me. "Are you the police?"

"No."

"You are not member of law enforcement?"

"No, I'm not law enforcement."

His eyes return to his phone. "Who is this Bonnie?"

"Cyrus knows who she is. I'd like to make a deal with him, if he's willing."

"I don't know if he is willing. He may be willing, he may not be. If he is not, you will be sorry that you asked."

"Well—"

"Ten o'clock Monday night, Mr. Leo. Ten o'clock Monday at the strip club. Do you want this meeting?"

"Yes."

"But I tell you, if he is offended by the request, you will be the one who is sorry."

"I understand."

"You will be searched. If we find a weapon, or a recording device, you will be the one who is sorry."

"Fine."

"Fine? Okay, *fine*, he says. Fine." He looks up from his phone. "Listen to what I am saying to you, Mr. Leo. If Cyrus is unhappy with your visit, he will make you very, very sorry."

"I understand. I accept those terms."

The man nods toward the door. "Mr. Leo, go out this door, turn left, follow the hallway. Go through that next door and you are inside the club. Go have a drink. Enjoy yourself. And think about what I say to you. If you change your mind and decide that you do not want this meeting, knock on that same door and tell the man inside you have changed your mind."

I won't change my mind. I should, but I won't.

But I wouldn't mind a drink, so I head down the hallway, the floor vibrating from the pulse of the bass in the dance music. I push open the door. I don't spend a lot of time in dance clubs, so I didn't really know what to expect. But probably something like what I find: a two-story monstrosity, cast in a hazy, dizzying, purplish glow, music blasting from gigantic speakers. The top floor is a series of rooms, private and semiprivate. I scan the ground floor for a bar. There must be one somewhere, amid the high-top tables, even a few booths in the corner, but it's all about the dance floor, at least three hundred people inside, more than enough to make a fire inspector break out in a rash.

I locate the bar, shout my order of a double bourbon with one rock, and take in the scene around me.

Cyrus must make a fortune at this place. And it's an ideal vehicle to launder money.

I do a lap, watching the hardbodies in their scanty club attire lose themselves in the deafening music, the lights bouncing around from color to color, occasionally going strobe. Envying them, wishing I could lose myself that way. My way is a lot less fun.

I turn as if summoned, as if a radar has gone off, and I see her. Coming off the dance floor, laughing with her friends, wearing a tight silver dress and wearing it very well—

No.

I don't move, though my heart climbs into cardiac-arrest gear. It always does, when I see her, no matter how long it's been.

Andi.

11

Leo

I met her on a Wednesday night. I was a college kid working the kitchen at D.C. Hubbards on Sixth Street in Champaign. People came up to the bar to order, then I prepared the food and delivered it to the tables. I spotted her straightaway; she was hard not to notice. Large dark eyes, ink-black hair straight to her shoulders, a gentle curve to her face. She was dressed casually in a purple long-sleeved shirt and running tights and wore a white stocking cap on her head. She could've been wearing a garbage bag for all the difference it would have made. Striking, in a word. Beautiful, but more than beautiful—different, unique. Striking. To this day, I can't find a better word to describe Andi.

"*Sa oled eriline*," as Katye would say.

She was sitting with two other women her age—college age like me, I assumed—but she caught my eye and seemed to watch me as I delivered baskets of breadsticks to a table. I glanced in her direction as I made my way back to the kitchen, and yes, she was still tracking me, though she looked away when I caught her eye.

I did okay back then with the fairer sex, but I was no lady-killer. I was awkward. The phrase *painfully shy* was invented for me. So our little game of peekaboo—well, it was fun, ego-soothing, my little moment of fantasy in an otherwise tedious night of work, but nothing more. There was no chance anything would come of it, and that made it easier to enjoy.

It went like that the rest of the night. The kitchen closed at eleven, and Peekaboo Girl stayed the whole time, always making subtle eye contact with me as I entered the dining area, always watching me as I left. I'd occasionally glimpse out the rectangular window of the kitchen to see if she was still there. One time, I thought, she caught me.

I thought I knew myself well enough by then. I made an okay first impression, by which I mean the impression you formed before I opened my mouth and spoke. A former girlfriend of mine, in a moment of drunken but stark appraisal months after we'd split, told me I was "a dork trapped in a hottie's body." I thought she was being generous with the latter, but we found common ground on the "dork" part.

So there I was in the kitchen after close, not rushing to finish up. Stalling, in fact, taking more time than necessary to shut down the kitchen, preparing more wraps for the next day's lunch rush than needed, scrubbing the ten-year-old grill until it looked recently purchased.

I figured either Peekaboo Girl would leave before I was finished, or it would be so close to last call that, even if I mustered the courage to talk to her, I'd have a quick out if I screwed it up too badly.

It wasn't until twelve minutes after midnight that I left the kitchen. That felt like a lucky number—72 minutes after close, the time 12:12—not only were they all divisible by 3, but there are 12 factors in the number 72. To say nothing of the fact that 72 is the sum of both four consecutive primes (13, 17, 19, and 23) and six consecutive ones (5, 7, 11, 13, 17, and 19), which is almost unheard of.

Like I said—Dork City.

All the more reason why I was relieved when I emerged from the kitchen and she was no longer upstairs. I headed downstairs. I'd decided that I would walk straight out the door without looking back. "Later, Randy," I said to the boss, who was behind the bar.

"Stay a minute." He nudged forward a draft beer he'd poured, a good inch of foam, some dripping down the sides. He nodded to his left. "Some girls were asking about you."

Randy was like that, always looking out for me. He once told me he used to be shy, too. He was one of those college students who liked it so much he never left campus, an Ag major who worked at D.C. Hubbards all four years, becoming general manager and now, ten years later, a part owner as well.

"That can only mean trouble," I said.

"Yeah, but whaddaya got to lose?"

I looked to my right, and there she was, still with her two friends, standing by a high-top, chatting with each other and two guys.

"Just walk up and say hi." Randy worked a rag along the bar.

"Who asked? There's three of them."

"The blond with the streak of pink in her hair and the nice caboose. She said, 'Who's the cute guy in the kitchen?'"

The girl with the streak of pink. Not Peekaboo Girl. I was immediately disappointed.

Randy put down his rag and leaned toward me. "Seriously, dude. Just walk up and say hi."

So I did. I'd made it about as easy as possible for myself. It was nearing last call, so a quick exit wouldn't be odd. But I also had Randy's eyes boring through the back of my neck, and I usually preferred my humiliation without witnesses.

She made it easy. Peekaboo Girl, that is. She saw me awkwardly ambling forward and opened herself up for conversation. She even smiled. It struck me at that moment that smiling did not come easily to her, which made me more intrigued than ever.

"You're the guy from the kitchen," she said. "Leo."

"Hey, how's it goin'?" I really was not a hey-how's-it-goin' guy, but simple and easy was the best approach. "I don't think I've seen you on campus."

I silently congratulated myself for that line. An icebreaker. Conversation! I was a conversationalist!

"We go to ISU." She nodded toward her friends. "Road trip. I'm Andi Piotrowski."

"Leo." I felt myself sliding into the pool. This wasn't my thing. I met girls on campus by seeing them a lot, usually sharing a class. And almost every time, the girl made the first move, or at least mutual intermediaries assured me that a forward move was welcome. I wasn't a pickup artist, a one-night-stand guy; I had no game whatsoever.

"You don't look Polish," I said.

See?

If there were an invisible lasso I could throw over words that leave my mouth, reining them in and pulling them back. Or if there were some kind of a three-second delay, like they have for live television to block out cusswords. But alas.

She took it well, even smiled for the second time. "I get that a lot."

"You're beautiful," I said.

So if we were keeping score at home, and the standard was cringe-inducing comments, I was 2-for-2. At least the second one was flattering, if unsolicited and way too soon. Unless, of course, you strung the two comments together, as if one logically followed the other, in which case it sounded like I was insulting the Poles as a people.

The second comment in particular seemed to pain her, or at least flummox her. "Thank you," she said, as if I'd just served her food.

She was trying, though, to make it easy for me. I'd already decided that she was far too composed, too mature, and too gorgeous.

She smelled fresh. I couldn't pin down a scent beyond that. I, on the other hand, was relatively sure I smelled like fried food.

"I'm not . . . Sometimes the filter between my brain and my mouth doesn't work so well."

Her head angled. "I never would've noticed."

Yeah, she was way, way out of my league in every way. Beautiful and cool and composed. Which itself brought a sense of relief. I felt myself easing up.

"So what's your major?" I said.

At least this time the humor was intentional. She picked up on it.

"Criminal justice," she said. "You?"

"Me? Oh, I'm not a student. I'm an astronaut."

"Really?" Her thick eyebrows arched.

"Yeah, I just work this kitchen to pass the time."

"I see. The commute from Champaign-Urbana to NASA must be a bitch."

Randy bellowed it out, last call. You don't have to go home, but you can't stay here.

I took a slug of my beer. "I should probably quit while I'm ahead."

Her eyes flickered. I couldn't read her. "You consider this being ahead?"

"Well, I haven't given you the chance to reject me yet. Plus, I think that whole astronaut thing went over pretty well. You bought that, right?"

"Absolutely." A big nod, eyebrows knit together, a whole show.

And then something came over me. Like I said, everything was stacked in my favor—I had an easy exit and absolutely nothing to lose. "Can I ask you a question?" I said, before I could talk myself out of it. My heart started banging a drumbeat, but I was too far in to back off now.

"Sure."

"Do you date dorky, insecure guys?"

Her mouth moved in the wrong direction from a smile. Not a frown so much as a transition from upward curves to a straight line. I instantly knew I'd missed. I was sure of it.

Before I could recover my dignity, her eyes dropped and she leaned in toward me. She lifted her chin, as if to kiss me, but she wasn't aiming for my lips or even my cheek.

"I have a question for you, too," she whispered into my ear.

My life was never the same.

I watch her as she comes off the dance floor now, what feels like a lifetime later, the athletic top and running tights replaced with a tight silver dress. I turn my head a quarter and raise my phone to my ear, all to cover my face in case she glances over.

But she doesn't. She heads to the bar with her two friends. Two people I don't know. Once upon a time, back when we were "Pio and Leo," I knew all her friends. They were my friends, too. And now they're strangers, just like Andi. She has a different life that doesn't include me.

My insides roiling, I slip out of the bar through the crowd. Andi can't know I'm here.

She can't know what I'm about to do.

12

Chris

Chris gets home after the gym, eager to listen to his electronic surveil-lance. He pulls out his phone and plays the audio, fast-forwarding through it, looking for the bounce in audio waves indicating when Cyrus is talking inside his strip-club office. Usually, he has to wade through hours of nonsensical talk with Cyrus's goons in Estonian, but he gets lucky tonight. It doesn't take him long to get a conversation in English, clearly over the phone, which all but guarantees that it's of interest to Chris—a phone call between Cyrus and Nico.

He sits on his bed and touches his earbuds while he listens to Cyrus's words from only hours ago:

"Hey, is me." Pause. *"Is okay, is okay. You will not believe who wants to meet with me. Leo Balanoff. Leo Bal—the lawyer for that woman. You re-member the woman? A year ago, the woman, Bonnie . . . Yes, yes, this one. He is coming to see me Monday night."* Pause. *"I do not know why. What? Yes. Hard to say. My guess is he wants protection for his client, Bonnie's son, but this I do not know."*

Wait, what? Leo Balanoff, Bonnie Tressler's lawyer, wants to meet with Cyrus? Why on earth would he do that? Is it what Cyrus is guessing—he wants assurances for Bonnie's son? God, if Leo Balanoff thinks he can reason with Cyrus, he has lost his mind.

"I call you because this gives me idea," says Cyrus. *"This lawyer Balanoff might be useful for that other job. We know about this lawyer, yes? Yes, ex-*

actly. Maybe this is something we can think about for this man. Maybe I will try to see how tough he is."

Jesus. He's talking about Project Nano. Cyrus already told Nico he doesn't want to be the middleman on that job. He's talking about Leo for that role. That must be—

"Hel-lo-oh!"

Chris all but jumps off his bed. Mary, walking into his condo with groceries. He kills the recording and dumps his earbuds. "Sorry."

"You feds and your overhears. Why don't I ever get to do stuff like that?" She pulls out some chicken, veggies, and a bottle of wine. She buys; Chris cooks; they both clean.

She's been coming by far more than she should since cancer entered his life. He appreciates the company but can't shake an underlying guilt.

"So who are you surveilling this time? One of the gangs? A big shipment coming in you're gonna intercept?"

"Something like that." He pushes himself off the bed. "I'm gonna jump in the shower before I cook."

"Yes, please do. I can smell you from here. I'll get started on the wine."

Chris starts the shower. First, an injection. Slipping the syringe into the vial; removing an air bubble; sanitizing the spot on his glute; plunging the needle in, checking for blood, then depressing the syringe. A quick disposal, then a pill of Diana down the hatch, no water.

"Remind me to tell you about *my* exciting day," Mary calls out from the bedroom. "Here's a preview: it involves a grown man pissing himself."

He gets in the shower, chuckling. Mary's a saint. She went to every doctor's appointment, drove him to and from every chemo session— sometimes staying with him—and was always there when he was so weak he could barely crawl to the bathroom to vomit. She was his cheerleader, nurse, cook, cleaning lady, and near-constant companion through the whole thing. The kind of thing you can never repay. Sure, they're siblings, but what she did—not everyone would do. To top it off, she played the same caretaking role five years earlier, when their mother fought and lost her own battle with cancer. There's a special place in heaven for that woman.

When he kills the water and grabs a towel, he hears her voice in the bedroom.

"Holy *shit*."

"What, holy shit?" he calls back through the foggy bathroom.

He dries off, throws on a T-shirt and sweatpants, and opens the bathroom door, finding Mary wearing his earbuds and holding his phone.

"Hey. What the fuck? Eavesdrop much?"

She looks up at him, mouth open. "Is this Cyrus Balik? It must be. He's talking about Bonnie Tressler and Leo—"

"Yeah, okay, it is."

"Is he talking to Nico?"

"Hey, y'know—this is confidential work."

She waves him off. She's his sister and she's a cop. They've shared plenty of secrets in the past. "You're on their trail again. I didn't know that."

"I don't tell you everything."

"I know the pattern of your bowel movements, kiddo."

Yeah, well, that was post-surgery stuff. "I'm gonna start dinner. Did you get breadcrumbs?"

"No, just grill it. But don't avoid me. This isn't a phone tap. It's a bug. What, in his office at the strip club? Or the warehouse in Deemer Park? Sounded like the strip club—the music."

He heads into the kitchen, pulls out a pan and some olive oil, unwraps the chicken.

"You got an intercept on Cyrus," she says. "How'd you get a judge to authorize it? What was your PC?"

"Y'know, I was gonna make chicken cordon bleu. You just want grilled chicken?"

She goes quiet, leaning against the wall, arms crossed, while he pulls some garlic and onion powder from the cupboard and starts preparing the meat.

"Put on some music or something," he suggests.

"You got a Title III intercept on Cyrus Balik. How'd you do that?"

"Can I just cook? I don't wanna talk about work."

She helps herself to more wine, a Chardonnay with the red price sticker still on. "Seems like a simple question to me," she says. "How'd you get a judge to sign off on a T-3—"

"I didn't." He throws down the spatula. "I didn't get a warrant. Happy now?"

She almost spits the wine out of her mouth. "What? Hello?"

"I'm just gathering intel. I know I can't use it in court."

"But you can't do it, *period*, Chris. Have you lost your mind?"

"Maybe I have." He nods, dropping the chicken onto his small grill. "Maybe I'm tired of Cyrus Balik and Nico Katsaros breaking about every law on the books and getting away with it. Maybe I'm tired of playing fair."

"But you could . . . you could lose your *job* over this. This isn't like you."

"Yeah, well—the old me has tried to catch those assholes for years and failed. Maybe the new me is gonna put 'em behind bars. And don't—don't give me that look."

She spreads her arms. "What look?"

"That look of disapproval. These guys are up to something big, Mare. Big even for them. And the only reason I know about it is this intercept. I'll use the information and massage it into something I can use for a warrant."

"You'll lie, you mean. Claim you have a CI or something."

"I won't lie. I'll take what I learn here and follow it to some other source. I'll leave out the part about the intercept."

"Which is lying."

"Which is finally putting away those lowlifes. I know what I'm doing."

"Okay, just . . ." She makes a calming gesture with her hands. "I know you're trying to make up for lost time—"

"Hell yes, I am." And he wouldn't mind proving—to himself, if no other—that he's capable of greater things.

She lets out a sigh. "You really should talk to Levi."

"I wouldn't talk to my chemo partner about *this*."

"About things, generally, I mean," she says. "Levi always kept your head on straight."

"My head's on straight. Truly." He puts his hand on his heart. "I'll do this the right way. I just needed to get a foothold. I have a feeling about this. I think this will be it."

They eat in relative peace. She finally calms down. He lays out the general parameters of what he's investigating.

"So Nico's going to steal some big medical discovery and sell it to the Chinese government," she summarizes. "And Cyrus is the one who's delivering it."

"But Cyrus wants someone else to deliver it. I'll bet Nico does, too. They're too easily connected, those two. They want someone outside their circle."

"And now here comes Leo Balanoff. Wanting to meet with Cyrus, probably to protect Bonnie Tressler's son. And you think Cyrus likes the idea of Leo being the new delivery boy?"

Chris spears some asparagus with a fork. "You heard the audio. Isn't that what it sounded like to you?"

"Yeah, it did." Mary leans back in her seat, her glass of wine poised. "Leo seemed buttoned-up. Back when we met with him, he seemed like he'd done his homework on Cyrus."

"Agreed."

"So he has to know that sitting down with Cyrus, trying to negotiate with him to leave Bonnie's son alone—he's walking into a lion's cage. That's lunacy."

"Borderline suicidal," says Chris. "The risk he's putting himself in, waltzing into that pit of vipers. He must really care about that son."

"Same thing I was thinking." Mary empties her glass of wine. "Bonnie's son, whoever he is, must be very important to Leo Balanoff."

30 YEARS AGO

1994

13

June 4, 1994

Marilyn

"You shouldn't be doing this, Marilyn," she whispers to herself. But what the hell does *should* mean anymore?

Marilyn takes the last sip from her glass of wine. Across from her, resting precariously on the dirt mound of the grave, is another glass half-filled with 1988 Finch Hollow Chardonnay—Fred's favorite if you pressed him, if you got him to admit he was actually kind of a wine snob.

The flame of the candle flickers in the gentle wind. She'd prefer to leave it there with the glass of wine, but she doesn't want to risk the chance of a grass fire, given how hot and dry it's been. That's all she needs, setting a cemetery ablaze in the middle of the night.

Channeling Fred's trademark dark humor—*At least everyone would already be dead*—doesn't cheer her up. She takes one last look at the headstone, animated and haunting through the dancing flame:

FREDERICK MARTIN BALANOFF
July 1, 1962–April 2, 1994
Devoted Husband and Father

She blows out the candle, plunging the Upper Alton Cemetery into darkness. She gets to her feet with the empty wine bottle and glass, holding them in one hand like Fred used to do. "Happy anniversary, Fredo," she whispers, using the nickname he hated. *Fredo was the pansy of the Corleone family,* he'd complain. *Why not Sonny or Michael?*

Her footsteps are plodding, unsteady. Too much to drink. But the drive home is only ten minutes. It's not like cops get DUIs, anyway.

The path back to the car is difficult to navigate in the dark, the only illumination the headlights from her car, still running, parked on the driving path that winds through the cemetery. In the distance, she hears the faint but lively chatter of young people. Teenagers, probably, sneaking into the cemetery to get drunk, exactly what she used to do at that age in this very place.

She gets inside the car and checks the rearview mirror. Her boys, Leo and Trace, are asleep in their car seats, Leo in his St. Louis Cardinals baseball cap, with his teddy bear dressed in a matching Cardinals uniform. "Leocorn," Fred used to call him, short for Leo the Unicorn, their left-handed boy with hair of bright red curls. His younger brother leans on his shoulder, brown-haired Trace with his blankie, some cheap thing they picked up at Walmart that he treasures more than anything else they've bought him, for reasons neither Fred nor Marilyn could decipher.

She probably shouldn't have brought them, all things considered. But the original plan was just a quick stop here at the gravesite, a toast on their tenth anniversary, a spontaneous idea after she took the boys to dinner. And they were asleep in their car seats by the time she got here, anyway. That toast turned into two hours and three glasses of wine, the boys none the wiser in their blissful slumber.

She drops the empty wine bottle in the footwell of the front passenger seat, next to a few cards, notes of consolation on elaborate stationery that fell out of the bundle she carried from the funeral home. *It's been two months since the funeral, Marilyn,* she tells herself. *Clean the car up already.*

It happened nine weeks ago today. It was a Saturday, like tonight. There had been *weather,* as people in town liked to say, a significant thunderstorm with high winds. Fred wasn't at fault; it was a teenage boy, driving too fast and losing control, hitting Fred's car head-on. She remembers the phone call, dropping the phone, feeling herself go down, down, down, down—

She opens her eyes, shakes herself alert. Yes, too much to drink. She buzzes down her window for air, even though it might wake the boys, then puts the car in gear and starts driving.

The roads are empty. Her eyelids heavy, her thoughts meandering from the morbid to the melancholy, she slowly navigates the curves on Oakwood. They really should light this road better. She leans forward, hands gripping the wheel with white knuckles, bright beams illuminating the dark streets as she makes the three turns toward home.

Finally, she pulls into her driveway, the suspension bouncing, and punches the button to raise the garage door. She eases the car into the garage but knocks over a bike against the far wall. Jesus. Well, she made it home safely, at least. The boys are fast asleep.

She puts the car in park, kills the headlights, and breathes out a sigh.

She punches the button and watches the garage door lower in the rearview mirror, grinding downward and landing with a conclusive thump. Fred was always adamant about closing the garage door as soon as the car was inside; you leave it up even a minute, next thing you know a mouse or chipmunk from the woods behind the house skitters in.

Fred. Ten years ago today, they said their vows under the cottonwood trees on Miss Agatha's Family Farm, Fred's forehead shiny with sweat in the searing heat. They'd planned a trip to New Orleans this weekend for their tenth anniversary; they'd leave the boys with Fred's father, the only living grandparent, in Huntsville. Now that she thinks of it, she forgot to cancel that hotel reservation, which Fred had secured with a credit card months ago, when he was alive and well and they were a family.

On the radio, the soothing voice of the DJ. "*WLUV-FM, playing only your favorite love songs as we approach the midnight hour . . .*"

She reaches for the keys in the ignition as the next song comes on the radio.

"You're My Best Friend." Queen.

"Oh, seriously?" she whispers, releasing her grip on the keys, laying her head against the cushion. Fred's favorite song, his vote for first dance at their wedding. Marilyn had wanted Van Morrison instead, "Crazy Love." Fred had taken it well: *Tie goes to the bride*, he'd said.

The overhead light, activated by the garage door closing, turns off, leaving her again in all but complete darkness, save the light of the radio and the digital clock: 11:57 p.m.

She closes her eyes and listens to Freddie Mercury's voice. *"I want you to know that my feelings are true."*

"I really luh-uvvv you," she sings along, her head swaying side to side.

I really love you, Fredo.

I really, really—

—really luh-uvvv you . . .

"Whuh . . ." Her eyelids flutter open.

She lifts her chin off her chest with a moan. A dull ache in her neck. The smell of oil and exhaust. Her head throbs with pain, tiny hammers pounding against her temples. Nausea surges to her throat as Michael Stipe sings *"everybody hurts"* on the radio, the vibration of the engine running—

The car. The garage. Darkness. The engine still running.

The time on the dashboard clock, 1:32 a.m.—

"No!"

She reaches for the keys, shuts off the ignition. Hits the button to open the garage door, to bring in fresh air. "Trace! Leo!" she screams, looking into the back seat.

"Boys!"

Two Months Later: August 1994

Leo

It's so hot in here, it's hard to breathe. I know it's hot outside because it's "summer," that's the American word, and when my *emme* and I go outside for our walks or play in the courtyard, it's really hot. But it's even hotter inside the back of this truck.

And dark, too. The only light peeks out from a rectangle on the wall that separates the back of the truck from the front. They told me to sit on a crate, but it was unsteady and uncomfortable, so the man in the back of the truck with me said it was okay if I just sat on the floor. He tried to be nice to me. He smiled but wasn't very good at it. He asked me my name (Rauno), my age (six), and if I liked sports (I'd only seen them on TV and didn't understand them). Then he stopped talking and just sat down across from me.

There are 42 boxes in the back of this truck. That means there are three sets of 14 boxes or six sets of 7 boxes or two sets of 21 boxes. Or vice versa.

"*Kas te räägite inglise keelt?*" he asks me.

"*Jah.*" Yes, I speak English pretty well. My *emme* wants me to know English, not just Estonian. She says I was born in America, so I'm American, and I must speak English. She knows English but not that well, and she wants me to be really good at it. So she makes me watch TV and listen to American music and read American books.

My *emme* tries to speak English with me, too. But mostly we just do numbers together. She says math is an international language.

"*Kas tunnete end paremini?*" the man asks.

He wants to know if I'm feeling better, now that I stopped crying.

"*Ma tahan Emme näha,*" I say. *I want to see Mommy.* That makes me want to cry again.

"*Sa näed oma ema varsti,*" he says. *You'll see your mother soon.*

He looks away as he says it. But it makes me feel better, because my *emme* was screaming and crying and begging and fighting after the men came in and took me and carried me down the stairs and put me inside this truck and drove away. Even from inside the truck, I could hear her screams. *Palun ärge võtke mu last! Palun ärge võtke mu last!*

The ride is long and bumpy. But he said I'll see my *emme* soon.

"*Ärka üles. Ärka üles.*"

I open my eyes. The man is nudging me awake.

The back door of the truck slides upward. Sunlight pours in. I raise my hand to my face.

The man pulls me to my feet and holds my arm. His fingers wrap all the way around my arm but he doesn't grip it hard, like the men when they took me. He walks me along the bed of the truck, our footsteps causing echoes, until we reach the edge, where another man, who is much bigger and also doesn't smile, grabs me and holds me in big arms and then sets me down on the ground.

I don't know where I am, but it's so bright I have to squint. It's hot but not as hot as inside that truck. We're in a wide-open space with a black surface and some kind of a store that has a broken window and looks empty.

"Oh, there he is!"

I turn and see a woman, who is squatting down to my height. She has hair that's kind of red and kind of brown. She has a lot of makeup on her face and big eyes. She also has a big smile, but it seems weird, like she really likes me even though she doesn't know me. She seems kind of scared but pretending not to be.

"They said you speak English," she says to me.

"Yes."

"What's your name, honey?"

"Rauno Invernenko," I say.

"I'm Marilyn, Marilyn Balanoff." Her smile widens and her eyes glow, like she has a big surprise for me. "You can call me 'Mommy.' And how do you like the name 'Leo'?"

Two Months Later: October 1994

Leo

A surprise, she said. I'm "in for a big surprise." I guess I'm kind of excited, sitting in the back of the car, strapped into a seat. We're going somewhere for a surprise.

I've lived with Marilyn Balanoff for 61 days. The number 61 is a prime number, which means it can't be evenly divided by any other number besides itself and the number 1. *Emme* says she likes prime numbers because they stand on their own without any help.

Marilyn wants me to call her "Mommy." I don't want to, but I do it because she tells me to and because I call my real mommy *Emme*, so it's a different word, at least.

I don't like staying with Marilyn because I miss *Emme*, but she's been nice. She asks me what food I want to eat and tries to get me what I want. I like the potatoes at McDonald's that they call "hash browns" that are oval-shaped, so we've eaten that a lot. She lets me watch TV and gives me books to read. She hugs me a lot, too.

But there's stuff I don't like. She puts something in my hair that makes it turn red. And sometimes she puts curlers in my hair to make it look curly. I have red curly hair now. And she makes me use my left hand for everything. I want to write and color and draw with my right hand, but she makes me use my left. She tells me I'm left-handed now.

I don't want to be left-handed. And I don't want red curly hair.

The only time she isn't nice is when I cry and tell her I want to go back to *Emme*. She gets sad and worried when I say that. She says she's protecting me. She says she's a police officer, and police officers protect people. I kind of know what police are from television.

The room where we live is part of a "motel." I'm not sure what that means, but it's a little bigger than the room where *Emme* and I live.

Marilyn is singing along to music while she drives. She has a pretty voice when she sings. Not as good as *Emme*'s, but pretty.

Marilyn says we're going to live in a nice house soon in a town called "Galesburg." I don't want to live with her there or anywhere. I want to be with *Emme*. I tell her that every day. Maybe I've told her enough now. Maybe that's what she means by the "big surprise" I'm in for. I cross my fingers, because people do that for luck.

The car slows down, and she turns left. I see it. The black surface. The store that looks empty and beaten-up. This is the place. This is where I first met Marilyn, 61 days ago.

And there's the truck! That's the same truck that I was in. My heart starts beating really fast and I start crying without meaning to.

I'm going home. She's letting me go. I'm going home to *Emme*. My body starts shaking, I can't help it.

Marilyn parks the car and looks back at me. She is smiling, but then she sees my face. "Oh, don't worry, Leo, you're going to *love* this surprise. Mommy will be right back."

I'm not . . . ?

I try to speak but my voice doesn't work. Marilyn gets out of the car but keeps it turned on, the music playing.

I watch her walk away. She has her winter coat on because it's cold outside but not that cold. She walks up to the truck and goes around the other side of it, so I can't see her. Is *Emme* going to come out of the truck—

No. I see Marilyn again. Holding a boy in her arms. He's little, like me, except he has brown hair. He's crying. She's talking to him, whispering to him, but he starts crying harder.

He stops crying as they reach the car. He sees me sitting in my car seat.

Now, I guess, I understand why there was another car seat back here next to mine.

The door opens. Cool air rushes in. She places the boy into the car seat and locks him in. The boy's face is streaked with tears, but he is silent, his eyes wide.

"Leo," she says to me, "this is your brother, Trace."

Two Months Later: December 1994

Roger & Leo

After a while on the job, you get a feel for it, you can spot the lifters long before they make their move. Little things, really. The stiffness of their posture, their casual glances in all directions, the shuffle of their feet.

Usually they're older than this kid on the black-and-white screen wearing a St. Louis Cardinals hat, who looks all of five or six years old, standing alone in the aisle. There must be a parent somewhere around here, probably lost track of the kid.

Roger Artest, the security guard in the back room of the store—Brandenberry's Grocery and General—swivels in his chair and picks up his radio. "Gino, I got a possible lifter in aisle six. A boy, young kid, Caucasian, red curly hair, wearing a hoodie and jeans and a St. Louis Cardinals baseball cap."

The boy looks left, then right, hands tightly in his pockets. He turns his head upward. When his eyes stop moving, he's looking straight into the security camera in the corner.

It's like Roger and this boy are making eye contact through the fuzzy screen.

"Don't do it, kid," Roger whispers. "It'll be just as much a hassle for me as you."

Problem is, it's not shoplifting until they leave the store. You can't bust them until they've walked out with the merch. That never made sense to Roger. Would make a lot more sense to give them a friendly reminder, at the checkout line, that they must have accidentally dropped that tube of deodorant in their purse, or hey, remember to pay for that candy bar that you absentmindedly shoved into your pocket.

But Mr. Brandenberry will have none of it. Company policy. Something about legal liability, about harassing customers while they shop, before they've committed a crime.

So Roger and Gino, they have a thing they keep between the two of them. Roger will send Gino over to whichever aisle to make an appearance, to ask the would-be shoplifter if he needs help finding anything, to courteously warn him he's being watched.

Before Gino can make it, a woman appears in the aisle—the boy's mother, obviously—holding the hand of another boy wearing a puffy jacket, who looks even younger than the boy in the Cardinals cap. They walk down the aisle toward the Cardinals boy. The mother says something to him. He nods his head, but when his mother turns, he grabs two packs of baseball cards off the shelf. He slips one into his back jeans pocket and the other into his little brother's coat pocket.

Damn. He wasn't even subtle about it. You want to steal a pack of baseball cards, take them off the shelf, walk with them as if you're planning on paying for them, then slip them in your pocket many aisles away, several minutes later. Don't be so obvious.

Roger lifts the radio again. "Gino, you missed him. He already lifted. He's heading to checkout with his mother and little brother. He stuck a pack of baseball cards into his little brother's jacket pocket and put one in his own back jeans pocket."

"Copy that. Let me know which line."

Roger makes a copy of the video. He plays the tape over from the start, stops it again at the point when the boy's face is turned to the screen, looking directly into the camera.

Looking right at Roger.

"This is so embarrassing," says the woman once she's pulled back inside the store. She holds out her driver's license to the assistant manager, Jason Kay.

"My name is Marilyn Balanoff," the woman says. "This is my son Leo, who is six, and this is his brother, Trace. Trace is five. We're new here. We just moved up to Galesburg a month ago."

"St. Louis?" Roger asks, nodding to her son's Cardinals hat.

"Close. East Alton. Southern Illinois. I was with the police department there, and I'm with Galesburg P.D. now."

"Oh, you're a police officer," says Roger.

"Yes. Look, I'm sure they didn't realize what they were doing," Marilyn says. "And of course, I'll pay for some silly baseball cards."

"Actually, ma'am," says Roger, "it was your older boy. Leo took both packs and slipped one in Trace's pocket, one in his own."

The mother turns and looks at Leo. "I *see*," she says with an icy tone reserved for disapproving mothers. .

Roger looks at Leo, a cute kid with messy red curls of hair. His eyes glued to the floor. But not staring aimlessly. His eyes are clear and intense. He is listening carefully to the adults.

"The boys lost their father eight months ago," she says. "That's why we moved here. A change of scenery. The boys . . . It's not an excuse for what happened here, but . . ."

"Oh, gosh, I'm sorry to hear that." Jason Kay lets out a sigh. "Well, welcome to Galesburg. Let's just call this a misunderstanding."

"Again, I'm so embarrassed and sorry."

The three of us leave the grocery store together. Marilyn pushes the grocery cart with one hand, her other clutching Trace's hand, while I walk next to Trace. We move through the parking lot to our car, a four-door sedan. "And here I thought we were in the Christmas spirit," she says. "I guess not."

She leaves the grocery cart by the rear of the car and gets us into our car seats. Then she shuts the door, loads the groceries into the trunk, and finds the nearest aisle to discard the cart.

When she returns to the car, she opens the passenger-side rear door, where I'm sitting.

"Nice try, Leo," she says.

I don't look at her. "My name's not Leo. And he's not Trace."

She leans in and whispers in my ear, "God gave us a second chance, and you're going to blow it?"

She works the buckles on my car seat, locks me in tight, and looks me over. Leans in again. "You know what would happen if anyone discovered you? You know, don't you?"

I squeeze my eyes shut, a tear rolling down my cheek.

"They'll kill you," she hisses. "They'll kill you and Trace both."

THE PRESENT DAY

JANUARY 2024

Five Weeks before Valentine's Day

14

Leo

Time to meet Cyrus. The man who fathered Trace, then snatched him away from Bonnie and sold him to Marilyn. The man who snatched me away, too, and sold me to the same woman. The man who is now trying to find Trace and kill him.

Should be fun!

The "gentlemen's club" Cyrus owns, *Seksi*, is on the outskirts of Calumet City in unincorporated Cook County. Men in tuxedos stand at the entrance, a semicircle drive-up for those wishing to valet their cars. VIP treatment, naturally, for such a classy joint.

The parking lot is full, forcing me to street park. A bunch of kids, college age, have poured out of an SUV, but the guy at the door is balking. "We require collared shirts, gentlemen," he explains, because of the whole classy, VIP thing.

I check my phone for the time. It's 9:58 p.m. 958 is the product of two prime numbers (479 and 2).

Another guy, also dressed like a penguin, holds the door open for me, the classy guy in a suit. "Welcome to the club, sir."

I shake my head. "I'm here to meet Cyrus," I say.

"Cyrus who?"

"You have more than one owner named Cyrus?"

Maybe that was unnecessary. But I don't like this place. I don't want to be here.

"He's expecting me," I explain. "I'm Leo."

"One moment." He presses the bud in his ear and speaks while turning away from me. The college boys, one of whom isn't wearing a collar, aren't getting anywhere with middle management.

The man nods to me and points around the corner. "There's a rear entrance," he says.

Of course there is.

I walk around to the side of the club and stop, breathe out, take a moment to ponder what I'm about to do.

I'm pretty sure this is the dumbest thing I've ever done. And that's saying something.

The rear entrance of the strip club is decidedly more private, only a single light over a door without fanfare, a security camera peeking down on me. I stand there with my phone. 10:03. The number 1,003 is divisible by 59 and 17, both primes.

The two men who answer the door are not dressed for a night on the town like the guys up front, unless your idea of a night on the town is a back-alley brawl.

They frisk me and take my phone. The one guy, the shorter of the two, examines my iPhone like he's never seen one before.

"This way." I follow large guy number one to a door and walk in.

I've seen him in surveillance photos and mug shots, even some news articles. But this is the first time live, sitting behind a desk, a bank of security monitors behind him.

Cyrus Balik, in the flesh.

15

Leo

I have represented murderers and drug dealers, swindlers and gang-bangers, men who robbed and cheated and maimed and killed. But this is the first time I have looked into the eyes of pure evil. A man who imprisoned young women—runaways like Bonnie, foreign girls lured to America like my mother—drugged them up until they were addicts, then turned them into prostitutes. A man who impregnated these girls, then sold their children to the highest bidder. A man who chewed up and spat out human lives like they were sticks of gum.

He has long, dark, wavy hair parted off the center, a scraggly beard that is showing signs of gray, a scar on his cheek, and a nose that looks like it's seen its share of battle. His face is worn, as I would expect of someone in his late fifties living a life like his. He wears a number of chains around his neck, one a crucifix. His right eye is small and puffy and bloodshot.

His artificial left eye, earning him the nickname "Cy-Bal," has a front plate of small diamonds over the acrylic surface, or at least legend has it that they're diamonds. All I can say for certain is it's very sparkly, and anyone who would go to that trouble is a complete douchebag.

Trace doesn't look like Cyrus, fortunately taking after his mother instead. But as best I can tell, there's no obvious resemblance between Cyrus and me, either. I have no idea who my biological father is. Unlike

Trace, who got to meet and know his true mother, I never got to see my *emme* after she was taken from me.

Cyrus greets me with a smile, his hands out, sporting cuff links of diamonds (of course) on his purple silk shirt. "A special guest, I see," he says, chuckling. A thick Eastern European accent; he's Estonian by birth, same as my *emme*. He doesn't offer a chair, so I don't take one.

"Where is he and what is his name?" he asks me. "The son?"

"You mean *your* son, don't you? The one you're trying to kill?"

Cyrus works his jaw. Glances over at one of the guys behind me. "*Ma peaksin ta kohe tapma*," he says.

Didn't catch every word of that. But I'm pretty sure he said he should kill me.

"*Ole ettevaatlik*," says the man behind him. "*Ta on jurist.*"

Be careful, the other guy's saying. He's a lawyer.

If Cyrus wants to kill me, I highly doubt that my status as an attorney is going to deter him. If anything, it would make him choose a more painful manner of death.

"I want to know where he is, mister lawyer," Cyrus says. "I want to know who he is."

"I didn't come here to tell you who he is or where he is. I came here to resolve this problem. My client is tired of looking over his shoulder. He wants this over. He is prepared to make a deal."

"Well, then." Cyrus throws his hands up in the air. "Let him come here himself and tell me he wants to make a deal."

"That's why I'm here," I say. "I'm representing him."

"I want *him* here."

"And I want to throw a fastball a hundred miles an hour. Neither one is gonna happen."

He cocks his head, resting it on his hand. I'm beginning to think he's on something. The whole thing with his eyes not moving in sync is starting to mess with me, too. Personally, I'd have gone with an eye patch.

"Okay, not a baseball fan," I say. "But you are a businessman. I came here to make you a proposition."

Cyrus stares at me, his lips moving, playing into a smile and then a frown. "Now you insult me," he says. "I show you great courtesy and ask one simple, reasonable question, and you insult me."

"You asked two questions," I say, because it's getting hard to be civil to this asshole. "And they weren't all that reasonable, if we're being honest."

Cyrus isn't entirely sure what to make of me. He bangs his hand on his desk and points at me, some kind of a goofy smile on his face. Yep, he's definitely on something.

"I'm here to make us square," I say. "My client agrees that he will never cooperate with the FBI. He will never provide evidence against you. And out of respect for you, in exchange for you leaving him alone, he's prepared to compensate you. He's willing to give you fifty thousand dollars."

I almost throw up in my mouth, uttering those words. But I couldn't come here with just a naked promise that Trace won't try to press a case against him. Cyrus has to win. There has to be something else, and the only thing that a guy like Cyrus understands is money.

Really, from his perspective, this should be a no-brainer. Without Bonnie, Trace isn't much of a threat to Cyrus. Trace could prove he is Cyrus's child, yes, but that is not a crime in and of itself. It was the combination of Bonnie and Trace that threatened him. With Bonnie gone, Cyrus is in the clear. However much he might consider Trace an enemy, he gives up nothing by making this deal, and he's fifty thousand the richer.

He gives me a long look, then glances at his comrades again and says something to them I don't understand. But he doesn't respond to me.

"You get what you want," I say. "He won't pursue any charges. And for your trouble, a generous offer of cash."

"But that is not what I want." Cyrus places both hands on his desk. "I ask you one more time nicely. Where is he and what is his name?"

"You don't actually think I'm gonna tell you."

He tries on a few different smiles, each one wider than the next. By the end, he's grinning ear to ear, his beady little predatory eye lit up while the diamond next to it sparkles.

"I *do*," he says. He nods to the guy behind me. The door opens. Two more men shuffle in. Four standing behind me now, maybe five. It smells like a locker room. I don't like my odds. Maybe if I knew tai chi or kung fu or some Jedi mind tricks. Or if I were Batman. That would be cool.

Cyrus reaches below his desk, producing some article of clothing or something that he slips over his head, some kind of apron—

A smock. A smock with dark red smears and spatters on it. Either this is an impromptu art class or I have overplayed my hand.

The men behind me force me down into a chair, then tilt it backward. Before I know what hit me, they are pinning me to the chair, angled backward at sixty degrees from the floor.

And now Cyrus himself is standing over me, holding a pair of pliers, wearing the bloody smock. "His name," he says.

"I urge you to reconsider," I say.

He blinks. "He urges me to reconsider!" he laughs. Then he says something in his native language that my rusty Estonian doesn't completely catch, but I'm guessing it's along the lines of *He urges me to reconsider!*

After the laughter dies down, he holds up the pliers. "I will pull out one tooth at a time until you tell me," he says. "You *will* tell me, believe me, so better for you, you do it now."

It's hard to argue with his logic. I'm a wimp when it comes to pain. My heart is pounding against my chest cavity, pleading with me to be reasonable. Sweat beads have sprouted from every pore on my body. I took this too far. Didn't handle it right. I was dumb. But I'm stubborn, too. There's no way I'm giving him the name he wants.

Cyrus shouts something. I clamp my jaw down tight. I try to struggle but these men are far too strong, holding me in place dangled backward.

Cyrus grips my mouth and pries it open, holds the pliers before my eyes. My head is being held in place by at least four hands between the three of them. I can't move.

"A hundred," I manage to say. "A hundred thousand."

The pliers snap open and closed, open and closed like a Pac-Man.

"Now this is *really* your last chance," he says, easing up on my jaw. "Because I am a nice man, I give you this one last chance. Do you have a name for me, mister important lawyer? Who is your client? Tell me his name."

I take a couple breaths, work my jaw.

"Vladimir Putin," I say.

He stares at me, then breaks into a wide grin. "This guy." He throws up a hand. Then he turns to me again. "You know why they knock your teeth out in prison, Mr. Leo?"

I do. Because it turns your mouth into the functional equivalent of a vagina. Because it makes you the belle of the cell block.

"Better blowjobs," Cyrus says, preferring to leave nothing to the imagination.

He calls out to his crew. A moment later, the door opens, and more men come in. I've lost count, but there are enough to secure both of my arms and legs, hold the chair steady, and force my mouth open with the strength of a vise.

Cyrus clasps the pliers onto my front tooth. "You had many chances, my friend."

He leans back to anchor himself, like he's readying for a tug-of-war.

"How many teeth are there, I wonder?" he says.

Twenty-eight. I have twenty-eight teeth.

"Let's find out," says Cyrus.

I hold my breath, squeeze my eyes shut, wrap my fingers around the arms of the chair in a white-knuckle grip.

28 is a perfect number the sum of its factors 1+2+4+7+14=28 the sum of the first primes 2+3+5+7+11=28 the sum of the first non-primes 1+4+6+8+9= 28 the square root is 5.2915 the square of 28 is 784 the sum of the digits of 784 is 19 the sum of the squares of the first 19 primes is divisible by 19—

"Or."

27, the sum of all numbers between and including its digits 2+3+4+5+6+ 7=27 the smallest composite integer not divisible by any of its digits wait, what, what—did he—

Did he say *or*?

I open my eyes, release a long breath.

"Or we come to a different agreement." Cyrus clacks the pliers a couple times. "As you say, I am a businessman."

16

Leo

They sit me upright, hand me a bottle of water and a towel to wipe the sweat off my face and neck. One of the thugs, who could break me in half over his knee but leaves something to be desired in the area of personal hygiene, stays in the room to keep watch while Cyrus leaves.

I'm not free to leave. I know that much. The man doesn't seem tensed up or ready to spring into action, though the firearm on his hip is probably enough of an advantage.

At the moment, I'm just happy that all my teeth are intact.

The door opens again about twenty minutes later. Just Cyrus, minus the bloody smock. He sits back behind his desk. The other guy leaves, so it's just Cyrus and me.

"You." He wags his finger, smiles at me almost with admiration. "You were going to let me pull out your teeth."

"I was hoping you wouldn't. You'll recall I said so."

His eyes narrow. Could be, he thinks I just insulted him. Or maybe he's simply trying to figure me out. If he does, I'd appreciate him letting me in on the secret.

"I have a job for you," Cyrus says. "A simple job. You make . . . a delivery for me. This is all you do. And I forget about your client. All is forgiven."

"A delivery. A delivery of what?"

"Not your concern."

"It's very much my concern."

He lifts his shoulders. "We cannot have everything in this world we want."

I look him over. He's in no mood for negotiation.

"You want a canary," I say.

"Why . . . do you say this?"

"You already move drugs and guns and women. You don't need me for that. This is something different. Something important. Something very, very big. You think you're being watched. The feds, probably, with all their resources. You want me to be the canary in the coal mine. If I get caught, only I go down. You have no known connection to me. I'm not one of your guys. I give you plausible deniability. How am I doing so far?"

Pretty well, judging from the expression of approval on his face.

"You will do this for me," he says. "A man willing to do what you were willing to do to protect your client—I assume you are willing to do this favor for me instead. Or . . ." He reaches down and produces the pliers, working them, snap-snap-snap.

Well, if you put it that way.

"You'll stop looking for Bonnie's son?"

"I will. This, I promise."

A promise from Cyrus Balik is worth about as much as investment advice from Bernie Madoff. But he has me over a barrel. If I don't say yes, I'll never leave this room alive. Or if I do, I'll never eat solid foods again. "Fine. Okay. When does this happen?"

"Soon," he says. "Very soon."

17

Chris

From his SUV, Chris keeps an eye on the west corner of the intersection, where his snitch, a low-rank West Side Cobra, takes cash from cars that pull up before he sends them down the street for their merch. One tug of his hat for one packet, two tugs for two.

But what really interests him is the conversation in his earbuds—the audio inside Cyrus Balik's strip-club office.

"Brother, you got some serious brass balls," he mumbles as he listens to Leo defy Cyrus time after time, while Cyrus tries to get him to cough up the name of Bonnie Tressler's son. Things got pretty tense with the pliers and the threats of coerced orthodontic work. But Chris knew Cyrus was never going to follow through with it. Cyrus just wanted to see how Leo held up under pressure. It was a test. An audition. And apparently, Leo passed:

"I have a job for you," says Cyrus. *"A simple job. You make ... a delivery for me."*

And ultimately, all that matters, Leo's answer: *"Fine. Okay. When does this happen?"*

Chris slaps his hand on the steering wheel. "Well, Cyrus," he whispers, "looks like you got your canary."

18

Leo

I woke up that morning, some thirty years ago, curled up at the foot of Trace's bed inside Marilyn's home. It was the fifty-sixth day since Trace arrived, since he was strapped into the car seat next to mine.

Trace cried every night for his mommy and always wanted me to come down from the top bunk and sit with him. Usually, I'd just sleep at his feet. It was hard to fit in his bed, but Trace couldn't fall asleep otherwise. It got so I just waited for Marilyn to say good night and lock us in the bedroom, then I'd climb down.

"When can I go home?" Trace whispered. I didn't realize he was already awake. "Do you think I can go home soon? I want to be Malcolm again. I want Mommy, not her."

Marilyn hadn't unlocked the bedroom door yet, but I could hear the clanging of pans as she made breakfast. I could smell the pancakes and bacon. She would come up soon to wake us, so I climbed back to the top bunk.

The night before, after she put us to bed, she'd said she was taking us to some fancy grocery store today called Branden-something, the nicest store in Galesburg. It had a sundae bar, and we could have fudge sundaes after shopping.

"Do you think she's going to let me go back to my mommy?" Trace asked.

"I don't know."

"Can you do something?"

I heard Marilyn on the stairs, coming up to wake us. "Boys!" she sang. "Time to get ready for our trip to Brandenberry's today!"

Trace looked at me, desperation in his eyes.

"Maybe I can do something," I said. "I'll try."

Well, I tried with shoplifting the baseball cards, but I choked in front of the security guards. When we got home from that debacle, Marilyn unstrapped Trace, then me, from our car seats. "You boys march right into the kitchen and wait for me."

We did. We sat at the kitchen table. The wallpaper was yellowish, with painted vines branching off in every direction with leaves and flowers. On the walls around us, 24 vines wound upward with 864 branches, 5,184 flowers, and 10,368 leaves.

Marilyn went upstairs, then came down into the kitchen, holding something in her hand. "I didn't want to do this, but you leave me no choice. First of all, whose idea was that little shoplifting stunt? Was it both of you—"

"Me," I said. "Just me."

Her hands dropped to her sides. "Brandenberry's is the nicest store in town. And now we can never show our faces there again."

"I don't care," I said. I surprised myself, saying that. It just came out.

She shook her head. "Then I guess you really *don't* leave me any choice." She opened a folder in her hand and pulled out photographs. "Do you boys have any idea what could have happened? Do you not believe me when I say I'm protecting you? Do you know what they'll do to you if they find you? This. *This* is what happens to the boys who didn't get away."

She dropped two large, shiny color photographs on the table.

Little boys, dead. One curled up in a bathtub, one lying face up on a tile floor. Pools of blood, lots of wounds.

A chill rippled through me. Then my undies were warm and wet as I soiled myself. Trace started sniffling and sobbing and then began to wail.

"Do you want them to kill you, too?" Marilyn said, tapping the kitchen table. "Do you? Because I'm trying to keep that from happening. Do you understand?"

She took away the photos after a few minutes and made macaroni and cheese on the stove while we settled down. Eventually, we both stopped crying. But I still couldn't speak. I couldn't stop shaking. Neither could Trace.

She set down the food, bowls for each of us. I wasn't hungry.

"Eat," she barked. I picked up my spoon. "No, no, *no*, Leo. You're *left-handed*. God bless it." She grabbed the spoon out of my right hand and put it in my left.

"Now." Marilyn sat at the kitchen table like us. "It's just a couple weeks until Christmas, and after that you're going to start school. Leo, you'll be in first grade. Trace, you'll be in kindergarten. And we have a *lot* of work to do before that. Especially you, Trace."

"My name is Trace Balanoff."

"That's right, honey," said Marilyn. "How old are you, Trace?"

"Five."

"What is my name?"

"Marilyn."

"And who am I to you?"

Trace looked at her.

"I'm your mommy," she said.

"You're my mommy."

"And who is he?" She gestured to me.

"That's Leo. My brother."

"Exactly. How old is Leo?"

"Six."

"Yes! And what is your daddy's name, honey?"

"Fred."

"Where is he now?"

"Heaven."

She smiled. Her eyes looked tired. She always had bags under her eyes, but when she smiled, the skin folded up several times. "Where did we live before Galesburg?"

Trace blinked. He looked at me.

"728 Windsor Lane," I said.

"Well, the street address isn't import—how did you even know that, Leo?"

I had seen it on an envelope from her mail back when we lived at the motel. 7 goes into 28 evenly. 72 divides by 8 evenly. The difference between the numbers backward and forward is 99, but that's always true when a three-digit number's first and last numbers differ by one.

"You're good with math." She smiled. "Trace, what town did we used to live in?"

"Al—Alton," he stammered.

"East Alton, but that's close enough, probably. Great, honey." She clapped her hands quietly. "Isn't he doing great, Leo?"

19

Leo

Now, decades later, as he looks out the window of his hideaway apartment in Old Town, my little brother isn't doing much better. He's been cooped up here in this apartment, all of one couch and a functioning fridge and tiny kitchen and sink and bathroom, since he got into town. It's probably overcaution, holing Trace up here. But then, I don't know how close Cyrus has come to finding him. "I'm gonna kill him," he says.

"No, Trace. No."

"His warehouse," he says. "Cyrus's warehouse in Deemer Park. That's where you said it has to happen? If we do it?"

"Emphasis on *if*," I say. "If we do it. We shouldn't. It's a terrible idea. Go home. Sneak back into Mexico the same way you snuck in. As far as Border Patrol is concerned, you were never here. Go back to your life."

He turns to me. "He killed Bonnie. He's looking for me so he can kill me, too. That's two reasons right there. And who's to say he won't kill you?"

"He'll never find you," I say. "He doesn't know your name. As for me, let me figure it out. He's roped me into this job. I can handle it. But you have to leave."

"Why? Why do I have to leave? It's okay for you to be in danger but not me?"

Like I'm being selfish. Like I'm getting picked over him for dodgeball. Like Mom gave me a bigger helping of mashed potatoes.

"I'm *already* in danger," I say. "I have been since Bonnie and I started this whole thing. I can't help it now. But you can."

"That's not it," he says, pointing an accusatory finger. "You think I can't handle it. You think it'll screw with my sobriety. That I'll feel guilt or remorse for killing that piece of shit."

That's a lot of it, yes. He's four years clean, but it's always a question, always a fragile thing. Could he handle that kind of weight on his shoulders?

"This isn't time to play the protective brother," he says. "This guy ruined Bonnie's life. Then he killed her. He fucked with my life pretty good, too, if you didn't—"

"I was snatched just like you," I say. "I was sold to Marilyn, too. So? Let me handle it. Killing him isn't the answer, Trace."

"And what—you'll send me a postcard? I just sit on the sidelines?"

I drop on the couch, exhausted, and put my head back. Trace has wanted to put an end to Cyrus since the day Bonnie died. He's no killer. It's not his way. But I've represented a lot of people who weren't killers until they were. Most of them are currently enjoying an extended stay in a friendly neighborhood penal institution. Either way, get away with it or not, it changes you. That's what my clients—the ones who've admitted their guilt, anyway—tell me. It haunts you.

Trace sits down next to me.

"You ever think about what would've happened if that shoplifting thing at Brandenberry's had gone differently?" I ask. "If I'd had the guts to tell those security guards that Marilyn—"

"Don't. Don't do that. You were *six*, Leo. It wasn't your fault."

Yeah, but still—what if? It's a question I've asked myself every day since. If only I'd said something. *This woman is not our mother. I'm not Leo. I'm Rauno Invernenko. He isn't Trace. He's Malcolm Tressler. Please help us!* What would have happened?

True, Marilyn was a cop, which can be intimidating, but the security people had a basis to hold us for shoplifting and probably would've decided, out of caution, to call the police. I'm not sure what the cops would've been able to find out about Katye Invernenko, other than the record of her flying from Tallinn Airport to O'Hare on April 9, 1985, never to be heard from again. But Trace's mother, Bonnie, gave birth in a hospital. There's a birth certificate for a Malcolm Tressler. And I know now—though I didn't at age six—that a simple DNA test would have confirmed that Marilyn was not biologically related to either of us.

Marilyn would've gone to prison. Would we have been reunited with our mothers? Would Cyrus and all his scumbag crew have been brought to justice? There are too many variables to know. But it hasn't stopped me from speculating, every single day. If I'd had the guts to spill out the information to those security guards, would Cyrus have been stopped decades ago? Would countless young girls have been spared?

Instead, I choked under pressure. And then Marilyn brought us home and showed us those photographs. I relive that moment every day, too. Why didn't I question her? Who were these mysterious men who, for some random reason, would kill Trace and me if they found us? Every day, I transplant an adult's critical thinking into my six-year-old brain back then. But what can I say? We believed her. She scared the shit out of us.

"Go back to Mexico," I say. "Let me try it my way first. Give me that chance."

Trace gives me a long look. Then he pats my leg. "Fine," he says. "I'll go home."

20

Andi

Andi swipes the touchscreen of her laptop, showing a woman, early fifties, with thick glasses and a sweep of gray hair. She turns to Jack Cortland, her boss, the small movement causing a larger quake between her ears. Too much wine last night.

"Debra Klonsky," she says. "Deputy chief engineer in Tissue Regen. Earns two seventy-five a year. Divorced with three kids in college. Gets twenty-five hundred a month in maintenance. Two days ago, she reported her laptop stolen from her locker at the gym where she works out in Rolling Meadows."

Jack leans forward. "I've met Debra. Seems nice enough. Any interesting expenditures?"

"Not that we know of."

"What was on the laptop?"

"Some specs and drawings. Something about shock wave technology to heal wounds. But her boss says the specs on her laptop were preliminary, first gen, and now they're onto second gen, so he's not worried."

"What do you recommend?" Jack asks.

"Monitor bank and credit card transactions. And surveillance."

"Surveillance? No, uh-uh." Jack shakes his head. "We only have so many resources for surveillance, Andi. We're not Johnson & Johnson. Stick with monitoring. This feels low-risk."

"You think?"

"Doesn't sound like she had anything of value on the computer. And computers do get stolen. It doesn't always mean corporate espionage." He touches her arm. "Look, I'm not trying to douse your enthusiasm. You're smart and aggressive. You're not just a pretty face, though your face *is* quite pretty."

He grins. Andi doesn't return the smile. But she's used to it by now. Jack grew up under different rules, where comments like that were an everyday occurrence.

"You might be running this department soon, Andrea, and if you are, you'll want people who are smart and aggressive like you. But you'll look at what's budgeted, and you'll have to allocate resources. What are the odds that Debra here is trying to sneak information to a competitor? Pretty low, I'd wager."

"Maybe so, but we need to be tighter," she says. "These scientists and engineers and doctors—they're so free with their information. They talk about this stuff all the time. They text each other day and night. They walk around with sensitive information."

"They're not secretive by nature," says Jack. "They're *collaborative* by nature. And the upper management at QCI has apparently made the decision that fostering that kind of creative environment is more important than a few added restrictions that probably won't stop the stuff we're most afraid of, anyway. You know what our biggest worry is, right?"

"The MSS, obviously," she says, referring to China's spy agency. "Foreign theft."

"Exactly. Domestic competitors aren't the real threat these days. It's the foreign markets. The Chinese government, mostly. So we firewall off all our stuff. As long as we keep our networks off the grid and monitor who downloads what, we've insulated ourselves from foreign theft as best we can."

"That's the thing, Jack. We're *not* doing it as best we can. We should ban phones from their areas. We should search them when they come and go."

"We do searches on eight," he says. "The SCIF for Project Nano."

"But nowhere else?"

"No." He swivels in his chair. "Look, I hear you. I've said all of this to upper management. It's a give-and-take with these guys. We have cameras and we restrict access and we search employees when they leave the SCIF. But identity management is our principal protection."

Andi paces the room, stewing. "'Identity management.' Meaning we just make sure authorized people are in those areas. And then we trust them."

"Right."

"My friend Agnes used to tell me, 'Trust is the hardest thing to give. Even harder than love.'"

"Agnes must have been a cynic."

Yes, more than anyone Andi ever knew, Agnes was a cynic. "But she was also right," Andi says. "I don't trust anybody."

A knock on the door. In pops a man wearing the staff QCI security uniform, the name "Brett" stitched above the shirt pocket. "Sorry to interrupt—the incident report you wanted?"

"Great. Brett Holliday, Andi Piotrowski." Jack waves his hand as he takes the report.

Andi turns and gets a good look at the man—tall, dark, and handsome. Bodybuilder, no question, his chest and arms straining against the cotton shirt, a neck the size of a tree trunk, a five-o'clock shadow of dark whiskers. He probably does well with the opposite sex, though it's hard to imagine that anyone loves him more than he loves himself.

"Nice to finally meet the new deputy." A firm handshake, his blue eyes sparkling. He gives her a once-over. "*Very* nice."

Jack gives an appreciative chuckle. "I told you, brother, I told you."

Andi swallows twenty different objections. What, do they teach misogyny in orientation around here? They actually expect her to feel flattered.

How about we compare IQs, gentlemen? she wants to say.

Instead, she says, "Nice to meet you, Brett."

"Brett's a good man," says Jack. "Just don't play poker with him. He cheats."

The two men get a chuckle out of that. "I just read faces well," says Brett.

It's a good thing neither of them can read Andi's face right now.

Men will underestimate you, Agnes used to always tell her as a child. *Let them. Wait for the moment to show them what you're capable of.*

That day will come, Andi knows. She just hopes it comes sooner than later.

21

Andi

"Time for our big date," Jack Cortland tells Andi. "Dr. Valencia and Project Nano."

"Project Nano," she says. "I'm finally going to hear what the big to-do is about this."

"Right. I've had a briefing, but I only understand about a tenth of what they tell me. We're going up to the SCIF."

The sensitive compartmented information facility, he means.

"I've been wanting to see it," she says. "It wasn't part of the tour."

"You're gonna love it, Andi. It's your kind of place."

They head up to the SCIF three floors above, swiping their key cards and placing their thumbs on the scanners for access. They step off the elevator onto the eighth floor. Nothing on the walls, only a single metal door with the words:

Warning—Biohazardous Material
Chemical Disposal
Do Not Enter

Andi rolls her eyes. Seriously? If anyone gets far enough to access this floor, they're not going to fall for that sign. They'll know what's behind these doors.

They repeat the process of swiping cards and impressing thumb-prints. The door pops open.

Inside, a long, well-lit hallway full of ceiling cameras.

"Welcome to FutureTech," says Jack, squeezing her arm. "Now *this* floor should make you happy, Andi. A certified SCIF."

"It does make me happy, Jack, yes."

"Everything self-contained," he says. "All electronic and communication systems dedicated and contained within this floor. No outside cellular or Wi-Fi reception. An entirely internal computer network. Even the ductwork." He points up at one of the ceiling ducts. "All the openings are equipped with steel bars, welded together, extending in every direction from the center, along with inspection ports and audio- and electronic-suppression systems. There is no way to get on this floor other than through the elevator. No way to hear what goes on in here. No way to send a signal out. Only one entrance that's also the exit, protected by thumbprint and card access."

"We could do more," she says. "Random polygraphs, for one—"

"I'm telling you, Andi—you're preaching to the choir, but it was hard enough to get people to work on this floor all day, unable to use their phones. We already search them before they leave. We make them empty their pockets, take off any coats, turn over their bags for inspection. They hate it but they do it. We start interrogating them or giving them lie detectors—they'll leave. And then we won't manufacture revolutionary products like . . ." He waves his hand. "Like Nano."

Dr. Allan Valencia, skinny and beak-nosed, eyeglasses the thickness of an ice block, looks away from his computer monitor. His desk is piled high with paperwork, the cushioned cubicle walls full of more paper still, pinned up. How does he find anything in this mess?

"The designs have been with the lawyers for months now," he says. "The patent application was filed last summer."

Which is the first line of protection against corporate espionage, right there. Any domestic competitor who tries to copy the product will run headlong into a patent-infringement lawsuit. But of course, foreign countries like China and Russia don't care about U.S. patents.

Andi picks up a copy of the design specs. Twenty pages, front and back, of words and symbols that might as well be hieroglyphics to her.

"We're finishing up stage three testing," Dr. Valencia says. "Animal testing mostly. Mice. A small subset of humans. The results have been impressive. And that's being modest."

"And this list here is the list of everyone working on Nano?" Jack shows him the paper.

"That's everyone," says Allan.

"Can you explain Project Nano to me?" Andi asks.

Not surprisingly, he is more than happy to. Jack was right; these doctors and scientists and engineers are eager to share their information. Wind them up, they'll talk all day about it.

"When you break it down, it's quite simple," he says. "Think of cancer drugs like rescue workers. Firemen putting out fires. But in reality, we're just putting those drugs into a bloodstream. A lot of the drugs get washed out by the circulatory system and never reach the fire—the tumor. Right?"

"I guess so, yeah."

"So in the past decade, scientists have invented nanoparticles that act as vehicles—the fire trucks—to better deliver cancer drugs to the tumor. Problem is, many of *them* can't get past the first line of defense in our immune system—the proteins in the blood serum. The serum proteins attach to the nanoparticles as potential invaders. So still, a very low percentage of these nanoparticles are reaching the tumor."

"That much I can follow," she says.

"Well, we've come up with an ionic liquid coating that acts as sort of a force field around the nanoparticles. It allows them to bypass the serum proteins and attach to red blood cells. Our lab studies show a fifty percent improvement in efficacy. It could be watershed."

Jack looks at Andi. "No wonder the top brass is having orgasms over this."

"How close to final design or prototype?" Andi asks.

"If all goes as we expect, somewhere around two to four weeks," says Allan. "Then we run clinicals and submit to the FDA. This could be . . ." He takes a satisfied breath. "This could forever change how we treat lung cancer. And lung cancer's just the start. Project Nano could revolutionize the treatment of all cancer."

Back on the fifth floor, Jack and Andi stand at the bank of monitors, watching the guard station in the SCIF as an employee leaves for the day.

The employee approaches, carrying a briefcase and holding his suit jacket over his arm. He places his jacket on the table by the station and hands his briefcase over.

The guard pats the pockets of the jacket and hands it back to the man. He opens the briefcase and looks through it. Removes some papers and flips through them. Pulls out a cylindrical thermos and sets it on the table.

"He should check the thermos," Andi says. "The guy could download Nano to a thumb drive, wrap the thumb drive in plastic, and hide it inside the liquid."

The guard runs his hands through the remainder of the briefcase, which contains very little. Then he unscrews the top of the thermos, holds it over a garbage can, and turns the thermos upside down, ensuring it's empty.

"Well, look at that." Jack nudges her with an elbow. "Maybe we aren't so backward."

"I still give you a B minus," she says. "I admit, good job with that thermos. But if he's smart enough to download to a thumb drive, he could hide that thumb drive anywhere. He could stick it in his sock. He could stick it up his you-know-what."

Jack laughs. "You think someone's gonna shove a thumb drive up their ass?"

"For twenty, thirty million dollars?" She whacks his arm. "What's the going rate for specs that are worth a billion dollars? Damn straight they would."

"Okay." He blows out air. "So what's your idea? Cavity searches for every employee?"

"No, we *stop* doing physical searches," she says. "We'll never do them reliably enough. I mean monitoring every download, every manipulation of the Nano file on computers. So we'll *know* if they put it on a thumb drive. I'm talking about specialized paper for the specs, once they go to prototype. Watermarked paper that can't be photocopied, with sensors that trigger alarms at the exit. So it will be impossible to get the specs out."

"Stop the physical searches. Replace them with sensor detectors." Jack thinks it over and nods. "I like it. Makes sense. Looks like I put the right person on this assignment."

"No one's stealing Nano," she says. "Not on my watch."

22

Andi

Andi pops her head into Jack Cortland's office. He's inside with that same guard she met yesterday, Brett the Bodybuilder. They're by Jack's desk, looking at something on a phone. Probably something involving flirty, buxom women and a hot tub.

"Yes, Andi?" says Jack, setting down the phone like a kid who's been busted.

"I found a product," she says. "Watermarked paper with a built-in sensor. It's incapable of being photocopied, and it will trigger the sensors at the door. It will be impossible to physically remove from the SCIF."

He shakes his head in admiration. "I love it, Andi. You continue to impress."

"Beauty *and* brains," says Brett. "Now *that* is one wicked combination." He smiles at her while chomping his gum.

"Um . . . yeah." She closes the door behind her. What next—are they going to ask her to spin around?

Patience, she tells herself. Her work here is too important. Nano is too critical for her to rock the boat right now.

When the time comes, she'll be sure to rock the boat.

After work, Andi parks her car outside her condo building. She lives near UIC in Little Italy, an area that's developed a lot over the last few years.

College students are milling about, walking to or from a night class or hitting one of the bars or coffee shops on Taylor Street.

She drops her bag down inside her condo. There on the kitchen table is a bottle of red wine and a glass from last night, still bearing her lipstick and tiny remnants of Cabernet.

She sits down at the table, uncorks the bottle, and pours her first glass, then walks into her family room. There, on the mantel above the fireplace, a series of photos of Mama, Agnes, or all of them together. After Andi's parents split up, it was just the three of them, at least before Agnes passed.

She picks up the photo of Agnes, taken a few years before she died, waving and smiling at a Sox game, though the darkness of illness had already crept into her eyes. Agnes (short for Agnieszka, her Polish mother's name) came from a shelter for immigrants as a domestic worker—housekeeping, cooking, helping with Andi.

"You call me Agnes," she said to Andi in her accented English, tapping Andi on the nose with a smile. But she called Andi *kallike*—KAH-leek-ah—a term of affection, she later learned after looking it up. At age nineteen, Agnes was only twelve years older than Andi. They were more like sisters than anything else. Agnes, alone in this country, could talk to Andi in a way Mama couldn't. She understood how it felt to be a cast-off, to feel truly alone.

Sometimes, like now, it really hits Andi, how alone she is. "Miss you, Ag." She kisses her photo, returns it to the mantel, and goes back to the kitchen.

23

Chris

Chris, eyes still shut, pats for the phone buzzing somewhere on his bed. He untangles the bedsheet and finds the phone just as the buzzing stops. He throws on his cheater glasses from the nightstand and checks the time—3:09 a.m.—then the caller ID: Mary.

He punches the phone to call her back, props himself up on an elbow.

"Hey," he says. "You okay?"

"I'm fine, but guess who isn't?" she says. "Someone buried a knife in Cyrus Balik's neck."

He pops awake. "Jesus," he whispers. "I'm on my way."

Chris makes it to Deemer Park before four in the morning. He pulls up to the industrial shed on Wentworth that Cyrus Balik sometimes called an office, units from Deemer Park and Calumet City P.D. already there. He immediately regrets his choice of a leather jacket when he's out of the car, pelted by the whipping wind on a frigid January night.

Mary emerges from the shed, lowers her head, gathers her long coat around her.

"Cameras?" Chris shouts over the wind, pointing to the mounted security cams over the shed door.

"Live feed only! No recording!"

"All right. Let's go inside!"

Heads bowed, they hustle into the shed, where a forensics team is dusting and photographing and bagging.

Chris shakes off the cold as he looks around the airy shed with its twenty-foot ceiling, maybe a couple thousand square feet in total, a small area off to the side where Cyrus held court, some tall cages and a wall of shelves in the back.

By the office area, beneath multiple posters of naked women, a desk rests against the wall—undisturbed, a couple stacks of papers, some pencils and a calculator, a ledger that Chris will want to look through to see if there's anything he doesn't already know about Cyrus Balik.

Away from the desk is where the action is. The card table Cyrus used is on its side, one of the legs broken in half. The chair he sat on, a simple folding chair, is soaked in blood.

Cyrus fell not far from that spot, landing face down on the concrete floor. The knife is still lodged in his neck, sticking out horizontally. The blood must've eventually stopped pumping from his wound, the combination of gravity and the ceasing of his heart functions, but not before a significant pool formed beneath him.

Chris can't see the knife's blade, only the hard rubber handle. Probably a five-, six-inch blade, he'd guess.

"Cause of death?" Chris asks, kneeling down by Cyrus. One of the techies glances at him to confirm he's joking.

Looks like Cyrus broke his nose, probably when he face-planted. But no bruising under the eyes, meaning he died almost instantly after hitting the floor, before bruises could form. No other visible marks on the one side of his face that Chris can see. No sign of bruising on his knuckles or fingernails, either. Not much of a struggle.

"Figure he was jumped from behind," says Mary. "The offender surprised him. Looks like Cyrus managed to connect with his elbow behind him, but once the knife sunk in, he probably dropped right there."

Chris sees it, a bloodstain on Cyrus's white shirt at the elbow joint. Probably just as Mary said: Cyrus got jumped, threw back an elbow and connected with the attacker's mouth or nose, drawing blood. Then the knife went into his neck and ended the struggle right there.

"FBI gonna snatch this from us?" asks one of the techies, gesturing to Chris.

"Let's see what happens," says Chris.

Chris and Mary take a walk to the rear of the shed, not as well lit. They end up by the cages, four of them, with heavy locks. "Those are for the girls," he says. "For discipline."

"Yeah, it's a real shame Cyrus had to meet his maker. He was such a swell guy."

"Speaking of. Have we narrowed the list of suspects?"

"I have it down to eight or nine hundred people who will not be weeping at the funeral."

Chris purses his lips. "I was thinking of one in particular."

She turns to him. "What—Leo Balanoff?"

"Why not? He probably still sees Cyrus as a threat to Bonnie's son. He's making him do that delivery job he doesn't want to do. Killing Cyrus solves a whole lot of Leo's problems."

"Maybe. Hard to see, though."

He shrugs. "He punched a cop in college."

"A drunken bar fight doesn't make him a cold-blooded murderer. And didn't he plead that down to simple battery?"

"Yeah, and I have to say, that's the first time I've heard of a guy punching a cop and getting only simple, not aggravated. But you know what's my favorite part about that arrest in college?"

"No, little brother. What's your favorite part?"

Chris whacks her arm. "He had to submit to DNA and fingerprints."

"Ah, okay, okay." She nods. "And let me guess. You want me to call my ex at the crime lab and get a rush on the DNA."

Chris puts his hands together. "I would be forever in your debt."

"You're already forever in my debt." She shakes her head. "You really like Leo Balanoff for killing Cyrus?"

He lets out a long sigh. "My investigation of Nico? It's on freakin' life support after tonight. Cyrus was my way in. His death may be game over for me. But if prints and DNA come back for Leo Balanoff—"

"Then you're back in the game," she says. "You'll use him as your way in."

Chris looks over the warehouse. "Leo Balanoff may be my only chance now."

"Well, if he ends up being your guy," she says, "maybe he can explain to you how he managed to strike a cop and convince a judge to give him simple battery."

FOURTEEN YEARS AGO

APRIL 2010

24

Leo

"*People versus Leo Balanoff,*" the clerk calls out.

Well, this should be interesting, if nothing else.

The courtroom has all but emptied now, most of the preliminary hearings already completed. A few police officers remain, seated along the side of the courtroom, chatting in hushed voices with the courtroom deputies. Otherwise, a prosecutor and public defender remain at the bench, as they have throughout the hearings today, flipping from one file to the other in their stack of paperwork, just another day at the office for them, though not so for the various defendants, mostly young and Black, scared and despondent, awaiting their fates at the hands of the justice system in Illinois.

I rise from the pew in the second row of the gallery and approach the bench of solid walnut, behind which sits the Honorable Nathaniel P. Rose, one of the felony trial judges in the Circuit Court of Champaign County, a sweaty, red-faced, middle-aged white man with an unpredictable temperament, based on what I've seen over the last hour.

I don't know why *he's* sweating. I'm the one looking at prison.

Already at the bench is the prosecutor, about whom I've managed to learn a few things and discern a few others. His name is Jackson Dower, he's built like a linebacker, and he doesn't particularly care for what he perceives as snot-nosed college kids like me. I know that last fact because he made that very clear when I first walked into court, before the session began, trying to figure out if I was supposed to sign in or some-thing. *Let me take a wild guess*, he said to me. *Frat boy who got drunk?* I told him I wasn't a frat boy.

"Jackson Dower for the People," he says for the eighteenth time this morning. That's a good start for me, the number 18, both because it's di-visible by 3 and because it's the only number where the sum of its digits is exactly half of the number itself.

The judge looks at me.

"I'm Leo Balanoff," I say.

"Mr. Balanoff." The judge peers down at me over his reading glasses. "Do you have counsel?"

"Do I have what?"

"A lawyer," he clarifies, though I knew what he meant.

Everything you do, do for a reason.

"Do you have a lawyer?"

"No, sir. No, Your Honor."

"We can appoint the public defender for you."

"That's okay, Judge. I don't need a lawyer. I don't want to waste any more of the court's time or resources."

"Your time is my time, sir. Would you like the public defender ap-pointed?"

I glance over at the assistant public defender, a nice guy by all impres-sions, skinny and dark-haired. If he didn't have a goatee, I might have predicted we'd be friends.

"No, thank you, Your Honor," I say. "I'm here to plead guilty."

"Now." The judge raises a hand. "Now let's just hold on a second, Mr. Balanoff. Son, before anything else, you need to understand that you should have a lawyer. You don't have any legal training, do you?"

"No, sir. I'm in college here at U of I."

"Which is exactly why you should not handle this case on your own. You wouldn't perform surgery on yourself, would you?"

That doesn't strike me as a serious analogy, but okay.

"Your Honor, I don't want to waste anyone's time. I want to plead—"

"Mr. Balanoff, I need to make sure I admonish you. You need to understand the stakes involved here. State," he says, turning to Jackson Dower, "what is the exact charge?"

"Aggravated battery," he says. "Battery of a peace officer. It's a (d)(4), Judge, based on status of victim. It's a class 2."

"Mr. Balanoff," says the judge, "you are charged with aggravated battery of a peace officer. That's a class 2 felony. You face a minimum sentence of three years in the penitentiary and a maximum sentence of seven years. Do you understand that?"

Yes, I understand that. I looked it up. Reading the criminal code and the sentencing laws in Illinois was only slightly less fun than parsing the IRS Code of Regulations, but I got there eventually.

"Wow," I mutter under my breath. "Three to . . . *seven*?"

The judge sits back, waiting for me to fold.

I let out a long sigh, then shake my head. "I don't care. I'm not going to fight this. I'm not. If I have to go to prison, then so be it."

"Do you also understand, Mr. Balanoff, that if you're convicted here, the DNA sample you gave when arrested will remain in the Illinois State Police database forever? As will your fingerprints?"

DNA. Fingerprints. Stored forever. Forever is a mighty long time.

That could be problematic down the road.

"I do," I say. "That's fine."

"Well, Mr. Balanoff, I can't force you to take a lawyer."

I know you can't. I have a constitutional right to self-representation. This law stuff isn't as hard as lawyers make it out to be. They just use formalities and Latin words to intimidate us and make us *think* it's hard, so they can feel exclusive and make us hire them.

"But I can strongly urge you to get a lawyer. You don't know what you're doing, son, and this is a serious charge. You will get no leeway from me because you're appearing pro se."

Yeah, exactly, like that. *Pro se?* Just say I'm representing myself. English does just fine there.

"I appreciate that, Your Honor. I know you're just looking out for me. But if the officer says I battered him, then I want to be respectful of that. I don't want to contest a police officer's word in any way."

The judge tosses his hands. "Very well, Mr. Balanoff. I will let you represent yourself. Are you telling me now that you wish to plead guilty?"

"Yes, sir. Yes, Your Honor."

"You understand that means you are giving up your right to a trial by jury or by the court."

"Yes, I want to give that up. There's no need for a trial. If the officer says I hit him, then I guess I hit him."

The judge does a double take. "You don't know if you hit him?"

"I trust his memory more than mine, sir."

"Well." The judge looks at the prosecutor, then back at me. "What is your memory?"

I pause a moment, as if struggling. "I didn't think I hit him. All I know is, someone at the bar said something about my mother, and I—we started shoving each other, and then someone came up behind me and grabbed me. I struggled to sort of free myself, and whoever was grabbing me from behind slipped on the floor of the bar. It turns out, it was a police officer. I didn't think I threw a punch or anything, but if he says I hit him, then I believe a sworn police officer's memory over mine that night."

"State, give me some context."

The prosecutor clears his throat. "This was a fight in a campus bar. Officer Vitello and others responded. While Officer Vitello was trying to separate the individuals, the defendant threw an elbow into Officer Vitello's face. Officer Vitello fell to the floor."

"Is that correct, Officer?"

I hadn't noticed the officer walking up from the side seats in the courtroom. Decent-sized guy, clean-cut and serious.

"Yes, Judge, that's what happened," says the cop.

"And the defendant here is the individual who struck you?"

We both lean forward so we can see each other. He blinks twice.

I wonder—does he really recognize me? It's been ten days since the arrest, and I can only imagine how many other people he's arrested, how many other situations he's handled. Does he really remember me, in particular, as the person he arrested that night? Or do the circumstances dictate that result—the fact that I'm standing up here, saying it was me, and I generally look the part, the white college-age kid with short brown hair?

"Yes, Judge, that's him."

Anyway.

"Your Honor," I say, "if the officer says that's how it happened, then I believe that's how it happened. I'm—I'm embarrassed. Of all people to have struck, of all people to have disrespected, on that night in particular, the last person in the world I would've disrespected was a police officer. If I had any idea that the person behind me in that bar was a police officer, I would've never struck him or even struggled. But he says I did, so I completely believe—"

"Mr. Balanoff, you're telling me you didn't know he was a police officer?"

"Well, of course not," I say. "I'd never hit a police officer. Not on purpose. But I did, so I'm guilty, right?"

Wrong, actually. The judge is starting to get it.

"State, this is a (d)(4) agg bat, right?"

"Yes, Judge."

"Not serious bodily injury."

No, I'm not charged with aggravated battery based on inflicting serious bodily injury. I'm charged with simple battery, which was then *elevated* to aggravated, because the person I hit was someone I knew to be a cop.

"Correct, Judge. It's a status-of-victim, (d)(4)."

The judge turns to me. "Mr. Balanoff, if you didn't know the person you battered was a peace officer, then you are not guilty of this form of aggravated battery. The law does not allow me to accept a guilty plea when what you're telling me is that you're *not* guilty."

"But I'm pleading guilty, Judge."

"Yes, but the facts you are reciting to me"—he glances over at the court reporter, who's taking down everything for the record—"the facts you are reciting to me would indicate that you're *not* guilty."

I throw up my hands. "I'm willing to plead guilty. I will not contradict this officer's testimony."

"Officer," says the judge, "you came up behind him and tried to separate him from someone he was fighting with. Did you announce your office?"

"I believe I did, Judge."

"And if he says so, I accept that, Judge," I say. "I should have known he was an officer. Isn't that good enough? That I should have known?"

(No, actually, it's not.)

"It's not should-have-known," says the judge. "You have to *know* he was an officer. It's an element of the offense. And you're telling me you didn't know. So I can't accept this guilty plea when the facts you state on the record do not show your guilt."

Right. The judge is in a box. If I say on the record, with the court reporter typing away on her tiny machine, that I didn't know the guy was a cop, the judge can't accept my guilty plea.

I look up at the judge. "Okay, then I did know," I say.

"No, no, no. No, no, no. We're not playing that game, Mr. Balanoff. You only tell the truth in this courtroom." The judge zips a straight line with his finger. "If you didn't know he was a police officer, you're not going to say you knew."

All right, then. Glad we got that settled.

"How about this," I say. "We have a trial, the officer testifies, and I don't. Then you could find me guilty of that, whatever you called it, that (d)(4) charge."

The judge sits back in his chair. "You seem to really want to plead guilty. Why?"

"Because I believe him when he says I hit him. Because I've always—"

I bow my head, take a moment. I raise my hand, finding the words.

"My mother was a cop," I say. "East Alton P.D. and then Galesburg P.D. She died from a pulmonary embolism when I was eighteen. But I promised her I'd become a cop, too. It's the only job I've ever wanted. And the last thing I'd ever do is come into a courtroom and say a police officer wasn't telling the truth. If I hit one, which apparently I did, then I should answer for it. Even if I . . ." I flip my hand. "Even if I blow my chance of probably being a cop."

The judge looks at me for a long time, peering into my soul, I guess. If he finds anything in there, I'd be curious to know what. Then he glances around the courtroom. At the prosecutor, at the cop, at the gallery behind me.

"Well, *this* isn't something you see every day. Let's take a five-minute recess."

The judge pushes himself up from his chair. I head back to the front row of the courtroom, where the public defender with the goatee is sitting. He smiles at me and shakes his head.

"Something funny?" I ask.

"No, no." He waves a hand. "I just enjoyed the music lesson."

I sit down next to him and stare at him. I don't follow.

"You just played that judge like a fiddle," he whispers.

"I don't know what you mean. I'm just a college kid. This legal stuff is a little overwhelming."

He likes that, actually laughs. "Yeah, overwhelming. You looked *real* overwhelmed up there." He leans into me. "You managed, without going to trial, without even testifying—through a *guilty plea*, no less—to convince the judge, first, that you're *not* guilty of aggravated battery of a peace officer, and second, that you're an upstanding citizen who shouldn't go to prison."

Good thing this guy wasn't the judge, then.

"So what's gonna happen now?" I ask.

"I think you know exactly what's gonna happen, college boy. What you wanted to happen from the moment you walked in here."

Simple battery, probation, was always my goal.

"The judge can't take your guilty plea on agg battery. You made sure of that. And by now, he doesn't want to, anyway. He'll convict you of the lesser-included offense of simple battery and give you probation. Did your mom really die of a pulmonary embolism when you were eighteen? Was she even a cop?"

I glance around, make sure we have privacy. "She was a cop," I say. "That part was true."

That makes him want to laugh even harder, but he buries his face in his hands. "No pulmonary embolism, though?"

"No. She died in a freak accident. She was in a pottery class. Kiln explosion."

He does a double take. "A kiln exploded?" He doesn't know what to make of that. Or of me.

"Yeah, she'd gone back to college. She was a sophomore at Faber. She was making a pot for me."

His face flush from laughter, he reaches into his pocket. He fishes out a business card and hands it to me. His name is Montgomery Morris, an assistant public defender for Champaign County. "Call me Monty," he says.

"Why are you giving me your card, Monty?" I ask.

"Look me up someday," he says. "Either you're gonna become a criminal defense lawyer, or you're gonna need one. Or both."

THE PRESENT DAY

JANUARY 2024

Four Weeks before Valentine's Day

25

Leo

I reach under my bed and pull out the battered case. I open it and remove my violin. I take a soft cloth and wipe down the reddish-brown, fine-grained spruce, the chin rest and fingerboard. I clear the rosin dust off the strings and wipe the bow with a separate cloth before rosining the bow hairs.

I need something soothing, calming. Somewhere I can escape. Because nothing else is working. The waiting, the anticipation, has loomed over everything, an ever-present shadow. Not knowing if they'll come, when they'll come, where they'll show up, who "they" will even be. Every time I hear the ground-floor security door buzz open or footfalls on the staircase, each time my phone rings, whenever I step out of my condo or open a door or approach my car or turn a corner. Every time, I brace myself.

Today, Sunday, is the worst, as I have little to occupy myself outside the office. No court appearances, no conferences with clients. In my condo, there are only so many loads of laundry I can do (two), so much surface area I can vacuum or wash (1,063 square feet or, obviously, 153,072 square inches), so many times I can add up the first fifty prime numbers (5,117) or all the circular primes below 200 (1,086).

Booze is no good, either. When the moment comes, however and whenever and whatever—a gun aimed at my head, handcuffs and a jail cell, or anything in between—I need to be sharp, on my toes. So I opt instead for my preferred tonic, one I can only do during normal hours without drawing complaints from my neighbors.

I lift my violin, a beautiful Guarneri reproduction, made in 1930 in the German town of Markneukirchen near the Czech border by the renowned luthier E. H. Roth, first purchased by my violin teacher's father in New York City. My instructor, Mr. Dingel, stooped, shaggy-haired, passionate Mr. Dingel, played it until his death and passed it on to me.

I start with something gentle, "Meditation" from *Thaïs*, the soft fade into the first note, the light, hypnotic vibrato, getting lost in the pure bliss of it. Some people think of the piece as maudlin, but to me, it's like a massage. Then "Ari Im Sokhag," a soft and sweet lullaby with a hint of rebellion. And finally, "Der Erlkönig," only because it is the single hardest piece I've ever played, forcing me to focus on triple stops and tenth stretches.

It helps. But there is no cure for the roiling in my stomach, the incessant waves of adrenaline-fueled dread. The not-knowing is pure agony.

It's been three days since Cyrus Balik drew his last breath. Somehow, in some way, I know I will have to answer for that.

26

Chris

Chris walks into the war room, where the task force supervisor, Manning, with his buzz cut and lined face, is about to start. "Okay, boys and girls—so what are we gonna do with our third-year med student?"

The photo of the kid is pinned to the corkboard. Manning is old-school that way; he'll use whatever surveillance technology they'll give him, but when he's talking strategy with the task force, it's still corkboards with pins, whiteboards with markers.

"Take him and shake him." This from Agent Rosalyn Dietrich from DEA. "See how many other interns and doctors and nurses are in on the action."

That idea gains traction in the room. Now that the task force has traced a fentanyl user to a med student in clinical rounds at a major Chicago hospital, they have options. Most people seem to like the idea of flipping the kid, wiring him up, sending him back into the hospital to see if he's selling to any of his colleagues in the medical profession. Imagine the headlines—a fentanyl ring inside one of the biggest and most respected health-care institutions in the city.

"What do you think, Roberti? You're the one who found this kid."

True. Chris went old-school himself on surveillance, the rinse-and-repeat method. So many of these users fall into the same basic cycle on an almost daily basis: purchase the fentanyl; use it; overdose; get rescued via paramedics or cops using Narcan, if not a trip to the ER; get released; go back to their dealer and buy some more. Chris just followed an addict out of the ER until he spotted him making a purchase behind the hospital near Racine.

"I say we follow him up the chain but leave it at that," he says. "Let's see where he gets his supply. Then we bust him and the supplier."

"Yeah, but that's no fun," says Dietrich.

"Getting soft on us, Roberti?" Manning, the supervisor, smirks.

Chris puts his feet on a chair. "When this kid's in the hospital, he's supposed to be taking care of patients. You want him wearing a camera and mike, walking around all day trying to work off his beef? No thanks, but if I'm in the hospital, I want doctors whose only focus is making me better, not worrying about getting their prison sentence reduced. The day we bust that kid should be the last day he practices medicine."

The room goes quiet. His idea isn't sexy, won't grab the same headlines, but he's right, and everyone in the room knows it. But he's the wet blanket, as usual.

Getting soft. It's not the first time he's heard it since he came back. That's how they all see him now, whether it's giving him the outer perimeter on a bust instead of the in-the-shit stack or delegating him the paperwork instead of the street action. Poor Chris, weakened from cancer. So fragile he might break in half if he's not careful.

God, he's sick of this bullshit, chasing low-rung drug dealers who will be replaced as soon as they're locked up, being handled with kid gloves by people with half his talent.

But maybe, just maybe, he'll get lucky with the forensics from Cyrus's crime scene and find his ticket out of Organized Crime.

Chris drives to Mary's house after work. She still lives in Deemer Park, the home on the cul-de-sac where they grew up, 523 Finlay Court. He can't imagine living here as an adult. Mary moved back in temporarily after her three-year roller coaster of a marriage imploded. Then their mother got cancer, almost five years to the day before Chris did. Mary played live-in nurse as best she could. Mom didn't last two years.

When Chris got sick, he spent most of his time here, too, with Mary. Why she still chooses to live here now is beyond him. It feels more like a convalescent home than a place to live.

He pulls into the driveway, takes a look at the place. Pretty basic yellow-brick Georgian. The front porch needs some work, and the gutters were probably installed during the Nixon administration. They need to get rid of this place. Mary could use the fresh start.

"Hey." He walks in with groceries, some tuna steaks he picked up. He finds her in the sunken family room, papers spread out around her. "Notice I'm not asking."

Chris has been hounding her since the night they found Cyrus dead. But a "rush" on forensics means whatever the forensic techie decides it means. If he's even rushing it at all.

On the mantel above the fireplace, the family photos, including one from his days at St. Ignatius (recalling the brutal hour-plus commute every day), looking so young and clueless in his football jersey. He was a scrapper more than a pure athlete, but boy could he cover, sticking to wideouts like glue. Enough for a scholarship to Madison, though he rode the pine there. At least he got a free education; no chance his family had the money to send him anywhere.

Chris preps the tuna steaks with salt and pepper and some olive oil. He got thick, sushi-grade cuts, perfect so they won't cook through. He preheats the pan—nonstick, of course—with a tablespoon of vegetable oil. He drops the tuna steaks into the pan with a sizzle. And he watches until the steaks cook about a quarter inch in before he flips them.

He hears Mary stomping into the kitchen in her bare feet, reading glasses tucked into her sweatshirt. Mary Roberti Cagnola always drew plenty of attention from the boys, even if her choices weren't the best. But since her divorce, rather than going wild, reliving her days as an eligible twenty-something, she has opted to be a stay-at-home recluse.

"Get ready to be happy," she says.

His head whips around. "No. Yeah?"

"Fingerprints and DNA," she says, allowing a small smile. "Both matches for Leo Balanoff."

"Oh, fuck, tell me you're not kidding."

"I'm not kidding."

He puts his hands on top of his head, as if in surrender. "I . . . got him."

"You got him," she agrees. "Dead to rights."

27

Leo

I walk into the office at ten, after a hearing at 26th and Cal that lasted all of five minutes.

"Avery, how are we this morning?" I say to our receptionist.

"Just fine, princess," she says to me. Avery's a single mom with two teenage boys at home, so her drill sergeant demeanor comes easily. She keeps Monty and me organized and on schedule, which is no easy task. Most of our clients are afraid of her. Monty and I are, too.

"You have a ten-thirty, a new intake," she says. "Francis Garza? Says he got arrested for assault and battery."

"Okay, I'll screen him. Where's Monty?"

"Court this morning. A prelim, I think, at Twenty-Sixth and Cal."

"Right." I walk into my office and lose my coat. I put my iPhone down on the desk, followed by my burner phone. I'm researching a motion in an aggravated DUI case involving *Brady* violations when my work phone's intercom buzzes.

"*Francis Garza,*" Avery squawks through the speaker.

The man who enters my office is taller than me, six three at least, but dumpy, with a long, sad face, a salt-and-pepper goatee. He is wearing a puffy vest over a flannel shirt that hangs beyond his jeans. He offers me a limp handshake.

"Mr. Garza, I'm Leo Balanoff. Have a seat, please."

He settles into the seat across from me, looking me over. Most first meetings, the clients are sheepish, embarrassed about the fact that they've been caught doing something wrong, or at least that the government thinks they did. This guy, not so much. He seems to be sizing me up.

"Why don't you tell me what happened?" I say. It's usually easier if I let them start wherever they want to start.

"I got arrested in . . . bar fight," he says. "I hit . . . police officer."

A bar fight. He hit a cop.

Gee, that sounds familiar.

Someone's done their homework. And wants me to know it.

I pictured many different outcomes. I didn't picture this, showing up at my law office as a potential client. Smart, I suppose. A lawyer's office would never be wired.

"They charge me with aggravated battery," he says. "I hope to plead down to . . ."

"Simple battery." I finish his sentence. Now I place his thick accent and clipped speech. This is one of Cyrus's guys.

The man reaches into the pocket of his vest, removes a folded sheet of paper, and slides it across the desk to me. It contains a phone number, nothing more, with a Chicago area code.

"We're exchanging numbers now?" I ask. "No offense, but you're not my type."

"This is the number you need to call," he says. "He is expecting your call."

I know he can't mean Cyrus.

"Who is expecting my call?"

He smiles at me. "You promised to do a job. You have not forgotten?"

"No, but . . ."

"But what?" he says.

"Nothing," I say.

"A promise is a promise. You will do this job for Nico."

"For who?"

"Nico," he repeats.

"Nico? Who the hell is Nico?"

He likes that, chuckles to himself. "He is the man you do this work for.

The man you always were doing this work for. Cyrus was here." He holds his hand at eye level. "Nico is here." He raises his hand above his head.

I fall back in my chair, pushing my hair off my face. "Cyrus had a *boss*?"

"Yes. Call that number. You agreed to do job and you will do it."

"Okay, listen, Igor. May I call you Igor?"

"Yes, the jokes, I remember this. The man who's lucky he still has his teeth."

So he was there that night, one of the goons holding me down. I didn't get a good look at their faces. I had more pressing matters on my mind. Like whether I'd have to be fed through a straw for the foreseeable future.

He pats his vest as his phone buzzes. He pulls it out of a pocket and answers with a guttural noise. "*Ma andsin selle talle. Mitte veel.*"

Didn't catch all of that. All I could make out was *Not yet*.

Whomever he's talking to, he's telling him I haven't said yes . . . yet.

He puts away the phone and stares at me again.

"I've never heard of this 'Nico' guy," I say. "I made a deal with Cyrus. If Cyrus is no longer around, there is no deal."

"There *is* a deal," he says. "With Nico. Call that number. Do not make us come to you again." He stands up.

"Let me summarize my answer in two words," I say. "The second word is off. The first one starts with an *f*."

His lips curl up, a grudging smile. "You want I should tell Nico to fuck off. That is the answer you wish me to give?"

I get to my feet and open the door for him to leave.

"That is the answer I wish you to give," I say. "I'm not doing it."

28
Andi

Andi sits in Dr. Valencia's carrel in the FutureTech wing, right hand on the computer mouse, looking at the computer screen. She finds the icon for "Nano.3.0" and double-clicks on it, watching it spin and upload.

Her phone *dings* with a message. In her earbud, the voice of Jack Cortland, who is sitting back in the security control center. *"Target file being opened at Dr. Allan Valencia's desktop,"* he says.

"Good." She closes the file, then clicks on the same icon again. But this time a single click. She drags the icon into a different folder, marked "Miscellaneous."

Another *ding* on her phone.

"Target file being moved from 'Valencia' folder to the 'Miscellaneous' folder."

"Roger that."

She pulls up Allan Valencia's email and attaches the "Nano.3.0" file. Her phone *dings*.

"Target file has been attached to an email from Dr. Allan Valencia, no current addressee, not sent."

She repeats similar maneuvers over the next hour, nearly every imaginable way someone could attempt to manipulate the Nano file on the system: emailing, printing, downloading, transferring, renaming, converting—same result, a *ding* on the central security server.

"Anything someone tries, we'll know in real time," she says to Jack over the phone. "Absolutely anything intra-office, we'll catch."

"And they can't email anything out," Jack says. "We're firewalled. So we're locked down."

"Totally locked down. There's no way to mess with this file without us knowing it immediately. We'll know who's doing it, what they're doing, and precisely when."

"You guys are thorough, I'll say that," says Dr. Valencia, standing behind Andi. "And just in time."

"Yeah? Why's that, Allan?"

"I'd say Nano will be ready to go to prototype within two weeks."

"All right, then," she says. "Good for us."

"Andi, the security looks terrific," says Jack.

"You think that's terrific?" she says. "Come up to eight and see what's even better."

Jack enters the SCIF. Standing with Andi is the security staff assigned to FutureTech, twenty-four in number. "Okay, let's see it," he says.

Andi hands him a sheet of paper.

"This is the fancy new watermarked paper?"

"It is. Throw that on a Xerox machine, it won't copy. It will be hopelessly blurred. But that's not my favorite part." She waves down the hall, where five QCI employees stand. "We have printed out five copies of the Nano specs on our new paper. These five employees have been gracious enough to volunteer to sneak a copy past our sensors. You guys ready?"

They all nod.

Andi holds up a wad of cash. "A hundred bucks to anyone who gets through. I guess that doesn't really make you volunteers, does it?" She smiles. "Okay, Anthony, you first."

Anthony walks toward the exit carrying a briefcase. When he passes through the brackets, a buzzer goes off and a light flashes atop the bracket.

"Sorry, Anthony. What did you try?"

He opens up a briefcase and pulls out a *Webster's* dictionary. "Stuck it square in the middle of the thickest book I could find."

"Okay, no hundred bucks for you." She pats him on the back. "Richard?"

Richard from Human Resources, wearing his winter coat, crosses through the brackets to another buzz and flashing red light.

"What did you try, Richard?"

"Separated the document into pieces," he says. He pulls wadded-up pages out of his pants pockets, out of his coat, even out of his socks.

"Good thought," says Andi. "But every single page is watermarked and contains a sensor. Okay, Eileen?"

Eileen, one of the biotech scientists, catches a buzzer and red light with the briefcase she's carrying. "I balled it up and put it inside a metal thermos in my briefcase."

"Put magnets on each side of it," says Louis, an engineer.

"Wrapped it in tinfoil," says Margaret, a hematologist.

"Nothing," says Andi. "*Nothing* gets through this bad boy. And team," she says to the FutureTech security squad gathered around, "who has to pass through those brackets?"

"Everyone!" they bark.

"Wait. But . . . What about me? I have rank on you. You can trust me, right?"

"No!"

"No?" Andi gestures theatrically toward Jack. "Well, surely, our director of security, Mr. Jack Cortland, standing right over there, can walk around those brackets—does he have to pass through?"

"Yes!"

"Wait a second. Hold on." Andi waves her arms, gaining steam. "What about the CEO of our company? She signs your paychecks. Certainly *she* could go around those brackets, couldn't she?"

"No!"

Andi, moving among the staff now, puts her hands on her head. "But what if she said she'd fire you on the *spot* if you made her go through those brackets? What would you say to her then?"

"Call Andi!" one guy shouts.

"Me?" She places her hands on her chest. "Oh, so now it becomes *my* problem?"

"Yes!"

Andi holds out her hands for quiet. "Ladies and gentlemen of the FutureTech security team . . . do you mean to tell me . . ." She walks over to the exit, grips one of the brackets. "Do you *seriously* mean to tell me that even the president of the freakin' *United States* would have to pass through those brackets?"

"Yes!"

"Now *that's* what I'm talkin' about! That's why I love you guys." Andi starts high-fiving the staff. Then she turns to Jack, who is laughing and clapping along.

"Jack," she says, "nobody, and I mean *nobody* is moving a physical copy of those Nano specs out of this SCIF!"

"I believe it, I believe it!" Jack puts up his hands in surrender.

"Okay, everyone, that was a lot of information I just gave you. Let me summarize." Andi looks over the room of seventy-three scientists, engineers, technicians, doctors—all people with more degrees than her, and the only people in the company besides security and the CEO with access to this SCIF. They've all sat through a forty-five-minute talk inside one of the FutureTech conference rooms.

"Number one, every action you take on the Nano file will be accompanied by a notification to security. Number two, if you print out a copy of the Nano specs, your watermarked copy will contain a unique encrypted identifier attributable to you and only you. If that copy is lost, it will be your responsibility. We will open an investigation. If you want to destroy your copy, you must shred it under the supervision of security. Number three, when you leave for the night, you will be required to store your copy in the small safes we will be putting on each of your desks." She takes a breath. "On the bright side, because the prototype specs will only be printed out on this paper with sensors that will trigger an alarm at the exit, there will be no more physical searches when you leave the SCIF."

A man who doesn't seem to be looking on the bright side raises his hand. "What do you mean, you'll open an investigation if we lose our copy?"

"Just that. We will open an investigation. We will have to consider the possibility that this draft has been turned over to our competitors. All available disciplinary remedies will be available. We will consider alerting the authorities, state and federal."

"We could go to jail? Just for losing track of a copy?"

"Treat it like the prized possession it is," Andi says. "Treat it like your phone."

Nobody seems very happy.

"Guys, people," Jack chimes in. "Just keep track of your copies and toss 'em in a safe at night. No big deal. If you do that, none of this other stuff will be a hassle."

Jack's biggest problem is that he worries about everyone's opinion. Andi understands—the brilliant scientists can't feel like they're working under the thumb of Big Brother—but this is a billion-dollar piece of technology they're discussing.

You get to be the good guy, Jack.

At lunchtime, she drives to her gym, only a mile from work in the South Loop. "Health club" is probably a more appropriate term, swankier than she'd normally go for. She needs a gym, meaning free weights, and a running track when the weather's too shitty to run outside. She doesn't need the sauna or juice bar. But this place is so close, and with the money she makes now, she can afford it.

She walks in and shows her ID to the front desk. She heads into the locker room and throws her gym bag into her designated locker. (They designate lockers here.)

Then she heads past the free-weight gym to the rear exit of the building.

A car is waiting there, a black town car. She gets in the back seat, where Nico Katsaros sits with his legs crossed.

"How's my favorite deputy director of security?" he says.

29

Andi

Yeah, well, not everything or everyone is as they appear.

When she started as a rookie in Deemer Park P.D., Andi really did have only one goal—being a hardworking, honest cop. She'd *always* wanted to be a cop, from the time she was a little girl.

The first time was her second week on the job, her star still shiny. She'd been pulled in for the rear stack on a bust on Astor, a stash house they'd found after following a dealer on an undercover buy. Performance adrenaline rushing through her, her gun drawn but down, her heartbeat pounding in her temples as the team leader yelled, "Go!"

The bust itself was not memorable. One kid tried to run but was easily put down. When it was all said and done, there were five men in handcuffs, dozens of packets of heroin, razor blades and baggies and scales. And piles of cash on a table in the kitchen.

Andi helped toss the men in the paddy wagon. She thought she'd follow it to the station, but one of the sergeants waved her back into the house. Inside, the money had been organized into piles. Some of the officers were already stuffing their stacks inside their flak vests.

Hers, apparently, was one of the smaller stacks, as she was a rookie. The sergeant held it out to her in front of a half dozen other officers, all of them senior to her, all of whom, it seemed, suddenly became very interested in her response. "Hazard pay," the sergeant said.

Her guess, looking back, she waited no more than five seconds to answer. But it felt like a lifetime. Like a dozen decisions were made, multiple debates held, before she spoke.

"Nah, I'm good," she said, her voice nearly catching. "I'm gonna follow the wagon and process 'em." And she walked out, her heart pounding harder than before the bust, her chest burning, feeling all eyes in the room trained on her.

It took less than twenty-four hours before she was pulled aside. "People are worried about you," said her partner, a guy named Billy Esrig, who was putting in for sergeant. "They're not seeing you as a team player."

She hadn't walked into the job with rose-colored glasses. She knew there'd be those who took detours, even a few who dipped their beak into places it didn't belong. But she hadn't expected it so soon, hadn't realized how brazen it would be.

Or the rationalizations. How stealing from drug dealers wasn't like stealing from innocent people. Or that they were underpaid, putting their asses on the line for an unappreciative public, and what's the harm if they tuck away a little tax-free contraband to help pay the rent?

It took three years and a reassignment before she finally changed her mind. But not because anyone forced her, or because she was trying to fit in.

The timing? Her change of heart? Probably a combination of several things.

One, it was right after she broke up with Leo. That's what Mama would say—that Leo, for all his oddities, kept her grounded, and when she cut him loose, she drifted into uncharted waters.

And not long after that, she met Nico Katsaros.

30

Andi

She first met Nico at a bar on the southwest side, an introduction made by another cop on the force at Deemer Park P.D. He was seated at the bar. He had pretty classic Mediterranean features, dark in the eyes and a prominent nose. He was balding, as if someone had run a razor right over the center of his head. But he kept the sides stubbly short, like five-o'clock shadows on each side. He had a way of making it look neat and classy, even sexy.

"You're Sergeant Piotrowski." He set his drink down on the bar. His intel was good; she'd only recently been promoted. "Captain Laughton is a friend," he explained. "He speaks highly of you."

"Someone wants to speak highly of me, I'm not gonna stop 'em."

He smiled, showing no teeth. "Would you have any interest in joining me for a drink?"

The mannerly way he said it almost made her laugh. The bar was pretty much a dump. Nico, in fact, seemed entirely out of place with his crisply pressed shirt open at the collar, expensive designer jeans, and Armani loafers.

They settled into a corner booth, which she had to admit was a lot more pleasant than the torn seats at the bar.

"Let me guess," he said. "You're a former athlete."

She rolled her eyes.

He picked up on Andi's reaction. "That was not a racial comment, if that's what you're thinking. It's the way you move, actually. You're grace-ful, agile. You seem athletic. Tell me I didn't offend you with the first words out of my mouth."

She was the one who felt silly. Maybe she'd overreacted. Either way, Nico had a way of making the moment vanish in an eyeblink. He spoke slowly, with precision, in a way you might equate with femininity, though he was masculine through and through.

A powerful man who knew how to handle the power.

"No worries," she said.

"I should probably tell you, Sergeant—"

"Andi."

"Andi." His eyes gleamed. "You should know, Andi, because you're someone with an impeccable reputation, that not everyone views me in that same way. I'd understand if you'd rather not be seen consorting with me."

Interesting how he'd put that. Giving her an out but making it too intriguing for her to walk away. At least without knowing more.

"Is that so?" She pulled on the straw in her drink. "Do tell."

"Oh, in truth, there isn't much to tell. But in my business, there are alliances, powerful people, and people who wish to be powerful. And whenever there are alliances, there are adversaries as well."

"You work on the set of *Game of Thrones* or something?"

"Not far off." He allowed a smile. "I'm in many businesses, but most recently gaming."

"Gaming." Gaming was a fancy term for gambling. She never under-stood why they didn't just call it that.

"I have an ownership interest in Five Oceans Casino in the Quad Cit-ies," he said. "The Iowa side. Davenport. I'm hoping to get a foothold in Illinois as well. There are people who would rather I did not. And the best way to deny someone a casino license is, well . . ."

"To impugn their integrity."

He raised his glass in salute. "Precisely. So. Now's your chance to run from a man who makes money on other people's gambling habits."

Andi had been poor her entire childhood, and not much better as a young cop. The one thing she hated more than being poor was how

wealthy people condescended to them, looked down on the poor as perpetual victims.

Anyway, they were just having a drink.

"Nobody put a gun to their head," she said.

So one thing led to another. Eventually, he made the pitch to her to go on
his payroll. A small monthly stipend in exchange for the occasional piece
of information. Mostly she was still just a cop, true and blue, but he'd
reach out to her with a question, or ask her to keep an eye out for certain
things.

Four hundred a week, tax-free. She went through one of Nico's guys,
a brute of a man, former Golden Gloves boxer apparently, who went by
"Trader Joe." If her information was particularly beneficial, she'd know it
by the bonus in the next envelope.

This thing with QCI came up a little over a year ago. An opportunity,
Nico called it—"an opportunity for both of us." Andi would no longer be
a cop. She would be a deputy chief of security at a medical technology
company. He didn't name the company, Quigley Crowe International, at
that moment—he wouldn't unless Andi said yes.

"Stealing trade secrets," she gathered.

"One in particular," he said. "One extremely valuable one."

She sat back in the chair in the office where they were meeting—a
back room in some tavern in the south suburbs, all stained oak wood. "I
give up my gig as a cop for a one-off job?"

Nico allowed a brief smile. "A one-off job for which your reward will
be five million dollars."

He knew very well that a number like that would knock her backward. But she didn't answer right away. She wanted to run it by Brando
first. She was pretty sure he'd tell her to say yes. And after some initial
balking, that was exactly what he did.

But no excuses, she reminds herself. The decision was hers and hers
alone. She knew her life would never be the same if she took the job. She
knew there would be tremendous risk.

Including the fact that, when the job was over, when the deal was done and she was of no further use to him, Nico might consider her a liability.

She returned to him a week later. A different place. Always a different location. But still that calm and cool Nico, with that implacable expression, legs crossed, hands on his knee.

"Ten million," Andi said.

31

Andi

"How are you?" Nico asks once Andi's settled inside his town car. The interior smells of his cologne. If you pushed her, she'd guess some combination of wood and vanilla and maybe a bit floral. More than anything, it smells like money.

"Bored as shit," she says. "Deputy director of corporate security at a medical technology company?"

He smiles obligingly. "I assume by now you have them eating out of your hand."

Pretty much. It wasn't hard to nudge her way in. She knew she had the job after her interview with Jack Cortland. From what she could tell, with all her experience in surveillance at DPPD and a joint task force she worked on, she was by far the most qualified applicant. But she could read Jack from the moment he walked in. He was less concerned with qualifications and more interested in checking out her ass. That was fine. He'd underestimate her for that very reason, like many men. She preferred to be underestimated. Especially for this gig.

The notion that she was attractive did not come easily to her. As a child, she felt the complete opposite, the outcast in every way. Growing up on a block in Morgan Park that was all white, attending a private Catholic school, Blessed Sacrament, with only a handful of minorities, Andi, a biracial kid, was viewed with suspicion by Black and white kids alike. She was "whitey" to the Black kids and a "zebra" to the white kids. Her second-grade teacher, Mrs. Sangmeister, tried to guess what she "was"—Filipino, Puerto Rican, or "half Black." She was tall and strong enough to fend off bullies, but it did nothing for her acceptance. She was the insular, quick-tempered tomboy, grudgingly respected, even feared, but not liked.

You're beautiful in every way, kallike, Agnes used to tell her while brushing her hair, reading stories to her in bed while Mama worked a second shift. *One day you shine. This I know.* But Andi grew up feeling like the odd girl out, the ugly duckling.

"I have some news," she tells Nico. "Project Nano could go to proto-type as early as two weeks from now."

"That *is* news." He works his jaw. "It dovetails into my news. Cyrus?"

"Yeah? What about him?"

"Cyrus is dead," he says.

Huh?

"The . . . Our courier? Our courier is dead?"

"Our courier, yes."

"Oh, fuck, you're *kidding* me." She falls back in the seat. "Sorry." For some reason, the way Nico carries himself, the calm, mannerly de-meanor, Andi always feels wrong when she swears in front of him.

But shit! Cyrus Balik is dead? The man who, about two weeks from now, was going to deliver the specs from her to the Chinese MSS agents— is *dead*?

"We're weeks away, Nico. And now we don't have a courier?"

Nico glances up at her, a hint of amusement, or something—it's so hard to tell with him. "You've processed your grief awfully fast."

"I mean, no offense, but—I never met the guy. Just knew him by rep-utation."

That's the way Nico runs everything. He has tentacles everywhere, but one tentacle doesn't interact with the other. Ne'er the twain shall meet. They're all his mushrooms—feed 'em shit and keep 'em in the dark.

"How'd he die?" she asks.

He shakes his wrist, loosening free his watch, then shoots the cuffs on his shirt. "Murdered. He was found dead in one of his offices. He had a shed in that industrial district in east Deemer Park. Your old stomping grounds."

So Deemer Park P.D. has that murder. "Any word on suspects?"

"Not that I know of."

He knows more than he's letting on. Nico has his hands up, down, and inside out of that department. She's tempted to use a puppet analogy, but that's not necessarily fair to her former colleagues. Nico has a way of putting things. He could talk a starving lion out of his dinner. He understands better than anyone that people believe what they want to believe.

When he finally made his pitch to Andi to get on his payroll, for example, it was more about how DPPD can't keep their best and brightest because the pay is so low. If there were a way to supplement that income, though. Just some information, once in a while—not hurting anyone, just a whisper in Nico's ear every now and then, a heads-up when needed—and otherwise go on doing your good work as a cop for the people of Deemer Park, but maybe now you can afford a modest mortgage, help your kids through college, too.

He had a way of making it sound reasonable, even righteous. Andi said yes, back then, and she was far from the only one. And her guess is every one of them, every copper in DPPD on Nico's payroll, tells themselves some version of the same thing—all things considered, they do more positive work than negative, they're good cops just trying to provide for their families.

"If you knew Cyrus," he says to her now, "you'd know that he had a habit of making enemies. The list of suspects would be long. But that's hardly our concern at this point."

Right. Their concern is who's going to deliver that package now.

"Maybe I'll just deliver it," she says.

Nico gives a curt shake of his head. "Absolutely not. Out of the question." He examines his fingernails. Manicured, she always thought, meticulous as they are, though she doesn't know if he goes to a place or does it himself. Probably the latter. "I have someone in mind. He may be perfect. He was someone Cyrus, in fact, wanted."

"Will this someone do it?"

Nico blinks. "So far, he's been reluctant. I expect that to change."

"Okay, well, I need to know his name. Once you've decided on someone."

He doesn't immediately answer.

"We've been through this, Nico. I need to know who it is. If he's not reliable, I'm screwed. I need to vet him. Cyrus was one thing. You knew him and trusted him. But if it's someone new and last minute—"

"He won't know who you are." It's not like Nico to interrupt. "He won't know your name, he won't know where you work, he won't even know what you're handing him."

Maybe that's true, but her point remains. "I need to vet this guy. I need to trust him."

His expression softens. He touches her arm. "This discussion is premature. Let me ensure that I have the right man first."

"When will that be?" she asks.

He nods, thinks about that. "Very soon," he says.

32

Chris

"That's it, that's it, you're up. Now do it, Chris. You got this!"

Chris lowers the barbell to his chest, back straight, and presses upward, his spotter's protective hands cupped beneath the barbell. *It's just a number just a number—*

"Earn that shit, earn that shit, *earn* it," says the spotter. "Breathe!"

More than the spotter, he hears the words of his chemo partner, Levi, in his head: *Nobody will give it to you. You have to take it. Get out there, be hungry, take it—*

With a grunt, Chris fully extends his trembling arms, then drops the barbell into its cradle with the spotter's help.

Two-fifty. Once upon a time, he could put up a set of eight reps at that weight without breaking a sweat. Now it's a one-off max. But it's a start. It won't come back all at once. He pops off the bench, slapping hands with his spotter.

Chris takes a breath, catches himself in the dusty floor-to-ceiling mirror. For the first time in years, he's not seeing a victim, a man who shed over eighty pounds, muscles shriveling, while fighting for his life. Now he sees a man on his way back. Not all the way yet, but getting there, scratching and clawing.

Inside the bathroom stall in the locker room, Chris jabs the needle full of Tren into his buttocks, looking back to ensure there's no blood in the syringe before pressing down on the plunger. He removes the needle and drops it in the hard case. He grabs the single pill of Diana he brought with him and swallows it with water from the sink.

Back home, Chris puts his head against the wall of the shower, letting the hot water scald the back of his neck. He runs a hand over the scar on his abdomen, his only remaining physical reminder. Cancer was so different in that way. He's had all kinds of bumps and bruises and sprains and broken bones in his life, but cancer felt so alien, something invisible, intangible, viewable only on a scan, yet wreaking so much havoc inside his body.

"Yeah, but I fucking beat you." He punches off the shower, gets out, dries off.

"I'm here!" Mary calls out.

"Give me a minute." He looks at himself in the mirror. Maybe that scar isn't the only reminder. He does look different, he thinks, some darkness and baggage under the eyes. But at least his body's starting to return to form. It's been a very long time since he was able to stomach the sight of himself in the mirror.

"Why do you have so many phones?" she calls out.

He throws on some clothes, finger-combs his hair, and finds her in the bedroom. "This, my friend, is what happens when you make a preliminary pitch to the National Security Division of the Department of Justice."

She picks up the phones. "This is DOJ shit?"

He sits down on the bed. There's no point in trying to keep it from her. He's going to be carrying these phones around all day every day, and he spends so much time with her. "This phone," he says, holding a gray one, "is what I call my 'Leo' phone. If I can flip him, this will be the phone he and I call each other on."

"Okay, cool. And the black one?"

"The black one, I use to talk to DOJ."

"Main Justice?"

"Main Justice, baby. I mean, this is freakin' spycraft shit, Mare. I don't call a person. I call a flower business. A front. Check this out. I mean, obviously, this is totally confidential, but—"

"But I'm your sister and a cop and you trust me with your life."

"Yeah." He shows her the name of the last caller on the phone: **Flowers Anywhere.**

"Flowers Anywhere?"

"It's a dedicated, secure line to a senior assistant attorney general with the National Security Division. We talk in code, a password and number. I feel like I'm in the damn CIA."

Mary leans back on the bed. "Cool. So, how'd you—I mean, how do you go straight to DOJ—"

"I ran it through our SAC," he says, meaning the special agent-in-charge for Chicago. "She's the only one in Chicago who knows. She patched me through to Justice. She and I are it."

"Your buddies in Organized Crime—"

"Oh, hell, no. OC doesn't know a thing about this. Those numbnuts?"

"And you're . . . operational?"

"Well . . ." He pats the air with his hand. "It all depends on Leo Balanoff. Cyrus's death screwed the whole thing. If I can flip Leo, if I don't fuck it up—"

"Don't talk like that." She takes his hand in hers. "I don't like it when you talk like that. You're not gonna fuck anything up. Let's celebrate. Wine."

They decide to go out for dinner, a hole-in-the-wall Italian place in downtown Deemer Park. Chris even allows himself a glass of Merlot from the bottle Mary buys.

"Okay, let's get it out of the way," says Mary.

"Get what out of the way?"

"Your joke. A dumb joke a day keeps the bad thoughts away, right?"

Courtesy of Levi. He'd zing one-liners and riddles at Chris right and left while they sat for chemo sessions, IVs in their arms, fluid running through their veins, fighting for their lives.

Chris dunks some bread into a saucer of olive oil and Parmesan. "I saw this old man carrying a wheelbarrow full of four-leaf clovers, rabbits' feet, and horseshoes up a steep hill. I thought to myself, wow, that guy's really pushing his luck."

She hoods her eyes with her hand. "Glad we got that done."

Chris looks over the menu, then peeks at Mary. "So you're not mad? You're okay with the FBI scooping this from Deemer Park P.D.?"

"Am I okay with a homicide with a guaranteed solve, slam-dunk forensics, being ripped out of my hands?" she says. "The better question is whether Dignan is happy about it."

Right, Mary's partner. "Tell Digs when I'm done with Leo, you guys can have him back. I won't immunize him. You can still charge him."

"Yeah, but if the guy acts as an undercover operative on a sensitive national-security investigation, we're not gonna turn around and charge him with M1."

"But you'll get your solve, Mare. That's what matters. The state's attorney, yeah, you're right, they probably won't charge him with first-degree. Probably second-degree or involuntary. Or who knows, maybe nothing. But what do you care? You put down a 'solve' in the books."

She allows for that.

"So . . . do I need to go to your lieutenant with this, or are we good?"

"My lieu? I can handle my own cases, thank you very much." She pours a second glass of wine. "Besides, I already told him the feds were scooping this. Deemer Park P.D. is officially not investigating Cyrus Balik's murder until your investigation is over."

"Good. Great." Chris sighs. "That's assuming I flip him."

Mary laughs. "You think you won't? If he refuses to flip, we have him cold on first-degree murder. He'll spend the rest of his life in prison." She pats his hand. "I think Leo will take your offer, little brother. He won't have a choice."

33

Leo

Saturday night. The wind howling and whining outside, rocking the windows of my condo.

It's been four days since "Francis Garza" paid me a visit and told me that I still had to do the job Cyrus signed me up for, even if Cyrus was dead. Four days since he put a phone number in my hand and told me if they didn't hear from me, I'd be hearing from them.

I grab my step stool and place it under the smoke detector centered between my kitchen and living room, near my couch. It's been giving off periodic beeps to inform me it's time for its six-month testing. If I don't manually test it, soon it will go off on its own. As wired and on edge as I am, the last thing I need is a surprise like that. So I climb the step stool, unscrew the cap, punch the red button, and endure the chirping scream for thirty seconds to get it over with.

A cold, gloomy night with a chance of danger calls for something light and airy on the violin, don't you think? So I go with a short, single-movement work by Williams called "The Lark Ascending." It was one of my instructor's favorites. When he wasn't incessantly harping on me ("Round thumb, Leo, round thumb!"; "Watch your tension, boy!"), Mr. Dingel taught me to give life to the music, to transcend the sense of sound, to feel it within you.

Can you hear the larks, Leo? Can you see them soaring into flight?

When you play it well, I mean when you're really on your game, you can.

I close up my violin case and look again at the phone number "Francis" gave me on that piece of paper. Not because I have any intention of calling it. And not just because the suffix, 8317, is a prime number. No, I'm looking at it because if you double 8,317, you get 16,634, and the sum of that number's divisors is 24,954, and among the divisors of 24,954 are 2, 3, and 6—which are the numbers in the prefix of the phone number. So.

I decide to do a little work, a new section of a brief that's due next week. I'm scribbling notes on a pad of paper; I still prefer pen and paper to a keyboard, at least for first impressions, spitballing. The pen I'm using is a deep blue ballpoint that I love, an XQ-1080 that Trace bought me for a Christmas present. X is the 24th letter in the alphabet, Q is the 17th. Put them together and it's 41, which, when added to 1,080, gets you 1,121, which is not a prime number but is divisible by 19—

Stop. *Stop.*

Okay, back to the violin again. One more piece before it gets too late to play and the neighbors gripe. Thinking the fifth movement of Bach's Partita No. 2 in D minor, a much longer piece but—

Boom-boom-boom.

Someone at my door. Near ten on a Saturday night. People don't pop in unannounced in the city, especially at this hour. And I live in a condo building with a locked security door that only opens with a key or a resident's buzzer. How did they get past that and up to my door?

Is this Nico's crew, stopping by to urge me to reconsider my "no"?

Maybe. But I don't think so. For one thing, I doubt they'd knock. For another, they wouldn't want neighbors around.

And me with nothing but this ballpoint pen clipped to my shirt collar.

I set down the violin and bow and take a deep breath. I was pretty sure this hammer would come down. I just wasn't sure who'd be holding it.

The door pounds again.

"Who's there?" I call out, not ready to move in front of the door just yet. I've seen too many movies.

"Vladimir Putin," comes the reply.

That voice. Yes. I recognize it. I move to the door and look through the peephole.

I should be surprised. But I'm not.

I bend over at the knees, breathe out, give myself a quick pep talk. Then I open the door.

Special Agent Christopher Roberti, wearing a wool overcoat, a suit underneath.

"Remember me?" he says.

34

Leo

Agent Roberti is all dressed up for a Saturday night. He looks different, though. Last I saw him, nearly a year ago, he seemed gaunt, his face drawn; his clothes didn't quite fit. Like he'd recently experienced a substantial weight loss. An illness, was my guess at the time.

Now he looks bulked up, healthier, a glow to his face. Or maybe that's just excitement.

"Yeah, I remember you. You're the FBI agent we came to for help. And all my client Bonnie got for her trouble was a needle rammed in her arm and a crack house to die in."

That seems to take the wind out of his sails. "As I said at the time— I'm sorry about that. If I could've proven it was murder, I would've. You *know* I would've."

"Yeah, so . . . why are you here now?"

He gives me a look. "You know why I'm here, Leo."

I do, but there's no way I'm saying so.

He removes his phone from his coat and pushes a button. An audio recording, voices I recognize. One of them Cyrus Balik. The other one, me.

"Because I am a nice man, I give you this one last chance. Do you have a name for me, mister important lawyer? Who is your client? Tell me his name."

"Vladimir Putin."

"This guy. You know why they knock your teeth out in prison, Mr. Leo?"

So Roberti was up on Cyrus. A bug in his office. I didn't see that coming.

"I was trying to nail Cyrus for *years* before I met you and Bonnie Tressler," says Roberti. "I told you that. All I needed was time. And then you had to go and make yourself the villain." He shakes his head, wipes his mouth.

"I had to what?"

He lets out a low grunt, eyeballing me. "Cut the act. You killed Cyrus. What, did you forget your arrest in college? That your DNA and prints are in the system?"

No, I didn't forget that.

"I got your prints on the murder weapon. A ten-point match of your thumb on the knife. The knife we found sticking out of Cyrus Balik's neck."

It's not in my interest to respond, so I don't.

"And the prints aren't even my best evidence," he says.

See previous thought. "I'm not gonna be your straight man, Roberti. Say it or don't."

One side of his mouth curves upward. "We have your DNA on Cyrus's shirtsleeve. A bloodstain."

I always knew I'd be a suspect in Cyrus's murder. That isn't a surprise. I worked through various permutations of how this could go. I might be one of many suspects. I might be one of a few but with nothing more than flimsy, circumstantial proof against me.

The one playing out before my eyes—this one went under the category of "worst-case scenarios." It was a category of one. This couldn't be worse. Prints, DNA, and my motive on audio, sitting right on that phone in Roberti's hand.

"The lab has you narrowed down to one out of two trillion male Caucasians who could've left that DNA sample," he says. "And seeing as how there aren't two trillion other male Caucasians on this *planet,* I'd say it's game, set, match for you. Deemer Park P.D. is chomping at the bit to put you in handcuffs. They have a slam-dunk case."

Roberti crosses the threshold of the door, entering my condo. He can't legally, but the Fourth Amendment is about the furthest thing from my mind right now.

"And yet you're not here to arrest me," I note.

"And yet I'm not."

Fingerprints matching mine on the murder weapon. DNA matching mine on Cyrus's shirtsleeve. But I'm not under arrest. It's not hard to connect the dots.

"No way, Roberti. I won't do it."

He walks past me, making himself at home in my condo, one of those little power plays that FBI agents so adore. "You agreed to do a job for Cyrus," he says. "You're going to do it. Only now you'll be working undercover for the FBI."

35

Chris

"No chance. No way." Leo shakes his head, stuffs his hands in his pockets.

Leo's no babe in the woods. No criminal defense lawyer is. But the color is draining from his face. It's not the same thing when it's you as opposed to a client. Leo Balanoff is not immune to fear, and it's showing.

"I don't suppose anyone's come around yet to remind you of the promise you made to Cyrus?" Chris turns around and looks at Leo. "No? Yes?"

Leo is leaning against the wall by his front door now, stooped at the waist, hands on his knees, reminding himself to breathe.

"How about the name Nico Katsaros? Familiar with that name, Leo?"

Leo's not dumb enough to volunteer information.

"Okay, well. Nico is Cyrus's boss. Remember when Cyrus had those pliers wrapped around your tooth? But then he left you in his office for half an hour? What do you think Cyrus was doing for thirty minutes?"

Leo looks at the door, anything to avoid eye contact. "A wax and pedicure?"

"Nope. He was getting say-so from Nico. You were always doing this job for Nico. You just didn't know it. And believe me, Nico is going to enforce that agreement."

Leo takes a long time with that. He's doing well enough with the brave front, tight-lipped and stoic. But the weight is too much. He sinks to the floor, hands on his face. "Good for Nico."

"Yeah, but not so good for you, Leo. You think Cyrus was a savage? Nico makes Cyrus look like Mother Teresa. He may dress nice and mingle with the beautiful people, but Nico Katsaros is a merciless fucking animal. He will get what he wants. If you turn him down, he'll ring you up without batting an eye."

"Great. I look forward to meeting him."

Yeah, but Leo's voice is getting shakier. "Let's review your options," says Chris.

Leo doesn't answer but turns his head in Chris's direction.

"Door number one, you get arrested by Deemer Park P.D. for murder, probably tomorrow. They have motive, your prints on the weapon, your DNA on the victim. No chance to argue self-defense, not when you snuck up behind him. So you're toast. You spend the rest of your life in a cage. And Nico, he will see all this. He'll know. Maybe he thinks you know too much about Cyrus and the whole operation. Or maybe he's just flat-out pissed at you for killing his lieutenant, his number two. Maybe you get a shank in county lockup before you ever see a trial. Death or life in prison, that's door number one for you.

"But behind door number two, Leo, you tell Nico you'll do the job. You do it with me hiding behind you. We take Nico down. You wanted to take down Cyrus's operation, right? A bad guy who traffics young women? Here's your chance to get the *real* boss. And I put in a word with the state's attorney when this is over. Maybe they don't charge you at all. Or maybe you get charged with something, but a lot less than murder one. Maybe, I don't know, involuntary—"

"I want immunity." Leo, still crouched in a ball, turns to Chris. "Full immunity."

"No. I can't give you cross-jurisdictional immunity."

"Sure you can. Just get the state's attorney's agreement. You can do that."

"But I won't. I can't read them in. When it's over, sure, but not before. Not now."

"Can't . . . read them in?" Leo gets to his feet. "What does that—are we talking about national security here?"

Chris looks at his shoes.

"Whoa, whoa—hang on a second, Roberti. Tell me more about this package I'm supposed to deliver. Is this some formula for a mass virus? The U.S. continuity-of-government plan? The codes to our nuclear arsenal?"

"Calm down. No." Chris frames his hands. "Okay, I can tell you this much. It's corporate espionage. IP theft."

That seems to give Leo at least a bit of comfort. He looks off in the distance, a sour look on his face. "What, the MSS wants to steal some intellectual property?"

Chris can hardly deny it. Leo's smart enough to figure it out, anyway. It's not exactly a huge leap. And Chris knows that Leo's law firm once represented a Chinese-American businessman who was accused of being an agent of the Ministry of State Security, China's version of the CIA.

"China is eating our lunch with IP theft," says Chris. "We have the chance here to take down a huge operator. A top MSS agent living here in Chicago. Nico Katsaros is on the other side of this. Nico's just the appetizer, if you can believe it. The foreign agent's the meal."

"Shit." Leo runs his hand over his mouth.

"So now you have an idea of the stakes, Counselor. If you deliver this package, you help us take down a major foreign operative *and* Nico Katsaros. The U.S. government will show its appreciation, believe me. I doubt Deemer Park P.D. will even prosecute you for Cyrus's murder."

"But you can't promise it."

"No, I can't. I'm not making any promises. We have to be square on that."

Leo walks into the kitchen, opens a cabinet, and pulls out a bottle of bourbon. He fills half a glass and drains it in one gulp.

"Just deliver a package from point A to point B, Leo, and there's a good chance you can put all this behind you."

"Yeah, sure." He pours himself a second glass.

"Don't drink that. I need to know you're sober when we make this deal."

"The fuck do *you* care if I'm sober?"

"I *do* care. Because the details matter. We're doing this deal by the book."

Leo pushes the glass away. "A deal that ends my legal career, right? Word gets out that I worked UC for the feds, no one will ever hire me. I might go to prison, might not—but I will *definitely* lose my career."

Chris shrugs. *Hey,* he'd like to say, *you did kill a guy. You wanted to get off scot-free?* But there's no point in rubbing alcohol in the wound.

"This is a Saturday-night-only special," he tells Leo. "I walk out this door without a deal, there's no deal ever. Deemer Park P.D. arrests you, and all bets are off. You go to prison, where you look over your shoulder every day for one of Nico's goons."

Leo puts his hands on the counter, his head dropping.

"No point in pretending you have a choice," says Chris. "I'm it. I'm all you got."

36

Chris

Leo, still standing in the corner of his kitchen, twirling a pen in his hand, slowly shakes his head. "I am so royally fucked."

This is what happens after you drop the bomb on them, after you show them how much evidence you have against them, how tightly you can turn the screws. Chris has seen it a hundred times. "Doesn't have to turn out that way, Leo. Help me catch Nico and I'll help you. So . . . you said that guy who called himself 'Francis Garza' left you a number to call? Show me."

He follows Leo into the living room, where Leo scoops a piece of paper off his coffee table. Chris photographs the number. "Monday morning, I'll come by at eight. You'll call that number. They'll probably give you a time and place to meet."

Leo has that look, the look Chris sees whenever he confronts someone and flips them. Like they still can't believe they're agreeing to it. Like they're praying it's all a dream.

"You're doing the right thing, Leo. See you in two days. You've got my number. Use it any time, day or night."

"You're my handler."

"I'm your handler. Any time, day or night, kiddo."

Chris leaves by the back stairs, the fire escape, to his car parked in the alley. He lets out a long breath of relief. He did it. Cyrus died, which could have fucked the whole operation, but Chris managed to fish this thing out of the sewer.

He pulls out his black phone and dials the only number he has dialed or ever will dial on it, the front company they've set up.

"Flowers Anywhere. This is Caleb. How can we make your day beautiful?"

"Hi, Caleb. I want to order flowers for delivery."

"Are you a first-time customer?"

"No, I'm not."

"Great! What is your last name and the last four digits of your card on file with us?"

"Last name, Grimsley. The last four digits are 4-1-2-1."

"Happy to take your order," says the man.

"You have a salesman named Roy?"

"One moment, please."

Oh, so the big man's there to take the call. Not terribly surprising. He knew Chris was making his move tonight. He breathes in and out.

"Chris," he says when he comes on the line. "How'd it go?"

"We got him." Chris can't contain a swell of pride. "Balanoff agreed to cooperate."

"That's good news. Does he want a lawyer?"

"No. He's willing to go without."

"And you can trust him?"

"I can trust that he all but soiled himself, he's so scared of prison. He's a defense lawyer. He knows a rock-solid murder case when he sees it."

"Yes. Okay. When does he meet with Nico?"

"We'll reach out on Monday morning. Then I'll know."

"Good. You stay on him, Chris. He's your assignment. We have Nico covered."

"Understood."

"And the woman, the security person at the company—"

"Andi Piotrowski."

"Right. We're watching her, too."

"Great."

"You have one job, Chris. Leo Balanoff. You just worry about him."

"Got it. Thank you."

"Don't thank me yet. Just keep him straight. He seems . . . unpredictable."

That he does. A bit of a checkered past, that guy.

"Do I have the right man for this, Chris?"

"Absolutely," Chris says, maybe too quickly. "I can handle him. I *will* handle him."

37

Leo

With Roberti gone, I sit in the kitchen, double-clicking the XQ-1080 ball-point Trace bought me. My favorite feature of this pen is not its ink quality but its superior audio—nice and clear with a noise-reduction feature. Good enough to capture every word Roberti just said. I push a button for the auto-download. I created an email account for this purpose. Every conversation I record on this pen will be emailed straight to that account. Just in case all these assurances Roberti just gave me happen to slip his mind one day.

Trust but verify, I always say.

I sit on my couch and send a text message to Trace: Call when you can.

Trace is surely asleep right now—his healthy/sober regimen has him down by ten every night. I doubt the beep of the text message will wake him. We'll talk tomorrow. He'll worry. He'll want to come. That can't happen.

I stretch my arms, releasing nervous energy. Roberti has me boxed in pretty tight. But I'm on my own. This can't involve Trace.

No, it's just you and me, Agent Roberti. You may have some leverage, but this isn't my first rodeo.

Then again, that last rodeo didn't turn out so well.

SEVEN YEARS AGO

MAY 2017

38

Leo

The attorney-client consultation rooms at Stateville penitentiary are full today, so they allow us some time in a staff room that looks like an old kitchen. My client, Eric Putnam, keeps his shackled hands locked together before him.

"We'll file the appeal next week," I say.

"But you don't think we'll win."

I sigh. "Post-conviction petitions are tough, Eric. Everything is stacked against us. But I do think we have an argument."

"And it . . ." He raises one shoulder. "It doesn't matter that I'm innocent."

Just another Black man spending his life in a cage for something he didn't do. In Eric's case, seven years in prison so far, as of tomorrow. Seven years down, sixty-three to go. Eric wasn't a perfect seventeen-year-old, but he wasn't a killer.

"It matters to me," I say.

He flashes me a smile. The kid, now age twenty-four and handsome, has a wicked smile and an even better sense of humor when the mood strikes him. "I know, Leo. Hey, man, you're the only one giving me hope in here."

"I'm not giving up. We'll keep working on those witnesses. Something will break."

He nods for too long, trying to convince both of us. "Hey, where's Mr. Senior Partner?"

Donovan Savage, he means, the head of our firm, Brown Savage. Our representation of Eric Putnam is part of a pro bono program Donovan spearheads and for which he very much enjoys taking credit. Technically, he is the lead counsel on this case, our attempt to prove that Eric Putnam has spent the last seven years in prison for a crime he did not commit.

But the work, naturally, will roll downhill to a young associate like me.

"That's okay," he says. "You're my man, Leo B. You're my believer."

The man walking out of the Missionary Baptist Church in Crestwood, a small child in his arms and family around him, is named Darius Norton. Nine years ago, he killed a man named Lawrence Grover, though everyone called him Groovy.

Darius killed Groovy because they were fighting over a corner—which of them would have the right and privilege to sell heroin to willing buyers at the intersection of Jackson and Kostner in a pocket of the city of Chicago known as K-Town.

But Darius didn't go down for the murder.

Darius stops on the steps of the church and speaks to the minister, showing the preacher the child, who I assume is his grandson. The three adults around him are younger—his two daughters and one son. Darius's wife died of cancer three years ago.

I'm across the street in the church's parking lot, but I move toward the church itself, crossing the sidewalk on my side and standing in the grass near the street.

Well, this should be interesting, if nothing else.

When Darius turns, his eyes catch mine, or at least my sunglasses. The only white person in sight, wearing a suit and shades, focusing on him—he already has an idea. I brush my suit coat at the waist just enough for him to see the badge pinned on my belt for confirmation. And

I nod. He pauses a moment, losing his smile, then nods back. He hands the baby to one of his daughters and whispers something to them.

I move away from the parking lot but slowly, trying not to draw attention to myself, waiting for him to catch up to me.

"What kind a police are you?" he asks me when he reaches me a minute later.

I pull my credentials out of my coat pocket, open them cupped in my hand, blocked by his body from anyone else's view. "FBI," I say.

Darius is now fifty-three years old, with a heavily freckled and lined face, pouches beneath his brown eyes, a receding hairline of short gray curls. He looks older than his age by a good ten years. The gangster life will do that to you. He's out now, by all accounts, but the wear and tear stays.

"Special Agent Krannert," he says, reading my credentials.

I like that last name, Krannert. It's the name of one of the concert venues in Champaign, where I went to college. It sounds like a name you wouldn't make up.

"Okay, Agent Krannert," says Darius, "you had to come to my church to talk to me?"

"Better than showing up at your house."

He seems to agree with that. "You look young," he says.

"I'm thirty-four," I tell him, an exaggeration by several years, but in my experience, older people have a harder time pinning down the ages of the younger generations. "Eight years with DEA, five with the Bureau," I add.

I don't think I would've enjoyed working for the DEA. The whole war-on-drugs thing seemed overblown to me. But the FBI might have been cool, depending on the assignment.

He nods. "Okay. Well, Krannert, what do you want with a broken-down horse like me?"

We keep walking, like two friends strolling down the street.

"Groovy's murder," I say.

"Groovy?"

"Lawrence Grover. Groovy. You know him. Do not play games with me, Darius, or I'll take you into custody right now."

"Okay, what about it?"

"What-about-it is that you shot Groovy. Your people went to bat for you and put the whole thing on Putty."

"Putty?"

I stop walking. "Darius, I swear to God, you play dumb with me one more time, and I stop deciding to be a nice guy about this. I'm trying to throw you a lifeline here, not that you deserve it. You know who Putty is."

He takes a breath. "Eric," he says. "Eric Putnam."

"Your boys put the whole thing on him. Hixon, Williams, and Trager. They all gave statements to the cops and put the gun in Putty's hand. Three eyewitnesses. You got a two-for-one there, Darius. Groovy's dead and Putty's away for the next seventy years. You kill one rival and frame another one for the murder."

"All right, all right," he says. "Why would the FBI even care about this?"

"They don't," I say. I point to myself. "I do. I was DEA back when this happened. I knew all the players. The Insane Warlords, the Carneys, the K-Street Crew. I knew Eric Putnam. He wasn't a killer. I knew the murder beef was bogus. But nobody would listen to me, because I was young, and it was a state matter. But now people will listen to me. And I'm not letting this go, Darius. Not again."

"So what do you want from me?"

"Your boys are falling apart now," I say. "Hixon got recorded yapping to his cellmate in Tamms that he and his buddies framed Putty. He said Putty was nowhere near the murder, that Putty was across town with himself, Williams, and Trager at the time of the shooting, but all three of them put the case on Putty. The whole thing was a setup."

"Hixon." Darius rubs the back of his neck. "That's a name from the past."

"I have the recording right here, if you want to listen to it," I say.

I show him the audio file in my hand, but he looks away, his eyes cast downward. "No, I don't need to listen."

That's good, because it's a recording of a continuing legal education seminar on choice-of-law provisions in arbitration agreements. I'm behind on my CLE credits at the law firm.

"And Williams," I go on, "he's trying to get some relief on an armed-habitual charge that will make him Class X. He's looking at life in prison. He's already proffered to CPD, and it sounds an awful lot like what Hixon told his cellie: Putty was across town with Hixon, Williams, and Trager at the time of the shooting. And Williams'll do better than that. He says *you* were the one who ordered them to put this on Putty. And he says you, Darius, murdered Groovy."

Darius looks past me, staring into the horizon. "What about Trager?"

"Trager's dead, if you didn't know. Overdosed a couple years ago."

"Jesus." Darius brings a shaky hand to the top of his head, patting gently. "Jesus, the drugs. The shit they made us do."

"Looks like you cleaned up *your* act, though," I say. "Moved out here to Crestwood. Helping raise a family. An honest job. A man of God, too. You've moved on."

"I have." His shoulders rise and fall as his eyes fill with tears.

"Personally, Darius, I'm not shedding a lot of tears over Groovy. The guy had four or five kills of his own under his belt before he got a taste of his own medicine. If Groovy's real killer is never brought to justice, I could probably sleep at night. But you know what I can't let go?"

His eyes glance at mine, then down to the sidewalk. "Putty."

"Correct. Eric Putnam. He's been in the can since he was arrested, since your boys framed him. Seven years, for a crime he didn't commit. He's gonna die in there before they let him out. That, I won't let go."

"I have . . . I have people counting on me," he says, his voice choking up. "People who need me."

"Eric has a daughter who's never seen her father outside a prisoner visiting room," I say. "Listen, Darius, one way or the other, Eric has to get out. Whether it involves you taking his place in the penitentiary or not is up to you."

He turns to me.

"Three options," I say. "One, you cop to it. You do the right thing. This man of God stuff, if it's real, then you do the right thing and admit you shot Groovy. Option two, you don't admit to killing Groovy."

"No?"

"No, but you *do* admit that you ordered Hixon, Williams, and Trager to pin this on Eric. You saw a chance at knocking out a rival by falsely accusing him, and you took it. Doesn't make you a killer. Means you obstructed justice. You'd probably do some time. But not compared to murder. And less time if you come forward voluntarily."

"Voluntarily," he mumbles.

"Leave me out of it. Act like you did it on your own. An act of conscience. You can't live with the guilt, et cetera. I'll pretend this conversation never happened. You have my word. You can be the reformed criminal who just wants to do the right thing. And it *would* be the right thing to do, Darius. You've let an innocent man sit in prison for seven years."

Darius works his jaw, tears running down his face now. "And three?" he whispers.

"Three, you do neither of those, because I can't force you. I'll go back to Williams and take his official statement. He'll swear under oath that you killed Groovy, and my guess is, so will Hixon. You might get charged with first-degree murder, you might not; it won't be my call. But if you do get charged, Darius, it won't be you coming in voluntarily, as an act of conscience, so you won't get any leniency at all."

Darius bends over, putting his hands on his knees. He was probably planning on a little Sunday brunch after church. Instead, the heaviest debt of his past has suddenly come due.

"I don't have to admit to the murder?" he asks. "Just to the frame-up?"

Stateville again, only this time we get one of the attorney-client visitation rooms. And this time, the senior partner, Donovan Savage, with his immaculate suit and coiffed silver hair, is with me.

Eric Putnam's mouth hangs open. "Say it . . . say it again," he says. "Darius . . ."

"Darius Norton walked into the Crestwood police station on Monday and gave a full confession," says Donovan. "He confessed to killing Groovy to take over his drug turf, and he confessed that he had his lieutenants pin everything on you."

"That's what I've been . . . That's what I've been . . ."

That's what Eric's been saying since the day I met him, eighteen months ago.

"What—what—why?" Eric can no longer keep his composure, his face streaked with tears, his voice closing down, sobbing so heavily he can hardly speak. "Why . . . now?"

"An act of conscience, as far as we can tell," says Donovan. "Just out of the blue, he decided to come clean."

Eric looks at me. I simply shrug. "He probably couldn't live with the guilt," I say. "Sometimes people do the right thing."

"You wanted to see me, Mr. Savage?" I poke my head inside Donovan Savage's palatial corner office, views of the lake and north side of the city. I've been summoned for the first time since Eric Putnam's conviction was overturned three months ago.

He waves me in. "Sit, Leo, sit." He looks over his reading glasses at me. "I'll get right to the point. There's been a . . . complaint filed with the ARDC."

The Attorney Registration and Disciplinary Commission. The cops for lawyer misconduct.

I'm midway through the act of sitting down and freeze. I look at the senior partner.

"Darius Norton's daughters filed it," he continues. "They say you im . . ." He struggles to finish the sentence. He removes his glasses and pinches the bridge of his nose. "They say you impersonated an FBI agent?"

THE PRESENT DAY

JANUARY 2024

Three Weeks before Valentine's Day

39

Chris

Here we go.

Chris takes the steps up the front walk of Leo's condo building. Four steps, one of them with a diagonal crack, each of them crunchy from salt that has managed to melt the remnants of ice. Up at the security door, he pushes the button for "Balanoff" and waits. Leo buzzes him in without saying a word; Chris grabs the door to push it open. Inside, a vestibule with twelve small mailboxes lined against the wall like safe-deposit boxes, secured by locks, a slot for outgoing mail below them. In the corner of the tiny entrance, beyond the dingy carpet, is a large rock. Probably used to prop the door open for bigger deliveries.

Chris pauses, blinks. Then he picks up the rock and wedges it between the security door and the frame.

He takes the two flights of stairs up to the third floor. He finds the last door on the left and knocks. He hears "It's open!" and enters Leo's condo.

Leo is sitting at the kitchen table, head propped on a hand, elbow on the table. His hair hangs in his face, greasy and unkempt. A weekend's worth of stubble on his face. He looks up at Chris with sunken eyes. And yes, he's wearing the same shirt and sweats he was wearing two days ago.

Jesus. This guy looks like shit. Has he slept at all in the last two days? Did he ever leave the kitchen?

"Ready to rock?" he asks. "We have a few minutes yet."

Leo is doodling, as far as Chris can tell, writing with that same pen on a sheet of paper. Chris moves in closer and sees that Leo is not aimlessly scrawling. He's making a list:

Executor—Monty
Condo—proceeds to DJK Foundation
Car—Kars4Kids
401(k)—DJK Foundation
Violin—CYSO

"Whatcha doin'?" he asks Leo, but it's not hard to tell. Leo is writing the outline of a will and testament—the executor apparently his law partner, Montgomery Morris.

"That's all I can think of." Leo puts down his pen, rubs his face. "Those are all the assets I have to show for thirty—"

"Don't be so melodramatic." Chris pats Leo on the back, then takes one of the chairs at the kitchen table. "Nobody's dying any time soon. Least of all a witness of mine."

Leo gives him a look.

"DJK Foundation? What's that?"

Leo's eyes are bloodshot. He looks like he's recovering from an all-night bender. "They help kids who've been trafficked. Find them shelter, reunite them with family—"

"Well, hey." Chris throws up a hand. "What better way to help the cause than taking down a human trafficker like Nico Katsaros?"

Hard to argue with that. Leo nods.

"No family?" Chris asks. "Parents, siblings?"

"Nope. My dad died in a car crash when I was young. Don't even remember him. I have a brother, but I haven't seen him in over a decade. Don't know where he lives. Or if he's even alive. Drugs." He looks at Chris. "I tried many times. I finally had to give up."

"Sorry about that. Your mother?"

"She died, too. She drowned."

"Oh—oh, wow. How'd that—I mean I guess it's none of my—"

"She fell off a platform during a rehearsal of *Oklahoma!* Community theater. She played Aunt Eller."

"I . . ." Chris cocks his head. "And she drowned?"

"We think that's when the bleeding on her brain started. She had a stroke about a week later."

"Oh, and she was swimming or something?"

"She was golfing." Leo shakes his head. "She went to retrieve her ball near a pond on the course and went face-first into the water. By the time anyone could reach her, it was too late."

"Well . . . I'm sorry to hear that." Chris stares at his hands. "Um, so . . . it's time to make the call. It's eight o'clock sharp."

Leo picks up the phone, looks at it.

"You got the number right there, kid. Call him. Call Francis Garza or whoever he is."

Leo nods but makes no move to dial. Chris looks at his phone; the digital clock switches from 8:00 to 8:01. Leo starts dialing. Chris moves over and puts his ear close.

The call rings and rings. After ten or eleven rings, Leo punches out.

Chris sits back in his chair. "He'll call back."

Leo puts down the phone. "I hope it's soon. I have a hearing at ten at Twenty-Sixth Street."

"Hey, why'd you wait until 8:01 to call? You waited until the time changed to 8:01—"

"I like the number better," says Leo.

Chris draws back. "You . . . like the number—"

"I don't like round numbers. Tens and hundreds. 800? That's the product of a bunch of other round numbers like 10 and 20 and 40 and 50 and 80. But 759? That's the product of three prime numbers. How many numbers can say that? And 801 is the product of three primes, too, though technically two of them are the same, so—"

"Are you puttin' me on right now? Like, this numbers stuff?"

Leo messes up his hair. "It's my curse. Most of the time, it drives me crazy. But it calms me when I'm on edge."

"You're on edge, huh?"

Leo gives Chris a look. "I'm about to set up a meeting with a gangster who probably thinks I killed his right-hand man. And who, if he's as good as you say he is, will likely make me for an FBI mole right away. And who, even if neither of those things is true, will probably want to kill me anyway, once I perform a job for him, just so I can't testify against him. So yeah, I'm not exactly feeling . . . serene."

Right. Obviously. Chris knows a thing or two about mortal fear. "For me, it's humor. Silly shit. Dad jokes. Helps take the edge off."

"Try me," says Leo.

Chris thinks a moment. "My neighbor bought me a new roof. I offered to pay him, but he said it was on the house."

Leo tries for a smile.

"Centuries ago, scientists got tired of watching the earth turn. So after twenty-four hours, they called it a day."

Leo lets out a breath. "I feel better already."

The phone rings. Chris jumps up and gets next to Leo again. Leo answers. "Hello?"

A moment later, a recorded voice, something robotic: *"Ela on Halsted, tomorrow morning at eight."* The line goes dead.

"Ela," says Chris. "That's a diner in Greektown."

"I know it."

"All right. So it's game on." Chris lightly grips Leo's shoulder. "You good? This is good. You're on your way to putting this behind you."

Leo pushes himself out of the chair with a moan. "I gotta shower. I'm gonna be late."

"Okay. Listen to me, Leo. If they call back for any reason, first chance you get, you call and tell me. Otherwise, I'll come here tomorrow morning at 7. Or how about 7:01? You like 701 better than 700?"

Leo almost smiles. "It's a prime number, so."

"Prime, meaning it's only divided by itself and one."

"Exactly."

"Kind of a loner in the numbers world, is that it?"

Leo shrugs. "I guess."

"Okay. Well, 7:01 tomorrow morning, then." Chris starts for the door, then stops. Thinking of that word. *Loner.* He hadn't thought much about

Leo's station in life. No girlfriend, no family. "Y'know, you can call me for any reason, Leo. Even if you're getting freaked out. My job is to make sure *you* do *your* job. That includes listening, if you just need someone to listen."

Leo thinks about that for a second. "I don't need you to be my friend. I just need you to keep me alive. Think you can manage that?"

"Flowers Anywhere. This is Caleb. How can we make your day beautiful?"

Chris, back in his parked car, clears his throat. "I want to order flowers for delivery."

"Are you a first-time customer?"

"No, I'm not."

"Great! What is your last name and the last four digits of your card on file with us?"

"Last name, Grimsley. The last four digits are 4-1-2-1."

"Happy to take your order," says the man.

"You have a salesman named Roy?"

"One moment, please."

Chris keeps his eye on the alley behind Leo's building. It's been twenty minutes since he left. Leo should be leaving any minute to drive to the criminal courts building at 26th and California, quite a hike in traffic.

"Chris. How'd it go?"

"Leo's set to meet with Nico tomorrow morning at eight."

"Good. Where?"

"A Greek diner. Ela, on Halsted. But I'm sure they'll move him from there."

"No doubt. Are you going to follow Balanoff?"

"I don't think so. Not worth the risk. Do you agree?"

"I do, yes. We'll be watching Nico. How *is* Balanoff?"

"Spooked. Normal stuff. I'm prepping him tomorrow morning before he goes."

"Keep me posted. Good job, Chris."

Ten minutes later, Leo comes bounding down the fire escape. He jumps in his car parked in the alley and drives away.

Chris kills the engine, pops the trunk, and gets out. He grabs his gym bag out of his trunk and heads around to the front of the building. The rock he wedged inside the security door is still there. He waltzes into Leo's building like he belongs there, placing the rock back in the corner of the vestibule. It was a gamble; he bet that nobody in the building would notice the front door ajar, that most residents leaving their condos would head out the back way to the alley for their cars.

The lock on Leo's door on the third floor is a standard lock-and-tumbler, nothing Chris can't handle in five minutes' time. People who live in buildings with security buzzer doors tend to spend less time on the doors to their personal units.

He's inside. He needs a central location. But he already picked the ideal spot, earlier today, square in the middle of the condo, right between the kitchen and living room, and not all that far from the bedroom, either.

The smoke detector on the ceiling.

He finds Leo's step stool, climbs up, and unscrews the cap. As he figured, the smoke detector is wired up to the power. Perfect. It won't take long. Thirty minutes, tops, to plant the eavesdropping device. And he'll have ears inside Leo's condo.

You seem like an okay guy, Leo, he thinks. *But I'm not trusting you as far as I can throw you.*

40

Andi

Andi leaves QCI for the day and heads to her car, bracing herself against a merciless wind. She starts up her Jeep and heads for Morgan Park. It takes her close to an hour to reach 111th Street. She gets the same twitchiness in her nerves every time she returns to the neighborhood where she grew up.

"Oh, *there* you are," says Marni when Andi comes through the front door, as if Andi's late. As if she didn't battle nightmare rush-hour traffic to get here. As if there were a set time she was supposed to arrive. Marni Piotrowski, queen of passive aggression.

"C'mere, let me see my formidable daughter." Her standard line. She takes Andi's face in her hands and kisses her forehead, humming to herself. Marni has shrunk over time, from pear-shaped when Andi was a kid to downright slender now. Her hair has largely grayed and is still parted on the side and combed over in swooping fashion. She's wearing circular, cobalt-blue eyeglasses she saw on some home shopping network and a knitted sweater she probably saw on TV, too. "You look tired, baby girl. You're not getting enough sleep."

"I'm fine, Mama."

She hums again. Her mother has varying tones of humming, from good-for-you to don't-bullshit-a-bullshitter.

Andi follows her into the kitchen, where her laptop rests on the table. The computer is "acting up," Marni claims, and she lives in perpetual fear of hackers and scammers in her email. She doesn't trust anybody but Andi to look at it, as if her daughter possesses some keen level of skill.

Andi awakens the computer by touching the mouse—Marni still uses a mouse—and is startled by the screensaver. It's a photo of Marni and Agnes, cheek to cheek, looking at the camera.

That came later, years after Agnes was firmly ensconced in the Piotrowski household, much more than a domestic worker trading work for shelter, truly part of the family. When Andi first saw Agnes, she thought she was beautiful—her delicate, sculpted features, the graceful way she carried herself. Not that she did anything to glamorize herself. Far from it; she was subdued and shy, wore ill-fitting clothes, did nothing to her hair other than let it hang down around her face, never wore makeup.

She was submissive at first, avoiding eye contact, cautious with every move she made. That was okay with Andi, who was suspicious of everyone not named Marni Piotrowski; keeping a bit of a distance worked for her.

They eased into things together. Their first week, they didn't say ten words to each other. They found their groove in the summer, when Andi was out back trying to practice volleyball spikes on their makeshift net. She'd throw the ball up to herself, jump and spike it, and hope it didn't bounce over the fence into the neighbor's yard.

Agnes used that as a way in. She looked up the dimensions of a volleyball court and staked them out, so Andi could work on angles and placement in a real court setting. Then she learned how to be a setter, mostly by practicing with Andi, so instead of Andi throwing the ball up to herself, Agnes could set it for her.

And then it became their thing, as Andi grew and blossomed, Agnes and Andi—A-squared—out in the backyard, every day of the week, ten months of the year, rain or shine.

"If you want to do things other people cannot," Agnes would remind her every day in her stilted English, "you must work like other people will not."

It was later, a good five years in, when things developed between

Mama and Agnes. Maybe Andi had seen it coming. Maybe she sensed it without realizing. But she can still remember the first time she saw them holding hands, the first time she saw them nuzzle faces, the first time she saw them kiss. What she doesn't remember is being surprised. It just felt natural.

The rest of the neighborhood—well, who knows what their little white Catholic neighbors said behind their backs. First the Pios were a mixed-race couple, and now they were a mixed-race *gay* couple with an age difference of sixteen years.

Andi never knew traditional, anyway. All she knew was Marni was the happiest she'd ever seen her. And Agnes? Either way, she was family.

When Andi fixes Marni's computer problem—by rebooting the computer and cleaning out the garbage in her email—she's back to that screensaver, that beautiful photo of them.

Agnes was the love of Marni's life, no question. Marni was never the same after Agnes died, ten years after she entered their lives, when Andi was seventeen and a year away from college. That spark, that smile, never returned.

Andi's phone buzzes. It's Brando on a text: **Got here early. Ready when you are.**

"Work?" Marni asks.

"Just something I have to do."

"They're not paying you enough, baby girl."

"You don't even know my salary, Mama."

"Well, it's not enough. Calling you at all hours."

Andi kisses her on the cheek. "Gotta run. Love you."

Brando is waiting for Andi in a booth at the bar, a place four blocks from where she lives, just off the UIC campus. The place is dark and moody, with brick walls and wood tables and a popcorn machine. Not too crowded and not too loud, especially on a midweek night.

A glass of red wine is waiting for her. Brando is looking at his phone. His hair is combed, at least, though it doesn't look all that different.

"Did you shower today?" she asks. "Do you ever shower?"

"Americans shower too much."

"And what are you, European? You were born in Oak Lawn."

"Yeah, but I'm . . . refined." He works the toothpick in his mouth. "Did you tell your mother you were coming to see me?"

"Of course not. She doesn't know about the things we talk about. You know that."

"Yeah, she probably wouldn't approve none too much."

That's an understatement. Marni's head would explode if she knew that her daughter was involved in an international espionage operation. Not that Brando doesn't worry, too. He's more protective than he'd ever admit. When she told him she was going to leave Deemer Park P.D. and go to QCI to do this heist, he was skeptical. Too risky, he said. Too many variables, too little control. But once she decided, he respected her choice. He is literally the only person she can talk to about this.

"Cyrus Balik is dead," she tells him.

"I heard. Not exactly a secret. Did Nico tell you?"

She nods.

"This is a problem, Andrea. A big one. Cyrus was supposed to be the courier."

"Tell me something I don't know."

"So what's he gonna do?"

"Nico can be so annoyingly calm," she says with a shrug. "He said he's got someone in mind."

"Yeah? Well, it better be someone good. This isn't the time to be bringing in the junior varsity. This is the whole fuckin' enchilada. This is the whole reason you left the force."

Don't remind me.

"Nico will get someone good," she says. "All I know is he said he had someone he wants for the job, but the guy was 'reluctant' so far."

"Reluctant? Nico told somebody to do something, and they were 're-luctant' to do it?"

"That's what he said."

Brando leans forward. "That doesn't sound like someone who works for Nico. Nico tells one of his guys to do something, they do it. 'Reluctant' gets you the morgue."

He's right. She hadn't considered that. Nobody says no to Nico. At least, not anyone who knows better. "Maybe it's someone with no connection to him at all?"

"A canary," says Brando.

"Maybe. That would actually be pretty smart."

"Yeah, well." Brando raises his glass. "This is a fifty-million-dollar job set to go down in two weeks. It's getting pretty late in the game to find a canary."

41

Chris

Inside his bathroom, Chris sticks the needle into his butt, looks back and sees no blood in the syringe, then injects the trenbolone.

He can't shake his nerves, an underlying sense of dread. He has Leo Balanoff cornered, locked down as much as any cooperating witness could be locked down. And yet.

He sits on the bed and awakens his "Leo" phone, which is receiving the audio from the bug he placed inside Leo's smoke detector. Leo should be home from work now. He puts the phone on speaker and fast-forwards through the audio, through the dead time during the day when Leo was at work and nothing was happening in his condo, until he sees a spike in the sound waves around seven o'clock this evening.

The sound, at first, is nothing of interest. Leo coming home from work. Dropping down his bag. The clatter of a pan, the sound of a television—*SportsCenter*. He fast-forwards again.

He sees the sound waves bounce at one particular spot and stops to listen. But it's not conversation or even a TV. It's music. Classical music. Violin without accompaniment. Right—Leo had written down a violin as something he wanted to donate in that makeshift will and testament he was putting together. So, Leo's a violinist.

And to Chris's amateur ear, quite an accomplished one, too. A slow, melancholy piece that seems like something you'd hear in a tearjerker movie. Emotional music played by an expert hand.

The violin music eventually stops, and Leo's condo is relatively quiet again. Chris blasts the phone's volume so he can listen while he starts a series of ab crunches. Abs are one of the few muscles you can't overwork. He rises and lowers, rises and lowers, feeling the burn of his abdominals shaping and chiseling—

"Hey, it's me. I tried to reach you last night but you were probably asleep. I didn't want to text you. This isn't something you text. Call back, man. I'm in big fuckin' trouble. The FBI's on me. It's about . . . It's about Cyrus. They think I killed him."

Chris pops back on the bed and replays the words—Leo's words, apparently leaving a voicemail message for someone.

A shiver of panic races through him. Leo can't talk to anyone about this—not even a lawyer, unless the lawyer gets cleared. This is national security. Leo knows that. He specifically promised that he wouldn't talk to a soul about this, that it would be a breach of his cooperation deal if he did.

Then again, what can Chris do? He can't very well *confront* Leo on this. Not without admitting he's running an illegal eavesdrop inside Leo's apartment.

Take a breath, he tells himself. *This is exactly why you installed the bug in his condo. Just wait and listen. Whoever it is will call back. Maybe there will be more to learn. And then you can decide what to do about it.*

The time on the audio is 8:07 p.m. Chris sits and waits as the audio rolls on. He hears typing on a keyboard. Leo's doing some work. He's probably sitting on the couch in the living area, right by the kitchen. Right by the smoke detector. Then again, everything's pretty much right by the smoke detector in that condo.

Chris fast-forwards through the audio recording until he reaches the next spike in the sound waves. He backs it up and listens. And hears a sound he hasn't heard in years. Music.

But not violin music this time. Music of a particular kind, deep bass notes easily recognizable as the theme music to *Jaws*.

Duhhh-NA . . . Duhhh-NA . . .

Then the pace picking up. *Duh-Na-Duh-Na-Duh-Na-Duh-Na—*

"Hey, thanks for calling back."

Okay—it's a phone ringing. The *Jaws* music is Leo's ringtone on his phone. Got it. And not a bad choice, considering that Leo probably feels like he's swimming with sharks right now.

"No, I wouldn't say I'm okay. I'm actually freaking the fuck out." Pause. *"Don't ask me that, okay? I mean, that's the one question—don't ask."*

Chris nods. Leo's friend must have just asked him if it's true—if he killed Cyrus.

"Let's just say they have a strong case. DNA, fingerprints, even me on audio talking to him. It couldn't be more of a slam dunk for them. No chance I win at trial."

Good. Leo fully understands how cornered he is.

"Monty? Hell, no. I can't tell him. He'd cut me loose."

Okay, so it's not his law partner, Montgomery Morris, on the other end of the call. Leo's afraid that he'll lose his career if Monty knows.

So who's he talking to? *Cyrus*, Leo keeps saying. Just a first name. Someone who knows about Cyrus Balik without having the context explained—

Oh. Oh, of course. Leo's talking to his client. He's talking to Bonnie Tressler's son, whoever he is.

"Don't even get on me about this, okay? I know it was stupid. I know I should've talked to you about it first. But guess what? I didn't. So can you at least be someone I can talk to, or are you gonna just bitch at me?"

A longer pause, the sound waves dipping, but Chris can hear Leo's stilted breathing.

"No, the FBI doesn't wanna charge me with murder. The local cops would do that. The FBI wants me to work for them. They want me to do the job Cyrus asked me to do. They want me to agree to do the job while working undercover for the feds."

Pause.

"Yeah, you'd think so, wouldn't you? No more Cyrus, no more job. But that's the thing. That's the thing I didn't know. He has a boss. Yeah, Cyrus

has a guy above him on the ladder. And that guy still wants me to do the job. You getting it now? The FBI wants the big boss, and they want me to help take him down. And it gets better. Apparently, this job they want me to do involves stealing some big trade secret or something. Something the Chinese government wants to steal."

Pause.

"I know." Leo lets out a frustrated chuckle. *"I walked into the middle of a damn national-security investigation. You getting the idea of how screwed I am now?"*

Pause. Chris has to remind himself to breathe. How much is Leo going to tell this guy?

"Don't ask me names," says Leo. *"Better you don't know. It's bad enough you know about Cyrus. Believe me, you don't want to get anywhere near this."*

An even longer pause, while the other person talks. Malcolm. That was the name they found on the birth certificate. The little boy born to Bonnie Tressler who completely disappeared afterward. Was he sold to a pedophile ring? A desperate family?

"Yeah, of course I'm gonna do it," says Leo. *"What choice do I have? Either I help them and pray I come out of it alive, or I spend the rest of my life in prison."*

At least Leo's on board. As if he had a choice.

"The agent? It doesn't matter. No names, remember? Anyway, he's standard-issue FBI, straight as an arrow, just the facts, the whole routine. I'll say this much—the guy has terrible breath. I mean, serious halitosis."

Huh? Chris cups a hand around his mouth and breathes out. He has bad breath? He's never heard that before. Not once, ever in his life, has someone told him that. But then again, who would want to break that news to you?

"All right, man, well—needless to say, you can't repeat any of this. I'm not supposed to talk to anyone about this shit. The agent would have my ass if he knew I was talking to you. It's just . . . nice to have someone to vent to. I'll call you tomorrow, if that's cool."

The call ends. Leo goes quiet.

Chris will replay the whole thing, make sure he didn't miss something. But all things considered, it could have been a lot worse. Leo could've given out names—Chris Roberti, Nico Katsaros—and forced Chris's hand.

But either way, it sure would be nice to know the current name and whereabouts of the person Leo called, Bonnie's son, Malcolm.

42

Leo

Chris Roberti pops yet another breath mint into his mouth, the third he's consumed since he's been in my condo this morning. "So we're good?"

"We're good," I say.

"It's okay to be nervous. He'd expect you to be nervous."

"I got it."

"Good." He puts a hand on my shoulder. "Now let me tell you how I think this will go."

I make it to the diner on Halsted at eight sharp. The step count from my car to the restaurant door is 213. If you add those digits, you get the same number you'd get if you multiplied them. Not many three-digit numbers can say that. And it's divisible by 71 and 3, both prime numbers.

I'm not nervous.

I normally like Greek diners, menus that serve just about anything, waitstaff always topping off your cup of coffee, cooks shouting to each other in the kitchen. Somehow it doesn't feel so warm and comforting today.

"I'm Leo," I say to the woman with dark circles under her eyes and a prominent mole on her cheek who is doubling as hostess and cashier.

She waves with the back of her hand, which doesn't tell me much until she says, "Downstairs, downstairs, go around rope."

I find the staircase by the bathroom. A velvet rope blocks access, a sign reading **EMPLOYEES ONLY**. I unclick the latch on one side, step down, and re-click the latch. I take two more steps and stop, my heartbeat drumming so hard I have to force a breath.

It's not too late to change my mind. I don't have to do this.

Fuck it. I've come this far.

I walk downstairs into a hallway with two doors, one marked **STORAGE**, the other **MANAGER**, next to which two men are standing, each wearing a long-sleeved sweater stretched out by muscles at the shoulders and a protruding stomach at the waist. They make a point of looking serious, so I take them seriously.

"We need to pat you down," one of them says. "Take off your coat. Empty your pockets. And give me your phone."

They'll frisk you, Roberti told me. *And they'll take your phone. So don't bring it.*

"I didn't bring a phone." But I did wear a coat, so I take it off. I empty my pockets of my wallet and keys and raise my arms. The second guy feels me up like we know each other a lot better than we do and puts my wallet and keys in a bag. "I keep for now. Come with us."

They'll move you, Roberti predicted. *That's normal. Don't freak out.*

I follow the guy down a hallway to a fire exit. He pushes through the door and walks up a flight of stairs, with me following. Once we're back up at ground level, he pushes open another door. We are in an alley, and I'm without my coat. But it's only a few steps into a waiting car.

I ride in the back of an SUV, a Chrysler, I think. My colleagues, the two thugs, are in the front. They are not conversationalists.

No hood over my head or anything, so I'm able to see where we're going. Which means they don't care that I know. Which could mean, if I let my imagination run wild, that they don't plan on my leaving this meeting alive.

With those warm thoughts percolating in my head, somewhere near the corner of Racine and Washington, the SUV pulls into a parking garage, heading down a ramp. The driver pulls a ticket, waits for the gate to rise, and drives into the basement.

They'll take you someplace where a recording device would lose its transmission signal, Roberti said. *Probably a basement garage.*

Like I couldn't have figured any of that out for myself.

We park in a spot next to a black town car. Someone opens my door and directs me into the back seat of the other car.

When I first slide into the leather seat, I think I'm alone. Then I see him, sitting across from me, on the other side of a rear cabin that smells like expensive cologne and Italian coffee.

"Good morning, Leo Balanoff." Nico Katsaros is not especially handsome, with a bald crown, large nose, and thin lips, dark through the eyes, but he does know how to carry himself, radiating ease and power, his gold cuff links gleaming on his crisp white shirt as he drinks from a paper cup of what is probably some espresso drink.

"Thank you for coming," he says. "I was surprised that you accepted. My understanding was that your first answer was not yes."

That provokes a burst of laughter from me. My first response to Nico's goon, if memory serves, included an F-bomb. Maybe this guy's got a sense of humor.

But I think it's too early to predict we'll be friends.

"Why the change of heart?" he asks.

Because the FBI made me an offer I couldn't refuse. Probably not a good answer.

I try this instead: "When your guy first approached me, I didn't know of your involvement."

"Yes, yes. Cyrus originally discussed it with you. Had he not died, he would have been the only one you'd have ever dealt with."

And Nico undoubtedly would have preferred it that way. Layers, buffers, are the beating heart of an operation like his. It's exactly why Cyrus, and now Nico, want someone like me to deliver the package.

"I've looked into you, as you can imagine," he says. "The incident that resulted in your license suspension. You pretended to be an FBI agent to elicit a confession from a guilty man in order to free an innocent man."

"That about covers it, yes."

"In the course of your disciplinary proceeding, you were analyzed by a psychiatrist who diagnosed you as a pathological liar."

That wasn't my idea. That was my firm, Brown Savage. More specifically, the senior partner, Donovan Savage, but not because he gave one tiny shit about me; he wanted to minimize any embarrassment to the firm. *Illness plays better*, he said. Sickness breeds compassion. Treatment, not punishment. So Donovan tapped one of his hired-gun experts, who spent all of one hour talking with me before coming up with his brilliant conclusion.

The irony is that, although the diagnosis was preordained, it wasn't that far off the mark. The problem is the labels. I don't go for terms like *pathological* or *compulsive*. I don't feel some overwhelming urge to lie for its own sake. Nor is it out of my control. I'm just good at it. My whole childhood was a lie. And I don't have any compunction about doing it if the situation presents itself. Why would I? Everyone else lies all the time.

But this, of course, makes me an even better candidate—ideal, really—for Nico's purposes. I have no known connection to him, already making it easy for him to plausibly deny any relationship with me. But as a cherry on top, I'm a pathological liar? Anything I say would be immediately discounted. If the worst case happens—the feds catch me delivering the package and I point the finger at Nico—it becomes a he-said, he-said, and he figures nobody will believe me.

I am the perfect canary for this job.

"As I understand it," says Nico, "as a precondition to restoring your law license, you had to undergo treatment, some counseling."

True. The shrink they appointed almost immediately realized that my diagnosis was bullshit, that there was nothing pathological about me and I only had one compulsion. She learned a lot about prime numbers before she signed off on me.

"But my question is whether it was ever true," says Nico. "In my experience, people facing legal consequences raise issues of health and competency to . . . mitigate the consequences. I'm wondering if that's all that was."

"You're asking whether I'm really a pathological liar, or if I just said that to get a lighter penalty."

"I am."

"And you think you could trust my answer?"

He bows his head slightly. "I see your point. That might put a gloss on my other questions."

"You want to know if I killed Cyrus."

Nico takes a sip of his drink, savors it, looks me over. "You seem awfully good at predicting my questions."

"I didn't kill him."

He holds his stare on me, eyes slightly narrowed. The man obviously prides himself on revealing nothing, remaining a mystery. He enjoys his power, and he likes making you guess what he's thinking. Every change of expression, every gesture, carefully considered.

"I think you did," he says.

"I know."

"Am I the only one who thinks that?"

Okay, so we're done flirting. He's making his move.

"Could you be more specific?"

That actually provokes a smile from him, though one with little merriment, more of impatience. He's one of these guys who's taught himself to smile when he gets irritated. "You know what I'm asking, Leo. You're a defense attorney. A good one, I'm told."

"Do the cops have their hooks in me? Do they think I killed Cyrus, and now they're flipping me to help catch the big guy at the top—you? Is that what you're asking?"

"Exactly," he says. "The local cops, the FBI, law enforcement of any kind."

"Nobody flipped me," I say. "I'm no snitch. You can decide whether you believe me."

He nods, setting down his cup of coffee.

"I will do that, Leo." He looks up at me. "I will do just that."

43

Chris

"Roberti. You're still here."

Chris looks up from his report, scoots back his chair. Agent Alvarez, with his crew cut and goatee, chomping gum and leaning on the side of the carrel, grins at him.

"Finishing up some 302s," says Chris. He checks the time—nearly nine at night.

"Wanna help us out tomorrow on an arrest warrant?"

Chris perks up. "Sure. Love to."

"We need some outer perimeter."

The outer perimeter. Always the easy stuff, ever since Chris returned. Like Chris is a fragile doll who will break at the first hint of contact. "How about the stack?"

"No, we're good there. Just some perimeter down in Lansing. Leaving here at ten."

"Sure," says Chris. "Whatever you need."

He watches Alvarez walk away. He counts the days until he'll be done with this piddly shit.

Speaking of. Leo should've been home a long time ago. Did he make another call to his friend—or more likely, his client, Bonnie Tressler's son?

Leo debriefed Chris after he met with Nico this morning. More of the same paranoia—*he knows who I am, he knows I'm undercover, he's gonna kill me*. But Chris wants to hear what Leo said to his buddy. He pulls out his "Leo" phone, sticks in his earbuds, and runs through the audio from Leo's condo tonight. He fast-forwards through the recording until he sees sound waves popping up at the 7:41 mark.

It begins, again, with the *Jaws* theme song. *Duhhh-NA. Duhhh-NA.*

Leo answers more quickly this time. *"Hey."* He sounds more resigned, deflated.

"So I met with Cyrus's boss today," he continues. Good. Sticking with the no-names thing. *"How did it go? I'll tell you how. I think he knows. He knows I'm working for the feds."*

The audio goes quiet, the sound wave flatlining. It could be that Leo's listening, but after a while, Chris begins to wonder if Leo has ended the phone call.

"He didn't have to say it. He just stared at me and asked questions. Guys like this, they just smile at you and then, one day, wham! A bullet to the brain. I'm a dead man walking. And you know what the most ridiculous part is? I'm going to do the job for the FBI anyway, because if I have to choose between a bullet and life in prison, I'd take the bullet any day."

"Flowers Anywhere. This is Caleb. How can we make your day beautiful?"

After running through the routine, Chris sits on his bed and waits.

"Chris. How did it go?"

"As good as it could. He's spooked, right? But he feels locked in. Out of options."

"Keep it that way, Chris. Make sure he's more afraid of you than Nico."

44

Leo

"So what's the latest?" Trace asks me while I'm driving to work. I don't have the burner synced up to earbuds, so I put it on speakerphone.

"The latest since last night? Nothing. It's all fine."

It's quite a distance from *fine*. I couldn't see *fine* with a telescope. But it's what he needs to hear.

"I'm still thinking I should be there. I could come back."

I turn onto Madison. "Then you're *not* thinking. Your presence here can only hurt me."

"Of course you're gonna say that."

He's right to expect that I'd protect him. It's ingrained by now. The kid finally has a normal, healthy life—sobriety, stability, a small business he runs. He's never had the chance to be normal.

Not that life with Marilyn in Galesburg, Illinois, was as terrible as it may seem. It was relatively stable. She played her role well. She cooked meals, helped us with homework, put Band-Aids on our boo-boos. She sat in our room if we were scared at night, listened attentively to our tales of school and play, worried about us if we were home late. She bought us new clothes. She enrolled us in extracurriculars, made sure we practiced our instruments, attended our recitals and sports outings. She held us when we cried and celebrated our successes. She basically organized her entire life around us.

What do you call someone who does all those things? You call her "Mom."

Years passed, and Trace and I, like all other kids, became enmeshed in our little worlds of discovery and insecurity, of ups and downs, joy and pain. Questions of how or why we all got to this place seemed to fade into the ether. It just became normal. Trace and I were brothers. Marilyn was our mother.

I mean, it wasn't paradise. I had to walk around as a lefty, for one. Try throwing a baseball with your nondominant hand. My teachers at school couldn't understand why my grades were stellar but my penmanship so atrocious as to border on illegible. One of them even suggested that I might be right-handed; that parent-teacher conference did not go well.

And the hair. The stupid hair. Twice a month, she'd put my hair in curlers and dye it under the sink. As I got older, she started worrying about my eyebrows, too. (Thank God I didn't have pubic hair yet.) I fussed and moaned and, the older I got, the more I questioned why taking the ruse to this level was necessary. Trace didn't have to color and curl his hair; why did I?

And then, one summer afternoon in Mikey Panczyk's bathroom, staring at one of those heavy-duty razors belonging to his father, a retired Marine, I realized that the best lie was the one I didn't have to tell.

Imagine Marilyn's horror when I came home with my hair shaved down to a nub. What could she do? She couldn't put a wig on me. I had her over a barrel. So she dealt with it like any mother disappointed with her son. And that's how I left my hair, from age eleven through high school, with a buzz cut. Problem solved, if you count having to look like a boot-camp recruit for most of your adolescence a "solution."

Trace, he was another story. He struggled. I didn't question why at the time, whether it was genetic or the product of our circumstances. He didn't do well in school. He was quick-tempered and thin-skinned, erratic and unpredictable.

Looking back, it was obvious he had what we would now call mental health issues. He needed therapy. But that was where Marilyn drew the line. In every other aspect, the role she played was indistinguishable from other kids' mothers. Marilyn didn't mind doctors treating our illnesses and injuries. But looking inside our minds? Confidential conversations full of probing questions dating back to one's earliest memories? Marilyn wouldn't allow that.

And Trace suffered for it. The fights began as early as sixth grade, the most notable of which involved a boy a year younger than Trace, Tommy Guiliardo. To this day, I don't know what would have happened to Tommy if I hadn't peeled Trace off him; Tommy's shirt looked like it had been through a paper shredder, his face like it had hit a brick wall.

The drugs started in junior high. Trace was suspended twice, nearly arrested each of those times for possession, spared only by the grace of being on school grounds when he was caught with the weed (and probably because Marilyn was a cop herself, though I never knew that for sure). His first three years of high school, when I was there with him, I basically followed him around and made sure he didn't do anything that would get him expelled.

And then Marilyn died when I was a freshman at U of I and Trace, a senior in high school. I skipped the second semester of my freshman year and all but forced Trace at gunpoint to finish out the year and get a high school diploma. But that was the most even I could do.

I returned to U of I the next year, a semester behind, and brought Trace with me to campus. I'd hoped that the new surroundings, and perhaps the absence of Marilyn, would lead Trace to better choices.

I was wrong.

"Everything will turn out fine," I say now into the speakerphone. "I have it under control."

That's a bit of a stretch, too. A hyena trying to ride the back of a wild boar has more control than I do over my current situation. There are third-world democracies that are more stable. There are so many permutations of what could happen to me that I can't even count.

Actually, I have counted. So far, 19 possible scenarios—most of them involving me going to prison, some in the morgue, and some with Trace and me both going down. At least it's a prime number.

"*What are the odds that you're prosecuted for murder when this is over?*" he asks me.

Assuming I live that long? "I won't be prosecuted, T. Don't worry. This will all work out. But hey, let's talk about the current plan. You remember what I told Roberti about you?"

He sighs. *"You haven't talked to me in a decade. The last you knew, I was addicted to drugs. For all you know, I'm face down in a ditch somewhere."*

"Right," I say. "So if he finds you and contacts you, what do you say?"

"That I've been speaking to you regularly, and I have important information about your involvement in Cyrus's murder?"

Funny, that one. Always with the jokes.

"I haven't talked to you in a decade," he says. *"You're a piece-of-shit, ungrateful brother who abandoned me, and I hope I never talk to you again."*

"Good."

"You're a useless, pathologically lying, number-obsessed loner whose idea of fun is counting the fibers on his area rug."

"That'll do."

"A pathetic, selfish—"

"We're good."

"—awkward loser with intimacy problems."

"Glad we talked," I say.

He goes quiet. The fun is over.

"Everything's gonna be fine," I tell him. "I promise."

Still, I'm hoping Special Agent Chris Roberti never bothers to inquire about Trace.

Or if he does, that he doesn't look too closely.

FOURTEEN YEARS AGO

APRIL 2010

45

Andi

In her dream, the phone is ringing, though it doesn't make sense. It's not until she hears Leo's voice answering the phone that she snaps free of slumber, catching the tail end of his words.

"Where?" he asks, sitting up in bed, clutching his phone, his hair hanging in his eyes. "Okay. Don't—don't say anything. I'll be right there."

By now, Andi's eyes have managed to find the bedside clock. It's three in the morning.

"Trace was arrested," Leo says. "Champaign police."

"God, for what?"

Leo gets out of bed, throws on a shirt, finger-combs his hair off his face. "Couldn't understand him. He's wasted. But take a wild guess."

Drugs, would be Andi's not-so-wild guess. Trace has adamantly denied it, but Leo is sure that Trace is using again. Frankly, it's a miracle Trace hasn't been arrested before tonight.

"I'll come with," she says, sitting up in bed.

"No room. He'll ride on the back of the scooter. Go back to sleep."

She wakes up when they return, talking in hushed but harsh tones in the main room. She can tell, just from their whispers and clumsy footfalls, that Trace is still not sober.

Andi gets out of bed but decides against going into the main room.

She's a guest. Well, okay, more than a guest; she and Leo have been to-gether for nearly two years, inseparable at this point, divided only by the fifty miles between the campuses of U of I and ISU. Still, if Trace is mak-ing a spectacle of himself, Leo will be protective. This is better handled among brothers.

When Leo finally returns to the bedroom, he looks as exhausted as he probably feels. He falls on the bed next to her.

"He's in big fucking trouble," he says.

"You mean the charges or just gen—"

"I mean every way." Leo turns to her, his eyes shimmering.

In all their time together, he has shared with her his deepest and darkest secrets, the details of his and Trace's upbringing—but never once has she seen Leo cry.

"I gotta get him into rehab," he says. "Right now. The criminal charges—I don't know, we'll have to figure something out. If he doesn't get cleaned up, nothing else will matter. He'll end up—I'm gonna lose him."

"Okay, then." She touches his face. "We'll find him a place today."

His face screws up with emotion, tears falling. "I have Marilyn's life insurance money."

Leo had planned to use that for Trace's college tuition, if Trace ever actually tried to attend college. But she knows Leo would spend every penny of it on rehab, if that's what it takes. Leo is still just a boy in most senses, though technically an adult. Long hair hanging down like a grunge rocker, a who-gives-a-shit attitude about pretty much anything that does not involve his little brother. But that little brother, he's a dif-ferent story for Leo.

"He's my responsibility," Leo whispers.

"He's twenty years old now. All you can do is your—"

"He's still a kid. He never had a chance at being one. Not a normal one."

Andi doesn't argue the point. She's sure as hell no expert on "normal."

The next day, they drive northwest to the rehab facility in Leo's crappy sedan. Trace offers her the front seat but she declines, letting the brothers sit up front together to talk. The sky is gloomy, promising rain. The radio is dialed into pop hits, which feels inappropriate for the mood.

"I'm gonna make this right," says Trace. "The court stuff."

"I know." Leo glances over at him. "Don't worry about that now. That'll work itself out."

Leo's eyes make contact with Andi's in the rearview mirror.

"I could go to prison, y'know," says Trace.

"That won't happen. We'll get you a lawyer. I talked to one this morning. He said for a first offense, you might be able to avoid it."

"You talked to a lawyer? Did you tell him everything?"

"Just kind of a general summary, but yeah. We'll worry about that later, T. For now—"

"But there's no doubt I could go to prison," Trace says. "I mean, it could happen."

"It could. It won't." Leo catches Andi's eyes in the mirror again. She shakes her head. *Don't make him promises like that*, she thinks but does not say.

"I really don't think I need rehab." Trace stands in the reception area of the rehab facility near Peoria. "I just messed up. Royally messed up, but still."

"It'll be good for you, brother." Leo puts his hand on Trace's shoulder. "Besides, I'm kinda sick of your ugly mug."

"Yeah, right." With his crew-cut hair and collared shirt, Trace looks more like he's ready for the first day of a private prep school than entering an addiction recovery center.

Andi gives him a hug. "See you soon, kiddo."

"I'm sorry. Sorry about all this," he whispers into her ear.

Leo claps his hands together. "All right, Romeo, she's my girlfriend."

Trace smiles. He doesn't want to be doing this, but he listens to Leo. He trusts Leo.

"So there's a court hearing next week," says Trace. "Remember—"

"The attorney I talked to," Leo says. "He said it's easy to get the date moved. They call it a continuance. If you're in rehab, they'll wait to hold the hearing until you're out."

"Okay." Trace nods.

"Hey." Leo grabs Trace's arm. "Don't worry about that now. The only thing that matters is getting back on your feet. That other stuff will work itself out. I promise."

An orderly dressed in all white escorts Trace down a hall. Trace doesn't look back.

"He'll turn it around," she tells Leo. "I know he will."

Leo nods absently. "He's scared to death. He won't show it. But he's terrified."

They walk out together. Andi loops her arm in his as they walk. "You talked to a lawyer this morning? When did you have time to call a lawyer this morning?"

"I didn't," he says. "But I will soon."

THE PRESENT DAY

FEBRUARY 2024

Two Weeks before Valentine's Day

46

Leo

I get to work and gather my stuff for a nine-thirty at Dirksen, a suppression hearing before a judge who'd rather swallow his tongue than follow the dictates of the Fourth Amendment. But I have to make a record, if nothing else, for appeal.

I'm not five steps out of my office building, the temperatures brittle and the sky gray, when I see Nico's guy, the giant oaf who first came to visit me at the office—"Francis Garza," he called himself, surely not his name. He's standing in the middle of the sidewalk, hands stuffed in the pockets of a parka.

I try to move past him, but he shuffles left and blocks me.

"I have court," I say.

"You have court? Where is the client?"

"The MCC," I say. This guy's English might not be so good, but I'm sure he's familiar with the Metropolitan Correctional Center, the federal prison in downtown Chicago.

"He wants to speak with you now."

"Who?"

He lowers his chin. "Get in the car." He nods to his right, a sedan idling along the curb.

"Maybe you didn't hear me, Brutus. I have court."

"Now." He grips my arm, though the expression on his face doesn't change. "It will be fast."

I don't move, but I don't fight, either. It's not in my best interests to struggle with this guy, not that I'd win, anyway. My guess is, he has orders not to make a scene; if I made a real fuss, he'd probably let me go. But all things considered, I'm going to have to do this sooner or later. Nico and I didn't resolve anything the first time we met. About all we settled is that I said I wasn't working for the government undercover, and he was deciding whether to believe me.

Maybe he's going to tell me his decision now.

Maybe I'm going on a one-way trip.

I get into the back of the sedan. The goon, "Francis Garza," climbs in next to me. Another man is driving, someone I've never seen before.

"Where's Nico?" I ask.

"We take you to him."

We do a quick tour of the Loop, culminating in another parking garage, this time off Randolph, west of the river. Again, the car veers down, winding around two floors of ramps, putting us well underground before we park in a space.

If they want to kill me, this isn't a bad spot to do it.

But it's also an ideal place for Nico to secretly meet. One, he doesn't have to drive a car into the lot that's traceable to him. Someone else drives a different car, and Nico just walks into the lot. And two, this parking garage, like the last one we met in, is attached to a building, so you can enter through the building and reach the parking lot by elevator. Play your cards right, and someone following you might not know you even were in the parking garage at all.

"So where's Nico?" I say.

Francis doesn't answer at first. Eventually, he turns to me. "You should not lie, Mr. Leo."

That's not a good start. "Lie about what?"

"About anything. Did your mother not teach you this?" He chuckles and says something in Estonian to the driver, who laughs. Then the driver says something more urgently, and both he and Francis Garza pop out of the car and stand next to it. What's—

The front passenger door opens, and Nico Katsaros gets in and closes the door. "Morning, Leo." He adjusts the rearview mirror so that he can see my eyes and I can see his, dark as coal.

I wish I had one of those lines like *If my people don't hear from me in an hour, that letter gets sent to every news outlet in the city.* But alas, I have no leverage on this guy.

"I'm due in court" is the most I can say.

"My time is short as well. I have two questions for you. That is all."

"Shoot." (Probably not the best choice of words.)

"Did you kill Cyrus?"

His eyes remain on mine.

"Of course I did," I say.

He double-blinks, then nods. He didn't expect me to admit it.

"Are you, or are you not, cooperating with the FBI?"

I sigh.

"I'm not." I meet his stare through the mirror.

He shifts in his seat and turns to me, so we are now face-to-face. "Let me explain something to you. You think I'll kill you if you're working for the FBI."

"That's true, I do."

"But I will not. That would be sloppy and risky. I am neither sloppy nor a risk-taker. I will *use* that information to my advantage. You'd still be able to tell the government you're cooperating. You'd still get your deal from them, which I assume is to avoid prosecution for Cyrus's murder. For all the government will know, you've cooperated. But in reality, you'll have helped me."

He'll use me as a decoy, he means. I'll lead the government to a whole bunch of nothing, while he slips under their nose and gets his package to the MSS operatives some other way.

"I only kill people who lie to me," he says. "So answer my question again."

I figured he must be pretty sharp. He's better than I thought.

"I'm not cooperating with the government," I say.

His eyes go cold. Whatever bullshit he may be spewing right now, I do believe that he doesn't like it when people lie to him.

He will kill me when this is over, if given the chance.

"I am satisfied." He gives a curt nod, then returns to his seated position, staring forward. "This will happen sometime in the next week. It may be tomorrow. It may be two days from now or six. You will be contacted. You will be given notice, but it might be very little notice, perhaps no more than half a day. You will do what is requested."

"Deliver a package," I say.

He pauses. "This overcoat you're wearing. Olive, is it?"

I look down at my coat. A bit tattered at this point, ripped at one sleeve, one of the buttons dangling by a thread. A gift from Andi, what, nine, ten years ago? Back when things were very, very different. It doesn't take Freud to figure out why I haven't replaced it.

"Be sure you're wearing that coat. And make sure you're wearing this on your lapel." He hands me one of those breast-cancer-awareness pins, a large pink ribbon that intersects at the bottom.

I take the pin and stuff it in my pocket. So I'll be a white guy with a long olive coat and a breast-cancer pin on my lapel.

"Do you have a blue Cubs hat?"

"Um . . . yeah, I think I do. I'll get one if not."

"Be wearing that as well."

Olive coat, pink lapel pin, blue Cubs hat.

"I'm delivering a package," I repeat.

"Good luck."

He leaves the car without another word.

47

Andi

The prosecutor, an assistant U.S. attorney whose name Andi has already forgotten, flips a page in the notes before her on the lectern. "Sergeant, why were you called to the scene?"

"Normally, I wouldn't be." Andi leans forward into the microphone from her seat on the witness stand. "But the motorist refused to roll down his window. It's department policy to call in a supervisor in stalemate encounters with citizens."

"I see. And had the search of the vehicle taken place yet, to your knowledge?"

"No."

Andi glances at the clock on her phone. This is the last thing she needs, being called in to testify on a gun case from two years ago, back when she was on the force, finally making its way into court. Worse yet, the feds scooped the case, hoping to tack higher penalties onto the defendant, believed to be one of the top members of the K-Street Crew. The AUSAs always overprepare. So Andi had to spend the entire morning prepping her testimony.

Her time on the witness stand, cross-examination included, consumes an hour. She can't get out of there soon enough.

When she reaches the bottom floor of the Dirksen building, bathing in midafternoon sunlight, she stops in her tracks.

He is standing not far away from her, talking to an older woman, his hand on her shoulder. It looks like he's delivering bad news, consoling her. A court appearance that didn't go so well.

Leo.

He sees Andi and does a double take. Then his expression eases.

She feels her guard rising to full mast, her heart rate at maximum throttle.

Just like her heart pounded six years ago, when Leo broke the news. "You . . . you impersonated . . . an FBI agent?" She looked up at him, unable to continue, unable to think of any way that could be possible.

"It worked." Leo shrugged. Standing there in his business suit, tie pulled down, looking so young and handsome.

"But . . ."

"But what? Darius needed a push. That's all I did. I pushed him in that direction. He confessed of his own free will. The state's dropping the charges on Eric."

"But . . . how could you . . . You could—you could go to *prison* for this."

"I won't go to prison. For getting a guilty man to confess and freeing an innocent man?"

"Yes." She walked up to him, put her hands on his shoulders. "Absolutely, yes. Have you *completely* lost your mind?"

He cupped her face with his hands. "Possibly. But there was no other way. Eric was gonna spend the rest of his life in prison for something he didn't do."

She peeled his hands off and backed up.

"What?" he said.

"*What*? You could—you'll lose your job over this. You could lose your law license. You could get prosecuted for this. You just go and play hero because . . . because—"

"Because somebody had to do something. I couldn't let that kid rot in prison for a crime he didn't commit."

"We're not in college anymore, Leo. We're adults. We can't just do whatever we want whenever we want. There are rules."

"Fuck the rules."

"Fuck the rules?" She threw up her hands.

"Fuck the rules when they land an innocent kid in prison for the rest of his life. Yeah. Yes. Fuck the rules."

She couldn't catch her breath. She couldn't believe what was happening.

"While you were formulating this . . . plan," she said slowly. "This plan to break the law and violate about a dozen ethical rules. Did I ever enter into the equation?"

"This isn't about you, Andi."

"No? Is it about *us*, at least?" she said. "Because last I checked, we're engaged." She held up her ring. "We're a team. We depend on each other."

"Andi—"

"So before you went off and did something so categorically stupid and reckless, did it ever occur to you that losing the job you've worked so hard for, risking prison—maybe that was something I deserved to have a vote on?"

That, in the end, for Andi, was the deal-breaker. He didn't even discuss it with her first. He was willing to throw away everything he'd worked so hard to become just to right a wrong, to remedy an injustice. Noble? Yes, very. One of the many reasons she loved him—but the reason, ultimately, that she knew they were not going to make it. No matter how much she appreciated his outsized sense of fairness and justice, she couldn't be with someone willing to exalt it over everything else in their lives. There was no room for "us" in Leo Saves the World.

"It won't happen again," he said.

As much as her heart was twisted up, as off-kilter as her world had suddenly become, that last comment almost made her laugh.

48

Andi

"Hi, handsome," she says to Leo now. She immediately regrets using a throwaway line like that. Too forced, too flippant. Trying too hard to keep a distance.

Trying, no matter how drawn to him she still is, no differently than when she first met him at the bar in Champaign—those warm eyes that smile before his lips, the unmanageable cowlick where he parts his hair, the lopsided curve of his mouth that always makes it seem like he's the only one in on the secret.

He's wearing the olive coat Andi bought him many years ago, after he passed the bar exam and became a lawyer. It's frayed at one of the sleeves, and one of the buttons is about to fall off. He's probably due for a new one.

But he's kept it, she notes. It's probably ten years old now, bordering on ratty, but he's kept it.

"What are you doing here?" he asks. "Testifying on an old case?"

"Yeah. A gun charge the feds scooped." She smiles, realizing that she hadn't done so upon seeing him. He hasn't smiled, either. This is not easy for either of them.

"How's Trace?" she asks. "Still in Mexico? Still . . . doing okay?"

"Still in Mexico, still sober. Seems fine. Seems happy."

"Tell him hi for me."

Leo angles his head.

"Or don't," she says. "If it will unleash a tirade of insults."

Trace, of course, never forgave her for ending things with Leo. She can't blame a protective brother.

"I miss you," he says.

That hits her like a forearm shiver. She blinks and looks away. Oh, that's *so* Leo, to just blurt something loaded like that out of the blue.

The years have flown since they broke up, but the days have been long. She hasn't met anyone else like Leo. She never will. She wishes she could say why.

They fit. That's the best she can say. Their jagged edges fit together. Leo could reach inside her and find that place she didn't want anyone else to see and say, *It's okay, I like your scars, I love your scars, your scars are you, and you are beautiful.* He could make her laugh so hard she couldn't breathe. He touched her and she lit up. He put his arms around her, and nothing could hurt her.

"Was it worth it?" she asks.

God, what is she doing? Why is she plunging the shovel in so deep, when this is a quick hi-good-to-see-you moment?

Because it isn't that for her, clearly.

"He's a restaurant manager," he says. Eric, he means. Eric Putnam, the man—the kid, really—he saved. "He's going to night school for a degree. His daughter's in third grade. They just had a boy."

That's Leo's answer. It was worth it because Eric Putnam got out of prison and now has a life. Pretty hard to be against that, right? The hero puts everything on the line, risks his livelihood, and ultimately gets disbarred, all to spring an innocent man from prison. The kid goes free, and the hero is awash in noble suffering as the credits roll. A Hollywood ending.

Unless you're the girlfriend of the hero, who has to watch her fiancé lose his career.

She knew Leo would do something like this again. She couldn't live permanently on the tightwire, always wondering when Leo would perform his next stunt and how hard he would fall.

Leo moves closer to her. Her heartbeat kicks up. "I would ask you about work, but I know you won't—"

"Right, I can't," she says.

He looks into her eyes, and everything comes crashing back, all the good parts, the intimacy, the laughter and tenderness, the sex, like nothing she's ever experienced with another man—

"For what it's worth," he tells her, "you made the right decision. It's just a matter of time before I crash and burn again."

She feels the emotion rush to her face. She starts to respond but her throat closes. They are so close now, close enough that she could lean forward, just this one time, no matter how right she was to break things off, no matter what the future holds, and just this one time lean forward and kiss him—

"I should get running," he says. "It was good seeing you."

49

Andi

Fourteen years ago, Andi and Leo, still just college kids, stood in the parking lot of Trace's rehab facility, having just dropped him off following his arrest. "It's only an hour from here," she said. "I'd like to see it. But only if you would."

Leo pushed back the long hair hanging in his face. He looked like the college junior he was, but he was far from young. Indifferent, sometimes, fuck-it-all as a defense mechanism, but he carried some pretty heavy baggage. Even his long hair. He joked that he was making up for lost time after those many years when he shaved it down to a nub so Marilyn couldn't curl it and dye it red. But Andi thought it was Leo's way of shedding the past, if not giving it the middle finger.

"You don't go back ever?" she asked as they got inside Leo's sedan.

"To Galesburg?" He put the car into gear and started driving. "I went back for Marilyn's funeral. I came around enough to get the house sold. Then there was no reason to go back."

His would-be mother, Marilyn, died when Leo was a freshman in college and Trace a high school senior. So yeah, once he took care of the funeral and sold the house, and with Trace living with him in Champaign, he probably saw no reason to return to Galesburg.

"When did you find out the truth?" she asked him as they drove. She knew the basics of the story, of course, but not every detail.

"June 4, 2003," he answered.

"Wow, that's specific."

"It was the anniversary. June 4 is the date her kids died inside that garage with the car running." Leo glanced over at Andi. "June 4, 1994. Nine years later, she finally told me everything. I mean, by that point, I was, what, fifteen? I wasn't falling for this bullshit that scary men were after Trace and me. She'd try to put off my questions, but it was becoming ridiculous. So yeah, she gave it up to me. Mostly. She said we were 'at-risk kids' and she took us in. She said she couldn't go through normal adoption procedures. She said, technically, it was illegal. 'Technically illegal.' The fucking understatement of the century."

"And . . ." She didn't know how to finish the question.

"Did I race to the authorities and turn her in?" He let out a bitter laugh. "She probably wouldn't have stopped me if I tried. But no, I didn't do shit. I can only imagine how that sounds to someone else."

She leaned over and nestled against him while he drove. "It sounds like a young boy who stayed with the only person he knew as a parent. And took care of his little brother at the same time."

"I guess."

"At least she finally told you."

"Yeah, nine years too late. After Trace had nightmares basically every night, thinking some boogeyman was coming to kill him. Thanks, Marilyn."

She kissed him, then wiped the lipstick off his cheek. "I'm sorry, babe."

"It's fine. I'm fine. Wish I could say the same for Trace."

She wished she could say that for Leo. But *was* he okay? By all accounts, he seemed to be. He aced his classes at school while holding down a job and doing his best to look out for his little brother. That was more than a lot of college kids could say.

"How'd she get away with it?" she asked.

"Oh, I mean, think about it. Her husband, Fred, had recently died. There's no playbook for how people deal with shit like that. So one day, she ups and says, 'We're leaving. We need a change of scenery.' Something like that. Suddenly, without notice, without goodbyes, she moves out of the home in East Alton. She doesn't give anyone time to figure out that her children were both dead from CO poisoning. And nobody seriously questions the actions of a recent widow, right? So she holed up in a hotel for a while until she got both Trace and me. Then she shows up in Galesburg with two kids named Leo and Trace. Nobody knows that we aren't her biological kids. Nobody would think to question it. She just needs the kids to go along with the ruse. And we did."

Andi stroked his hair. She thought *her* childhood was messy.

"Here we are," he said as they exited off I-74 onto the ramp for Galesburg.

"We don't have to do this," she said to him. "Maybe this is a bad idea."

"It's okay." He looked over at her. "I . . . I like that you want to see this."

To someone who grew up in a narrow house on the south side of Chicago, Galesburg looked like a slice of Americana, peaceful and idyllic, a small town with mostly generous plots and tree-lined streets, a cute downtown.

Leo pulled the sedan over in the middle of a block on Broad Street. "There it is," he said, gesturing out her window. "The scene of the crime."

It was a split-level house of stucco and stone painted a light gray, set back off a large front lawn, a winding stone walkway and manicured landscaping. The kind of house you'd expect to be inhabited by a close-knit, upstanding nuclear family with 2.5 kids. "It's beautiful."

When Leo didn't respond, she turned to him. He wasn't looking out the window. He had his head back and eyes closed.

For a long moment, she said nothing. Then she took his hand in hers. His eyes opened. He tried to be casual—"Yeah, it was a nice house"—but Andi could see that this had been a bad idea. She leaned in and kissed him.

He smiled at her and drove away. Soon they were in a remote area, navigating through tiny roads surrounded by woods. Leo stopped the car. "You mind if I just . . . have a minute?"

"Sure, of course. Whatever you need."

Leo got out of the car and walked down a narrow path between the trees.

She waited in the car for what seemed like half an hour. Finally, she ventured down the path and saw Leo sitting by a small creek. She sat down next to him.

This beautiful boy, so strong and loving, looking so broken and lost in that moment. He chuckled without humor. "You know the fucked-up part of all this? It really could've been so much worse for Trace and me. I mean, a lot of kids who get sold on the black market, they don't end up with a woman who wants to raise them. They get tossed into some perverted pedophile sex ring or something. They live a life of hell. I mean, half the time I can't decide if I should've thanked Marilyn or wrung her neck."

They held each other there by the creek, listening to the slow ripple of the water, the sounds of birds, a light breeze flittering past them. "I never thought I'd need another person," he whispered. "I always thought I could get through life with just my brother. Trace and I against the world. But now, I . . . I don't know what I'd do without you, Andi."

She leaned her forehead against his. "You'll never have to find out," she said.

50

Andi

Today. *Today* has to be the day she runs into Leo? She's down to brass tacks now, final preparations, on the verge of pulling off a heist she's planned for a year, and she has to deal with her past rushing back like this?

But that's the deal, she reminds herself. That's the gig. Time to pretend. She can do it. She's been doing it so long now, she can turn it on and off like a spigot.

So that's what she does, returning to the QCI campus after seeing Leo at the courthouse. Hollowed out and reeling on the inside from that encounter, but wearing a mask of confidence, put-together, a suppressed smile on her face like she has life wrapped around her finger. She gives a thumbs-up to security and strides across the marble floor to the elevator bank.

First stop, the SCIF on eight, FutureTech. She swipes her card and presses her thumb in the scanner. The door pops open.

The guard at the door is Brett, now assigned to FutureTech. That was Jack's idea, but she assumes it was at Brett's request, as these two jocular souls seem to hit it off so well.

"Here comes trouble," he says to her, grinning while chewing his gum. The man is so desperate for female attention, Andi wonders if he's ever gotten any in his muscle-bound life. Giving him a bit of validation can't hurt. She'll use him, all right, but not in the way he hopes.

"So you're up here now. Good." She wags a finger at him. "The day of the party for Nano, I'm going to need a personal assistant. What do you say, hotshot?"

"I'm your man." Unfortunately, he grins even wider, his gum peeking through his teeth.

"Yeah?" She holds her stare on him a little longer. Just an extra beat or two. That's all it takes.

"Whatever I can do to make you happy," he says, "just say the word."

She tries not to gag.

But now you're on the hook, Brett. You're going to help me steal the Nano specs.

She takes the long corridor into the room where all the geniuses work. Dr. Seth Hargrave is at his carrel, typing an email. "Hi, Seth."

"Huh? Oh, Andi!" He scoots his chair around to face her, pushing his glasses up to the bridge of his nose.

"I'm here to scold you." She gives him a stern look but with a smile. "Every draft of the Nano specs is assigned to you and has to be logged in and out. And every time you print out a new version, it gets—"

"Assigned a new number, and I'm responsible for it." He removes his glasses.

"It's a pain, Seth, I get it. But we have to maintain the integrity of these documents. And if someone as senior as you isn't following the rules, nobody will."

"Sorry, Andi. And I found the copy I misplaced."

Andi does a quick glance around Seth's cubicle, the L-shaped desk. On the left, there are two folders. One has the words "Nano Previous Gens" on it. The other, "Nano Gen 3."

She's pretty sure she knows what that means, but she asks, anyway. "Seth, 'Nano Previous Gens'? You keep a folder for that?"

"Huh? Oh, yeah. We're on Gen 3 now. The prototype is Gen 3. Those are the Generation 1 and 2 specs. We didn't perfect the ionic coating until Gen 3."

"You keep those old specs lying around?"

"Yeah. I keep them here in the SCIF for now. Some day, when we're patented, when the product is out on the market, I'll probably make a scrapbook or something. You know, the story of how Nano was created."

"But from a security perspective," she says, "should I be worried about these versions? All of our focus is on the prototype, Gen 3."

"As it should be." He shakes his head. "Gens 1 and 2 are functionally obsolete. Well, okay—not obsolete. But anyone getting their hands on the Gen 1 specs would be five years behind us. Even Gen 2—a couple years behind us, at least. And by then, the product will probably be on the market. We'd certainly have our patent."

Andi chews on that. More inspiration, juices flowing.

"From a security perspective," says Seth, "Gens 1 and 2 are a non-issue."

Right. Exactly. That's it.

This has certainly been a productive visit to the SCIF.

"Hey, we have the rehearsal tomorrow, right?" Seth says. Andi has created a little skit for the celebration party when Nano goes to prototype.

"Yeah, that's right. I've put together scripts. Unless tomorrow's inconvenient."

"No, it's convenient," he says. "In fact, we better not waste any time."

"No? Why?"

"Well . . . You didn't hear this from me." He leans toward her and lowers his voice. "I think we're announcing tomorrow."

"Announcing . . . It's going to prototype?" she whispers back. "Already?"

He nods. "We're just double-checking everything now. But you didn't hear that."

It's ready. The specs are ready.

She can see the excitement on his face. Project Nano is the culmination of a decade of research, toiling, trial and error, dead ends, and discoveries. For most of these scientists and engineers and doctors, it has been their life's work, a drug that will dramatically improve the treatment of cancer. To say nothing of the financial perks. The bonuses the principal scientists on this project will make when the project receives FDA approval will dwarf their annual salaries.

But there's no point in sentimentality. She's going to steal those specs, and she's going to do it soon.

And she just figured out how.

51

Leo

It could be any time, Nico told me. It could be today, it could be tomorrow. I should be focusing on that. I should be preparing for that. Instead, all I can think about is seeing Andi today.

I leave work early, unable to concentrate. When I get home, I reach for the violin. Tchaikovsky's only violin concerto, the first movement in D major. Breezy, romantic, but technically demanding in parts, with scales and other ornaments, a cadenza ending in a trill (before the orchestra's cue to reenter) that I usually botch. This time is no exception.

But Andi didn't care. It was the piece she always requested. She'd close her eyes and let the music sweep her away, her hands air-conducting, a content smile on her face. I loved seeing her let go like that. Andi had a very, very hard time letting go.

When the piece is finished, I'm spent, drained. But pining for her isn't going to help any, and besides, I still have work to do.

I walk down the street to Bar Lucy, an old-school place more my speed, dark wood and low lighting and mood music, photos of famous Chicagoans on the wall. It's doing a decent business on a Thursday night. I need that. I need a crowd.

"Double bourbon," I say, slapping down my credit card. "And keep the tab open."

52

Chris

Chris is on his couch, listening through earbuds to audio inside Leo's condo, when his front door opens. His sister, Mary, walks in with groceries.

"Didn't know you were stopping by," he says.

"Yeah, well, sometimes I feel like a loser sitting home alone on a Thursday night."

"And you think joining a fellow loser will make you feel better?"

"Good point," she says.

"Hey, let me ask you something. Do I have bad breath?"

She laughs. "What? No. Why? Did someone tell you that?" She pulls meat wrapped in paper out of her grocery bag. "Ribeyes."

"Now you're talking." He closes the laptop.

"Hey, you care if I take a shower?" she asks.

"What—a suspect vomit on you again?"

"Close. Don't ask. You mind?" She heads into his bathroom. She's never asked permission before. Why start now?

Chris prepares the steaks with some spice and sears them on the pan while he preheats the oven. He pops in his earbuds and uses his "Leo" phone to listen in on whatever might be happening in Leo's condo today. He's surprised to hear audio in Leo's place at four in the afternoon; Leo got home early. The sound is violin again, nothing Chris recognizes but, he must admit, quite beautiful.

But the music stops not long thereafter. He hears the sound of a door closing and nothing afterward. Leo left his condo at close to five.

He throws the ribeyes into the oven and sets a timer. Now it's time for the asparagus, dropping it into a pan with olive oil and—

Mary comes bounding into the kitchen, fresh out of the shower, still in her towel, her wet hair clinging to her cheeks. In one hand, she holds her phone. In the other, she holds his hard case containing the needles and the bottle.

"What . . . is this?" she asks.

"You're going through my cabinets—"

"I was looking for the skin cream I leave here," she says. "Don't avoid the question."

"It's . . . it's a supplement."

Her eyebrows rise, but her expression is less of anger and more of horror. "In a glass vial? That you inject?"

"Listen—"

"It's a steroid, Chris. An anabolic steroid." She holds up her phone. "I looked it up. What in God's name are you thinking?"

"I'm . . ." He puts his hands on the counter. "Look—"

"You're just recovering from a life-threatening disease, your immune system is just building up again, and you're taking—"

"Yes!" he snaps. "Yes, I'm taking steroids. Yes. I'm tired of looking like a shriveled little shell of what I used to be. I'm trying to get back to where I was. And maybe even something better, if that's okay with you."

She raises her hands. "I don't understand what's gotten into you with all these shortcuts. Illegal wiretaps and illegal steroids. That's not gonna get you where you used to be. That's gonna take you to a place you don't want to be." She takes a breath. "Look, you just need time—"

"Well, maybe I don't *have* time," he says. "Ever think about that?"

"Oh, Chris. Come on now." She takes a step closer to him. "The recurrence rates—"

"Are just a bunch of percentages. I got it once. It could come back tomorrow. It could come back in a year. The fuck do we know from recurrence rates? I *probably* won't die in the next five years? Wow, *that* inspires confidence."

An icy wave runs through him. He lives with this all the time. Mostly, it just hovers over him. Sometimes it sticks him right in the gut. But saying it out loud . . .

"I'm not walking the rest of this race," he says. "I'm sprinting."

The tension hasn't subsided while they eat dinner, though Mary grudgingly admits that he nailed the ribeyes, so tender you could cut them with a fork.

"So we agree that you'll *strongly consider* stopping with the steroids after this cycle is over," she says.

"Yes, sis, I will."

"Because you agree that it's probably not the greatest idea in the world to be taking a drug used for horses."

A phone buzzes in his pocket. He pulls them out, all four of them. It's the black phone, the caller ID **Flowers Anywhere**.

"DOJ," he says as he pops out of his chair and heads into his bedroom. "Hello?"

"This is Caleb from Flowers Anywhere. I'm calling to confirm an order."

"Uh, yes, yeah. The name's Grimsley. Last four digits of my card are 4-1-2-1."

"Thank you. Would you have a moment to speak to your salesman, Roy?"

"Yes, I would. I do." He takes a deep breath to calm himself.

The voice of "Roy" comes on right away. "Chris. Do you have an update for me?"

"Nothing, no."

"Have you spoken with Balanoff today?"

"No, I haven't," he says, filling with dread. Why the question?

"He met with Nico again. You didn't know?"

"I—no, I didn't."

Shit. He feels like a pupil being scolded, like when the nuns rapped him on the knuckles in middle school.

"One of Nico's men stopped him on the street and put him in a car. We lost the car, but our people tracking Nico picked it back up. They met in an underground parking garage."

That sounds like Nico. "I'm sorry, I didn't know that."

"I don't want apologies. I want to know that you have Balanoff under control."

"I do."

"You have him under control, but he's meeting with Nico and not telling you?"

"I'm sure he was gonna tell me. We were gonna talk later tonight."

Not true, but it is now.

Chris pinches the bridge of his nose, feeling stupid, inadequate. Why the hell didn't Leo contact him?

"Chris, if this is too much for you, now's the time to say so."

"No, no, it's not. I'll make this right. I'll get back to you."

The line goes dead.

"Fuck. Fuck, fuck, *fuck*." He puts away his black phone and pulls out his "Leo" phone. It rings six times and no answer. He calls him again. Same result.

He throws on a pair of jeans and grabs his coat. He dials Leo one more time.

This time, someone answers. "Hello?" A woman's voice. Crowd noise in the background.

Chris stops dead. "Hi, who is this?" he asks.

"Are you a friend of Leo's?" she asks.

"I am, yes."

"Well, you might want to come pick him up. He's in no shape to walk out of here on his own."

"That isn't true!" Leo's voice in the background. "That, madam, is a bald-faced lie!"

He's drunk. Off his rocker. "Where is he?"

"Bar Lucy. Uptown."

"I'll be there in twenty minutes."

53

Chris

When Chris arrives, a fresh breath mint in his mouth, Leo is at least up-right, if barely conscious. He's singing a song from *Annie*, though it's still many hours before the sun will come up tomorrow.

"There . . . he is! The man of the hour! Chris . . . topher Roberti!"

"He's all yours," says the bartender, pretty with light red hair and a seen-it-all smirk.

"Barkeep, a lager of your finest ale for my friend. And fresh horses for the men!" Leo drills a finger in the air. He almost falls off the barstool.

"Always a pleasure," she says.

"Madam, did I not pro—provide you with a gratuitous generous—a generous gratitude?"

"That's gratuity, tough guy." Chris hikes him up off the stool. "Let's go."

"Gratitude for the . . . gratuitous." Leo makes an attempt at a bow. "Madam, I bid you adieu. Tomorrow, I'll bid you another dieu. Ow, take it easy."

"C'mon, Leo."

"He's with the FBI," Leo whispers loudly to the bartender, his hand cupped over his mouth. "I'm undercover so don't tell anyone."

"How much did he drink?" Chris asks the bartender.

"Nine bourbons. Doubles."

"Did he settle up with you?"

"Sure did," she says. "And he gave me a very gratuitous generous."

They get outside, frigid air, hopefully enough to snap Leo awake.

"Jesus, Leo, what the fuck?"

"I'm out," Leo slurs. "I'm fuckin' . . . out, dog."

"You're out what? What does that mean?"

Leo spins, but Chris keeps hold of him.

"You know I never throw up when I'm drunk? Never." He wags a finger. "I mean if I have the flu or something but not from . . . not from . . ."

"That's great to hear, Leo. What do you mean you're—"

"Not from booze!"

They reach Chris's car. He pours Leo into the front seat and buckles his seat belt for him. He gets into the driver's side, starts it up, and blasts the heat.

"What do you mean, you're out?"

"I'm out, C! C.R.! C. Roberti!" Leo puts his head against the headrest and sinks into the seat.

It's a short drive to Leo's condo. Leo is mumbling and babbling, but a linear conversation does not seem to be in the immediate future. Chris helps him up the steps and gets the outside door open with Leo's key. Then they take the stairs up to his condo oh-so-slowly.

"Brings back memories, eh, Chrissy?" Leo laughs. "Chrissy, Chrissy, Chrissy."

"You're in rare form."

"This is where you . . . fucked my life up forev—ever."

He glances over at Leo. Fucked up his life forever? Sometimes he has to put himself in the shoes of the people he flips. The stress, the danger, the guilt and shame.

He pats Leo's back. "Your life isn't fucked up forever, guy. Just hang in there."

They make it to his door. Chris slides in the key.

"You, sir, are an agent of the law and you're for—for—you're prohib— you cannot make an entryless warrant into my home, sir."

"A warrantless entry?"

"That, too."

"Hey, Leo. Leo."

Leo's not really able to focus.

"You gonna be okay if I get you inside?"

"How could I be ... any ... worse?" Leo pushes through the door. Chris starts in, but Leo slams the door, leaving Chris alone in the hallway. He stares at Leo's door a long time.

What does Leo mean, he's out?

Well, he's sure not going to find out tonight. At least not straight from Leo.

But maybe Leo will talk to his friend with the *Jaws* ringtone.

54

Leo

"You gonna be okay if I get you inside?" Chris asks me.

"How could I be . . . any . . . worse?" I slur. I stumble through my front door. Chris tries to follow me in, but I shut the door on him. Rude, sure, but hey, I'm drunk, right?

Right?

Well . . .

. . . not so much. But really, it's not that hard to pretend being drunk. I've certainly been inebriated and seen plenty of other people the same way. And the circumstances helped a lot, too—the bartender telling Roberti to pick me up to get me home safely; the smell of booze on me; the fact that I'm under a lot of stress. Slurring and stumbling around is the easy part.

Compared to impersonating an FBI agent, feigning drunkenness is a walk in the park.

The bartender was right; I did order nine double bourbons over the course of four hours. But she never actually saw me drink them. I dumped three or four, bought a round for some guys I was talking sports with, and nursed one for good luck.

I stomp around my condo, as if I'm (all together now!) drunk and slur out a couple of cuss words for good measure.

And I take extra care to be noisy when I'm standing under the smoke detector between the kitchen and the living room.

The smoke detector, that is, where Roberti placed the eavesdropping device.

Like *that* was hard to predict. I mean, the guy hardly waited for me to leave for work—or pretend to leave—before he was sneaking back into my condo to install the bug.

"Fuck," I mumble, dropping onto the couch. "I am so fucked."

Delivered slurred and sloppy, of course. The eavesdropping bug is almost directly above my position on the couch. I assume that's why he installed it there, a nice, centralized location, and the couch in the living room being the most likely place I'd talk on the phone.

Ready? Time to "make a call."

"Fuck . . . where's your . . . here we go," I say.

To anyone listening, that's me looking up a number in my phone. Even though my phone is still tucked in my pants pocket.

But then, Roberti can't see what I'm doing, can he? He only gets audio on that device.

"C'mon, c'mon," I say. "Fuck, fuck—fuckin' answer your phone, asshole!"

That's me being impatient and loud because the person I'm calling isn't answering.

Then I pause—that's me waiting for the voicemail.

"Hey," I say into the empty apartment. "Fuckin' . . . call me back. Call me back!"

I let out a loud sigh, having left my "message."

"Fuuuck!"

That should be self-explanatory.

How long do I wait? Truth is, I'm tired. I wouldn't mind an early night. So let's get on with it.

By which I mean, it's time for the "friend" I just "called" to "call me back."

I fish my phone out of my pocket and scroll through the ringtones I've downloaded until I find the one I'm looking for.

The *Jaws* ringtone.

I push it, and suddenly the apartment is filled with the theme song from a movie that gave me nightmares as a child.

Duhhh-NA...Duhhh-NA... Then the increase in tempo. *Duh-Na-Duh-Na-Duh-Na-Duh—*

Right. It sounds to anyone listening like an incoming phone call. I wasn't entirely sure Roberti would fall for it—or that he'd hear it well enough via his eavesdropping device—until he showed up the morning after my first "call" with a mouthful of breath mints. I just about busted out laughing.

I pause the sound of the ringtone and say, "Hey, fuckin' finally."

Y'know, as if I just answered the phone. (And remember to slur a little—you're drunk!)

I shut off my phone and stick it in my pocket, so there's no chance the ringtone will start up again—that would kinda blow the ruse, right?

And I continue: "Man, I gotta—yeah, no, sorry, I know—"

I pause for the "other person" to "talk."

"I know, man," I say. "But I'm really in a lot of fuckin' trouble. Yeah, even worse."

55

Chris

When Chris returns home, Mary has left. Chris goes immediately to the audio inside Leo's condo. Best bet, he passed out, and there will be nothing to hear. But if he's really upset, he probably reached out to the friend he assigned the *Jaws* ringtone.

What the hell did Leo mean when he said he was "out"? Chris fast-forwards through the audio, looking for a bounce in the sound waves to indicate dialogue.

He startles as he sees a spike on the audio waves. He backs it up and starts listening.

"Fuck. I am so fucked."

Leo almost sounds like he's sobbing. The booze doesn't help. Certainly not the first time he's worked a CI who couldn't handle the pressure.

"Fuck... where's your... here we go." Pause. *"C'mon, c'mon. Fuck, fuck—fuckin' answer your phone, asshole!"*

Leo's reaching out, presumably to the same confidant as before. But getting no answer.

"Hey. Fuckin'... call me back. Call me back!" Pause. *"Fuuuck!"*

It goes quiet for a while. Wouldn't surprise Chris if Leo just passed out, right there on the couch.

But then Chris hears it—the ringtone, the *Jaws* music.

Duhhh-NA... Duhhh-NA...

"*Hey, fuckin' finally,*" Leo says, answering the call. "*Man, I gotta—yeah, no, sorry, I know—*" Pause. "*I know, man. But I'm really in a lot of fuckin' trouble. Yeah, even worse.*"

Now he's getting to it. Maybe he'll explain what he means by being "out." Did something happen?

"*I . . . saw him again today. The, y'know, gangster guy.*"

Yeah, and thanks for sharing that info with your handler. Chris was clear with Leo—any contact with Nico is followed by a call to Chris. So why didn't he do that?

"*He said it could happen any day now. But I think he . . . wants me to do something else. Besides delivering the package.*"

A pause. Nico wants Leo to do something else besides delivering the specs?

"*I'm telling ya, it's gonna be bad. It's gonna be . . . Oh, fuck, how did I get myself—*"

A pause. Leo's falling apart. But what is he talking about?

"*I gotta go, man. I'm gonna puke.*"

No further conversation. He hears Leo move into the bathroom and gag and cough. Then the flush of a toilet.

Then the sound of a grown man sobbing.

This can't end soon enough. Leo is coming unglued.

56

Leo

The sun actually does come up tomorrow. Friday morning, bright and early. Well, early, anyway; this is February in Chicago, so the sun plays a lot of hide-and-seek, if we see it at all.

I'm careful leaving my condo. Roberti's going to be worried about me after last night. He might want to catch me before breakfast. I doubt he'll expect me to be up and moving *this* early, though, before seven in the morning, after my "bender" last night.

He can't know what I'm about to do.

I gingerly slide open the glass door to my fire escape and sneak out. I head into the alley and tuck through the gangway between two condo buildings on the opposite side. I make it down the street to a Starbucks not that far from Marine Drive and dial up an Uber. The driver picks me up a few minutes later and drives me to my destination.

An old client named Ronnie Watts, one of the lucky ones, whom we managed to walk after twice hanging a jury on a gun charge, wipes grease off his hands as he strolls out of the auto body shop off Kedvale. "Leo Balanoff," he says, laughing, giving me a fist bump to keep the grease off me. "Leo B. You're looking good, man. Keepin' in shape and all."

"You, too, Ronnie. Sorry I don't have much time to catch up."

"No problem. I only have a ten-minute break, anyway. Let's grab a pop."

He means a can from the vending machine on the side of the shop.

But that's not what he really means. We pass the vending machine and move to the rear of the building, where Ronnie quickly removes three spare tires stacked against the wall and produces a black shopping bag, holding it with two hands and placing it in mine.

"Untraceable, right?" I ask.

"One hundred percent."

I plop four hundred dollars in the palm of his hand.

"Nah, my old lawyer gets a discount."

"No, no, I'll pay the freight. I insist."

"Okay, man, so listen up." Ronnie does a quick look around and bows his head. "You know how to use a Glock 17? How to pop the slide back and load the mag?"

"I know enough."

"Got a box of rounds for you. Magtechs. Enough for two magazines."

"That's more than enough," I say.

"And last but not least, the suppressor. You civilians call it a 'silencer.'"

I spot it in the bag. Black as the gun, long and sleek.

"It's a RAD 9," he says. "A personal favorite. But Leo, man, a suppressor? I mean, people usually want a gun for protection. For defense. But a suppressor? Man, that ain't for no defense. That shit's for offense. I mean, none of my business, but."

I shrug. He's right. It's none of his business.

And yes, that gun will be used for offense.

57

Chris

Leo climbs into Chris's car behind the convenience store. He looks like hell—hair mussed, wincing, a droop to his shoulders. "Okay, I'm here."

"How ya feelin'?" Chris tries to sound upbeat, though he's feeling anything but.

"Like I didn't get the license plate of the truck that ran me over." Leo puts his head against the headrest, closes his eyes. "I may have been slightly overserved last night."

"Yeah, I noticed."

Leo looks at him. "What do you mean, you noticed?"

"You don't remember?" Chris shakes his head. "How do you think you got home?"

Leo moans. "I called you?"

"No, *I* called *you*, smart guy. And the bartender told me to come get you. Do you wanna know why I called you last night?"

"I'm . . . filled with suspense."

Chris hits Leo's arm. "Because you met with Nico yesterday and didn't tell me. What the hell is *that* all about? You think I'm just playing?"

"Oh. That."

"Yeah, that. I couldn't have been clearer with you. If Nico reaches out, you tell me."

"Sounds like your surveillance team saw me, anyway. So? What's the problem?"

"The problem is *you're* supposed to tell *me*! I shouldn't be hearing it from the rest of the national-security team, asshole!"

"Oh. Okay. Now I get it." He rubs his temples.

"Get what?"

"You were embarrassed." Leo looks at him, self-satisfied. "You're worried your buddies will think you can't handle it. This is a big break for you, yeah? And you're afraid you're gonna blow it, and everyone's gonna say, 'Poor Chris, nice guy, but he fumbled the ball when he had his big chance.' Something like that?"

"No." Chris grabs his arm. "I'm just doing my job."

"Not very well, sounds like." Leo purses his lips. Challenging him. Baiting him. "And let go of my arm." He wrenches his arm free.

"I'll grab your arm if I *want* to grab your arm." Chris shoves Leo, harder than he intended.

"Fuck you." Leo's hand whips up, an openhanded smack to the side of Chris's head.

Chris comes out of his seat, grabbing Leo with both hands and forcing him against the door of the car. "Are you out of your mind? You're assaulting a federal agent? I could arrest you right now, you piece of shit!"

"Then do it! Arrest me!" Leo's face is hot, nostrils flaring. He puts out his hands, as if waiting to be cuffed. "Take me in. For murder and for bitch-slapping you. I'm done. You hear me? I can't do what he—I—I can't do this."

Chris freezes on those words. *I can't do what he*—that was the start of Leo's sentence, before he corrected himself. *He.* Meaning Nico.

"What happened at that meeting with Nico yesterday?" he asks.

Chris releases his grip on Leo and returns to his seat. Things got out of hand; he needs to restore order and trust. He has to be the leader. The voice of calm.

"Tell me what he said, Leo."

Leo straightens his coat and looks out the passenger window. "Just that the job was a 'go.' And it would be happening soon. Like, within a week, any day now."

"No, he said more than that. I can read it all over you. Something's changed."

"Nothing's changed. I'm still scared out of my mind. I'm still out of options."

"But now you're saying you're 'out.' The same thing you said to me last night when I picked you up at that bar. Why? What's bothering you so much?"

Leo closes his eyes. "I'm out, Chris. I can't do what you're asking."

"Sure you can, kid. Look, deliver the package, and I'll scoop you right into WITSEC. Or put you in protective custody. Whatever you want. Don't you want to put this asshole away? I'm telling you, whatever you had against Cyrus Balik, that guy didn't do anything without Nico's say-so first. Let's get this asshole, and then let's get you somewhere safe. There's an out here for you. It's not a bad one."

Leo takes a moment with that. Finally, he breathes out and looks over at Chris.

"But I need you to tell me what Nico said to you. What does he want you to do?"

"You have a salesman named Roy?"

"Yes, we do. Please hold."

Black phone in the other hand, Chris twists the rearview mirror to get a look at his face. Just a little mark. It wasn't a punch. Just a hard smack.

"Chris."

"Yeah, I just talked to Balanoff. Nico told him that everything was a 'go.' Sometime in the next week, he told him."

"And did Leo explain why he didn't immediately inform you of the meeting?"

No, he did not. Nor would he say what Nico said to him that upset him so much. He wouldn't tell his *Jaws*-ringtone friend on the phone last night, either.

Leo's keeping it close to the vest, whatever it is.

"He's . . . spooked, is all. He thinks Nico knows he's working under-cover. It's understandable. Nico's a sophisticated operator. But I walked him back. I told him I'd protect him, come hell or high water. Witness Security if need be."

A long pause. Chris would love to know what he's thinking.

"Tell me right now, Chris. The odds, one to a hundred, that Leo goes through with this."

"A hundred."

"Because if he doesn't, if he gets cold feet—"

"He won't. I've got this."

The pause that follows is longer than the first one.

"I'm telling you," Chris says. "I've got this under control."

"Chris, the reason we need to be certain that Balanoff is on board is that *we* think this is about to happen, too."

"Why do you say that?"

"Because I can't think of any other reason why the security officer from QCI, the Piotrowski woman, would be meeting with Nico as we speak."

58

Andi

At lunchtime, Andi drives to her gym. Nothing unusual about that. She's built up a consistent enough routine, working out every day at noon, that it should draw no attention whatsoever by now. She heads past the free-weight area to the rear exit of the building.

A car is waiting there, not the black town car from last time but a rust-colored SUV. Nico switches up cars frequently for obvious reasons. She gets into the back seat.

Nico turns to her with that practiced look of calm, cool, and collected. But he has to know what she's going to tell him. They've been careful to limit their contact. She wouldn't be reaching out if there weren't a good reason.

She doesn't waste any time. "I got word from the scientists yesterday that the prototype would be completed today. And this morning, they announced it. It's ready to submit to the FDA for trials."

"I see. Thank you." Nico, dressed in a suit with a perfectly knotted purple tie, raises his chin. "And your timetable?"

"Monday, I hike it."

"Good. Tell me what you'll be wearing on the train, so we can convey it to the courier."

"Long navy-blue coat," she says. "A mask on my face. Your basic COVID mask, something nice and big. Then a powder-blue wool hat. And tinted glasses."

"Ah, yes." Nico nods with approval. "Almost a complete cover-up. Hardly an inch of your face showing. Your beautiful eyes, even your lovely hair, for that matter."

Andi shoots him a look. "Yeah, that's why I came here today, so you could flirt with me."

"No need to be unpleasant, Andi. Now, you will be on the train platform at six-thirty Monday night. The El stop at Clark and Lake. The north side, as if you were taking the train west- or northbound."

"Got it."

"You will take the first Green Line train that arrives after six-thirty. You will enter the third train car from the rear."

"The contact will be inside the train car already?"

"Yes. The handoff will take place inside the train car. You will remove the envelope from your gym bag and hand it to him. Then you'll get off at the next stop of the Green Line, which is Clinton."

"Great. And?" Andi's eyebrows rise as she waits for the obvious. "Who'm I delivering to?"

"Of course." Nico hands her a piece of paper with handwriting:

white male, mid-30s
olive overcoat
pink breast-cancer pin on lapel
blue Cubs hat

"I wanted a name," she says. "This is just a description."

"You're better off not knowing the name," says Nico.

"That wasn't the deal, Nico. You promised a name. So I could vet him."

Nico nods his head. "You said yourself, this is happening Monday. It's too late to vet. And besides, don't you trust me?"

She hands him back the paper. "You promised me a name. Then you broke that promise. And now you ask me to trust you?"

"Andi, you know how I operate. It's best when the people doing their parts don't speak to each other and don't even know of each other."

Andi sits back in her seat. "We had an agreement."

"Please trust me, Andi. I would not use a man I could not trust. I can assure you that this man is the perfect person to be performing the task. He is in my debt, and he understands what it means to be in my debt. Yet he has no verifiable connection to me. And with his background, I can assure you that, even if something were to go amiss, his word would mean nothing to the authorities. I could not script a better candidate if I tried. Much better than our initial courier, Cyrus, in every possible way."

She thinks about it. "And what does he know?"

"Only that he'll be receiving an envelope on the train, and he is to deliver it to another person nearby. And then his debt to me is absolved. He does not know what's inside the envelope or who is delivering it to him. And with the outfit you plan to wear, he wouldn't be able to identify you, anyway."

She blows out air, giving up. "Fine." She reaches for the door. "We're on for Monday."

59

Andi

Andi returns to QCI's campus at one o'clock and heads straight to the eighth floor, the SCIF for FutureTech. "Okay, places, everyone, places. We don't have much time before Allan comes back."

The twenty doctors, engineers, and technicians they've selected for the skit are gathered with Andi. She hands out the scripts.

"You typed all this up, Andi?" one of them asks.

"Well—you guys were so fast getting Nano done, we didn't have much time to rehearse. And it'll be just as funny, even if you have to resort to your notes a little. I'm taking the scripts back when we're done rehearsing, though. So Allan never sees them."

"Are you going to encrypt them and lock them in a safe? Print them on watermarked paper?"

"Ha, ha, very funny, you guys. Okay, so do we have our fire truck?"

The fire truck costume is cut from boxes and painted, with room for four people to fit inside, complete with firefighter helmets.

"Rita, you're the tumor, right?"

"I am." She bows, as if it's an honor. She's wearing a big black blob of a costume that probably looks less like a tumor and more like a poop emoji.

Everyone's in a good mood, a general air of celebration permeating the entire eighth floor, people laughing and joking, high-fiving in their geekish way.

"Okay, and the serum proteins?"

The proteins are dressed in black with balloons of different colors and sizes pinned to their clothes; they look like characters out of the old Fruit of the Loom underwear ads.

"And now the nanoparticles," she says. The actors are going to look like beach balls with heads—the best they could come up with on short notice.

"Okay, you all look great," she says. "Start from the top. Seth, the first cue is to you."

"That was fun, Andi," says Seth as they walk back to his cubicle.

"It will be fun. It will help that everyone watching will be in a festive mood."

They reach the cubicle. Andi takes another glance at those folders on the long side of the L-shaped desk: "Nano Previous Gens" and "Nano Gen 3."

Then her eyes casually move up to the camera peering down on them from the ceiling.

Yes, this is going to work.

"Hey, Andi, all those scripts you're lugging around," Seth says. "They look heavy."

They are. She has twenty copies in her arms. She collected them after the rehearsal, cracking a joke about "securing" them so Allan Valencia doesn't see them.

"Rather than hauling that load back and forth," says Seth, "do you just want to leave them up here with me?"

No. Absolutely not. The scripts are key.

"I'm fine," she says. "Good exercise for me."

60

Chris

Chris drives through evening traffic, a pit of dread in his stomach. It's just nerves, he tells himself. That's all it is.

He pulls his car off I-294 onto the ramp for the oasis. Winds his car around and parks in front of the fast-food restaurant, buzzing with commuters.

He walks in through the west-side door, through the restaurant and its scent of greasy French fries and burgers, and out through the east-side door.

He gets into a car, alone in the back seat. The car turns into a parking spot and stops.

"Sorry I'm late," he says. "This isn't easy. Anyway, I'm here."

In the driver's seat, Nico turns around and gives Chris a once-over.

"Nice to see you, Chris," he says.

61

Chris

"You sure you weren't tailed?" Chris glances around the parking lot.

"I followed the protocol, not to worry."

"You went to O'Hare? Bought a ticket? The whole thing?"

"The whole thing. This car can't be traced to me. I was not followed. Now please explain to me why it's necessary for us to meet in person so close to the end."

"It was necessary to meet because I said it was."

Nico doesn't appreciate the comment, but he's too composed to show emotion. "You're on edge," he says. "Something's wrong."

"So are we? Close to the end?"

"We are. It's happening Monday. I've already given instructions to my asset. Monday, six-thirty p.m., Andrea Piotrowski will be at the Green Line at Clark and Lake, third car from the end. Everything we discussed. And I've given her Leo's physical description."

"So . . . she's all set? No further instructions from you?"

"Correct, Chris. Because unlike some people, I understand the importance of minimizing sensitive, face-to-face meetings."

Sure, nice rebuke. But the key takeaway—Nico's already given his asset final instructions. This is happening.

"Nico, what have you been saying to Leo? He's freaked."

"As he should be. He views both of us as threats. In different ways, of course."

"He thinks you've made him as an undercover."

"It would be natural that he'd fear as much. I've pressed him on that point, as he'd expect. Frankly, it would be more suspicious if I *weren't* skeptical of him."

"He thinks you're going to give him a different job, besides delivering the briefcase."

Nico's brow wrinkles. "A different job . . . such as?"

"I have no idea. But something's put a spook in him."

"Ahh, Chris, the big moment draws near. It's natural he would be nervous."

Not the most satisfying answer. But he's probably right. "There's nothing you can think of," Chris confirms. "Nothing at all."

Nico looks Chris over for a long beat. "He's your asset, Chris, not mine. My end of the operation is ready to go. If yours is not, I suggest you get your house in order soon."

Chris's eyes narrow. "Let's not forget who recruited who here, pal."

Nico allows for that. "Nevertheless. It's important to remember our roles."

"Our roles?" Chris feels heat rise to his face. "Oh, I know my role. My role *was* pretty simple—to be our eyes and ears in the Bureau, make sure nobody's watching us, which I've done. And *your* role, my friend, was to get those specs out of that medical company and into the hands of the MSS. But then your boy Cyrus got whacked, and you couldn't get Leo to take his place, could you? No, you couldn't. If memory serves, Leo told you to go fuck yourself."

"Chris—"

"So *I* had to step in and clean up your mess. *I* had to get Leo to do it, by threatening to prosecute him if he didn't cooperate in the undercover operation I had to invent. Which, by the way," Chris adds with a wave of his hand, "required me to play my FBI card with Deemer Park P.D. and get them to back off their investigation when they were about to arrest Leo. I had to involve my sister in this. My *sister*, who would shit a brick if she knew what I was up to."

"Chris—"

"Not to mention, I have to work my day job at the Bureau without them knowing what I'm doing with Leo, which is turning into more work than I expected." He sits back in his seat. "So yeah, I remember our roles just fine, thank you."

Nico's eyebrows rise. "Are you finished? The sooner we conclude, the better."

Chris feels a headache coming on. Maybe the nerves are starting to get to him, too. "When are you giving Leo his final instructions?"

Nico purses his lips. "My thought was tomorrow, Saturday morning. Give him the weekend to prepare, to make changes to his Monday schedule if need be. Give him time to confer with you, as well. I want him good and comfortable with the plan."

Makes sense. "What have you told him so far?"

"What to wear. His olive coat, a pink breast-cancer pin I gave him for his lapel, a blue Chicago Cubs hat. That will be more than enough, in a single train car, to distinguish him."

Easy enough. "You haven't told him where to be yet?"

"Not yet. I will tell him where to be and where to deliver the package tomorrow morning. And I'll give him the bag he should carry for the delivery."

All good. So far. Only one more important item. Very important, at least to Chris.

"Let's talk about what happens afterward. After the drop."

"What happens after the drop is what we've already discussed," says Nico.

"I'd like to discuss it again."

"Very well. I am responsible for my asset, Andi Piotrowski. And you are responsible for yours—Leo. It should be quick and clean."

"How quick? When do you plan on taking care of yours?"

Nico nods. "Almost immediately, of course. She'll be expecting payment. The longer I hold out, the more of a problem she becomes, the more suspicious she gets. So the sooner I take care of that problem, the better."

Chris figures the same with Leo. He can't leave Leo out there as a loose thread afterward. And if he needs to do something, it might as well happen right away.

Meaning Monday, right after the drop. Leo drops the package, Chris drops Leo.

Problem is, Chris has never killed anyone in his life. For Nico, it's another day at the office. And unlike Nico, Chris has nobody to do the wet work. He'd have to do it himself.

"I don't suppose you could help me out with that chore," he says. "Having all the resources you have and whatnot. I don't have anyone else on my end. It's not like I can ask one of my Bureau buddies to whack a guy."

Nico almost smiles. He's probably thought through this whole thing. "You want my people to take care of the Leo problem along with the Andi problem?"

"I think that might be preferable, yeah."

"That's certainly something I'd consider." It's clear by now that he'd *already* considered it. He was expecting it. "We'd just have to renegotiate our split."

"I was kinda thinking . . . Well, you remember I helped you out with that information about Bonnie Tressler a year ago."

"You helped *Cyrus* with that," Nico counters.

"Yeah, but helping Cyrus was helping you, right? If it weren't for my information, Leo and Bonnie could've taken Cyrus down, and he might have taken you with him."

Nico sighs. "Two million," he says.

Chris makes a face. "You're kidding."

"I don't kid about such things, Chris. These aren't junkies or street whores we're talking about. Andi Piotrowski is a decorated former cop and a top security officer with a respectable company. And Leo Balanoff, whatever his quirks, is a well-regarded defense lawyer in the city. When people like that disappear, it gets noticed."

Chris shudders through a chill. "Is that how it's gonna happen? They'll disappear?"

"You don't leave people like that lying on the street with a bullet to the brain. They disappear. People will look for them. Wonder about them.

You let time pass. And two such people disappearing on the same day? That is a far trickier proposition."

"All the more reason for the same person to handle both jobs," says Chris.

"All the more reason . . . for two million dollars."

"One million," Chris counters, because it seems like the thing to do.

"Two million, Chris. It's not negotiable."

Whatever. What's it to Chris, the difference between twenty-three and twenty-five million? Either amount is more than he's made his entire life, more than he'd ever dreamt of. If it gets him through this op without having to get his hands dirty, it's money well spent.

"Deal," says Chris.

62

Andi

Saturday morning. Her eyes stinging from the cold. She removes her headphones and stocking cap from her three-mile run and walks into Sal's Diner.

"Andrea!" Sal sings from behind the counter. "How we doin' this fine morning?"

"You know me, Sal. Every day's a gift." The cliché has a little more bite right now.

"Your pop's in the back. I should charge him rent."

"There she is." Brando pushes back his plate of eggs. He's wearing a faded baseball hat that looks as aged and beaten as his jowly face. "How's my favorite daughter?"

She takes a napkin and dabs at her forehead and face. She doesn't usually continue to sweat like this after a morning jog to the diner, once she's settled in. But she's feeling a little internal heat of her own, with just over forty-eight hours from the drop.

"Monday," she tells him. "Six-thirty p.m. The train car. The Green Line."

He lightly pounds the table with his fist. "Game on, then. You good?"

"I'm good." She's anything but good.

"And you'll be able to get the thing out of the building?"

"That's the plan."

"Y'know, kiddo, it might not have been the best idea to install so many safeguards like you did. Watermarked paper with sensors? Automatic security notifications the moment anyone touches that file on their computer? Ever hear of making it easier on yourself?"

She shrugs. "I . . . It's my job. I wanted to do it well. Laugh all you want," she adds as Brando does just that. "I like that company. My boss is a chauvinist pig and so is one of his lackeys, but most of those people—they bust their ass to make a product that will save people's lives someday. They're good people."

Brando sits back in the booth and whistles. "Conflict of interest, anyone?"

"Don't give me that. I know what I have to do. And I'll do it."

"Listen." Brando puts a hand down on the table. "I'm just messing with you. You're a good egg, Andrea. But now let's talk about the courier."

She knew that was coming. "A canary. A guy from outside the crew, like you thought. I got a physical description."

"But not a name?"

"Not a name."

"Andi, what the fuck? How are you supposed to vet this guy?"

"I can't. Nico said I gotta trust him."

"That's not acceptable."

"Okay, so go tell Nico that it's not acceptable."

Brando blows out air. "Fuck me." He nods. "How do we know this dipshit isn't gonna take the bag and run? Or stick a blade in your gut while you're standing in the train car with him?"

"We wouldn't know that even if we knew his name."

He allows for that. He runs a hand over his face. "I'm gonna tell you something you already know. The moment you hand the specs over, you have a target on your back."

"I know, I'm expendable."

"You're more than expendable." He comes forward, grips Andi's arm. "You're an instant liability. You could talk. And you'll be owed ten million dollars Nico doesn't wanna pay you. So when you get off that train, girlie, keep eyes in the back of your head. And pack your firearm."

63

Chris

Inside his car, the morning sun peeking through the buildings and hitting his face, Chris tries to contain his nerves, tries to rely on his training as an agent. He feels like one of those carnival performers, trying to keep a bunch of plates spinning all at once.

Just get through today and tomorrow, he tells himself. Saturday and Sunday. Leo will get final instructions from Nico's people this morning.

And then, hopefully, nothing—at least not until Monday, when everything happens.

He's parked around the corner from Leo's condo building, located in a spot where he can see enough of the building's front and rear that he could spot Leo leaving from either side. He can't think of anything that makes more sense than just sitting on Leo between now and the drop. Even if it means spending the better part of the next two days in this damn car.

Chris got here at six this morning, throwing in his earbuds and listening on his "Leo" phone to the audio inside Leo's condo.

At just after 7:00 a.m., Leo turned on the TV, some cable news. Chris heard the clank of a pan and the sound of running water and assumed that meant breakfast.

Another dreary day in February, gray and cold, the kind of weather that makes him question his choice of the Midwest for home. The cars parked along the street are dirty and grimy with salt, the roads bumpy and pockmarked from another abusive winter. Here and there a jogger or dog walker, their breath lingering before them in the freezing air; otherwise, the only signs of life are the delivery trucks clogging the streets.

Chicago will remain Chris's home short-term but not much longer. Once he pockets that money, he'll leave the FBI and live wherever he wants. He hasn't allowed his imagination to drift that far, not wanting to jinx anything.

He won't ditch the FBI immediately. Maybe in six months, maybe a year, Special Agent Christopher Roberti announces his departure after a lackluster career at the Bureau. Who knows, they'll say, maybe it was the cancer that changed him, that made him search for something more or different in life, to appreciate the scarcity of our time on this mortal coil.

As for Mary—that will take some work. It won't be hard to explain that the sting operation involving Leo went awry, and Leo got killed. And with the prime suspect in Cyrus's murder now dead, there will be nothing for DPPD to do but close that file as solved, suspect deceased.

But the money. He will be careful with his spending. Maybe over time, he'll come up with something—he took a gamble on a business venture that paid off big, something like that. Who knows? He'll figure something out. He has time. He won't do anything quickly, won't arouse suspicion.

Chris kills the audio on his phone and dials Leo. The phone rings three times before Leo picks up.

"Hey, Chris."

"Hope it's not too early to call on a Saturday." The time on the car clock is 7:40.

"No, I'm up."

"So listen, I have an update for you. We think it's gonna happen Monday."

"Monday—two days from now?"

"Yeah. Someone from Nico's crew will give you final instructions this morning."

"This morning? Should I do something? Go for a walk or something?"

Chris chuckles, playing the chill, experienced agent, the calming influence. "Sit tight and relax, Leo. If they want to talk to you, they'll probably call you."

Leo lets out an audible sigh. "Okay. Okay."

"You good, pal? Anything you need from me? Anything at all?"

"Um, I don't—I don't . . . think so."

"Leo, you're going to be totally protected. We'll be watching you every step of the way. You'll do a basic handoff somewhere, and you're done. You just sit tight afterward, and I'll come pick you up. And if you want witness protection, you got it. I'll drive you into protective custody my-self. By the time you hit your pillow Monday night, this will all be over. Nico will be under arrest. That scumbag will never see the light of day again."

"Yeah. Let's hope." The line goes dead.

That didn't sound good. But Leo's not the first CI to crumble as the big day nears.

Forty-five minutes later, after listening to the clanking of pots and pans, to the mind-numbing babble of one cable news commentator after another, Chris hears the sound of a phone ringing inside Leo's condo. Not the *Jaws* ringtone but an ordinary one.

"*Hello?*" Leo answers. "*Okay. Yeah. Okay. Okay.*"

Chris's own phone lights up with a call from Leo.

"You were right," says Leo. "They just called me. They want to meet."

64

Leo

I punch out the call with Chris Roberti. I throw on a hooded sweatshirt and leave through the front door, down the steps of the walk-up. I take a moment, as if to check for my wallet, just to make sure I'm moving slowly enough for Chris Roberti to see me from his spot around the block.

Yeah, he's not that sneaky. He probably figures, even if I catch him, he'll just say he's keeping watch over me, protecting me. But I know that's not the real reason.

He has trust issues. I can't imagine why.

I turn right, heading west down the sidewalk. My street spans a full city block before it hits a park and the street bends north. At the corner, right at the bend, is a new pastry shop, Torte de Lish, that I've tried a couple times. They have a kale-raisin scone that sounds gross but is terrific. The place is a lot more fun in the summer, when the tables come outside.

There are only five people in the place when I step inside to the smell of cinnamon and fresh pastries and strong coffee. One is Nico's guy, the big oaf with the bloodhound expression I've dealt with, "Francis Garza," sitting at a table with a cup of coffee and a gray gym bag. He pats the bag and nods to me without making eye contact.

I order a coffee. "Francis" is just getting up, leaving the bag behind.

I get the hint. I sit down at the table and unzip the bag. Inside there is a note, typewritten, which is smart:

```
Read these instructions. If you have questions,
call the number we have used to contact you.
    At 6:30 p.m. on Monday, you will go to the El
stop at State and Lake as if you were taking the
Green Line to Harlem Avenue. You will take the
first Green Line train that arrives after 6:30
p.m. You will wear your olive coat, your pink
lapel pin, and your blue Cubs hat. You will carry
this gray bag. You will get on the third car from
the left end of the train. You will take the
train to the next stop at Clark and Lake.
    At the Clark and Lake stop, a Black woman will
get on the same train car as you. She will be
wearing a long navy blue coat, a surgical COVID
mask on her face, a powder-blue wool hat, and
tinted glasses. She will stand next to you. She
will hand you an envelope discreetly. You will
take it and put it in your gray bag. She will get
off at the next stop, Clinton.
    You will stay on the Green Line train until
the Pulaski stop. You will take the stairs to
exit. On the landing halfway down the stairs,
you will see a white man wearing a red
Blackhawks cap. You will hand him the gray
bag and continue walking. Your work will be
completed.
```

Sounds easy enough, so I zip the bag back up and take my coffee with me. When I'm back inside my condo, I call Roberti. He answers on the second ring.

"I'm on my way," he says. "I'll be there in about ten minutes."

Jeez, he really doesn't want me to know he's parked right by my condo.

Back at my place, Roberti uses his phone to take a photo of the instructions I was given. "This seems simple enough," he says. "You know the State and Lake train platform, I assume."

I nod. "Hey, I have court appearances Monday. It's always a busy day."

"Okay." Roberti purses his lips. "When?"

"Three things, all at Twenty-Sixth Street. Should be done by two in the afternoon."

Roberti deflates. "That should be fine. Plenty of time. But I'm going with you," he adds. "I'm going everywhere you go Monday."

"Sure."

"So let's talk about the plan for Monday night," he says.

"Sure thing." I grab a pad of paper and pull out my XQ-1080 pen and click it, as if to take notes.

"Once you make the handoff," says Chris, "stay in your role. Leave the Pulaski station, walk out onto the street, open your phone, and make like you're dialing an Uber."

"Okay."

"I'll pull up with an Uber insignia on my car. Sell it, okay? Look at the license plate and match it up on your phone like you would a real Uber. Wave to the car. And ask my name when I show up."

"Got it." I roll my neck.

"Any questions?"

"What happens if some car skids up in front of me, and someone tells me to get in the car? Or doesn't even bother with that and shoots me right there on the street?"

"Leo, Leo, Leo." Roberti puts a hand on my shoulder. "You and your imagination. The only person who will be pulling up is *me*. Even if you're right about Nico—and you're not—"

"I am."

"—he wouldn't do something that dramatic and that quick. And anyway, there will be a dozen agents watching you. If you want to conceal yourself until I arrive, that's okay. I'll be there in a couple minutes."

I throw up my hands. "You're right, Chris. I mean, what could go wrong?"

"You'll be fine." He holds up his cell phone. "I'm a phone call away, any time you need me between now and Monday. Okay?"

"Right."

"Let's talk Monday morning. I'll call you. And like I said, I'm with you Monday, all day. I'll follow you to work and go to court appearances with you."

I wouldn't have it any other way, Chris.

When he leaves, I double-click the pen and download the conversation.

65

Chris

Sunday morning. Chris takes a sip of his Starbucks, unable to stop a little from spilling on his lap inside his SUV. Annoying, but the caffeine helps. It's gonna be another long day sitting on Leo's condo, probably all for naught. But now it's just one more day until showtime.

Leo awoke just before seven, or at least that's the first time Chris heard any sound inside the condo through his earbuds.

He hears now, live, some noises that he's come to recognize as Leo pulling out his violin. Then tuning it, a quick warm-up, a scale, sounds like. (Three years of piano as a child taught Chris that much.) Leo never talks about his music, but to Chris's untrained ear, Leo must have had a fair amount of instruction as a child.

He starts his piece, and instantly Chris recognizes something different. Nothing whimsical or vibrant.

The intro sounds like the opening to a horror movie, slow and eerie. Then it explodes into a fast-paced, urgent, almost angry frenzy, so fast as to be almost dizzying. Chris recognizes portions of it from a movie or something. He imagines Leo breaking into a sweat, exhausted, violently working his bow, finally reaching a furious crescendo—

"Shit. Shit!"

The music abruptly stopped. What—did Leo bust a string or something?

"Goddammit!" A crashing sound. Did he throw down his violin?

What the hell has gotten into Leo this morning?

Another banging sound. Leo collapsing to the floor?

Should Chris—should he do something? Should he call for a check—

Duhhh-NA. Duhhh-NA.

Chris jerks to a start. The *Jaws* ringtone.

Duh-Na-Duh-Na-Duh-Na-Duh-Na—

"Yeah." Leo, out of breath. *"No, I'm—just broke a string on—never mind. It doesn't matter."* A pause. *"Not exercising. Just playing some Vivaldi. Psyching myself up."*

Psyching himself up for what? The drop isn't till tomorrow evening. It's a little early for an adrenaline session.

"No, not yet. Soon, I think. They said it would be this morning."

Wait. *This* morning? Sunday morning. Who does he mean by *they*?

"No. Hell, no. I can't tell him. I'm screwed if he finds out. And he might. He's a smart dude." He grunts. *"Tell me about it. I keep wondering who I'm supposed to fear more—the gangster or my FBI handler."*

Panic flutters through Chris. Leo can't tell Chris what? *They*—meaning Nico and his crew? They're keeping something from him. They have something cooking. Something Nico doesn't want Chris to know about.

And whatever it is, it's going to happen soon.

"I'll call you when I'm done. Yeah. Yeah, okay, later."

Sounds like the phone call has ended. Leo lets out a loud sigh.

The minutes tick by. Coming up on nine o'clock in the morning, the sun starting to appear over the buildings. *Soon*, Leo said.

Chris checks himself for paranoia, but the burn in his chest doesn't lie. There must be something going on between Nico and Leo. Leo's about to go on the move, and Chris needs to follow him.

Will he go out the back way and grab his car in the alley? That's the best bet. But Chris has that covered—

He hears a phone ringing through the headphones, another call to Leo's phone. Not the *Jaws* ringtone but his standard cell phone ringtone.

"Hello? Okay. Yeah. Where? What kind of car will it be? Like, the make or the color." Pause. *"Okay. Okay. You want me—okay. Yeah, I understand. I got it."*

A pause. The end of the phone call.

Then hard footfalls, followed by a loud slam of the door. That must be Leo's front door. The back door is a sliding glass job. Probably the front door, then—

Not long thereafter, Leo pops down the stairs of the front porch and turns right, west. Away from Chris.

Chris puts the car in drive. If Leo's getting picked up by a car, Chris needs his, too.

He inches out onto the road and turns onto Leo's small, winding residential street. He keeps a distance, just enough to keep him in sight. It wouldn't be the end of the world if Leo turned around and spotted him, but Chris wants to stay concealed if possible.

He'd like to know where Leo's going.

Leo walks at a normal gait, wearing a hooded sweatshirt, which doesn't look warm enough for the weather, but it doesn't seem to bother him. Chris holds back, cruising slowly, eyes peeled for anything amiss.

Leo turns into the same pastry shop as yesterday, Torte de Lish, at the curve of the street. Shit. Chris is in his car, and there's no place to pull over.

Well, screw it. He pulls the car over as best he can, probably only barely leaving room for a vehicle to pass—but hey, it's the city. He wouldn't be the first to double-park.

He jogs around to the other side of the street and slowly moves down toward the pastry shop, not wanting to be seen, crouching behind parked cars. A few people are inside the shop, but he doesn't immediately spot Leo. He moves closer.

He's . . . not there.

Leo is absolutely not inside that shop.

But how could that—

He pops up. Only now does he spot it. The pastry shop has two doors, one on each side of the corner. Leo entered through the south door and must have exited through the west door.

Chris jogs to the corner and follows the bend. No sign of Leo.

He breaks into a sprint. Speed was never his thing, but panic propels him. But even as he runs, he realizes that Leo was told there'd be a car. And now Chris is far away from his own vehicle.

He passes an alley and looks down. Nothing. He runs to the next street and sees only one car, a sedan, heading east, way too far away for him to spot the plate.

He drops to a crouch. "Dammit."

He lost him.

66

Leo

Too bad Chris doesn't know my neighborhood like I do.

It's pretty simple, really. It's just a game of alleys, the real thorough-fares of city living.

First, I had to make sure Chris would follow me by car, not on foot. So on my "phone call," I mentioned that a car was picking me up; he'd need one of his own to follow.

The trick at Torte de Lish was simple enough, with the multiple doors. That gave me some time to turn right down the first alley, then cut north up another alley, and then turn right, east, through yet another alley.

By the time Chris got anywhere near that first alley, I was long out of his sight line.

Then it was just a matter of winding through the alleys in this little cocoon between Marine Drive and Sheridan until I was back at the rear of my building, sneaking up the rear fire escape and through my sliding glass door, which I left open.

Now I step into my condo as quietly as I can, like a pantomime. Chris is listening, or he will be soon, through his eavesdropping device, so I can't make any sound. I walk as slowly and gingerly as possible until I reach my bedroom, where I lie down.

I'll give it an hour. Maybe ninety minutes. I could use the rest.

After eighty-three minutes, I'm ready to do this. I walk carefully over to the sliding glass door and peek out. I wouldn't expect Chris to be standing right there in the alley, but just to be sure.

Then I loudly swing the door open and slide it shut, good and noisy for Chris to hear, as if I'm reentering just now from my trip. The door doesn't catch the first time, so I make a point of getting upset about it, shouting and cussing, then finally slamming it shut and punching the glass door. Then I pace back and forth.

To the ears of Chris Roberti, I sound very upset.

Time for another "phone call."

I continue pacing and curse and bitch when my "call" isn't answered.

"Do you, like, never answer your phone?" I kick the couch. "Call me back, man, ASAP, okay? Please."

Then more of the same. Pacing, moaning, bitching, cussing.

I let that go on for eleven minutes. Then I dig out my phone, go to "settings," and find the *Jaws* ringtone.

67

Chris

Now long returned to his vehicle, defeated, having no idea where Leo went, Chris leans forward as he hears, on the surveillance audio, Leo reentering his condo via the rear sliding glass door. The door apparently doesn't close so well on the first try.

"Close, you stupid—"

He slams it shut and pounds on the glass, cussing.

Another banging sound—Leo kicking the couch? *"Call me back, man, ASAP, okay? Please."*

Chris needs to make sense of this. Leo must have been meeting with Nico. But why?

"C'mon, call him back, Mr. Jaws Guy." Chris drums his fingers on the steering wheel. *"Call back."*

"I can't do this," Leo says to himself. *"I can't I can't I can't."*

Should he call Leo again? Just another check-in?

Chris feels a buzz in his pocket. The black phone. He pulls it out. A call from **Flowers Anywhere**. That's the last thing he needs right now.

He lets it ring and ring. It stops after seven times.

He puts his head back against the seat. What the hell could Nico be doing here? Nothing makes sense—

The *Jaws* ringtone plays through his headphones. Chris steels himself.

"Hey. Hey, man. I'm . . . I don't know what to do. I need your advice."

A pause.

"Yeah, it's—I can't even—it's like the worst thing I feared. I can't do it. He says I won't get caught. He says it won't be a problem. He says we'll be square if I do it."

Leo is speaking in a hushed but frantic tone, barely loud enough for Chris to hear.

"I can't even say it. What's the worst thing you can imagine? Yes. Exactly."

Leo is still pacing back and forth, the floor creaking and groaning.

"No, I mean, he gave me a gun and everything. Bullets, a silencer. This shit is real."

Chris starts forward. What? A gun? A silencer? Nico wants Leo to . . . *kill* somebody?

What the hell is going on?

"Yeah, I know. This is crazy, right?" Pause. *"You think? But what happens if I tell him? I mean, he's FBI, what's he gonna say? He's gonna say no. So then I don't do it, and the gangster freakin' kills me. Or at least he cuts me out of the operation, so then I don't get my deal with the FBI. I'm screwed however you slice it."*

Leo goes silent, listening to whoever is on the other end of the line.

"I don't know why. You think he's gonna tell me why? Well, actually, the one thing they said was that this person 'knows too much.'"

Someone knows too much? Who? What does that mean—

"I don't even know who the person is. No, I'm serious. They just gave me an address."

He needs to get in there and talk to Leo. He needs to figure out what's going on.

"Tonight," says Leo. *"He wants me to do it tonight."*

68

Leo

I figured Chris would rush straight to my condo after that phone call.
Two minutes, tops, would be all it would take for him to run from his
SUV parked around the corner to my front buzzer or, more likely still, up
my fire escape. But I was wrong.

He waited ten minutes. Ten minutes, before the sound of the buzzer
attached to the front security door zips through the condo.

I let it buzz. Then I let it buzz again. And again.

My phone rings. Chris is calling.

I'm tempted to wait longer, but he might actually break through the
door, and my neighbors in the building will be pissed. So I answer the
phone but don't speak.

"Leo? Leo?"

"Yeah," I whisper.

"You okay?"

"I, uh . . ."

"Let me up, Leo. I have information for you. I need to give it to you."

"I don't know. I . . ."

"Leo, let me up. I just need five minutes. It'll make you happy, I
promise."

I buzz him in. Then I open my front door and sit down at the kitchen
table. I hear his thunderous footfalls up the stairs. I rub my eyes hard
with my knuckles so they'll be red.

The door opens. Roberti comes in with his gun drawn.

But he drops it to his side after he sizes me up, closing the door behind him and locking it. "You have a firearm in here? They gave you one, didn't they?"

I look up at him. "How did you—" But I stop there. "I should've figured. You're following them?"

"Where is it, Leo?"

"The living room," I say. I point to the bag I got Friday morning from my former client behind the auto body shop.

Roberti walks over, goes through it. "Nine-millimeter Glock, suppressor, plenty of rounds, serial number scratched out." He pulls out the gun, removes the magazine, checks the chamber.

"How . . . did you know?" I ask.

Pro tip: Make the other guy think he knows more than you. It empowers him, makes him feel like he has the upper hand.

Roberti holsters his weapon. "Leo, this ain't exactly a one-man operation. You don't think we have intel all around this thing?"

"So you probably already know what they told me."

"Most of it," he says. "But tell me anyway. First of all, who talked to you today? Nico's people? Or was it Nico himself?"

"Don't know," I say. "Guys I've never seen before."

Another pro tip: Do not unnecessarily pin yourself down. If I say I met with Nico personally—well, maybe Chris knows that Nico is somewhere else right now, which would expose my lie. Same with any specific one of his goons. But if I say they were guys I've never met, how can he contradict that?

"I . . . I couldn't believe they were asking me—I mean, how am I supposed—"

"Leo, calm down, relax. Don't worry. You're not gonna kill anybody."

"But I'm supposed to do it tonight," I say. "Come tomorrow, Monday morning, if I haven't done the job—"

"He won't do anything to you." Roberti puts out his hand. "He needs you, Leo. He needs you to be the courier. He isn't gonna do a damn thing to you until you've delivered that package. And by that time, he'll be in federal custody. And *you'll* be in witness protection, if that's what you want."

I heave a relieved sigh. It's important that he thinks he's reassured me. People are inclined to believe things that paint them in a favorable light.

"Thanks, Chris. The weight of this thing ... I mean ..."

"Why didn't you tell me this? You see what happens when you keep things from me?"

No, but I've seen what happens when I fuck with your head.

Chris sits in one of the chairs. "Tell me what happened. Start from the start."

69

Chris

Chris draws it slowly out of Leo, who is totally spooked. "Nico said it to me the second time we met. When they grabbed me off the street and took me to the parking garage?"

"The time you didn't tell me about."

"Right. He said . . ." Leo shakes his head in disgust. "He said delivering the package wasn't enough to pay off my debt to him. That there would be one other task. That's what he called it, a 'task.' Like it was just a freakin' errand or something."

"Go on." Chris rolls his hand.

"He said the 'task' would be unpleasant. But he assured me I wouldn't be caught. I wouldn't be implicated. He had people in the police department who would make sure it didn't come back to me."

"You believed that."

Leo shrugs. "I'm telling you what he said. And it wasn't hard to read between the lines. He wanted me to kill someone."

Chris nods, tries to act natural, though he feels color rising to his face.

"He told me to be ready Sunday morning. He said he'd probably meet with me before Sunday, but that there would also be a Sunday meet. I don't get that. Why meet twice?"

Chris feels that burn again. Why would he tell Leo to meet again on Sunday? Because he told *Chris* the meet would be Saturday.

He didn't want Chris to know about this extra meeting.

"So, anyway—they called and told me to go to the pastry place on the corner. The same place as yesterday. They said to go in the same way, through the same door, but then cut through the shop and go out the door on the other side. Then jog up the street to the alley, and a blue car would be waiting for me. I'm not sure why all the cloak-and-dagger was necessary."

Same reason: they thought Chris might be following Leo.

"They didn't tell me who I'm supposed to kill. They just gave me an address and some instructions. They said I'd never be connected to it. Nico knew people in the police department who would protect me."

Chris thinks about that. "Did he say why he wanted you to kill this person?"

Leo picks up a piece of paper off the coffee table. "Something about someone 'knowing too much.' Could be anything. Nico's involved in all kinds of shit, right? Here's the address."

Leo hands him the paper, folded over once. Hard, like the back of a book of matches.

Chris opens it up and reads the address.

Chris is on his black phone as soon as he leaves Leo's. He calls Flowers Anywhere, where he goes through the required intro.

"You have a salesman named Roy?"

"One moment, please."

Chris tries to control his breathing.

"Yes, Chris?" he says when he comes on the line.

"We have a problem," says Chris. "A very big one."

70

Chris

The sun has fallen now. The streets are empty on a Sunday night. Chris slows the car as he approaches the bridge over the Cal-Sag Channel.

It wasn't easy, the first time Chris met with Nico. He'd spent the better part of five years trying to catch him, to bring down his operation, only to be thwarted time and again as cooperating informants wound up in a ditch or disappeared in the wind.

But then came the cancer. And everything changed.

Chris met Levi the first day of chemotherapy, took the cushioned seat right next to him. There were only two choices of chairs when he walked in, one next to a woman wearing headphones who was laughing at something on her phone, or the quiet Asian guy in the corner. Chris opted for the latter.

At first they didn't speak, but Mary, who accompanied Chris and was always the chattier of the two, in particular on a gloomy day like this one, started up a conversation with him.

"Levi, like the blue jeans," the man said. "That's what everyone calls me. My full name is Li-Wei. Li-Wei Kuo."

Chris didn't recognize the name. National security wasn't his area. He didn't know then that Li-Wei Kuo was believed by the U.S. government to be the most dangerous covert agent of China's Ministry of State Security living in the U.S.—here in Chicago, as it turned out.

"It's our first treatment," Mary told Levi.

"My third," said Levi. "My first alone. I told my wife I preferred to do this alone. It's not so bad. I just think of it as solving a problem."

"I like that. Solving a problem. Exactly." She patted Chris's hand. He had yet to speak. He was still in a state of disbelief over the diagnosis, like there must be some mistake.

It wasn't until his fourth treatment, when Mary couldn't attend, that they spoke. He ended up sitting in the same chair each time, some kind of comfort in routine, and Levi leaned over. "Can I ask you a question?"

"Sure," said Chris.

"What's your favorite swear word?"

He turned and looked at Levi. "What?"

"Mine's cocksucker," Levi said.

Chris shook his head, then chuckled. "Motherfucker, I guess."

"Yeah, I like that one, too," said Levi. "Maybe I'll start using that one more often."

Chris didn't know what to make of the guy. Then he stared down at his forearm, the fluids pouring into his body. "Fucknut works for me in a pinch, too," he told Levi.

They had the identical schedule, so they sat together every time. Levi brought a checkers board. Chris hadn't played checkers since he was a kid; he'd forgotten how fun it could be.

They shaved their heads together, two weeks later ("Fuck hair loss," Levi said). They talked tips and remedies, Levi always with better ideas than Chris, who found the research exhausting. "Bone broth," Levi said. "I swear by it. All the nutrients of a meal in a drink."

They got to talking, too, about their lives and their hopes and their fears. They talked about their work. Chris confided in Levi his frustrations at the Bureau, how he'd joined up to make a difference, to serve his country, to take down bad guys and be a force for good, all that star-spangled red, white, and blue crap, but instead he found himself simply putting away one drug dealer so another could take their place. And now cancer. "Now I'm a cripple."

Levi talked about growing up in the Henan province of China, becoming a naturalized American citizen over twenty years ago. He talked about his country, about the people back home. And the government. "I understand how America sees the Chinese government," he said. "But you probably don't understand how the Chinese see the American government. The truth is, from my perspective, the Chinese government fears America. Each is afraid of the other's intentions. I don't think either side is the big, bad wolf they're made out to be."

In hindsight, sure, Levi was probably working him—if not from day one, at least from pretty early on. But Chris was a willing participant. When the talk finally got around to ways to earn a living and provide for the people they love, to making meaningful changes in their lives when—not if, but *when*—they survived cancer, it was almost a seamless transition into playing hypothetical games of what-if.

What if there were a way to make some extra money and nobody got hurt?

What if an occasional piece of valuable information was exchanged under the radar?

It wasn't like they were talking about stealing nuclear codes or designs for an atomic submarine. Levi was talking about aeronautics or medicine or telecommunications. Nobody would get hurt. To the contrary: The technology was going to make it out into the world eventually, anyway, right? So maybe China gets it a little sooner, and some company with a patent loses out on some customers and profits. Was that the end of the world?

No, of course it wasn't. And the money Levi was talking?

It wasn't just an upgrade. It would mean an entirely new life.

And that, of course, was where Nico came in. Of all people—Nico Katsaros, the man Chris had chased for so many years. But he needed the best. And Nico was the best.

That was a year ago. He knew the approach wouldn't be easy. Nico would be highly suspicious. So Chris had to start with a gesture of good faith, a piece of information that demonstrated that he wanted to be a friend, not an enemy.

That gesture came in the form of a tip about a complaining witness named Bonnie Tressler. True, she and her lawyer, Leo, were after Cyrus, not Nico. But that was a distinction without a difference. Cyrus was Nico's top lieutenant. Helping Cyrus was helping Nico.

And then Chris was in. He would be the buffer only, connecting Li-Wei Kuo to Nico Katsaros. Nico would recruit the asset. Chris's only job, besides a finder's fee, was keeping an eye on the Bureau to make sure the FBI was none the wiser.

Yes, it got messier once Cyrus turned up dead. Leo was the perfect replacement, but he refused to do it. Which meant Chris had to force Leo's hand. Thank God he had DNA and fingerprints to implicate Leo in Cyrus's murder. Leo had no choice but to go along.

Chris crosses over the Cal-Sag Channel and turns off onto a frontage road for a marine terminal down the way. He pulls into an empty lot adjacent to the road, parking his car near the car that's already there, headlights beaming over the channel.

He leaves his car, feeling a blast of cold air, a merciless wind that mostly drowns out the sound of light traffic over the bridge. He pulls down his stocking cap and stuffs his gloved hands into his pockets. The back door of the Cadillac opens, and he slides into the back seat. Sitting up front is someone he knows only as Trader Joe, one of Nico's trusted lieutenants.

"The night before the drop, Chris? This better be as urgent as you say." Nico is bundled up in a long coat and scarf, though inside the car it's toasty. "Our MSS friends are concerned, you said?"

Chris hands him a photograph. "I'd say it's more my concern. Do you know who this man is?"

Nico takes the photo and peers at it. He won't recognize the man. He's a low-level gang member caught on surveillance a few years ago. It has nothing to do with Nico. That's okay. He just needs Nico to focus on something for a few seconds.

Because while Nico's attention is diverted, Chris slides free his right hand, gripping Leo's gun, equipped with the silencer, and aims it at the front seat. He pulls the trigger twice, *thwip-thwip*, Trader Joe's brain matter splattering on the window beside him.

Before Nico can react, Chris turns the weapon on him. *Thwip-thwip-thwip.*

Nico buckles three times in rapid succession as the bullets hit his chest and torso. His head falls back against the seat. He struggles to breathe, making nothing but a wet, sucking sound as blood spatters from his mouth.

Chris keeps the gun trained on Nico, though his hand is shaking. He slides away to avoid any blood that might pool below the man. Though maybe he's so bundled up, the blood will be contained by his coat.

"She didn't know too much," Chris whispers. "I never told her anything."

Nico doesn't respond, still struggling. But after a few spasms of wheezing, he goes motionless, his eyes vacant, blood dripping from his mouth.

Chris carefully removes the photograph from Nico's dead hand. Then, his gloves still on, he opens the door and goes around to the driver's side, where Trader Joe lies dead, slumped against the steering wheel. He puts his hand on Joe's shoulder and gives him a shove, enough to push him away from the gear shift. He reaches down and puts the gear into neutral before closing the door. He gets behind the Cadillac and gives it a push. It doesn't take much before the Caddy starts rolling toward the Cal-Sag Channel.

As he watches the car lumber toward the cliff, he feels the after-rush of adrenaline. He just killed someone, two people—the first lives he has ever taken. He reaches into his pocket to remind himself why.

He removes the slip of paper that Leo handed him earlier today with an address on it, the address of a home Leo was supposed to visit and kill the owner:

523 Finlay Court, Deemer Park

His sister Mary's house.

He doesn't wait to watch the vehicle topple over the edge into the channel. He hears the ugly crunch of metal when it lands as he's pulling out of the lot and back onto the bridge.

"Flowers Anywhere. This is Caleb. How can we make your day beautiful?"

Chris controls his breathing while he runs through the rigamarole, clutching the black phone against his ear. "You have a salesman named Roy?"

After a moment, he gets "Roy"—Levi—on the phone. "Chris."

"It's done," he says. "Thanks for . . . signing off on this. He was gonna kill Mary."

Levi pauses. That's usually how he shows displeasure. "You know how much I love Mary, Chris. But I only signed off on this because you assured me it wouldn't interfere with tomorrow."

"This won't come back to me. The list of people who'd want to kill Nico will be endless."

"And his girl at QCI?" Levi asks.

"She already has her final instructions. Nico wasn't going to talk to her again. She's ready to deliver tomorrow."

"And your courier is ready to receive it?"

"Yes, for sure," says Chris. "That's a guarantee."

"And what happens after the drop? Nico is no longer around to take care of your courier."

"I'll take care of Leo myself. I'll take care of everything." Chris takes a breath, convincing himself as well as Levi. "I've got it under control."

71

Leo

I open my violin case and pull out the instrument and bow. I use a soft cloth to wipe down the body, chin rest, and fingerboard, then clear the rosin dust off the strings and wipe the bow with a different cloth. Then I rosin the bow, hopefully not for the last time.

I chose violin by chance. I was in grade school, and the music department was encouraging us to play an instrument. Another kid in our class, a girl named Maura, whose last name I don't recall, wanted to play the violin. No, they told Maura, you're left-handed. You must be right-handed to play the violin.

That is not altogether accurate, but left-handed violins are hard to come by and can be impractical in orchestras, where multiple violinists must bow in sync in close proximity. Anyway, my ears perked up when I heard that. I chose the violin immediately and, when asked, told the teacher that, yes, ma'am, I was right-handed.

The first time I brought home that dinky little school violin and tried to play it, Marilyn knew. But for whatever reason, she forgave my small rebellion. Either I would lose interest or, if I took to it, it would just make her son Leo (and her by extension) all the more impressive, a left-handed boy who could play a right-handed instrument so well.

I tuck the violin beneath my chin and raise the bow. *Violins mourn the dead*, so the saying goes. I think it was a poem. It was a favorite line of my instructor, Mr. Dingel.

I start with "Kindertotenlieder" by Mahler, a vocal performance, not a violin concerto, but I play the vocal melody, to which I've always been drawn. Marilyn heard me playing it once and asked me what the German word meant. I told her I didn't know. I didn't want to tell her that the English translation was "Songs on the Death of Children."

It was a Wednesday morning—June 4, 2003—when she finally told me about her real children, the original Leo and Trace. School was out for the summer, but I woke up earlier than she expected. I found her in the basement, which was only minimally furnished. She had pulled a box out of storage, dusty and beaten. A scrapbook lay on her lap while she sat on the sofa, eyes closed and head bowed, mumbling words.

She heard me. She didn't protest when I came over and sat beside her. Maybe she was tiring of fending off my skeptical inquiries about scary people trying to kill us. Or maybe she was just ready to come clean.

The toddler in the photo, clutched in the arms of a radiant young Marilyn, had chubby cheeks and curly red hair. The baby, held by the father in his checkered shirt—that was Fred, Marilyn's husband—had no particularly distinctive features at that point. Next to it, written in marker beneath the plastic covering: **Leo and Trace 6-18-90**.

It was an accident, she said. An unforgivable, unspeakable mistake. I hardly knew what carbon monoxide was—but I was familiar with the cautionary note that you don't leave a car running in a closed garage.

That, of course, didn't explain why she had to replace her dead kids with Trace and me—Leo 2.0 and Trace 2.0—her best attempt at replicas. Was she so overcome with grief that she couldn't accept the thought of her children dying? Or was she just trying to cover up her criminal liability?

I never got that answer. I never asked. All she said to me, with her deep-set eyes, strands of hair stuck to her tear-streaked face, was "You saved me. And I hope I saved you, too."

In substance, that was all I really knew. She mentioned that Trace and I were "at-risk" kids whom she informally—though not legally—adopted, and God knows where we might have ended up had she not done so.

And I stayed with her. I didn't run to the police.

Instead, I took her hand and said, "Okay."

And now, things have swung full circle. The man who Marilyn never mentioned to me, the man whom Bonnie was too afraid to identify until a year ago, is now dead. And the man above him on the food chain, Mr. Nico Katsaros?

Well, I wonder how his night went. Chris Roberti sure seemed upset after seeing his sister's home address written on that scrap of paper.

Did my plan work? If it didn't, I'm in a world of trouble.

Then again, I could be in a world of trouble even if it did.

When I'm done playing, I dab some polish on a dry cloth to clean the violin, wiping along the grain of the wood in long, delicate strokes. Then I put the violin in the case and close it up.

Hope to see you again, old friend.

But I don't kid myself. Anything could happen tomorrow. There are so many moving parts, so many players, so much I don't know.

It's gonna be a wild ride.

THE DROP

MONDAY

72

Andi

6:00 A.M.

Andi is awake, staring at the ceiling, when her alarm blares at six on Monday morning.

"Olive coat, pink breast-cancer pin, blue Cubs hat," she says aloud.

She does two miles on the treadmill, then a hundred reps on the bag, to burn off some nerves. Then she showers and drives to the QCI campus. Today, she will steal the Nano specs.

The specs for which they have tightened protocols such that it is impossible to download, copy, print, email, or otherwise transfer the file without immediate detection. The specs for which they have created an encryption code for every copy of the file that is printed off, a file that is contained only on computers on a network dedicated to the eighth floor, itself a sensitive compartmented information facility with no possible outside access.

She strides into the building with two boxes of donuts for the party FutureTech is throwing for the submission of Nano to the FDA, plus a shopping bag.

She gets off the elevator on eight, setting down her shopping bag and balancing the boxes of donuts like a waitress while swiping her key card and placing her thumb on the scanner by the metal door.

Brett is at the door.

"Hey, I'm going to need you in a second," she tells him. "Get someone to replace you temporarily."

"Sure thing, boss," says Brett with a smile. And chewing gum.

9:13 A.M.

She walks the length of the well-lit hallway, filled with ceiling cameras, to the conference room that covers the entire east wall. The party, such as it is, is just getting underway.

Andi's accustomed to parties thrown by cops, which usually feature copious amounts of hard alcohol drunk from paper cups and at least one fistfight. And that's before noon, when they really get started.

These guys have a different idea. These doctors, scientists, and engineers are drinking coffee from boxes or nonalcoholic punch from a glass bowl and eating croissants, bagels, and donuts. There are streamers, balloons, and an oversized photo of Dr. Allan Valencia converted into a dartboard, even a piñata that is shaped, she is told, in the form of a mitochondrion.

Once she drops off the sweets, Andi swipes her way into the work area and winds through the cubicles to find Dr. Seth Hargrave, banging away on his computer.

She checks one last time, confirming that the two folders, "Nano Previous Gens" and "Nano Gen 3," are still sitting on Seth's desk.

Good. Andi pulls the scripts out of the shopping bag.

"Jeez, Andi." Seth glances back. "You made twice as many copies."

"A Girl Scout is always prepared." She drops the stack of scripts on the desk.

Right by the two Nano folders.

"Seth," she says, "you'll make sure Allan doesn't come back here, right? We are setting up everything for the skit in your cubicle."

"Right, right, no problem."

Andi returns to the exit, where Brett is waiting with his replacement, a man whose name is Hubert but whom they call Howzer.

"Go down to my office," she tells Brett. "There's a big box containing a video camera and tripod. Can you bring it up here to Seth Hargrave's cubicle? We're gonna make one exception to the rule of no cameras in the SCIF. We're going to record the skit."

9:57 A.M.

Brett arrives at Seth's cubicle carrying the long, heavy box. "Can you open it and get the camera out?" Andi asks him. "Careful not to destroy the package. We'll need it when we're done."

"Sure thing."

It's awkward, particularly within a small cubicle. Brett stands the box upright and rips at the seams, breaking apart the tape. Above the top of the box, Andi can still make eye contact with the security camera on the ceiling. But the rest of her, from the shoulders down, is obscured by the muscular security guard and the oversized box he's pulling apart.

For the sake of the camera, Andi chats with Brett—"This should be a fun party"; "I appreciate your help"—and stands almost completely still.

But her hand slips into the Nano folder and slides the document out and over to the stack of scripts.

"I know, right?" she says, laughing at one of Brett's comments that she didn't listen to. The box tilts and angles as Brett works it open. Andi adjusts, as one would expect, and takes that moment to slip the Nano specs into the bottom of the pile of stapled scripts in one fluid motion.

"Can I help more?" she asks. "I'm just sitting here not helping."

"No, that's okay." Brett pulls the tripod camera, its legs bound together, free of the box. "I'm done."

What a coincidence, she thinks. *So am I.*

10:21 A.M.

While Brett takes the tripod camera into the conference room to set it up, Andi waits in Seth's cubicle. The various actors in the skit filter in and put on their costumes. Andi pulls out copies of the script from the stack, bound together by a rubber band. In all, there are twenty actors. Andi has a remaining stack of twenty more scripts, with the Nano specs nestled inside, after she has handed them all out.

As it gets close to eleven in the morning, Andi gives them the thumbs-up. "It's time," she says.

Seth, dressed as Dr. Valencia—complete with the ugly tie and thick glasses, wearing a long white coat—says, "I'm not even sure I need a script. I've listened to that freakin' speech a thousand times."

The joke is that Allan Valencia's explanation of the Nano technology is always the same, down to little idiosyncrasies. How cancer drugs are like rescue workers, "firefighters putting out fires." How the circulatory system washes most of the drugs out before they reach the tumor. How nanoparticles are like fire trucks to transport the rescue workers, but still "the protein serums attack them as potential invaders and redirect them from the tumor." Or how they've come up with "an ionic liquid coating that acts as sort of a force field" around the nanoparticles and allows them to bypass the serum proteins and attach to red blood cells.

The actors, dressed in their various roles, sneak toward the conference room, with Andi following them.

She leaves behind the remaining stack of scripts in Seth's cubicle.

As the first speech inside the conference room is ending, one of the corporate executives speaks up, saying, "Can someone please explain this technology to me in simple terms?"

That's Seth's cue. "I can," he announces with faux authority, entering the room to much laughter and applause. "My name is Dr. Allan Valencia. And I have some experience in explaining this technology. I've done it once or twice, or perhaps seven hundred and ninety-seven times."

When the laughter subsides, Seth continues in Allan's voice. "When you break it down, it's quite simple. Think of cancer drugs like rescue workers. Firefighters putting out fires..."

The various cast members enter at the appropriate cues. People in the room are finishing the sentences for Seth, with plenty of laughter.

12:01 P.M.

The party officially breaks up around noon, after speeches by Allan, by the EVP in charge of RPD (the executive vice president and director of Research and Product Development), and even by the CEO and president of QCI, who calls the Nano technology a "watershed moment in the battle against cancer" but does not mention what excites her even more, the estimates of billions of dollars in profits over the life of the patent.

Through it all, Andi sits patiently, laughing with the others, socializing, pretending to enjoy herself, though she can think about nothing but the extra stack of scripts she left behind.

When it's over, Andi returns to Seth's cubicle with Brett, who is hauling the camera equipment. The box in which the camera came is somewhat torn apart, but Brett can still close the box around the tripod and camera.

"Okay, let's go back to my office," she says to him, leaving the cubicle.

"Oh, wait," says Brett. "Want to take the extra scripts with you?"

Well, sure, Brett, thank you for noticing. Because now it was your idea.

"Sure, probably shouldn't just leave them there," she says. She picks up the stack, bound together by a rubber band, a copy of the Nano specs nestled inside. "Let's go."

And off they go, heading for the exit. A number of people are leaving, passing, one by one, through the security brackets like people entering a courthouse.

She recalls the demonstration she did with the FutureTech security team for Jack Cortland. Everyone must go through the brackets— even Andi, Jack, the CEO of the company. And nothing can block the watermarked paper's sensors—not splitting the document into pieces or balling it up, not tinfoil, not a metal container—nothing.

"Keep it moving," says the guard, Howzer, as people pass through the brackets without a buzzer going off, without a red light flashing. Because who would be dumb enough to try to sneak the Nano specs past the sensors?

Slowly Andi inches forward in line, her heart banging a drum, because you never know. Finally, it's her turn to pass through the brackets. "Ladies first," says Brett.

"You're up, boss," says Howzer to Andi.

She nods and walks through the brackets.

No buzzer. No flashing red light.

She pushes through the exit and waits with the crowd for the elevator.

1:58 P.M.

Andi works at her desk for the next two hours, the stack of scripts resting on the corner of her desk. At close to two, she knocks on Jack's door. "I was thinking of heading out early," she says. "Feeling a touch of something."

Jack, at his desk, swivels around and faces her. "Then go ahead and get home. You've been working so hard on this Nano stuff, Andi. Really, the company's in your debt. I'm in your debt. I probably don't say that enough."

Andi feels a tiny lump in her throat, caught off guard by the sentiment. After all, though no one knows it, this will be her last day working at Quigley Crowe International.

"The pleasure's been all mine," she says.

She returns to her office, pulls the Nano specs out of the stack, and slides them into a manila envelope. She drops the envelope in her briefcase and leaves her office.

Sorry, guys, she thinks. *Maybe someday I'll explain what happened.*

Then she takes the elevator down to the lobby and walks out of the building.

73

Chris

2:04 P.M.

Chris, dressed down in a leather jacket and jeans, sits outside the court-room where Leo is handling his final court appearance of the day, some-thing about a post-conviction petition. He tries to remain still and calm. It isn't easy. But so far, at least, so good.

His phone buzzes. Another text message from the office. Everyone's been in a tizzy the last several hours, since they identified one of the bodies in the Cadillac at the bottom of the Cal-Sag Channel as Nico Katsaros. Anyone at the Bureau hears "Nico," the first thing they think of is Chris, who chased him in vain for five years.

Preliminary thoughts from all the messages he's received: it was a professional hit, a planned shooting, an ambush. Hard to think anyone will come to a different conclusion. Nico was obviously meeting in a se-cret, obscure location, and there's no doubt someone jumped his ride and unloaded on both Nico and his driver.

With a guy like Nico—no different than Cyrus—the list of suspects is endless. Only Chris didn't do something stupid like Leo and leave his blood and prints at the scene. No way they're getting any forensics off that Cadillac. Smart money says the murder of Nico Katsaros comes back unsolved. He reviews the latest text updates:

No weapon found

No official comment yet

Looks like one shooter

Possible suspects include every human being on face of
earth

All good news. Lots of suspects—check. And yeah, no shit, no weapon
was found. Chris didn't leave it behind. He's going to need it again.

The best news is the "no official comment yet." Meaning Nico's identity hasn't been released to the public—to people like Andi Piotrowski.

It's time to start planning next steps, after the drop. He'd delegated
the task of taking care of Leo to Nico, but that's for shit now. Chris will
have to kill Leo himself.

How and when are the questions. He's supposed to pick Leo up right
after the drop at the Pulaski station. He could whisk him away to an
"undisclosed location"—he has in mind a place on the west side he's used
for gangbangers—and take care of him right there. As much as he'd like
to put this off, that obviously makes the most sense.

He quietly shakes his head. Never, in his years of service to his country, has he so much as shot someone, let alone killed them. And now,
within the span of twenty-four hours, he has two kills to his name and
will be adding a third.

As Chris is finishing up his texting, Leo comes out of the courtroom,
dressed in his suit and his olive overcoat with the pink breast-cancer
ribbon.

"Ready to rock and roll, Counselor? We got . . . four hours. Wanna grab
some food?"

"God, no. I'm too wired up to eat." Leo shakes out some nerves.

Chris puts his hand on Leo's shoulder. "Tell you what. When this is
over, I'll get you whatever you want. My treat."

"Get me out of this alive and in one piece," says Leo. "That'll be enough."

74

Andi

It all feels electric, high-voltage and surreal. Any mistake now is not a bump or a miscue—it's a fall off the high wire, instant disaster.

It's just a one-mile drive from the QCI campus to the church, Immaculate Heart of Grace. A purple sash is tied to one of the elaborate front doors. That means she hasn't been followed. As if anyone can ever be sure of such things.

She parks in the church lot and enters through the side door, left ajar for her. She takes the stairs down to the basement, where Brando awaits, dressed in a sport coat and tie, hair combed.

"Wow, you showered? And a necktie?"

"Special occasions." Brando faux-knots his tie. "We're good?"

She pulls the manila envelope out of the bag. "Got 'em right here."

"How'd you do it?"

"It was easy. C'mon, let's go in."

"My ass it was easy." He taps her arm. "Hey, before we head in, I have some news. Your friend Nico? He's dead."

She steps back. "Seriously?"

Brando nods. "Found him in the Cal-Sag Channel this morning. Professional job."

"But . . . Who? Why? Why right now, before the drop?"

He shrugs his shoulders. "Too early to tell. Not necessarily related to our thing. Nico probably had enemies out the wazoo, right?"

"Yeah, but the timing . . ."

"I know, girlie, which is why I'm worried. This isn't how the MSS operates, but if they did this? Tying up loose ends so quickly? Think what they'll do to you."

He's right. But what can she do? It's not like she can turn back now.

"Anyway, let's go in." Brando guides her forward. "Don't wanna be late for the prom."

Inside the main basement area, a team of people, a good forty strong, some in suits or formal clothing, some in plain clothes, some working on laptops, some checking their equipment. They all snap to attention when Andi enters, as if a celebrity has arrived.

"Let me do some intros," says Brando, his hand still on her back. He extends a hand around the room. "Special Agent-in-Charge for the Chicago office, Amelia Braxton. United States Attorney for the Northern District of Illinois, Blair Hightower."

The top feds stationed in Chicago.

"This is Deputy United States Attorney General Lisa Tonyan. And this is Anthony Coyne, the assistant attorney general for National Security."

The number two at Main Justice and the head of DOJ's National Security Division, here in Chicago for this.

At least there's no pressure.

Brando turns to Andi. "And this, as you all know, is Special Agent Andrea Piotrowski."

75

Andi

"Okay, let's do the chain of custody." The Special Agent-in-Charge for Chicago, Amelia Braxton, nods to everyone gathered around Andi. "Agent Piotrowski?"

Andi detects a bit of a dagger thrown her way by the SAC. She isn't sure why.

She waits for the video camera to turn on before beginning. "I am Special Agent Andrea Piotrowski. The envelope in my hand contains specifications for a nanoparticle technology created by Quigley Crowe International for the treatment of lung cancer. In my undercover capacity as deputy director of security, I removed these specifications from QCI's sensitive compartmented information facility at approximately ten minutes after twelve this afternoon. Since that time, these specifications have remained in my possession."

Andi removes the specs from the manila envelope.

"I am now handing these specifications to Special Agent Michelle Renfus, who will emboss a latent strip on the back of each page of these specifications."

Andi hands the specs to the agent, a forensics specialist from Quantico, who will tag the specs. Once the chain of custody has been memorialized and the specs are out of her hands, she feels a whoosh of relief, though she knows they will be returned to her soon for the drop.

"Let's debrief," says the SAC, Braxton. "You need a minute first?"

"Just one," Brando pipes in. He pulls her aside.

"I gotta know," he says. "How'd you remove the specs from the SCIF?"

"Easy." She shrugs. "I stuck them in the middle of a bunch of papers and walked out."

"But what about the sensors? You said the specs would have sensors on each page."

"I said the *prototype*—the Gen 3 specs—would."

He slowly nods. "Ah, okay."

The plan all along was that the DOJ would not turn over the final prototype specifications for Project Nano to an agent of the MSS. There was too much risk. What if the sting operation fell through, and the MSS got away with them?

No, Andi is just handing off the Gen 2 specs to the MSS. Still proprietary information, still illegal to steal, and hard to distinguish, at first blush, from the prototype specs. But if worse comes to worst and the MSS agents get away with the information, it will be so far behind the Gen 3 prototype that it will be functionally worthless.

"Once we got to prototype, nobody cared about the earlier-generation specs," she says. "We only watermarked the prototype specs. And once we had the sensors on the watermarked paper, there was no need for physical searches at the exit anymore. That's what always worried me— the physical searches."

Brando smirks. "So by upgrading the security for the Gen 3 specs, you *downgraded* the security for the earlier version you planned to steal." He wraps his arm around her neck. "Anyone ever tell you you're a smart one?"

4:39 P.M.

"Nothing more you can tell us on the courier?" The SAC for Chicago, Amelia Braxton, is doing the questioning while Andi sits in a chair.

"White, male, mid-thirties, olive coat, pink pin, blue Cubs hat," she repeats.

"Okay." Braxton brushes her curls out of her face. "We have eyes on

Li-Wei Kuo as best we can, and we know which of his men is going to be in the field today to receive the package from the courier. We have everything else locked down. We just don't know who the courier is. That assignment was yours and yours alone."

"Whoa, whoa, whoa," Brando interjects. "Tell ya what, Brax. Try spending five years of your life pretending to be a cop who's working undercover for a ruthless gangster, when in fact you're working *double* undercover for the DOJ. Give up everything else in your life for that. Keep it all straight, live with that constant danger, pull it off, and somehow maintain your sanity along the way. Oh, and then, five years in, switch up! Sorry! Now the ruthless gangster is teaming up with the Chinese government, so now screw the corruption case you've built in Deemer Park P.D., now it's a national-security case, so quit your job as a cop—a job that was your first love, by the way—and instead go infiltrate a high-security medical laboratory and manage to sneak out the most sensitive and valuable secret they've ever had. When you do all that, Madam Special Agent-in-Charge, maybe, *maybe* you can start pointing fingers."

Braxton finds all this mildly amusing. She looks at Andi, eyebrows raised. "Protective."

"Almost like he really *is* my father," Andi agrees.

The truth is, though Brando posed as her dad for cover, he really has been more like family than Andi's real father, who left and never looked back. Sure, he's rough around the edges and looks like Father Time used his face as a doormat. But strip it down, he's fiercely loyal, true to his word, and so protective of Andi that she sometimes has to remind herself that the paternal connection is just a ruse.

The special agent-in-charge nods and turns to one of the techies. "Get her plugged in."

"Fuck her and the whole ungrateful lot," Brando mumbles when Braxton's left.

"She's not wrong," says Andi. "I was supposed to get the courier's identity. If I had, we could've started tailing him already. It's a miss on my part."

"Nah, Braxton's just being pissy," says Brando. "Chicago got cut out of this whole op."

"They did? I didn't know that." That explains the stink eyes Braxton's been shooting her.

"I . . . thought it was better I kept you away from the political bullshit. You had enough to do focusing on your work. But yeah, Main Justice wasn't taking any chances. They figured, Chicago had ten years with Li-Wei Kuo and couldn't get him. Nobody in the Chicago office knew this was happening. Even Braxton, the SAC, just got word yesterday. She's nursing some wounds."

Andi feels a chill. "So I guess I better not screw this up, huh?"

4:47 P.M.

"Okay, all set," says the techie, taking one last look at his work product. "It's all wireless. You don't have to do anything. We'll have to do some run-through checks for audio and vid before you go." He walks away, leaving just Andi and Brando.

The techie has attached a green shamrock pin onto Andi's blue over-coat. It will record video and audio. Eyes will be on the courier. And ears, too; whatever the courier says to Andi, and Andi to him, will be captured by the federal government.

She looks down at the pin. "A Black girl wearing a shamrock on her coat?"

"Breast cancer was already taken." Brando nudges her.

She looks around the room. A large projection screen's been set up, satellite imagery of the El trains running along the north side of the Loop, another one of an area that she assumes is where Li-Wei Kuo, their principal target, resides or works.

If all goes as planned, long before the MSS operatives figure out that they've been given an earlier, inferior version of Nano, they'll be under arrest and in custody of the government.

If all goes as planned. There's a lot of game left to play. Andi stretches her arms, releasing nervous energy. The drop can't come soon enough.

76

Andi

6:18 P.M.

Andi stands on Clark Street, looking over the river, bracing herself against the falling temperatures that accompanied the falling sun an hour ago. People are walking with heads low, avoiding the swirling winds, eager to get home to families and friends.

"*Proceed, agent.*" This through her earbud, hidden beneath her powder-blue stocking cap. The words of Amelia Braxton, the SAC for Chicago, who apparently decided that if her office got cut out of everything else, at least she was going to personally run the last leg of this op.

Andi starts walking, clutching the black gym bag with the billion-dollar document. The train stop is little more than a block away. The wind seems to have changed direction and now slaps her in the face as she heads toward Clark and Lake.

She pulls on her COVID surgical mask, then scans her phone pass and takes the stairs up to the Clark and Lake platform.

She looks at the sign for the arrivals. The next Green Line train arrives in twelve minutes.

Twelve minutes from now is 6:37 p.m. That would make it the first Green Line train arriving after 6:30. Her train.

77

Leo

6:21 P.M.

In his idling car by the train stop, Roberti pops another mint into his mouth. I really got into his head with that halitosis comment that he overheard on his eavesdropping device.

"You chew on mints a lot," I say.

"Just a habit, I guess. Want one?"

"No, I'm good."

"Actually, you should probably get going," he says to me, showing me his phone. "Next Green Line train arrives at State and Lake at 6:33. It arrives at *Clark* and Lake about 6:37."

"So that's my train. But I have twelve minutes. It will take me, like, one minute to walk up onto that platform."

"Yeah, but just in case you have a problem with your fare card or whatnot."

True enough.

"Third car from the end," he says. "Third from the left, if you're facing it."

"Got it."

"Black woman, wearing a blue coat, powder-blue hat, COVID mask, and tinted glasses."

I blow out air. "Okay. She hands me the envelope, I drop it in this gray bag"—right here in my lap—"and I give the bag to the guy in the Black-hawks cap at the Pulaski stop."

"Exactly. Easy." Roberti looks me over. "Olive coat, check. Cancer pin, check. Cubs hat, check. And you seem to be a white male in his thirties. So get up there, kid."

"Right. Hey, whatever happened with that person I was supposed to—y'know. Whoever lives at that address on that note Nico gave me. I think it was 523 Finlay Court in Deemer—"

"Nothing for you to worry about."

"But who lives there? Some colleague of Nico's? Some enemy?"

Roberti looks over at me. "Do not worry about it, Leo."

"Okay." I stretch my arms, working out the nerves. "I still can't believe I'm doing this."

"You're gonna be great, kid. Pretty simple job, at the end of the day. Then you're done, guy. Nobody will prosecute you for Cyrus's murder. I'll make sure of it. Do me righteous here, and your future is bright."

I breathe out. "Tell me a joke," I say.

"A joke?"

"Yeah, something funny. Make me laugh."

Roberti thinks it over a second. "All my jokes are dumb. That's kinda the point."

"The sillier, the better," I say. I put out my hand. "And maybe I will take one of those mints for the road. I hate to conduct a covert mission without clean, fresh breath."

He pops one into my hand. "Actually, that reminds me of one. You'll like this." Roberti adjusts in his seat. "You know the movie *Mary Poppins*? Julie Andrews? You know it?"

"Sure."

"So the story goes, she had this lipstick she loved. It was a combination of a bunch of different colors and she loved it. But there were two problems. One, it kept breaking off whenever she tried to apply it to her lips. And two, it gave her bad breath."

I nod, wait, then turn to him. "That's it?"

"That's it," he says. "Her . . . super-colored fragile lipstick gave her halitosis."

Not bad, especially delivered in song. Good for Roberti. I unhook my seat belt.

Roberti puts his hand on my shoulder. "You can do this, brother. Really."

I take a deep breath. "Okay."

I push open the car door.

"Wish me luck," I say.

78

Andi

"The Green Line train to Harlem is now approaching."

Andi steps forward, among a decent crowd, waiting for the train. Her heart pounding like it's going to break through her chest.

The train slides to a stop with a hiss. The doors open. She counts the train cars. The third one from the end—from the left—she finds it.

She steps inside, keeping her head down, letting herself be seen, not wanting to surprise him. Then she turns and sees an olive coat with a pink breast-cancer pin.

But . . . not just any olive coat. The same olive coat she saw the other day in the lobby of the federal court building, tattered at the sleeve, one button hanging by a string.

Leo's coat. The one she bought him a decade ago.

And then she looks up.

"You gotta be kidding me," she mumbles, though her mouth is obscured by the mask.

The man wearing that coat, and a blue Cubs hat and pink breast-cancer pin, is not Leo.

It's Chris Roberti.

79

Chris

"Her . . . super-colored fragile lipstick gave her halitosis."

Leo gives a perfunctory smile as he unhooks his seat belt.

Chris puts his hand on Leo's shoulder. "You can do this, brother. Really."

Leo looks out the car window at the train platform and draws a deep breath. "Okay."

He pushes open the car door. Finally.

"Wish me luck," says Leo.

"Good luck."

Leo gets out of the car but doesn't close the car door. He stands by the side of Chris's SUV, looking up at the train tracks. Nodding, mumbling to himself, a pep talk.

"You got this, kid!" Chris calls out, his neck craned forward, trying to make eye contact with Leo from the driver's seat.

Leo is quiet. Then he starts moving, like he's wiggling. Chris can't really see what he's doing. "Leo—"

Leo leans into the car, his coat bunched in his hands. "Sorry, I can't. I'll take my chances on a murder trial." He throws the coat onto the car seat, followed by the Cubs hat and the gray gym bag.

"What? Leo, *wait*." Chris grabs for his arm, but Leo yanks it free. "You can't pull out *now*!"

"I can't do it."

"They . . . the cops have you slam-dunked on a murder charge," he says, panic filling him. "You'll go to prison for life. This is ten more minutes of work and you're free, man—*free*. You'll be safe and out of prison."

Leo ponders that. Chris reaches for the door handle, ready to chase.

"I'm really sorry, Chris."

"Leo, Nico's dead!" he shouts, opting for a Hail Mary. "He's no threat to you."

Leo locks on that for a moment. Then he turns and starts running. Chris pops out of the car and starts to chase, but it's over before it begins. Leo's much faster than him, and anyway, the clock is ticking. Even if Chris could manage to catch Leo—which he couldn't—what's he going to do, drag him back, force the coat back on him, and push him up the stairs onto the platform?

He stands, helpless, watching Leo reach the corner of the next intersection and turn left, disappearing from sight.

He feels like he just got the wind knocked out of him. Did that . . . really just happen?

"You have *got* to be . . ." Chris puts his hands on his head, spins in a circle. "What . . . What the *fuck* . . ."

Five minutes away from completing this thing, and his asset bails?

He gets in the car, grips the steering wheel so hard it could yank free, too panicked to bellow out the primal scream building inside him. He pulls out his phone for the time. **6:25.**

He looks at the olive coat lying on the passenger seat, the Cubs hat along with it.

He grabs the coat, puts on the hat, grips the gray bag, and races for the train platform.

80

Andi

Andi braces herself as she moves toward Chris Roberti, his hand on a vertical pole by a row of seats on the train car, wearing Leo's coat, the pink breast-cancer pin, the blue Cubs hat.

Thank God for the tinted glasses and the COVID mask, concealing Andi's facial expression. For all Roberti knows, she doesn't recognize him.

After a stutter step, she regains her composure and navigates through some people toward Roberti. She doesn't look at him and, from what she can tell peripherally, he's not looking at her, either.

Andi takes the seat by which Roberti is standing. He probably sat in it until he arrived at her stop, essentially saving it for her. A pro move.

Seated, she unzips the gym bag in her lap. She places the envelope against Roberti's dangling hand. He takes it without a hitch and drops it into a gray gym bag, then zips it closed in what seems like an utterly casual way.

She's supposed to get off at the next stop, so she stands again and moves toward the door. She grabs a pole for balance and makes sure to turn just enough so she's facing him, so the camera in the shamrock is capturing Special Agent Christopher Roberti in all his glory.

"This is the Green Line train to Harlem. Next stop, Clinton. All doors open on the right at Clinton."

The train comes to a stop, the doors pop open, and Andi is out in the open air once more. She is alone getting off the train. Most commuters are traveling farther than one stop past downtown.

"You guys get a visual on him?" she says to Braxton in her ear as she walks toward the stairs, the mask concealing her mouth.

"That's affirmative. Positive ID."

Yeah, Braxton can't be too happy right now. One of her own agents, in on the plot with the MSS operatives. Doesn't make her office, or her personally, look so good.

Andi takes the stairs down from the Clinton stop and pulls off her mask. The cold air feels good on her face.

Chris Roberti. She still can't believe it. Christopher Roberti.

Leo was right. He was right all along.

ONE YEAR AGO
FEBRUARY 2023

81

Andi

Andi winds along the paved road within the cemetery, only scantly illuminated by occasional streetlamps. It's near eight in the evening, long past the time when Bonnie's funeral was held earlier today. She turns left at the first fork and parks by the row of hedges. She zips up her collar and throws on her hat as fresh snow begins to fall around her. She uses her phone for a flashlight and moves forward, looking for freshly dug earth—

"Andi."

She jumps, literally jumps. A cemetery is not the best place for a surprise. Especially under these circumstances.

Leo shines his phone light under his chin so Andi will see him, sitting by the grave.

"You scared me."

"Nice of you to come," he says, getting to his feet.

Sarcasm. She expected it.

"Couldn't tear yourself away from your fancy new corporate-security job and lifestyle to come to her funeral, I see."

Up close now, her eyesight adjusting, she really sees him. Still that handsome boy, though in many ways looking older, the weight of loss and sadness on his face. He dusts off his coat—the same olive coat she bought him so many years ago, now a bit tattered.

"I'm sorry I couldn't be there."

"No big deal," says Leo. "I mean, Bonnie was only Trace's mother."

"It's not like that, Leo. You don't understand."

"Whatever. You're here now. I'll leave you to pay your respects."

She grabs his arm as he passes. "I literally *couldn't* come, Leo. How 'bout you get your boot off my chest?"

"Fine. Whatever. Oh, and thanks for the recommendation for someone at Deemer Park P.D. Mary Cagnola? That worked out really well. She brought an FBI agent, too—Chris Roberti. They really helped out Bonnie."

"That was—you're talking about that text message you sent me a month ago? That was about *Bonnie*? You never said that. You said you had a law enforcement question for a 'client.'"

"Yeah, and you sent me to Mary Cagnola. Who gave us Agent Roberti. And instead of helping Bonnie bring to justice the man who imprisoned her and raped her and stole her child away from her, they killed her."

"Wait—Bonnie was killed? I thought she OD'd. And you're saying Mary Cagnola—"

"Either directly or indirectly," he spits, fire in his eyes. "They either did it themselves or they tipped off Cyrus."

"Cyrus Balik?"

Leo nods. "So you know the name."

"Just through . . ."

"Through Nico," says Leo. "You can say the name. Nico Katsaros. Remember him? The guy who sold Trace and me? The guy you and I made a vow back in college to take down?" He puts his finger to his chin. "If I remember correctly, the whole reason you wanted to be a cop was to stop these human traffickers. And the reason you joined *Deemer Park* P.D., specifically, was to stop Nico. Any of this ring a—"

"I *did* work to stop Nico," she says in a harsh whisper. "Will you keep your voice down?"

"Yeah, you did until you didn't. Did you ever, like, actually do anything to try to bust Nico during your time at DPPD? Before you traded in your badge for a bigger paycheck?"

She steps back. "What about you? You were gonna be a prosecutor, right? Put away the human traffickers? But then, hey, you plead guilty to punching a cop in college—so much for *that* dream."

"That's different."

"How? How can you compare our stories when you don't even know mine?"

Leo stuffs his hands in his pockets. "You're right. I don't. Not for the last five years, at least. Because you left."

She frames her hands in the air. "*Love* how you put that. After *I* left. Like I had no reason." She grabs his coat and gets in his face. "Within two months of our breakup, I was working undercover for DOJ, building a case against Nico. And I had him. Oh, I had him."

"Yeah? So what stopped you? The allure of a big payday at a fancy medical lab—"

"No, you idiot!" She catches the volume of her voice again, even though she's so close to Leo she could kiss him. "I was *moved* to that corporate job. Nico got himself into something bigger. Something with national-security implications. Justice wanted me on it. It was much more important to them than a local corruption case."

Leo blinks hard. "So you—you didn't leave law enforcement."

She releases her grip on his coat. "No. I went where DOJ wanted me to go. Where *Nico* wanted me to go."

"And that's—that's why you didn't come to the funeral. You couldn't be seen."

"I just have to be really careful with people who could blow my cover. I mean, Bonnie was one of the girls Nico trafficked. I doubt he'd remember her, but what if he did?"

"Then . . . why didn't you just tell me that, Andi?"

"Well, for one thing, I'm undercover. It's kind of the point that you *don't* tell people. And number two, we've been apart for the last five years. I have to give you constant updates on my life? Have you been giving me updates on yours?"

He allows for all of that. "They sent you to a medical tech company. An issue of national security." Leo does some quick math. "You're stealing IP. Selling it to the MSS."

She doesn't confirm or deny. But it's the most logical inference.

"And what about Cyrus Balik?" he asks.

"What *about* him? I've never even met him—"

"He's the one who raped Bonnie over and over again when she was fourteen, then knocked her up. And I'm sure he helped Nico with the black-market sale."

"I didn't know that. The only name I ever knew was Nico. How did you learn about Cyrus?"

"Bonnie. She finally told Trace and me a few weeks ago. That's when I texted you. Then we met with Cagnola and Roberti. And within a few weeks, Bonnie's lying dead in a crack house in Humboldt Park."

"Jesus. And you think Cyrus killed her? That Mary or Roberti tipped him off?"

"They're involved somehow. Cyrus, for sure. At least one of those cops. I don't know which. It was one or the other. Mary Cagnola or her brother, Chris Roberti."

Leo had been starting to calm down. But now his reservoir of anger is filling again.

"Look," she says. "I've never heard of Chris Roberti. And Mary—as far as I know, she's an honest cop. But I guess I can't be certain of that. Nobody in DPPD ever knew who was dirty with Nico and who wasn't. Nico wanted it that way. If I referred you to the wrong person when you reached out—if Mary burned you—I'm sorry, Leo. I didn't know this was about Bonnie. I figured you were trying to get some client off a DUI charge or something. Truly, I'm—"

"I should've been more specific. Just—it was a text, y'know? So I kept it vague. And things between us . . ." He shakes his head. "I didn't handle that right."

That seems to lower the temperature with Leo again. Speaking of lower temperatures, the bitter cold out here is starting to invade her bones.

"Can we—can we get in my car before I get hypothermia?"

Inside her Jeep, the heat blasting. You never realize how cold you were until you get warm.

Leo seems to have warmed as well. But she can't tell what he's thinking. She can't tell how things are between them, either, other than broken up as a couple. Maybe it doesn't matter. She's not sure they'd work as friends, and they definitely don't work as more than friends.

But God, would she like to kiss him right now.

"Here's what I know," she says. "I'm not supposed to be telling you this."

"Understood."

"You're right—I'm going to steal tech from the company and deliver it to a middleman, who's going to deliver it to an agent of the MSS. The middleman, currently, is Cyrus Balik."

Leo thinks about that. "When? When does this all happen?"

"Hard to say. At least a year from now. The tech isn't ready yet. It's not worth stealing until it's ready. I'd say a year, eighteen months."

Leo nods. "So when you take Nico and the MSS agent down, Cyrus goes down, too."

She pauses on that. Leo, of course, is quick to note her hesitation.

"I don't want to give you false hope," she says. "If Cyrus is the middleman, then yes, we'd take him down along with Nico. But Cyrus doesn't want to do it. Frankly, Nico doesn't want him to do it, either, because Cyrus is connected to him. But they can't find anyone else."

Leo's eyes rise upward. Thinking. "So there's no guarantee that Cyrus goes down when your operation is complete."

"No guarantee."

"Because they're trying to find another middleman," he says. "Someone they can trust to do it. A canary, preferably."

"Well, sure, a canary, if possible. But think about how hard it is to find someone from outside his crew that Nico can trust to do this."

Leo goes quiet, eyes intense, looking out the window.

"Yeah," he says, "that person would be pretty hard to find."

THE DROP
MONDAY

82

Chris

6:52 P.M.

"This is the Green Line train to Harlem. Next stop, Pulaski. All doors open on the right at Pulaski."

Chris moves to the train doors, clutching the gray gym bag with both hands, pulse thumping in his temples. The train hisses to a stop, the doors part, and he steps onto the platform.

He lets a few people pass so he's in the middle of the crowd moving to the stairwell heading down to the ground. On the landing halfway down the stairwell, before the turn, stands a white man, overweight, wearing a red Blackhawks cap and a dark puffy coat.

Chris hits the landing. He angles past one person and hands off the gray bag without breaking stride. Still walking down the final run of the stairwell, he doesn't look back.

He walks onto the dark street, releasing a long-held breath.

The weight is off his shoulders, unloading that package. He's done his part. Sure, it was a clusterfuck, but the package got into the hands of Levi's asset, one way or the other. That's all that Levi cares about.

Speaking of clusterfucks. He has to find Leo. There's no pretense now of witness protection, luring him into a safe house. Leo knows he violated his deal six ways to Sunday. There will be no sweet-talking him. Chris has to take him out as soon as he finds him.

6:59 P.M.

"State and Lake," he tells the cabdriver. Not an Uber. Nothing that can be memorialized.

He pulls out his phone—the one for Leo—and dials him. He doesn't expect Leo to answer, and he doesn't.

First things first. He needs to get back to his car at State and Lake.

Inside the cab, he pops in his earbuds and finds the link for the surveillance audio for Leo's condo. Leo ditched him around six twenty-five. He could've returned home by now, thirty-five minutes later, but with rush-hour traffic, hard to say.

He'll probably be getting home any minute, if home is where he's headed.

Chris could call in for a real-time cell-site location, track Leo's current whereabouts by phone. But that would be memorialized, too. How would he explain *that*?

He hears no sound inside Leo's condo. That could mean he's not home yet but will be soon. It could also mean he's not going home at all. Impossible to know—

Wham!

Chris alerts as he hears the sound of a door slamming inside Leo's condo. Then footfalls. Leo's home.

He hears the footfalls more loudly, Leo entering the living room, by the smoke detector.

"*C'mon, c'mon. Fuck! C'mon, c'mon . . . Hey! It's me.*"

Leo's on the phone. Talking to his friend?

"*You're not gonna believe this. I bailed. Yeah. What do you* think *that means? I couldn't go through with it.*" A pause. "*I just kept thinking, the moment I hand off that package, I get a knife in the stomach or something.*"

Well, in truth, Leo wasn't wrong about that.

"*Yeah, so fuck any cooperation deal. I'm getting charged. M1. Gotta be M1.*"

Yeah, first-degree murder would be the charge, all right.

"Listen, I don't—I don't know what to do, but I can't stay here. I'm at home right now. No. The FBI guy's looking for me. He just called me. I gotta get out of here and think about things. Can you meet me?"

Good. He'll get Leo out in the open. He'll take him into custody, then figure out what to do with him. Suicide would be good, if he could pull that off. Suicide with the gun used to kill Nico Katsaros.

"Sure, ten o'clock tonight is fine."

Ten o'clock. Okay, ten o'clock.

"Definitely not at your house. I wouldn't do that to you. How about . . ."

Pick someplace private, Leo. Someplace obscure.

"I agree, someplace totally random . . . Okay, here. You want someplace random?"

Chris lowers his head, covers the earbuds with his hands to push out traffic noise.

"Here's someplace totally random," says Leo. *"Let's meet outside 523 Finlay Court, Deemer Park."*

83

Andi

In the basement of the church where the DOJ has set up operations, Brando hands Andi a cup of coffee. "The post-adrenaline nosedive," he says. "You must be exhausted."

It's more than that. It's the surrealness of it all. Sitting in this chair while around her, the rest of the team is buzzing, issuing orders, conferring, banging on keyboards. And realizing that, regardless of the outcome, it's over. Six years of her life living a fake identity, first to expose Nico and corruption within the DPPD, then using her connection to Nico to break up a foreign espionage ring. She's done being that person forever. What's she supposed to do now?

"Eager for the finish," she says, nodding toward the two giant screens set up in the basement. The first containing satellite imagery of the location where the package has just been delivered—an industrial warehouse on Cermak. The other, video from the vest camera of the lead agent on the takedown, glimpses of his AR-15 and shield as he sits inside a wagon with the rest of the go team.

"So—Chris Roberti." Brando looks at Andi. "Never heard of the guy. Some line agent in Organized Crime."

She doesn't say anything. She'd rather not lie to Brando.

"So the idea was, Roberti keeps an eye out from inside the Bureau, making sure the coast is clear." Brando chuckles. "Meanwhile, the whole op's being run outta D.C., and he had no idea. Hey, you think he killed Nico?"

"No idea," she says. All she knows is that some way, somehow, Leo was around all of this—thus his overcoat on Chris Roberti's back. But what did he do?

She shakes her head. Why is she even surprised anymore when Leo pulls these stunts?

"I wanted to arrest him," she says. "I wanted to look Nico in the eye while he was inside a cell. And I wanted to tell him why."

Brando pats her leg. "I wanted that for you, too, kiddo. But wherever she is up there, she knows," he adds. "Agnes knows you brought Nico to justice, one way or the other."

The day Agnes passed, she'd been sick for months, but the turn for the worse had still felt sudden. She was home in hospice care, the early years of enforced drug abuse having finally taken their toll.

She was nearly gone, her eyes so sunken she was almost unrecognizable, the color of her skin so pale she looked like a ghost. She could hardly speak more than a few words. And when she did, the words were largely her native language, which neither Mama nor Andi knew.

"*Palun ärge võtke mu poega ära,*" she whispered. "Please don't."

Mama would cringe, tears squeezing out of her eyes, gently stroking Agnes's hand. "She's asking for him," she whispered to Andi. "She's begging them not to take him."

It was only two years earlier, when Andi was fifteen, that she learned of this chapter in Agnes's life. Agnes had first deemed Andi too young to hear something like this, but once Andi had matured, and Agnes had become more embedded in her and Mama's lives, Agnes wanted to share everything with Andi.

How she'd left her native country on the promise of a math internship but fell into the clutches of human traffickers who forced her into drug addiction and prostitution. How she'd managed to escape and found the women's shelter, where Mama ultimately found her and brought her in.

She told Andi about the man she feared, who filled her with such terror that she changed her hair color and used her middle name—her Polish mother's name, Agnieszka—so that he could never find her. So that Nico could never hurt her again.

And she told Andi about the secret scar that reopened every day of her life, wondering what happened to the beautiful boy they stole from her when he was six years old.

And on that day that Agnes, dear, strong, gentle Agnes passed, Andi watched her take her last breaths and beg for her son. Something came over Andi in that moment; a decision was made. She leaned close to Agnes, whose eyelids fluttered as she passed in and out of reality, as her final moments neared.

"Can you hear me, Agnes?" Andi whispered, her own voice trembling, her tears falling onto Agnes's cheek.

"Yes, *kallike*," came the faintest of sounds.

"I believe he's alive," she said. "And I will find him. I will find Rauno."

Something changes within the church basement. Everyone who was sitting is now standing, gathering around the body-cam footage from the agent and the satellite imagery of the warehouse. All extraneous conversation has been silenced.

The takedown. It's happening.

"That's a go, team leader." Amelia Braxton, the FBI SAC. "Go."

"That's a go. Go go go!"

The body-cam footage is clunky, nausea-inducing. The satellite imagery is easier to watch as two large vehicles converge on each side of the warehouse facility, agents pouring out of the back and crashing through doors.

"Federal agents don't move don't move—"

"—on the floor on the floor—"

From the shaky body-cam footage, the takedown turns out exactly how a shock-and-awe show of force should—six men lying on the floor in surrender, their hands quickly zip-tied. The place secured within the span of three minutes.

"Li-Wei Kuo, you're under arrest for violations of the Economic Espionage Act. You have the right to remain silent—"

Cheers go up. Applause. Hugs. Andi half expects streamers or balloons from the rafters.

Brando's arm comes around her. "This was you, kiddo," he whispers into her ear. "More than anyone else, this was you."

84

Chris

Chris, from his car, looks through his binoculars at Mary's home at 523 Finlay Court.

He's parked down the street a bit, behind another SUV, due east of Mary's house. This is where Leo will be meeting his friend in a little under half an hour. Leo will recognize Chris's vehicle if he sees it, so Chris has made sure that won't happen. You can only enter Finlay Court from the west, as it dead-ends into a cul-de-sac a block down. So he'll be able to see Leo, but Leo likely won't see him.

Chris doesn't know how this will go, exactly. If Leo arrives first, he'll arrest him and whisk him away before the friend even makes it here. If he has to do it in front of the friend, so be it.

He startles as a car, a sedan, pulls onto Finlay. The car stops short of Chris's position and pulls over to the curb on the opposite side of the street. Chris uses his binoculars but can't see inside the vehicle. Too dark out. Maybe the windows are tinted, too.

Given the cul-de-sac, there isn't a lot of casual traffic on this street. You don't pull your car over on Finlay Court unless you live here or you're visiting someone.

Or you're meeting someone secretly.

That's not Leo's SUV, and whoever it is seems content to just sit in the vehicle, so it must be Leo's friend. So much for getting to Leo before the friend arrives.

The car is pulled up too close to the car in front of it for Chris to make out the plates. Damn.

An SUV turns onto the street. But not . . . not Leo's. The SUV continues toward Chris, who turns and covers his face as it passes him. He checks his side mirror. The SUV proceeds eastbound, reaching the cul-de-sac and taking the circle, now proceeding westbound, back toward Chris.

That's . . .

Fuck.

Another SUV pulls onto Finlay but stops abruptly and turns sideways, blocking the road.

Chris reaches for his tool bag and pulls out a screwdriver, then thinks better of it and removes a hammer. He smashes his "Leo" phone before reaching in, with shaky hands, and removing the SIM card and snapping it in half.

In the side mirror, he sees the other SUV skidding to a stop not far away from him, people emerging on each side from the rear.

"*Chris Roberti!*" a voice bellows through a megaphone. "*Federal agents! Step out of your car and put your hands on your head!*"

He pulls out his black phone, for Levi, but his nerves get the better of him. The phone slips away and falls to the floorboard.

Agents inch forward on all sides, fanning out, weapons trained on him.

Chris grabs Leo's gun and puts it under his chin.

Then he sees her, rushing out of her house, down her beat-up front porch, wearing a sweatshirt and jeans, in bare feet.

Mary.

"*Step out of your car and put your hands on your head!*"

Mary, who was there when nobody else was. The one person, the only person . . .

He places the gun on the passenger seat. He picks up his personal phone and calls her.

Agents are converging now, encircling him. But they won't rush him. Not this quickly.

Mary looks down, then sees his call on her phone.

"*Chris?*" she says in a shaky voice. "*Is that . . .*"

"Don't say a word to them, Mare. This was all me! Promise me you won't say a word!"

"*What's happening, Chris?*"

"*Step out of your car and put your hands on your head!*"

"I love you, Mary. Always know that. You're the best person I know."

"*Chris—*"

He kills the phone call and pushes open the car door. He doesn't wait for them to force him to the pavement. He goes down all by himself.

85

Chris

11:41 P.M.

When it comes down, it lands with the force of a sledgehammer. He's seen it so many times, the light in a suspect's eyes going out when they realize their fate is sealed. How many times has he wondered what that would feel like, not dispensing justice but being on the receiving end, staring at years in prison, at a ruined life.

It's easier, he's discovering, not to think too hard about it, not to play out the string too far and think about day after day, month after month, year after year in a cage. To hold it at bay, at least for now, when you still have something specific you want to accomplish.

He hasn't lawyered up, so they can speak directly to him. He knows that everyone should have a lawyer. But most people haven't seen what he's seen. He wants to exert total control here, not delegate it to an attorney.

The door to the interview room opens. "Good evening, Chris." The woman, a prosecutor named Liz Weingarten, looks up at the clock on the wall. "Still evening, I guess."

A number of agents walk in behind her. But Weingarten sits directly across from him. "Are you willing to talk to us?"

"You give me what I want, I'll tell you everything."

She makes a face. Leans back in her chair. "I'll bite. What do you want?"

"A non-pros."

She all but laughs. "There is not one chance in a million that we give you a non—"

"Not for me," he says. "For my sister, Mary."

She raises her chin, eyes narrowing. "Sergeant Mary Cagnola. That's where you were tonight, right? Outside her house?"

He digs a finger into the desk. "She didn't know about any of this."

"I see. So . . ." She shrugs. "If she didn't do nuthin', why does she need a non-pros?"

"Because even the slightest hint that she's involved would tank her career. And she doesn't deserve that. The only thing she ever did wrong was have an idiot like me for a brother."

"Well, that's . . . that's gonna take some work. And some thought. I mean, you're acting like we need you. We don't. We have you on video taking the package from our UC. And we have you delivering it to Li-Wei Kuo's guy. I think it's in your own best interest to come clean for the sake of mitigating your sentence, but if you're gonna start putting *conditions* on it—"

"Oh, would you spare me the theatrical bullshit? I've given that speech a hundred times. You need me, and you know it. Levi isn't going to say shit to you. You need *me* to take him down. And I'll do it. But you leave Mary alone. I mean, you don't knock on her door, you don't execute a search warrant at Deemer Park P.D., you don't let anyone think you have the slightest fucking suspicion about her. You do that, and I'll be the best witness you ever had."

She gives him a sad smile. "Poor Chris, with no leverage, who thinks he has some."

Chris nods at her. "You got Kuo on video holding those specs in his hand? Huh? I'll bet you six days a week, and twice on Sunday, that you do *not*. He's not that stupid. He will plead ignorance. And his lackeys? They will fall on their swords before they'd give him up."

Weingarten gives her best impersonation of a poker face, but it's not really her thing. She's been sanitized in Washington too long.

"I, on the other hand, can give you chapter and verse on him and his participation in this whole thing. Start to finish. So all you need to do is the incredibly small act of *not* destroying the reputation of someone who had nothing to do with this. That shouldn't be too hard, even for the Department of Justice. And for that, I will hand you your entire case on a silver platter. So when you and all your colleagues with your fancy diplomas and alphabet-soup titles huddle together on this, try not to overthink it."

86

Andi

Andi winds along the paved road within the cemetery Wednesday morning, turning left at the first fork and following it along until the row of hedges. She parks behind Leo's car.

He turns when he sees her, a blank expression on his face. He doesn't look upset to see her, but he doesn't look happy, either. He's wearing a hooded sweatshirt with a puffy vest over it—not enough for this cold. Then again, he no longer has his overcoat, does he?

"We have to stop meeting like this," she says.

"Careful. You sure you want to be seen with me?"

"I doubt anyone's following my movements today."

"Not sure we can say the same for me. Congratulations, by the way. I read all about it this morning. 'Chinese Spy Ring Exposed in Chicago.' Nice headline."

"Thanks. Or maybe 'No thanks' is more appropriate."

He likes that, suppresses a smile.

"So can I ask?"

"Better you not," he says. "I wouldn't want you withholding knowledge."

"You mean knowledge like, when I handed him the stolen IP, Chris Roberti was wearing the coat I bought you ten years ago? That kind of knowledge?"

He bends down and uses his sleeve to wipe some dirt off the tombstone.

BONNIE LEIGH TRESSLER
A beautiful spirit

"Yeah, that kind of knowledge," he says, getting to his feet.

"Did you kill Cyrus?" she asks. "Is that how this all started?"

He thinks about whether he wants to answer. Or how he wants to answer. "I think a law enforcement officer has to read me my rights before asking that."

"I'll take that as a yes. That's not okay, Leo. That's not okay with me."

His expression adjusts in a way that tells her she landed a blow there. "Well, then it's a good thing I didn't ask for your opinion."

Okay. So it's going to be like that? Why did she even come here?

"Roberti was gonna walk," he says. "Cyrus might have, too. That wasn't acceptable."

That's what she figured. And thinking back a year ago to their conversation at this cemetery, she realizes that she's the one who gave him this idea.

"So with Cyrus out, you make sense for the courier. You're perfect. You owe Nico, you're smart, and you can be discounted as a pathological liar if you're caught. You knew Nico would think so. But how did you draw Roberti in?"

He hitches a shoulder.

"Oh." Now she remembers. "After Cyrus was dead, Nico asked you to be the courier. And you refused. Nico told me he had someone in mind but the guy was 'reluctant.' That's what you did, isn't it? You said no, and the only way they could make you say yes was by having Roberti come in as the big, bad FBI agent. He forced you to work undercover for him, pretending that he was trying to bust Nico. How am I doing?"

He doesn't answer, but his expression tells her she's doing okay so far.

She shakes her head in admiration. "Roberti thought he was roping you into this. But you were roping *him* in."

"Jeez, Andi, you're making me blush over here."

"You sneaky shit."

"I've been called worse."

He probably has. "And Roberti killed Nico? How'd you manage to pull that off?"

"Chris is a grown man. He can make his own decisions. Besides, I'm sure he's already answered that question."

True. He told DOJ he killed Nico because he thought Nico would try to kill *him* after the heist. But Andi thinks there's much more to that story—more that includes Leo.

"You were *that* sure that Roberti was complicit with Nico? I knew you had suspicions, but how could you be so sure?"

"Andi—"

"Just give me that much."

He deflates. "I knew it was one of them, Roberti or his sister. Whoever showed up at my door was the one. Roberti showed up."

"Ahh, okay." She nods. "That's why you picked the warehouse Cyrus owns in Deemer Park. Seemed like an awfully strange place for a murder. Roberti, it wouldn't matter, he's a fed with jurisdiction over all of northern Illinois. But Mary Cagnola—"

"Only has jurisdiction over her small town of Deemer Park."

She can't help but laugh. "Remind me not to piss you off."

"You could never piss me off, Andi."

"Oh, I think I've pissed you off before."

"What? When you left me?"

"For one, yeah."

"That didn't piss me off. That broke my heart."

Again he hits her out of the blue with that heartfelt shit.

"Y'know, it broke *my* heart, too, Leo."

He isn't sure how to take that. She senses something in the way he processes it. Maybe relief? Maybe he needed to hear that. He needed to hear that she loved him as much as he loved her, that it hurt her as much as it hurt him.

Leo reaches out and takes her hand. "You made the right decision to leave. And if there were any doubt, didn't I just prove that point? I mean, this is another line in a long list of me doing dumb, reckless shit. Isn't this exactly what you predicted?"

It is, of course, but—

But. She was right then, and she's right now. Isn't she?

"Anyway." Leo releases her hand, gets mock-serious. "You should apologize for calling me a 'sneaky shit' in front of my mother."

She turns, bends down, clears away some grass from the headstone next to Bonnie's.

KATYE AGNIESZKA INVERNENKO

A Mother to Rauno

A Loving Friend to All

"Sorry, Agnes," she says. "I meant it in the best way."

87

Andi

The first time she met Leo. That gorgeous college boy working in the kitchen at that shitty bar in Champaign. She'd convinced her friends to do a road trip and begged them to stay at the bar long after they wanted to, just so she could see him.

She'd seen photos and read about him. The private investigator had told her everything.

In person, he was awkward—God, was he awkward, trying to make small talk, trying to hit on her. But she liked awkward. She'd felt awkward her entire life. And then he lightened up, got just a little loose, made her laugh, claiming to be an astronaut, and laughter had never come easily to Andi.

"Can I ask you a question?" he said to her, after the bartender had announced last call.

"Sure."

"Do you date dorky, insecure guys?"

She lost her smile. He'd tell her later, long after, that he thought he'd blown it right there. But she didn't lose her smile because she wasn't interested. She lost her smile because that wasn't why she was there. And the reason she *was* there was not an easy one.

She leaned into him. "I have a question for you, too," she whispered. "Don't freak out."

"Okay, I promise I won't freak out."

He was going to freak out.

"Is your real name Leo?"

He stepped back. "That's an odd . . ." He couldn't finish the sentence. He saw the tears welling up in Andi's eyes. His expression froze.

"Your name is Rauno Invernenko. Yeah?"

He slowly nodded, his lips parting, chest heaving.

"*Ma tundsin su ema*," said Andi. She'd practiced it. Then, in case his Estonian was rusty, she translated. "I knew your mother, Leo. Your real mother. I promised her, before she died, that I'd find you."

88
Andi

"I should probably get going." At the cemetery, still standing by Bonnie's and Agnes's tombstones, Leo zips the puffy vest he's wearing in lieu of his olive overcoat. They have months more of winter; he'll need a new coat. "Congrats, Andi. What you pulled off after six years as a UC—that's gotta feel good."

No, it feels weird. Like she doesn't know what to do now. She's burned from further undercover work. For the first time in six years, she gets to be herself again. She doesn't remember how. And DOJ? Burned-out undercovers don't have a stellar track record.

"Leo, listen—Roberti's talking. He's spilling everything."

"Well, I guess that's good."

"But 'everything' might include Leo S. Balanoff, Esquire."

He sizes that up and wrinkles his nose. "Maybe. You know, he could pretty easily leave me out. The story is that he and Nico plotted this. Plus whatever Roberti and the MSS agent did together. Me, I'm just a detail. He tried to rope someone else into his plan, but it didn't work? Telling the feds that doesn't help him. It makes him look worse, defrauding an ordinary citizen into committing a crime—or trying to, at least. He'd be admitting to more misdeeds. My money says he leaves me out."

"Yeah, maybe," she says, "but you can't bank on that."

"I'm not banking on anything. I recorded every conversation he and

I ever had. Downloaded them and sent them to an email account I created for that purpose."

"Of course you did."

"And at the end of the day, Andi, did I actually do anything illegal? No. I *refused* to do it. I mean, the feds—I suppose if they even know about me, yeah, they could probably try to trump something up. But I'm probably okay."

He's likely right. Lending someone an olive coat probably doesn't qualify as a substantial step for a conspiracy charge. He's right about *that*, but . . .

"What about Cyrus? I believe there's the small matter of a murder?"

"Yeah." Leo rubs his face. "Yeah. I was kinda hoping, with all this shit raining down, with Roberti as tainted as tainted gets, maybe everyone decides that the Cyrus thing is better left alone. Leave it as unsolved. The guy was scum, anyway."

"That's your plan? Hope it gets wrapped up in the rest of the scandal and goes away?"

"Yeah, I mean, Mary Cagnola could end up just as screwed as—"

"Mary got immunity. That was Roberti's condition for talking. The feds won't so much as *mention* her."

Leo didn't know that, of course. Nobody does yet.

"So Sergeant Cagnola's in the free and clear," he says. "And bitter." He squints into the sun. "And here I thought February was looking up."

89

Leo

I hear them trudging up the back stairs, the fire escape. Cops, gotta be. But local or federal? I'm not sure which I should fear more. I pull out my phone and dial my law partner, Montgomery Morris.

"Happy Valentine's Day," he says.

"You busy?"

"On my way to the Bulls game. Why?"

"I'm gonna need a lawyer, Monty."

"You—what? Why?"

"It's a long story. They're about to take me into custody."

"Well . . . when?"

"In about eleven seconds," I say.

"Eleven sec—the Bulls are playing Giannis tonight. Is it serious?"

"Umm . . . probably. It depends on which crime they charge."

"There's more than one to choose from?"

"Depends on whether it's FBI or local cops."

"You don't even know that much? What did you do now, Leo?"

Here they come in three . . . two . . . one.

Two people appear at my back door. One is a guy I don't recognize. The other is Mary Cagnola. Both with their badges out so I can see them.

"Deemer Park P.D.," I say. I punch out the phone before Monty can object.

I slide open the door, a shock of cold air invading my condo.

"Leo Balanoff?" Sergeant Cagnola does the talking.

If I were cool, I'd say something like *What took you so long?*

"And here I didn't get a valentine for you guys," I say.

"No valentines, Leo. We have a warrant for your arrest for the murder of Cyrus Balik."

90

Leo

Deemer Park P.D. They run me through the traditional booking process and start with some general questions before taking my photo. They take my picture from both profiles and head-on. I don't think a smile is appropriate. I try to look innocent.

A female officer uses a cotton swab to sweep the inside of my cheek for a DNA sample to run through the system. Some of these stations have a Rapid DNA check now, though I don't know if Deemer Park is one of them. It doesn't matter. One way or the other, rapid or not, the DNA sample will be enrolled into the CODIS-NDIS database for a potential match.

The police already did this, of course, when they found Cyrus dead on the warehouse floor with a knife in his neck. They found blood on his shirt, culled a DNA specimen from it, ran it through CODIS, and got a match in the national database for the DNA profile of yours truly, Leo S. Balanoff.

Then fingerprinting. The officer makes me plant each finger on an ink blotter. Then I roll the finger, from one side to the other, into a designated square on the impressions card. She actually directs my fingers with hers, like I wouldn't know what to do otherwise. When we're done, she hands me a towel, but it doesn't come close to getting the full ink stain off my fingers.

That's okay. They'll probably make me repeat this step, anyway.

Then the enjoyable cavity search to ensure I'm not holding contraband. They make really, really sure I'm not. I can't decide whom I pity more—me, or the guy doing the searching.

Then they park me in a holding cell. Business must be slow, because I'm alone back here. Fine by me. The walls are bare, of course. The toilet looks decent enough, though the seat could use a good scrubbing. There's a bed built into the floor with a thin cushion. No bedsheet, though; you could tie a bedsheet in knots and hang yourself. They don't want a suicide. Stay alive, they say, so we can throw you in prison for the rest of your life.

I sit on the bed, put my feet up, and lean against the wall.

Monty comes in, wearing a suit but no tie. He takes one look at me and deflates. "Jesus, Leo. Murder? There's a story, I assume?"

"There's always a story, Monty. Isn't that what we tell our clients? In our story, the client is innocent."

Monty pulls up a chair. "Are you innocent in your story?"

"Well, 'innocent' might be a stretch. Would you settle for not guilty?"

Interview Room A of the Deemer Park police station. Cagnola and Dignan sit across from me.

"I didn't kill Cyrus Balik," I say. "I'm willing to listen to what you have to say, but this is a . . . gross miscarriage of justice."

Cagnola suppresses a smile. Shoots a look at my lawyer, Monty, and nods back toward me, as in *Do you believe this guy?*

"Okay, well, you can start by listening." Cagnola settles in. "But you already know what I'm gonna say."

She runs through the whole thing, good and bad. How Cyrus was a really, really bad guy, and she'd be happy to talk to the state's attorney about a lighter sentence—as long as I come clean and show contrition. Not a chance of that.

She does the old we-know-all-about-you routine—my criminal record from assaulting that cop, my misadventure impersonating an FBI agent, and how I was diagnosed as a pathological liar.

Then she tells me how substantial the evidence is against me. Motive—I blamed Cyrus for killing Bonnie; I met with Cyrus shortly before his death.

And then her version of a kill shot. "We found your blood—your DNA—on Cyrus's shirtsleeve. And we found your fingerprints on the knife sticking out of Cyrus's neck."

Both of those pieces of forensic evidence—truly unforgivable. Never should have happened. But the best-laid plans and all.

"So?" Cagnola parts her hands. "We have all kinds of motive, and we have forensic evidence putting you at the scene with the knife in your hand. We got you, Leo. You're done. Anything you'd like to say?"

I don't say anything.

"Maybe it was self-defense," she says. "Maybe it was a moment of panic."

No and no.

"This is a chance to help yourself," says Dignan. "Explain how it happened."

I look at Monty. Nothing I can say will help me. He knows it, I know it.

For the first time in my life, I can't talk my way out of something.

I stare at Monty. This is his cue. What's he waiting for, a director to shout, "Action"?

"Our position," he says, waking up from his nap, "is that the forensic evidence was planted. We plan a full inquiry into who processed that crime scene and who else may have been involved. Including federal agents working in coordination with DPPD."

Detective Dignan takes great offense at the suggestion, as I'd expect him to. Mary Cagnola doesn't say shit, but she gets the hint. She may have immunity from the feds, but she doesn't have immunity from me. A sheen of anger appears in her eyes.

But truly, this is all stalling, killing time. It's been 134 minutes since they processed me. It should happen any minute now, if these guys in Deemer Park are any good at what they do.

A knock at the door. An older guy pops in. "Sergeant, I need a minute with you."

There we go.

And he's going to need a lot more than a minute.

Cagnola and Dignan leave the room. They're about to get some bad news.

Monty leans into me. "Let me just take this brief opportunity to say that you are un-fucking-believable. And I do *not* mean that as a compliment."

I raise my eyebrows.

"Okay, maybe a little bit as a compliment," he says.

FOURTEEN YEARS AGO

APRIL 2010

91

Andi

"Well, you *do* look like a Boy Scout," says Leo into the phone, talking to Trace. "Me? What's wrong with my hair? I know, but that's just because I'm too lazy and cheap to get a haircut. Besides, Andi likes it. She thinks I look like a rock star."

"I do?" Andi looks up from her criminal investigations textbook. "I never said that."

The truth is, she does kind of like Leo's hair longer, hanging down almost to his shoulders. The Kurt Cobain look is kinda hot on him.

"It's tomorrow," Leo goes on. "But like I said, it's handled. The lawyer's getting a continuance. I know, T, but do not worry about this, okay? Focus on rehab, your recovery. Do not worry about a stupid court date."

Tomorrow is Trace's court appearance for when he was arrested.

"Good to hear your voice, too, little brother. Call me next Sunday."

Leo punches out his phone. "He sounds pretty good. I thought he'd hate rehab."

"What are you doing about his court appearance? You were going to talk to a lawyer?"

"It's covered."

"You're getting a continuance?"

"The . . . lawyer, he said a continuance is easy to get. No big deal. Hey, I'm starving. I'm gonna make some pasta."

He leaves the room.

"You sure everything's okay with court?" she calls out.

"I'm sure. You want marinara or meat sauce?"

Leo is up before her Monday morning, showered and shaved and dressed in a button-down white shirt and slacks—his only pair.

"You look nice," she mumbles. "What—what time is it?"

"Quarter to nine. Go back to sleep."

Her head falls back on the pillow. "Good luck."

Andi's up at ten-fifteen. She doesn't have to be back on campus at ISU until two, so she's good on time. She walks into the kitchen, hoping Leo made coffee.

Lying on the floor by the door is a slip of paper. Something for Trace and the court proceeding. Leo must have dropped it. She sees the bold-faced heading, "Summons to Appear."

It's summoning Leo S. Balanoff to appear before the Honorable Nathaniel P. Rose in the Circuit Court of Champaign County, blah, blah, blah, to answer the charge of violation of subsection (d)(4) of section blah, blah, blah—

Wait a second. What?

She rides her bike to the courthouse and makes it there by twenty to eleven. She finds the courtroom for the "Honorable Nathaniel P. Rose" and enters. She doesn't see Leo. There is a clerk at the front of the room and a number of people lining the pews in the courtroom, most of them looking on edge.

She approaches the clerk, unsure of what to do. "Excuse me."

The clerk, a young man, hardly looks up from whatever papers he's shuffling. "Do you have a case in here today?"

"No, I'm just . . . a spectator. But I wanted to make sure I have the right—"

"What's the last name?"

"Balanoff."

The clerk goes down a list, then nods his head. "Here we go. Yes. Leo Balanoff. Aggravated battery of a peace officer."

Andi waits outside the courtroom. He has to show up sooner or later.

A few minutes later, standing in the hallway, she spots him walking toward her, and whatever burn she was feeling becomes an inferno.

It's Leo, all right, the same handsome boy, with the same crisp white shirt and slacks he was wearing this morning. But that beautiful long hair is gone, replaced with a tight, cropped haircut. Almost to the point of military.

Almost to the point of looking like Trace.

He sees Andi and skips a stride, surprised and momentarily unsure of himself. "What are you doing here?" he asks.

She shows him the summons. "You dropped this," she says. "In the apartment."

"Okay, thanks. You can take off now."

"That is a summons to appear in court, Leo. A summons for *you* to appear in court."

"Umm . . ."

"Yeah, um. And the clerk in the courtroom just told me the case is against *Leo* Balanoff. Not Trace Balanoff. Leo Balanoff."

He doesn't have an answer for that one. Not even "um."

"Nice haircut, by the way."

He pats the top of his head. "Yeah, I figured, it's court, y'know, I should look—"

"Look like *Trace*?"

He deflates.

"Let me guess—he used your ID to get in the bar that night," she says. "Right? He's only twenty, but you're twenty-one. He swiped your driver's license and used it to get in. The resemblance is close enough. Then he gets shit-faced drunk, gets into a fight, a cop comes, he throws the cop an elbow and knocks him to the floor, and now he's charged with . . ." She looks at the summons again. "Aggravated battery of a peace officer."

"Andi—"

"So they get him to jail, and he's way too intoxicated to talk to them, so they pull his wallet out of his pants and find the driver's license. They process him that night as Leo Balanoff. Not Trace Balanoff. *Leo* Balanoff. And he doesn't correct them."

"He *couldn't* correct them," says Leo. "Not that night. He was so drunk he couldn't spell his own name. He didn't do it on purpose. It was an innocent mistake."

"Okay, fine, but instead of fixing that mistake, you're doubling down. You're showing up, making sure your hair is cut just like Trace's, so the cop will ID you from that night. You're gonna take the fall for him."

For a moment, he almost cracks. But he doesn't speak, which has the same effect, anyway.

"Leo—"

"Go home, Andi," he says. "I'm doing this."

"Are you *insane*? You could go to prison."

"No." He shakes his head. "I have a plan."

"A *plan*? A college junior majoring in poli-sci has a *plan*?" She throws up her hands. "Okay, what's—what's the plan?"

"I think I can get it pleaded down to simple battery, not aggravated. And the judge will give me probation."

Andi feels like she's about to explode. "I don't even know what 'simple battery' means. But I do know you're taking a *huge* risk—"

"I've done a lot of research. I know what I'm doing."

"Baby." She puts her hands on his shoulders. "You could go to *prison*. For something Trace did, not you."

"I'm not going to prison. I can make this work."

"But what if you can't?"

"Then it's better I go than Trace," he says. "He couldn't handle it. Rehab is gonna work for him. He can get a fresh start. But not with this hanging over his head. And prison would set him so far back, I'd lose him forever." He takes her hands. "I'm going to make this work."

She can't believe he's serious about this. But he's as serious as she's ever seen him. He's not the screw-it-all college kid with a smart remark for everything. He's a grown-up making a grown-up decision, however unbelievably idiotic it may be.

She steps away from him. "Even if your plan works, you'll have a criminal record."

"One little battery conviction. From college." He lifts a shoulder. "Not the end of the world."

"Will U of I kick you out of school?"

"I don't think so."

"What about law school?"

"I'll figure something out. It's not the end of the world."

"What about becoming a prosecutor? Everything we talked about. You become a prosecutor, I become a cop, we take down all those predators like Nico Katsaros. No prosecutor's office is going to hire someone who assaulted a cop."

"You're right." He chews on his lip. "But I'm still doing it."

She looks away from him, tears welling in her eyes. "Does Trace even know?"

"Oh, God, no. He'd never let me do it. But I've made up my mind. I'm sorry."

He heads into the courtroom. She doesn't—she can't—follow him in.

She walks in a trance out of the courthouse, feeling ripped open, having no idea what will come next. Will he even walk out of the courtroom? If his plan doesn't work, if he gets sentenced to two or three or four years of prison, will he get taken into custody immediately?

And best-case scenario, what if his plan works? Is this the man she was sure, until about an hour ago, she would marry? Who would be so willing to throw away everything he's worked for to help someone else?

It's not the end of the world, he said.

Is it the end of *their* world? Their world together?

She wanders the grounds of the courthouse in the unseasonably mild April air, aimless and foggy, unable to stand still, unable to go inside, but also unable to leave. Time passes. Enough for clouds to form, even a brief rainfall, then sunshine again, Champaign in the spring.

She doesn't know how long she's supposed to wait, how long things like this take. Maybe it's already over, and he's in some paddy wagon headed to jail. Maybe there's just a long delay—

She startles when she sees him, standing on the sidewalk, hands stuffed in his pockets.

"Oh, thank God," she whispers.

"Probation," he says. "Simple battery and probation. It worked."

She's so flooded with relief, she can hardly keep her feet. But it doesn't feel like anything "worked" here. It feels like something has broken that will take a long time to heal.

"So now you have a criminal record."

"It'll do a lot for my bad-boy image." He smirks. "A minor one, Andi."

"And they have fingerprints on file from the arrest. Trace's fingerprints."

"And a DNA swab from the night he was arrested, too," he says. "Yes. Trace's fingerprints and DNA have my name attached to them."

"And you're okay with that?"

He shrugs. "I have to be. Let's hope Trace doesn't kill someone or something."

The humor falls flat, even to him.

"I needed to do this for him," he says. "Just this once. But never again. I promise, Andi."

She holds up a finger. "Strike one," she says. "And this isn't baseball. With me, *two* strikes and you're out. You understand? You only get one strike with me."

"Strike one. I got it." He puts his hand on his heart.

"Strike two and you're out."

"Strike two and I'm out." He nuzzles up to her, then lifts her into the air.

"No, too soon," she says.

"I love you."

"Too soon," she says, but her defenses are already breaking down as he spins her around.

"You love me, too, Andrea. I know you do. Say it."

"No, I don't. I don't." But then she's laughing and wrapping her arms around him and pressing her lips against his. What is she going to do with this young man?

THE PRESENT DAY

FEBRUARY 2024

92

Leo

"I'm out for now," I say into my burner, using its version of a video call. "They couldn't hold me. The forensics they took from me don't match the crime scene forensics."

"But they didn't drop the charges." Trace runs his fingers through his buzzed hair. "They smell a rat. This isn't going away."

"Give me a chance, T." I step out onto the balcony of my condo, enjoying fresh air.

"That's what you always say."

"I was right, wasn't I? I could've done this without Cyrus dead. But you had to go ahead and do it. And without telling me, I might add."

"I told you," he says, as if scolded.

"Yeah, *afterward*, you told me. If you'd just—" I catch myself. No use pouring salt on the wound. But my God. If the boy had just listened to me. I told him I could do everything we wanted to do with Cyrus alive. Cyrus would recruit me to be the canary, I'd eventually say no, and they'd bring in Roberti (or Mary Cagnola, I didn't know which at the time) to force me to do the job. I'd make sure that Cyrus and Roberti both went down. And Andi had Nico covered.

But Trace didn't trust the plan. He didn't trust Cyrus. It was a lethal cocktail of fear that Cyrus would eventually find him, fear that Cyrus might kill me, and desire to avenge Bonnie's death. It drove him to do something I never thought he could.

"I'll come," he says. "I'll turn myself in. No way you're taking the rap for this."

I know he means it. "Give me a chance first," I say. "This isn't over yet."

93

Leo

"Well, isn't this quite the shit show." Montgomery Morris, Esquire, my counsel of record, crosses a leg. We're inside the office of the Deemer Park chief of police, Natalie Cottrell. "My client's DNA and prints don't match the crime scene DNA and prints. Which usually means, as far as I can tell, that you drop the charges against the suspect."

The chief, a Black woman with silver hair and an extremely good poker face, defers to the prosecutor in the room, an ASA named Michelle Moriarty, a southside Irishwoman whom I've seen around the courthouse but never tried a case against. She's a lifer at the office, a former first chair at 26th Street, and currently a supervisor in the Conviction Integrity Unit.

"Funny thing, though," says Moriarty. "The prints and DNA at the crime scene are a match in the databases for Leo Balanoff. That's a pretty big coincidence."

"A coincidence isn't a crime," says Monty. "Nor is it admissible in court. His forensics don't match the crime scene, Michelle. Whatever else, that's the bottom line."

Moriarty leans forward, eyes narrowed. "I admit, I've never seen anything like this before, and I've seen a lot. But there can only be one explanation. Somebody else got arrested in Champaign and submitted those forensics. And whoever that person is—that person killed Cyrus Balik."

"But that person was not Leo Balanoff." Monty throws up his hands.

"No, but it was someone *claiming* to be Leo." Moriarty's eyes widen. "A close buddy. His brother, maybe. This was college, Monty. Leo was twenty-one. This other person probably used his ID that night to get into the bar. And then got arrested. And didn't have the balls to man up."

Monty expels an exasperated sigh, though he and I have worked through this very exchange. Michelle Moriarty is no rookie and definitely no dummy.

"Someone close to Leo killed Cyrus Balik," she continues. "Which means your client sitting there all innocently? He probably had something to do with it. Even if he didn't plunge the knife in Balik's neck."

"Well." Monty claps his hands together. "So let's start, what, taking fingerprints and DNA samples of everyone Leo knew down in Champaign fourteen years ago?"

"Maybe so." Moriarty leans back in her chair. "Maybe so."

"Good luck getting *those* warrants."

I raise a hand. "Look, can I say something?"

"No," says Monty.

"It's a plea discussion." Meaning our conversation isn't admissible. Besides, it's not like I'm going to confess to murder. "We have it on good authority that Chris Roberti, disgraced agent and overall asshole-of-the-month, cut a deal with the DOJ that makes them leave his sister, your sergeant, alone." I'm looking at the chief. "Meaning your department gets to skate free of a messy, juicy scandal. But guess what? We're not letting you skate. You drop the charges right now, or we sue you for wrongful arrest. A nice Section 1983 lawsuit in federal court, naming both Chris Roberti and his sister, Sergeant Mary Cagnola, and of course your department. Fabricating evidence. Doctoring evidence. Planting evidence. And with Chris Roberti's name attached to it, that lawsuit will stick. The media will enjoy it. And what's your defense gonna be? No matter how you slice it, my forensics are not at that crime scene. You think something 'happened' in Champaign a decade and a half ago, Michelle? Even if it did, it doesn't change the fact that my prints and my DNA are not at that crime scene. I didn't murder Cyrus Balik. And everyone in this room knows it."

"Couldn't have said it better," says Monty.

"I don't know who you think you're dealing with," says the chief.

I get to my feet. "I think I'm dealing with a police chief who has a good reputation, who's trying to turn around a department that was infested by Nico Katsaros."

The chief's poker face serves her well, but even she blanches at the name. She knows what I'm saying is true.

"Your department is at a crossroads," I go on. "You have managed to dodge a lethal bullet with that deal Roberti cut with the DOJ. Nobody is talking about Sergeant Mary Cagnola. Nobody is mentioning Deemer Park P.D. in this scandal. But if we sue, they will. And you better be damn sure we'll shine a spotlight. I hope you enjoyed being chief, Chief. Because you won't be much longer. All the good work you're doing will go down the tubes. And why? For what?" I look at both the prosecutor and the top cop. "To solve the murder of one of the most vile, disgusting low-lifes who ever drew a breath. Whoever killed Cyrus Balik cut the crime rate in Deemer Park in half. You're gonna blow up your department for *him*?"

Monty nods and stands as well. "It can be a new day in Deemer Park," he says. "No more Nico Katsaros. No more Cyrus Balik. Or we sue, and you spend the next few years reliving that nightmare. You have until the end of the day to decide."

94

Andi

A light snow falls outside Andi's living room window. So peaceful. Everything's been so peaceful over the last week. So peaceful she could scream.

Andi being Andi. A new concept. You spend six years looking over your shoulder, keeping your stories straight, and suddenly you don't have any story. It's just you.

"I still can't believe it," her mother says over the phone.

"He didn't do it, Mama. That's the point of the agreement. They dropped all charges, and he agreed not to sue them for tampering with evidence."

"No, I mean, I can't believe anyone would ever *think* a boy like Leo could do something like that. Leo's no killer."

But his brother Trace is, apparently. Did Leo help plan it, help execute it? It's hard to imagine he didn't. But the interesting thing is that Andi is having a hard time calling what they did wrong. Cyrus was the worst of the worst. He ruined lives. He killed Trace's mother.

But that was true of Nico, too, and Andi didn't kill Nico. She waited patiently and built a case against him. Why do Leo and Trace get to skip the line and do whatever they please?

They don't, of course. But still. Despite the hardening of her core after years in law enforcement, it's difficult for her to feel any outrage over the murder of Cyrus Balik.

"You should call that boy, Andi. And tell him you were a fool to ever let him go."

"That's not gonna happen, Mama."

"And so . . . what, then? You live your life alone?"

"Are those my only two options? Leo or nobody?"

Marni lets out one of her hmmphs, this one indicating something between concern and disgust. "That boy is the love of your life, Andi. I had one of those. I only had her for a short time, but baby girl, she filled my world. She still does. I want that for you."

As if on cue, as if this conversation weren't turning emotional enough—violin music, sad and beautiful, almost wistful.

"Did you just turn on music?" Marni asks. "Are you making fun of me?"

"No, it must be my neighbor. That's obnoxious."

"I know that music."

Andi pauses and listens.

Oh my God.

"That's the song Leo always played for you."

Tchaikovsky's violin concerto in D major. "You gotta be . . ." Andi gets out of her chair and looks out the window.

Leo, on the sidewalk below, in twenty-degree weather, his breath lingering in the air, playing his violin. She opens the window, letting in the harsh air. He catches her eye but keeps playing that gorgeous, romantic song.

"He is unbelievable."

"Is that Leo?"

"It's a very long movement!" she calls down to him. "You'll get hypothermia!"

"I don't care!" He keeps playing. Oh, he plays so fluidly, so beautifully.

"He's serenading you?"

"Yes. Oh, I miss him."

"If you miss him, go down there, girl!"

"I—no, I meant—I miss the music. The *music*."

"You said you missed *him*."

"No, I said . . ."

"Andrea Lynn—"

She punches out the call and settles on the windowsill, watching him, drinking in his playing, remembering. Seriously, this isn't even fair.

But that was a different time, back then, uncomplicated.

We were just kids, she reminds herself as she opens the door to her condo.

Things were simpler, as she rushes down the stairs.

We have no future, as she opens the front door of her building.

She stands in the doorway, her heartbeat at full throttle. He spots her and turns. He stops playing. "I mean, if I can't get laid after *this*," he says.

She bursts out a laugh and waves him forward.

"I was thinking." He draws up to her but stops short, his face red, his eyes watering. "I understand all the strike one and strike two and strike three nonsense. I get it."

"Nonsense?"

"Well, not nonsense, but—well, yeah, nonsense. Have you been happy without me?"

Her lips part but words don't come out.

"I haven't been happy without you. Not for one day. Six years is a long time to get over somebody, Andi. And I haven't. I never will. I don't know how."

She grips the lapels of his coat. His new long coat, replacing the old one. But still olive.

"And I know you're afraid I might do something stupid again—"

She pulls him toward her, into the vestibule.

"—but isn't it more stupid to not—wait, should I stop, did this work?"

"It worked," she says. She presses her lips against his, wraps her arms around his neck, and holds on tight.

95

Leo

"I'm sorry, you know." Trace walks out onto his patio and hands me a beer, having retrieved a fresh one (of the nonalcoholic variety) for himself.

I take the beer bottle and put it against my face, sweaty while I soak in the sun.

"It's not that hot," he says, taking a seat in a lounge chair. "It's maybe eighty."

"It feels like a hundred compared to April in Chicago."

We're in the backyard of Trace's house outside Chihuahua, bordered with privacy shrubs, a hammock between a couple of trees, even a decent-sized pool. His door business is doing well.

He is, too. Sobriety suits him. He's in the best shape of his life; he looks tanned and refreshed, muscular and trim, a man firmly in control. He puts his bare feet up on another chair and lets out a pleasant sigh.

"What are you sorry about?" I ask. "Killing Cyrus?"

"Not so much doing it but putting you in a jam. I didn't even realize he'd drawn blood from my nose until I got back. And the fingerprints on the knife—well, what can I say? I'm not good at killing."

"Well, you're *pretty* good at it, T. He did die, after all." I look over at him. "We don't have to talk about it if you don't want to."

He sips from his non-beer. "One thing I've learned—talking about things is better than not talking about them. Even if they're not fun. And I screwed that up. I should've listened to you and not done it."

Damn straight. But there's no sense in rubbing it in. He's beaten himself up plenty over the decision. And he will always have to live with it. By that I mean not just the guilt, if he has any, but the fact that his fingerprints and DNA are now associated with a murder in the United States. The prosecutors dropped their case against *me*, but if Trace ever gets arrested and his prints processed, he will be handing them a gift-wrapped prosecution against him.

"But let's talk about something happier," he says. "Like your old-slash-new girlfriend. Everything good?"

I smile and nod.

"Yeah, look at you light up when I mention her. Well, brother." He raises his bottle. "I was pretty pissed when she dumped you six years ago, and I'll be pissed when she dumps you again, but in the meantime, enjoy."

"That's your toast? Enjoy it until she ditches me again?"

Not that I haven't thought the same thing. Andi and I, we're living in the moment. What I said to her the night that I serenaded her was true. We make each other happy. We love each other. And I keep telling myself that I won't do anything stupid again. But as good a liar as I may be, I'm not very adept at lying to myself.

"How long you been back together now?" he asks.

"Fifty-nine days today."

He gives me a look. "Y'know, you could've just said two months. A normal person would've said, 'I don't know, couple months.' So what's next? You're gonna tell me that fifty-nine is . . . actually, it *is* a prime number, isn't it?"

"Oh, it's not only a prime. It's a twin prime, an irregular prime, and a safe prime."

"A *safe* prime? As opposed to a dangerous one?"

"A number that, if doubled and added to one, yields another prime."

"Why the hell would someone want to double a number and add one to it?" he says. "And how in the—no, not how—*why* the hell do you know that?"

"Why the hell did you drink?"

He thinks about that. "Huh. Okay. Fine."

Only I'm not a danger getting behind the wheel of a car because I'm adding the sum of all twin primes under 100 (hang on . . . 488) in my head. And I don't end up elbowing a cop in a bar in Champaign because I'm counting the number of tiles on the ceiling.

"A twin prime," he mumbles under his breath, chuckling.

"It just means two prime numbers that are within two of each other, like 59 and 61. They're special. Other than 3 and 5, because they're too small, the sum of every twin prime is divisible by 12."

"I agree, Leo. They do sound special. Thank you for sharing that." He reaches out with his bottle to clink with mine. "Here's to you and your twin prime, Andi."

"I'll drink to that."

I close my eyes and bake for a moment in the sun, more wounded than I care to admit by Trace's prediction that Andi and I are doomed. He may well be right. But I prefer to believe that I've learned my lesson. No more wild stunts. No more reckless acts. Never again. That's in the past.

I'll try, at least. I probably won't do anything stupid again. There's a chance I won't.

Unless, obviously, I come across another wrongly accused client. Or a murderous, human-trafficking crime lord. Not to mention a corrupt FBI agent.

Sure, there could be other exceptions, too. You can never really know until the situation presents itself . . .

But I will never, ever lie to Andi. That is my vow.

If something comes up and I need to act, I'll talk to her first. I'll tell her, full disclosure. We'll make the decision as a team. I'll convince her.

And if I can't, well, then I simply won't . . .

. . . um . . .

I mean, obviously, I can't let an innocent man rot in prison. I can't just sit back and watch someone ruin other people's lives.

But I'll figure something out.

Yeah.

Yeah, I'm sure it will all be fine.

Acknowledgments

I am extremely grateful to many people who helped me through the journey that was this novel. On technical aspects, thank you to my friend Matt Stennes for giving me ideas and tips about corporate security. If I made any mistakes, blame me.

In developing the plot and the characters, I am indebted to my superstar agent, Susanna Einstein, and to my brilliant editor, Aranya Jain, both of whom spent hours and hours reading over different drafts and making each one better than the last. (There were a lot of drafts.) I am also grateful to my former editors, Danielle Dieterich and Mark Tavani, who provided incredible insight and suggestions. This book would not be nearly what it is without all of you.

And to my friend and author extraordinaire Hannah Morrissey, for taking a look at some early pages and smacking some much-needed common sense into my head that kept me on the right path. Hannah is such a terrific thriller writer that I would be tempted to hate her if she were not such a humble and generous person.

And as always, the final nod goes to my first reader and the best thing that ever happened to me, my better half, Susan.